Praise for the Novels of Stephen White
Cold Case

"Entertaining, insightful, and enlightening . . . extremely well-crafted and laced with humor and sensitivity . . . White keeps[s] the suspense percolating" —*The Denver Post*

"Elegantly plotted, with brilliant characterizations."
—*Cleveland Plain Dealer*

"White's style effectively explores all the complexities of the human psyche . . . compelling."
—*The Gazette* (Colorado Springs, CO)

"A page turner that immediately engages readers."
—*Chattanooga Free Press*

"White drives the story through agile plotting and fine characterizations to a clever surprise ending. . . . His fans will enjoy the action and the way the series' main characters evolve in this latest entry." —*Publishers Weekly*

"A gripping page turner." —*The Denver Business Journal*

"A great plot line . . . intriguing . . . clever and suspenseful." —*The Boulder Daily Camera*

Manner of Death

"Heart-stopping suspense." —*Cleveland Plain Dealer*

"Pulls readers along like a steam train. . . . Don't crack this thing unless there's nothing else to do, because once you get started, nothing else is going to get done."
—*Denver Post*

"A top-notch thriller." —*Chicago Tribune*

"Chilling. . . . The invigorating twists and turns . . . [will leave readers] gasping." —*Publishers Weekly* (starred review)

"Action-filled . . . White is so good at pumping up menace." —*Kirkus Reviews*

Continued on next page . . .

Higher Authority

"Sinister and scary." —*New York Times Book Review*

"A powerful piece of storytelling . . . tense . . . chilling."
—*John Dunning*

"Absorbing . . . intriguing . . . chilling."
—*San Diego Union-Tribune*

"As intricate as it is mesmerizing." —*Denver Post*

"Stephen White scores again . . . a captivating read."
—*Milwaukee Journal*

Harm's Way

"Gripping." —*New York Times Book Review*

"A genuine puzzle that should keep readers guessing."
—*Denver Post*

"Taut, tightly spooled storytelling . . . difficult to put
down." —*Rocky Mountain News*

"Engrossing." —*Publishers Weekly* (starred review)

"Superb . . . one of the best thrillers of the year."
—*Cleveland Plain Dealer*

Private Practices

"Detective writing at its best."
—*West Coast Review of Books*

"White weaves a near-flawless web of evil."
—*Publishers Weekly*

"A can't-miss read." —*Larry King*

"Intriguing. . . . Solid, satisfying entertainment."
—*San Diego Union-Tribune*

ALSO BY STEPHEN WHITE

Manner of Death
Critical Conditions
Remote Control
Harm's Way
Higher Authority
Private Practices
Privileged Information

COLD CASE

STEPHEN WHITE

A SIGNET BOOK

SIGNET
Published by New American Library, a division of
Penguin Putnam Inc., 375 Hudson Street,
New York, New York 10014, U.S.A.
Penguin Books Ltd, 27 Wrights Lane,
London W8 5TZ, England
Penguin Books Australia Ltd, Ringwood,
Victoria, Australia
Penguin Books Canada Ltd, 10 Alcorn Avenue,
Toronto, Ontario, Canada M4V 3B2
Penguin Books (N.Z.) Ltd, 182–190 Wairau Road,
Auckland 10, New Zealand

Penguin Books Ltd, Registered Offices:
Harmondsworth, Middlesex, England

Published by Signet, an imprint of New American Library,
a division of Penguin Putnam Inc. Previously published in a Dutton edition.

First Signet Printing, February 2001
10 9 8 7 6 5 4 3 2 1

 REGISTERED TRADEMARK—MARCA REGISTRADA

Printed in the United States of America

PUBLISHER'S NOTE
This is a work of fiction. Names, characters, places, and incidents either are
the product of the author's imagination or are used fictitiously, and any
resemblance to actual persons, living or dead, business establishments, events
or locales is entirely coincidental.

To Roes and Xan, the loves of my life

ACKNOWLEDGMENTS

Although I found Steamboat Springs on my own, Lester Wall pointed me toward the splendors of the Elk River Valley, and Larry and Marilyn Shames planted the seeds that led me from there to the blowdown in the Mount Zirkel Wilderness. Jeffery Deaver introduced me to Edmond Locard and to the quirky delights of Adams Morgan. I'm grateful for everyone's guidance.

While writing and revising, I received invaluable advice from trusted friends and colleagues Harry MacLean, Mark Graham, Elyse Morgan, Jamie Brown, and Tom Schantz. Over the years I've learned to rely on their counsel as I rely on their friendship. Each completed book reminds me of the first, which would not have been possible without the help of the Limericks, Patricia and Jeff. My gratitude to them continues.

My lasting appreciation, as well, to the supportive professionals at Penguin Putnam: Lori Lipsky, Claire Ferraro, Karen Murphy, and Sally Franklin. Louise Burke deserves special gratitude for her enduring faith. The same is true of Lynn Nesbit at Janklow & Nesbit Associates.

As always, my most precious thanks to my family, especially to my mother, Sara Kellas.

Shoot all the bluejays you want, if you can hit 'em,
but remember it's a sin to kill a mockingbird.
—*Harper Lee*

PROLOGUE

No one had anticipated the need for security, so there wasn't any. Briefly, back in 1988, things had been different. After what happened to the two local girls that year, some of the ranchers began carrying loaded rifles and shotguns in their pickup trucks. A few went so far as to strap handguns to their hips while they did their chores. But that geyser of paranoia didn't endure, and four years later, in the spring of 1992, Colorado's Elk River Valley just didn't feel like a dangerous place.

The Silky Road Ranch filled a horseshoe canyon on the west side of the valley. The ranch was rimmed on three sides by the gentle slopes of the Routt National Forest and shadowed by the high wilds of the Mount Zirkel Wilderness. The northern edge of the Silky Road abutted the banks of Mad Creek while the open end of the horseshoe lined the county road that ran along the swell of the Elk River.

The new ranch house—of logs and stone imported from southern France—was situated to the south and west of a thick stand of aspen trees, the dwelling meandering over 5,306 square feet on one level. The two housekeepers who managed the estate were a lesbian couple in their forties who lived a quarter mile away in the original frame house that had been built on the ranch when it was christened the Crooked Diamond spread in 1908. Care of the ranch's 316 acres of land and its twenty-seven horses required two full-time hands who bunked in better-than-average quarters adjacent to the modern stable.

Gloria Welle loved her ranch and treasured the house that she had designed, as she told the second of her three architects the day before she fired him, "to appear to have been built by someone who had moved gleefully from Provence to the Colorado Rockies." Her stable— she would never refer to the building as a barn—was designed to the same exacting specifications as her home. Gloria adored every one of her horses, confided intimacies to her two cowboys, and tolerated her rather apathetic gay housekeepers because she didn't want it to appear to anyone in the valley that she might be letting them go solely because of their sexual orientation. Sometimes she prayed at night that the girls, as she called them, would just see fit to resign. But Gloria prayed as she did most things not involving money, which is to say haphazardly, and the girls stayed on.

The day that Brian Sample knocked on the front door of the sprawling pseudo French country house, the housekeepers were in town running errands and the cowboys were in Gallup picking up the two new horses that Gloria had purchased on a recent trip to New Mexico. Gloria's husband, Dr. Raymond Welle, was at his clinical psychology office on the second floor of a nicely renovated old mercantile building on Lincoln Avenue in nearby downtown Steamboat Springs.

When Gloria threw open her front door she probably didn't know her visitor's name, though he might have seemed vaguely familiar to her. No doubt she had seen him once or twice around town. The person she greeted was a middle-aged man wearing freshly laundered Levi's corduroys, a neatly pressed blue chambray shirt, and good cowboy boots. For many of Steamboat's residents this outfit constituted their Sunday's best, and Brian Sample's presence at her door likely caused no alarm to cross Gloria's face.

People who knew him well say that Brian Sample

probably smiled in his own shy way—his eyes deflected off to one side—before he introduced himself and asked if he could come in. Given the events in his life over the previous year, though, he may have forgone the smile. If the worn black cowboy hat that he called his "day-off" hat was still on his head when Gloria answered the door, Brian would have removed it or at the very least tipped it as he greeted her. People who knew her insist that Gloria wouldn't have considered her alternatives for long. She would have quickly invited the stranger into her living room, which was a cavernous post-and-beam enclosure that was large enough to entertain most of a traveling circus. Gloria was especially proud of the room and loved to show it to strangers.

It appears likely that Brian Sample didn't display his true intentions to Gloria Welle for, say, twenty minutes or so. During that time, Gloria fixed them both some Celestial Seasonings tea—Sleepytime for herself, Red Zinger for him. Given that Ranelle and Jane, the house-keepers, were gone for the morning, Gloria went to some special trouble preparing the refreshments, cutting a slice of lemon for her guest to squeeze into his Red Zinger. Gloria didn't take lemon in her tea. She also set out some Girl Scout Cookies on a ceramic plate, one she had thrown and fired herself during one of her periodic self-improvement phases. The selection of cookies included both Trefoils and Thin Mints. Girl Scout Cookie deliveries had taken place a few months before, but Gloria always bought in quantity. The only surprise was that she was willing to share her Thin Mints with a relative stranger. Gloria's friends often joked about her addiction to Thin Mints.

Most locals assumed that if Gloria and Brian talked casually, they probably talked about horses. Perhaps they even discovered that they both used the same large-animal veterinarian, Lurinda Gimble. Horses was defi-nitely Gloria's favorite conversational topic. And it hov-ered somewhere in Brian's top three or four, though it certainly came in after his two boys—and after fly-fishing.

If Gloria was in one of her infrequent moods when she allowed herself to pay attention to her guest, as opposed to paying attention only to her own graciousness as a hostess, she would have found Brian to be a tired, sad man who had recently picked at his cuticles until they were cracked and bloody. She might have heard him talk about the family and emotional problems that had forced him to lose not only his business, but also, imminently he feared, his home. Although it wouldn't have been like him to go into it, he might also have mentioned his recent failed suicide attempt, a clumsy overdose of Valium and penicillin that had caused him more humiliation than medical risk. Virtually everyone with an opinion believes Gloria must have heard Brian Sample vent about his rage at his psychologist, who happened to be Gloria's husband, Dr. Raymond Welle.

Folks think that it was sometime after the tea was poured and before the cookies were gone that Gloria learned that she was being taken hostage. People in the Elk River Valley still argue about whether or not Brian initially had anything else on his mind that day or whether what happened later was just a sign that something went terribly wrong inside Gloria's home on the Silky Road Ranch.

At some point after the tea and cookies were served Brian revealed his weapon and stood by in some reluctant menacing fashion as Gloria called her husband at his office. She explained that one of his patients was visiting and that she would like him to come home and deal with this situation *right away.* Her voice was tight and pressured as she spoke. Raymond Welle had listened carefully for nuance and warning in his wife's words during that phone call. He was, after all, a psychologist. He'd even taken some notes. Twice Gloria implored her husband to hurry and twice she insisted that he must not call the police.

He wrote down her directives each time

Raymond Welle got the message loud and clear. The first thing he did when he hung up was call the Routt

County sheriff, a man named Phil Barrett, whom Ray Welle considered a friend.

There is not much to suggest what happened inside the stone-and-log house in the next half hour or so. At some point, Gloria was directed by Brian to move from the sofa in the living room into a closet in the guest suite that was down the hall from the great room. Gloria typically used the guest-room closet to store wine for her frequent parties. Brian graciously moved a chair into the closet for Gloria to sit on. He didn't bind her hands or gag her. But he did lock the door from the outside.

Ranelle—one of the housekeepers—was the one who mentioned later that Gloria usually just left the key in the lock.

The sheriff and his deputies arrived at the Silky Road Ranch a moment ahead of Raymond Welle, whose drive from Steamboat Springs to the ranch gate took a little less than fifteen minutes. The three sheriff's vehicles that bounced up the dirt road transported a total of five officers. The Routt County sheriff had already determined that he was going to treat the situation as a possible hostage crisis.

Before the authorities had time to accomplish much planning at the scene, and long before any detailed discussions took place about how best to handle this particular hostage negotiation, should those circumstances arise, the assembled officers heard three gunshots emanate from the house. The blasts were only seconds apart. The cops all instinctively dove for cover behind their cars. Raymond Welle reacted considerably more slowly.

Maybe thirty seconds later, while the group was still arguing about whether there had been three shots or four, they were startled again, this time by the sounds of breaking glass. Raymond sneaked a glance at the house and told the sheriff that someone had broken the small window that was above the utility sink in the laundry room.

No more than a minute after the glass broke, the windshield of one of the police department vehicles—the only one that no one was hiding behind—fractured into a starburst as another gunshot exploded The roar of this shot echoed and bounced around off the faces of the nearby mountains like a steel ball in a pinball machine.

One of the deputies said, "My dear God, is he firing a cannon at us?"

Another one replied, "Nope. I would say that boy's firing a .45."

The sheriff said, "How the hell did he get out here? Walk? Anybody see any cars or trucks that don't belong? Raymond?"

Raymond looked around. "Nope. But there's a dirt road that goes into those woods from Copper Ridge. His car could be in there."

"Or it could be in the garage, right?" the sheriff wondered aloud. He would later tell one of his deputies that when he first got the call from Raymond about the problem at his house he suspected that Gloria might have been having an affair and that either she or her lover had suffered a change of heart that had resulted in some impulsive actions that would surely be regretted later. The sheriff called those situations "domestics—once removed." For the participants he usually considered them more humiliating than dangerous.

Gossip around town was that Gloria's attention did wander occasionally, especially on those horse-buying trips she took out of town.

Raymond reached up and opened the door to his Chevy Blazer and pressed the remote switch that operated his garage doors. Immediately, the three doors swung up on the face of the garage, revealing one empty bay, one jam-packed full of junk, and one full of the rear end of Gloria's forest green Land Rover. Ray said, "That car there? The Rover? That's Gloria's. Whoever's doing this to her, his vehicle must be in the woods."

The sheriff said, "Say you're right, Ray. Is there a side exit to the house, I mean close to the aspens over there?

Some way for him to make a run for it up to a car on Copper Ridge?"

The garage doors came back down.

The chief asked, "Did you do that?"

Raymond said, "No. He must have done it. There's a switch inside the house. By the mudroom door."

"Well then. We'll have to keep an eye on the Range Rover, too. He may try to make a run for it in Gloria's car. But we'll have to be careful—if he does that he'll probably be using her as a shield. Now what about doors from the house that lead over to those woods?"

"That's the master bedroom on that end. There're big sliding doors that go out onto a deck on the side of the house just out of our sight. Your men should cover that and the garage."

On his radio the chief ordered that the dirt road from Copper Ridge to Mad Creek be blocked off. He ordered that the main gate of the Silky Road be covered. He also sent two of his deputies to set up cover on the deck by the master bedroom and the other two to drive around back to a safe location where they could watch the deck and the sliding glass doors. "Stay out of range as you're making your way. I'll get us some assistance from town."

Before the cops were even in position around back, Raymond Welle screamed, "There he goes. Look! He's running. There! See him?" He pointed in the direction of the master bedroom. Brian Sample was loping across the wide deck. With more deliberation in his movements than one might expect, Sample hopped the railing that led down to a neatly trimmed lawn of buffalo grass. He paused there, turned and faced the police vehicles, leveled his .45 in the general direction of the sheriff's car, and fired. The shot went high. To his men, the chief barked, "Open fire," and instantly his two remaining deputies returned fire with their scoped rifles.

Brian's left shoulder snapped back. One step later he stumbled. Two halting steps after that he fell and released his weapon. The heavy gun in his hand seemed

to float in the air for a second or two before acceding
to the laws of gravity and plummeting to the ground.

The sheriff's radio came alive. One of the deputies
who had headed around back wanted to know what the
hell was going on.

Raymond Welle was already running toward his house.

Gloria wasn't hard to locate. The pungent stink of
spilled wine provided a great olfactory trail that led
straight to the guest-room suite.

When he'd murdered Gloria Welle, Brian Sample
hadn't even bothered to open the closet. He'd shot his
hostage right through the door. The .45 slugs had shattered one raised panel of the pine door and two of the
three bullets had shattered Gloria Welle, one in the
upper abdomen and one in the neck. She was already
dead when her husband, Raymond, found her slumped
over the back of her chair, which had tumbled onto its
side. Her clothing was stained red with her own blood
and was washed burgundy with Robert Mondavi's wine.
It was party wine—not Mondavi's finest.

The deputy who was right behind him said that Raymond didn't touch his wife's body, didn't even leave a
footprint in the blood and wine that were consecrating
together on the hardwood floor.

Brian Sample died that night in the hospital in Steamboat Springs. He had not regained consciousness.

PART ONE

The Dead French Detectives

CHAPTER
1

The phone call that summoned us to D.C. came on a Friday evening in April. I was busy playing Frisbee with some pizza dough and Lauren was slicing garlic so thin it was translucent. Her hands were less sticky than mine so she answered the phone.

A moment later, with real surprise in her tone, she said, "Hi, A. J. No, no, no. You're not interrupting anything. Really. We're just throwing some dinner together. . . . Yes, in our new kitchen, it's wonderful. It's good to hear from you. . . . We're doing fine, thanks. You?"

I smiled. The only A. J. I knew was A. J. Simes, a retired FBI psychologist. The previous year she had been instrumental in helping me identify and track down someone who was eager to kill me. Before the adventure was over she had saved my life. Lauren and I had only heard from her once since she had left Colorado and returned to her home in Virginia.

"You still in touch with Milt Custer, A. J.?" Lauren asked. Milt was also retired FBI, and had been A. J.'s colleague the previous fall.

A. J.'s response to the Milt Custer inquiry took a while. Milt, a Chicago widower, had been sweet on A. J. during their sojourn together in Colorado. I fondly recalled his awkward flirting. But Lauren's next words yanked me back to the present.

"You want our help with something? . . . Both of us? . . . Of course I'll listen. Should Alan get on an extension? Good, yes . . . Hold on." Lauren covered the mouthpiece and said, "It's A. J. Simes. She wants our help with something. Why don't you get on the cordless and listen in to what she has to say?"

I grabbed the other phone from the front hallway and A. J. and I greeted each other. Immediately after the pleasantries she asked, "Have either of you ever heard of a man named Edmond Locard?"

I said no. Lauren said she thought the name was familiar.

"Well, have you ever heard of an organization called Locard? It is, of course, named after Edmond Locard. He, by the way, was a nineteenth-century French police detective."

We both said no, though Lauren had begun nodding her head as though she was remembering something about him.

A. J. sighed. "Does the name Vidocq ring any bells? An organization called the Vidocq Society?"

"Yes," I replied. "I've read something about them. It's, um, a volunteer organization of law enforcement officers and—what?—forensic specialists and prosecutors who try to assist local police in solving old crimes. Murders and kidnappings mostly. They've been quite successful, haven't they?"

"That's right, they have. Very good, Alan. Well, Locard is a group similar to the Vidocq Society and has similar goals, though a slightly, mmm, shall we say, different philosophy and approach. I am one of the founding members. We are not as well known as Vidocq, which is mostly by design. Our members are not as prominent. That, too, is partly by design. But as an organization we are very effective. The reason I'm calling is that we in Locard have just made a decision to consider involving ourselves with a case that involves a crime that occurred in Colorado over ten years back but that also has some intriguing contemporary Colorado connections. I suggested to our screening committee that I thought you could both be of some help in our efforts. You, Lauren, could advise us on the lay of the local prosecutorial landscape. And you, Alan, could help me with some aspects of the case that might involve your clinical skills. The screening committee has already looked—discreetly, I assure you—into your backgrounds and authorized me to invite you both to consider assisting us on the case. Should the case develop as we anticipate it will, you would each bring an important local perspective to our investigation."

A. J. told us little more that evening. She did explain that our participation was purely voluntary, and that we would not be remunerated for our time or for our expenses except for extraordinary travel costs, which would need to be approved in advance by the director of Locard.

We looked at each other and shrugged. Lauren told her that we would be happy to consider her request. A. J. explained that we would need to come to Washington, D.C., at least once and possibly twice or more but that the Colorado family that was imploring Locard to investigate the crime had agreed to provide transportation for the initial visit.

"When would this be?" Lauren asked.

"The first meeting is a week from tomorrow. You would need to be at Jefferson County Airport at six o'clock in the morning. That's close to your home, right? I'm told that it is."

"Yes, it's close enough."

"There will be a plane waiting for you there at a facility called . . ." She hesitated and I heard papers ruffle. ". . . Executive Air. The family name is Franklin. You should be back in Colorado the same day if you're lucky. Midday Sunday at the latest. If you're required to stay over, someone will make sleeping arrangements."

"And you'll be there, A. J.? At the meeting?" I asked.

"Yes, definitely. And one last thing."

We waited.

"Please don't tell anyone we've talked. Discretion is important. Essential. Agreed?"

"Yes."

                          *   *   *

"She doesn't want us to tell Sam," I said, a few moments after we hung up the phone. Sam Purdy was a Boulder police detective and a good friend. A. J. had become acquainted with him the previous autumn, too.

"I got that impression, too," Lauren agreed. "Any idea why?"

I shook my head. "Secrecy is its own reason. Can you finish making the pizza I want to check some of this out on the Internet."

I sat down at the kitchen table fifteen minutes later. "There isn't much about Locard as a group. A little about Edmond Locard as an individual. But the Vidocq society has its own Web page. Lot of heavy hitters are members. You know, CNBC types—the kind of people who had endless opinions about Monica Lewinsky. Some people who testified in the O. J. trial. Vidocq has a fancy meeting room in a town house in Philadelphia. There's some blurb on their Web page about 'cuisine and crime.' Apparently, they have fancy lunches while they sit around and discuss old crimes. The Web page makes it sound like some kind of club. A regular crime-fighters' Rotary."

Though Lauren was drinking water, she handed me a glass of red wine. "While you were on the computer I remembered where I'd heard his name before. Locard. He's the man responsible for what detectives and crime-scene specialists call Locard's Exchange Principle. It's the foundation for the science behind trace evidence. Locard's the one who theorized that when any two objects came in contact or stay in close proximity for an extended period, something, some material, either visible or microscopic, will always be exchanged between the two objects."

I smiled. "That's about all I learned on the Net, too. That and that Locard worked in Lyons. Can you believe we agreed to do this?"

"Yeah, I can. I think it sounds fascinating. I'm more

surprised that we were asked. Let's face it, Alan, our national reputation as crime fighters is, shall we say . . . nonexistent. I suspect that A. J. has an agenda that we don't know about."

"Do you think it will take up much of our time?"

She shrugged. "I know a couple of people who have done this sort of thing before. My impression is that it's more of a consultation thing. I don't think it will be too bad. Anyway, we owe A. J. big-time."

"Yes. We do owe A. J. big-time." I lifted the pizza to my mouth. "Gosh we make good pizza, don't we?"

We were in.

CHAPTER
2

Our flight from Jefferson County Airport in Colorado to Washington National was on a private jet that had room to seat ten or so, depending on how many people squeezed onto the leather sofa in the center of the plane. On this nonstop, though, Lauren and I had been the only passengers. The whole private-jet, flight-attendant-acting-like-a-butler thing had led us to conclude that we would be greeted on the tarmac at the airport by a shiny black limo with a liveried driver, or at the very least a Town Car with a chauffeur. Instead, as we descended the stairs from the Gulfstream and collected our bags from our always solicitous flight attendant, Ms. Anderson, we stood alone on the macadam watching the approach of a bright yellow fuel truck. After a minute or so one of the pilots followed us off the plane and suggested we might want to retreat to the waiting area that was inside the office of the company that was going to service the plane.

We were almost to the office doors when a voice behind us called out, "Yo. Al? Laurel?"

The experience of traveling cross-country on a private jet had left me feeling impervious to discourtesy. I turned and smiled and said, "Yes?"

The man behind us seemed out of breath. He was wearing flower-print shorts, old Tevas, and a dirt brown T-shirt that was so faded I couldn't discern what had once been silk-screened on it. I pegged his age at around thirty-five. "Whoa, glad I caught up with you. Traffic is something for a Saturday and I thought I was supposed to go to the terminal to get you. Had to find my way out here by Braille, I swear. Anyway, I'm your wheels. This way." He pointed behind him, pausing only to glance up at the Gulfstream and add, "Nice ride. Is it yours?"

He didn't wait to hear my reply, which was an amused "Hardly." We followed him to a red four-door Passat and loaded our own luggage into a trunk that was half-full of nylon ropes and harnesses, all neatly bundled. Lauren and I glanced knowingly at each other, recognizing the accoutrements of a rock climber.

Lauren patted herself gently on the bulge that barely protruded from her lower abdomen and urged me into the front seat. Our driver lowered some narrow sunglasses from the top of his head to his eyes and said, "I'm Claven, Russ Claven, by the way. I guess I should welcome you, at least unofficially, to the ranks of Clouseau. So . . . hey . . . welcome to Clouseau." He affected a pseudo French accent for his final pronunciation of Clouseau, and completed his welcome by saluting us in a quasi-military fashion.

"I'm Alan Gregory. This is my wife, Lauren Crowder. And . . . did you say Clouseau?" I asked. "We were expecting to be met by somebody from a group called Locard."

He laughed with a robust roar that came straight from his belly. "Clouseau . . . Locard . . . Vidocq. They're all just dead French detectives, right?" He laughed again, enamored with his own joke. "Some of us affectionately call the group Clouseau. You like *The Pink Panther*? Personally I think Sellers is hilarious. *'Does your dog bite?' Was* hilarious anyway. You guys ever do the dead pool? Do they do that in Colorado? I do it every year. I almost won that year—the year that Sellers died? If Sinatra had kicked on time, it would have been mine. And John Paul? The man seems immortal. I had him on my list every year until they put him on the zombie list. I got Sonny Bono right, though, if you can believe it. Just a premonition on that one. But I always pick the wrong dead Kennedy. Seems one dies every year but the rules say you have to pick the right one to get the points. And I can't tell you how many votes I wasted on Bob Hope before he got added to the cast of *Night of the Living Dead.*"

I waited for him to pause for breath. He didn't. "Anyway, welcome. You know the District at all? We meet in a place in Adams Morgan. Not too far. Then again, not too close." He hit the accelerator with great force, as though he were trying to kill a roach that was camping out on the pedal. "Tell me. Which one of you is the shrink and which is the DA?"

Lauren clenched the armrest with one hand and my shoulder with the other as she identified herself as the deputy DA.

"Boulder, right? Colorado?"

"Yes," Lauren responded, her voice tentative. I could tell she knew what was coming.

"Did you do JonBenet? Was that yours? And was it as crapped up as everybody says it was?"

"It wasn't mine," she said, smiling insincerely. "I was totally out of the loop on that one."

"You must hear things, though, right? That DA of yours pointing at the camera and saying he's gonna get his man. I loved it. *Loved* it. I have a friend who started calling him Wyatt Burp."

I knew Lauren desperately wanted Russ Claven to drop the JonBenet questions. To my surprise, he did. I couldn't decide whether he was displaying some sensitivity to Lauren's discomfort or whether he suffered from a congenitally short attention span.

Claven drove the Passat aggressively. Lauren and I learned quickly that the German car accelerated with élan and—thank God—braked efficiently. He took us into the city across the Arlington Bridge and circled the Lincoln Memorial at a speed that made me grateful for centrifugal force. "I'm avoiding construction," he explained as he downshifted and accelerated up Twenty-third, as though he feared I was going to question his choice of routes or argue the charge on the meter.

The morning in the capital was bright and warm. In some kind of seasonal time warp, Lauren and I had advanced a month further into spring by leaving Boulder, flying across country, and descending to sea level. She tapped me on the shoulder and pointed in the direction of the Tidal Basin and the sea of pink-white cherry blossoms. I heard her whisper, "Maybe we'll have time tomorrow."

I somehow doubted it.

In the next few minutes I recognized the fleeting images of the State Department, Washington Circle, and Dupont Circle, but we were soon traveling through the narrow, car-lined streets of an urban D.C. neighborhood that I'd never visited before. The way our driver was looking around from side to side I had the feeling he hadn't been here a whole lot, either.

"Parking's always a bitch around here, especially on weekends. Too many college kids live in this neighborhood. None of them are even up this early on Saturday morning, so none of them have moved their cars." The DJ on the car radio announced the time. In mock horror, Claven repeated, "Twelve-seventeen? Shit, we're late. God I hope the sandwiches aren't gone. I'm starving. Man can't live on potato salad alone."

He squeezed the Passat into an impossibly small spot between a bread truck and a Chevy Impala that should have been in a museum, then removed the plastic faceplate from the front of his car stereo and slid it into the glove compartment. He apparently noticed my questioning stare and explained, "This isn't the best neighborhood in a city that's known for not having the best neighborhoods. Why do I leave it in the glove compartment, you ask? I figure that if they bother to steal the whole car, the thieves deserve a radio that works, don't you think? I mean, I could carry it with me, but what good does the front panel of a car stereo do me after my car is gone?"

For two blocks we followed Claven on foot, at a distance. We hung back mostly because we were weighed down with our carry-ons and couldn't keep up with him. Finally, he ducked into the arched doorway of a stately old stone warehouse. He paused for a split second; I thought he wanted to be certain we were still on his trail. Once inside the building, there was again no sign of him.

Lauren said, "Poof. He disappeared."

"Back here," he yelled. "Behind the mailboxes."

Behind the wall of mailboxes was a beautifully carved oak door. Behind that door was a tiny elevator. Claven called for the car with a key, escorted us inside, pulled the oak door shut, and tugged the gate closed. The elevator was about the size of a vertical coffin, sans satin. "Can you get to that button?" he asked me.

"Which one?"

"There's only one button. Just lean against the wall until the elevator starts moving." I did. It did.

The elevator was patient. Russ Claven was not. He tapped his foot the whole time we were ascending. He was humming something by Bruce Springsteen. I couldn't remember the title, but thought Russ was carrying the tune quite well. Finally, I remembered the name of the song. It was "Pink Cadillac."

After a long, slow ride we exited directly into the foyer of someone's loft. Claven walked past us into a huge open room and explained, "This is Kimber Lister's house. Mr. Lister has good taste and the resources to indulge it. Family money."

Lauren was taking in the beautiful furnishings. She said, "Indeed he does. What floor are we on, Mr. Claven?" She had moved her gaze to a southern wall of metal-rimmed square-paned windows that revealed an admirable view of the distant government buildings and monuments.

"Russ. Call me Russ. What floor? Top floor," replied Claven. "We're on the top floor. Follow me. We shouldn't dawdle." He strode across a stunning old tribal carpet that was bigger than my office and up a ten-foot-wide staircase that was lined with banisters and handrails of exquisitely turned wrought iron. He waited for us at the landing and, with his arms parted, pirouetted to face a pair of heavy paneled doors. He said, "Voilà. Oh, wait, do either of you need to use the john?"

Lauren replied, "I do."

"That door, there." Russ pointed to the opposite side of the landing. "Alan, you're sure your bladder is up to it? Kimber doesn't like anyone to leave until the initial part of the meeting is over. It could be a while. He runs these things like he's Werner Erhard and we're all at an old-time est meeting."

Lauren disappeared into the bathroom. Russ asked me if I climbed rocks. I told him I didn't but that I had friends who did, mostly in Eldorado Canyon.

"Oh *maan*. Envy, envy. You should try it, you really should. You'll fall in love, I promise you. I'm going this summer for sure. First week in August, I'm climbing in Eldorado Springs. A longtime dream of mine. I'll tell you, if it wasn't for climbing rocks and windsurfing I don't know how I'd stay sane."

I told him I liked to ride bikes.

He nodded and said, "That's okay, too," but his voice conveyed the same kind of disdain that snowboarders routinely express for skiers. Lauren returned to the landing. Claven's last words as he placed his left hand on one of the ornate doorknobs were, "Don't worry about being late. They'll probably blame me. It's one of my primary roles in the organization. Designated screwup." He snapped his fingers and added, "Oh, and if anyone asks, tell them I checked your ID."

A second set of doors, these of some kind of metal, awaited us inside. Claven mouthed a profanity, added, "I knew it. They've started," and punched a code into a keypad mounted on the wall of the small foyer. Moments later the metal slabs slid open in the same silent, fluid motion as elevator doors.

The doors closed behind us just as the lights in the room were dimming to black. My retinal image of the scene in front of me was of nothing but silhouettes. The room was large, maybe thirty by forty, and appeared to have been set up as a small theater with perhaps two dozen seats. I tried to visualize the backs of the heads I had seen and decided that more than half the chairs were occupied.

Claven separated my hand from Lauren's and led her to our right. I grabbed her other hand and followed them to seats near the back of the room. The chairs were big, leather, and comfortable. Mine rocked gently as I sat down. A deep, unaccented voice cracked the silence in the room. "Nice of you to join us, Dr. Claven. You've gathered our final guests?"

"Yes, Kimber. All present and accounted for."

A spotlight clicked on and washed an uneven circle at the front of the room. At the bottom of the circle a man sat on the edge of a small stage, gripping a cordless microphone as though it were a cherished cigar. He was staring at the wall to our right. I was surprised to note he was no older than I was. His blond hair was thick, like his body.

"Good day, all. My name is Kimber Lister. To those of you who are visiting my home for the first time, please permit me to offer you a warm welcome to my dwelling and a gracious introduction to . . . Locard."

The *d* was silent.

CHAPTER
3

Kimber Lister's eyes never strayed toward the small audience as he addressed us from the diminutive stage. His voice was a resonating baritone that caused the subwoofer in the room's sound system to rumble. The rich timbre of the sound was an incongruous counterpoint to the body of the man who was speaking; Kimber was soft and round and appeared almost childlike and angelic, despite his size.

"As we have three visitors with us today, I will briefly survey our procedure. The Locard Acceptance Committee has already reviewed the case we will be discussing this afternoon. After contemplation and deliberation, the committee has reached a decision to permit the entire group to hear the details of the case and to render a decision as to whether or not to offer our expertise and make our services available to assist the local authorities in accomplishing a final determination of the issues that remain unresolved in the matters that will be before us today."

Russ Claven leaned my way and said, "He always talks like this when he's in front of groups. The man was born in the wrong century."

Lister continued to focus his attention on the wall. "The purpose of today's meeting of the complete membership—in consort with our invited professional guests—is threefold. First, we will use this opportunity to familiarize ourselves with the specifics of the case. That is . . . to review what is known, and to make an initial determination of the breadth and quality of the evidence that was developed during earlier phases of the investigation—those conducted by local authorities contemporary to, and subsequent to, the crime. Second, we will make a final determination as to whether or not to commit our resources to provide assistance toward further analysis. Finally, should we decide to proceed, we will endeavor to develop and implement a strategy that will permit us to take the investigation to a more fulfilling level. To further those objectives, we will use presentation, discussion, question and answer, argument, and deduction. Through the process that ensues, remaining investigatory tasks will be identified and fertile forensic pathways marked. Locard members and visiting experts alike will then use these guidelines to delineate tasks so that appropriate individuals might accept responsibility for making additional analyses and inquiries that are in line with their areas of expertise. As the developing evidence dictates, of course."

One of the effects of Lister's profundity was that I found myself attending vigorously to his words. His manner of speaking was so obtuse that it required additional concentration. He paused as my eyes began to adjust to the darkness. I tried to scan the room to find A. J. Simes. Based on my memory of her hairstyle I settled on two likely candidates who were sitting near the front of the room.

Before he resumed his soliloquy, Lister lifted his feet from the floor and turned so that he was in profile to his audience. His feet and buttocks now rested on the stage; his knees were in the air. He still hadn't looked our way.

Behind him, a large movie screen descended silently from a slit in the ceiling at the back of the narrow stage. Lister said, "We'll begin with a short film presentation."

Russ Claven leaned over again and whispered in my ear. His breath was fetid. "We always begin with a short film presentation. Mr. Lister would much rather be Ken Burns than Sherlock Holmes."

The first image on the screen was a close-up of the left hand of a woman. Her fingers were long and thin.

Only a solitary ornament—a delicate ring of silver and amethyst—adorned the hand. The ring graced the pinkie. The fingernails on the hand were manicured but not painted, the cuticles having been trimmed with some care. From the lack of wrinkles on the skin I guessed that I was looking at the hand of a young woman.

Lauren, sitting beside me, reached over and squeezed the wrist on my left arm. The gesture was a warning, a caution. The gesture said, Get ready, here it comes.

The camera pulled back slowly, revealing the woman's wrist and bare arm. A half-inch curved scar caused a quarter moon of silver to shine smoothly two inches below her elbow. The arm was trim, the biceps firm.

The theater was funereally quiet. I kept waiting for blood to darken the screen. I was sure there was about to be blood.

But instead we moved from fingers to toes. Brightly painted, beautifully proportioned toes. The color of the nails was turquoise, and the background skin tones were a gorgeous gesso of subdued gold and amber.

Immediately, I decided that this was a different girl.

The camera lingered for a few moments and then pulled back from the toes to reveal an ankle of perfect proportion, a slender calf and an unbent knee, and a seemingly endless expanse of unblemished thigh. The beauty of the leg distracted me, but not totally. I was still waiting for the blood.

The next image on the screen was a wagon wheel. Totally unlike the arm and the leg, the wagon wheel was old and weathered, the spokes radiating out from a rusted iron hub. Through the spokes, behind them, I could see the vertical shoots of out-of-focus golden grasses. Cultivated grasses. Hay.

Lauren squeezed my arm again, released her grip, and lightly caressed my forearm. *Wait, it's coming.*

Using the hub of the wheel as the center of the world, the camera pulled back again. Quickly this time. At one side of the spoke rested the hand with the silver-and-amethyst ring. Hanging beside the wheel was the exquisite leg and the foot with the turquoise toes.

Here comes the blood.

The silence ended and Lister's recorded voice forced its way into every cubic centimeter of space in the theater. "Colorado," he said as the wagon-wheel image exploded to a snapshot that showed two young women laughing deliriously, mugging for the camera. They were posing in a field on an old buckboard, the rolling mountainsides in the background dotted with strands of aspen. One of the girls was sitting on the buckboard, her legs draped over the side. The other was standing, leaning languorously against the wheel. The one whose hand we'd studied was an outdoorsy blonde. Her face was so vibrant and joyous I wanted to smile along with her. The one with the painted toes was of Asian ancestry. Japanese. On reflection, I decided that she was not quite so vibrant. I sensed some pressure in her mirth and her eyes were averted from the lens by a degree or two.

She was the follower.

Her friend was the leader.

"The Elk River Valley near Steamboat Springs, Colorado. Steamboat is a mountain town in the northern Colorado Rockies, founded by ranchers, but developed by skiers. Its residents call it 'Ski Town USA.'"

The camera closed on the blonde. "Steamboat Springs was the only home that Tamara Franklin ever knew. Everyone in town knew her and everyone called her Tami." The lens moved to the young Asian. "Steamboat was the home of Mariko Hamamoto for only eight months. Her new American friends called her Miko. Her family . . . did not."

The screen went suddenly white. So fine was the focus that I could make out the crystalline forms of snowflakes and ice crystals. I waited for the camera to pull back. It did. Protruding from an uneven bank of snow were a hand and, four or five feet away, a foot.

On the hand was a silver-and-amethyst ring.

On the foot were five toes with glistening turquoise nails.

I stopped worrying about the blood. Now that I'd had my first view of the murder scene, I was sure that every drop would be frozen.

The film lasted another ten or twelve minutes.

Tami Franklin and Miko Hamamoto had been juniors at Steamboat Springs High School. They were friends who were last thought to have been together on a November evening just before Thanksgiving of 1988. Sometime in the late afternoon Tami had driven her dad's pickup truck away from her family's cattle ranch near the tiny township of Clark, high in the Elk River Valley in the shadows of Mount Zirkel. Behind the truck she was towing a snowmobile on a trailer. She had told her brother that, snow permitting, she was going to meet Miko for an evening ride to one of the hot springs not far from town. Her brother, Joey, had thought she said she was heading to Strawberry Park. But he wasn't sure.

Mariko's parents had told investigators that their daughter had left home to meet her friend after completing her homework. They didn't know anything about a snowmobile outing. Mariko's mother guessed that her daughter left right around six o'clock. Maybe ten minutes before or ten minutes after.

That was the night the two girls disappeared. No witnesses reported seeing them together that evening. No one acknowledged seeing the truck. A massive search was mounted the next morning; attention primarily focused on the trails that led to the most popular of the nearby hot springs in Strawberry Park. The search continued for the entire day. But early that evening a memorable storm blew in from the north. Skiers waiting at he base of Mount Werner rejoiced. Nearby Rabbit Ears Pass was closed under forty-three inches of snow.

The girls were declared missing. A day later the snowmobile trailer was discovered in a parking lot near the gondola in Mountain Village. The snowmobile was not on the trailer. The pickup truck was found almost a month later in Grand Junction, hours away, abandoned.

The bodies of the two girls lay undisturbed until the springtime thaw of 1989 was well under way. A cross-country skier who had moved off of a main trail in order to find a secluded place to urinate spotted one of the skids of Tami's snowmobile as it was beginning to protrude from a snow-filled ravine above Pearl Lake, high in the Elk River Valley. The location of the snowmobile was not in the direction of the hot springs that Tami had told her brother was her destination. Not even close.

A bloodhound brought to the scene by the Routt County sheriff discovered the bodies about six hours later. The grave where the girls had been dumped was a natural hollow in the earth that had been created by the fall of a diseased fir tree as it broke free of the steep slope where it had been growing. The hillside to which the tree had tried to cling faced north. The location where the bodies were found was at least seventy-five yards from the overturned snowmobile. Due to the nature of the terrain, however, neither of the two crime scenes was visible from the other.

To investigators at the scene there did not appear to have been any attempt to bury the girls. The only shroud over Miko's and Tami's bodies was snow. A lot of snow. At the nearby ski area that winter, the official snowfall total on top of Mount Werner had been 361 inches.

When their inadequate graves were discovered by the bloodhound, the girls' bodies were still encased in snow and ice. Only Miko's once lovely foot and Tami's once elegant hand protruded. The exposure of the limbs to the elements had been recent; small animals had barely begun to nibble on the exposed flesh.

The crime scenes were complex and would have challenged virtually any experienced homicide-crime-scene investigator. However, no experienced forensic personnel were available that day either in Routt County or in nearby Steamboat Springs. The personnel who did arrive at the scene didn't correctly recognize the challenge they faced.

Especially after they discovered that the hand that protruded from the snow was the only one still attached to Tami Franklin's body. The other one was gone. As were the toes of her friend's left foot.

The primary focus of Kimber Lister's short film was to spotlight the forensic and investigatory shortcomings of the initial investigation. A litany of problems was listed. Poor crime-scene management. Careless recovery of the snowmobile. Possible contamination of both crime scenes by unnecessary personnel. Mishandling of the dead bodies at the crime scene. Incomplete laboratory analysis and mishandling of specimens from the autopsies. Witnesses who should have been interviewed, but weren't. Witnesses who should have been reinterviewed, but weren't.

The list went on. The more I listened, the more I wondered why I'd been asked to be a member of the team that would reinvestigate this case. Lauren's invitation made much more sense to me. She was a deputy DA in Boulder County with an extensive background in felony investigations. She could advise Locard on a myriad of local legal mores associated with the earlier and the current investigations.

But me? I didn't get it. I was a clinical psychologist in private practice. I had no formal training in forensic psychology. The crux of Locard's involvement in the murders of Tami Franklin and Miko Hamamoto appeared to involve the cutting edge of forensic science. I knew that I couldn't help them there.

The lights came up at the conclusion of the film and Lister announced a short break for lunch. An anteroom off the side of the theater had been set up as a sandwich buffet. Russ Claven made a beeline for it.

I was looking around the room for A. J. Simes when she approached us from behind.

"Hi, you two. Thanks for coming."

We both stood. Lauren and A. J. hugged awkwardly over the top of the seats. A. J. offered her right hand to me. I shook it. She said, "Bet you're wondering why you're here." She was looking at me as she spoke. I was trying not to focus all my attention on the four-point cane she was using for support.

"You're right about that, A. J. This"—I waved at the screen—"doesn't seem exactly up my alley."

"Do either of you remember the case? These two murders? You both lived in Colorado back then, didn't you?"

Lauren didn't respond. I said, "I remember it vaguely. Crimes back then didn't get the coverage they do now. My memory is that there was a little splash when the girls disappeared, a big splash when the bodies were found, then the fanfare kind of faded away when no suspect was identified."

A. J. said, "Well I wasn't there, of course, but that summary doesn't exactly surprise me. Do you mind if we sit?"

Lauren said, "Let's. Please."

A. J. moved around the seats and took the chair that Russ Claven had occupied. "Obviously, your participation in this inquiry was my idea. Please be assured that I wanted both of you to be involved. Lauren, your role is easier to define. It's typical for us to find a consultant in a local prosecutor's office to provide guidance for us on local legal customs. Okay?" Lauren nodded. "Alan, your role is less circumscribed. I suggested you for two reasons. First, it is clear to all of us on the committee that screens new cases that too little is known about the premorbid history of these two girls. At the time the bodies were discovered the local police approached the investigation as though they were looking for an opportunistic killer, either a serial killer, or a drifter, or whatever. They never adequately explored the possibility that there might have been a reason that these two girls collided with this killer, or killers. My own bias is that if you don't explore something, you can't rule it out.

"What I'm talking about, obviously, is a variant of a psychological autopsy. Typically, doing a psychological autopsy of these two girls would be my role. But I'm currently . . . unwell, physically unwell . . . and not in a position to do the traveling necessary to accomplish the tasks that are required to assemble such a profile. Based on our work together last year, I think you, Alan, have the skills and the demeanor to help me do it."

I found myself slowly inhaling, overfilling my lungs. I wasn't sure why. I didn't speak.

"But that's only part of it. The second reason I wanted you on board is that we already know that the background of one of the girls—Mariko—included a stint in psychotherapy with a psychologist who was practicing back then in Steamboat Springs. We're going to need to acquire permission from her family to get access to those treatment records. And someone is going to need to interview the psychologist who treated her to see what he can tell us about this young girl."

Lauren was a step ahead of me. She said, "And you would rather that be somebody local?"

A. J. said, "Exactly."

During the sojourn the prior year when she was trying to protect me from a killer, A. J. and I had gone a few rounds over the necessity of the confidentiality of treatment records, so I pressed her on that issue. "Do you have any reason to expect that her family will deny us access to their daughter's treatment records?"

"We don't really know. Locard's assistance on the case was requested by the new police chief of Steamboat Springs and by the family of Tami Franklin. The Hamamoto family no longer lives in the area—in fact they no longer live in the United States. Obviously we're anticipating cooperation, but those contacts are yet to be made."

I remained confused. "Why do you want a local psychologist to make the inquiries? I don't exactly follow."

"Surprisingly enough, the answer is political." She assessed our faces to see if either of us had guessed what she was referring to. When neither Lauren nor I responded, A. J. continued. "Why politics? Because it turns out that the psychologist that Mariko Hamamoto was seeing for psychotherapy in Steamboat Springs was Dr. Raymond Welle. That's why this thing is so damn political."

I said, "Representative Raymond Welle? That Dr. Welle?"

Before A. J. had a chance to respond Lauren's hand jumped up to cover her mouth and she emitted a little squeak from deep in her throat.

I explained, "She knows him. Raymond Welle."

My wife swallowed, exhaled once, inhaled once, and said, "Actually I was related to him. Kind of. Well, briefly."

A. J. looked my way before turning back to Lauren. "We know about Lauren's first marriage. It came up when we were vetting the two of you. Welle was your brother-in-law, right?"

Lauren said, "Yes. My first husband's sister was married to Raymond Welle."

"So do you know him intimately?" A. J. asked.

"Does anybody?" Lauren replied.

CHAPTER
4

Before we had a chance to talk any further, A. J. was called away by Kimber Lister. Lauren and I grabbed sandwiches and drinks and returned to our seats. Russ Claven didn't come back to join us. He was across the room, near the stage, his attention consumed by a woman with short, radiant bronze-red hair and a gold lamé patch over her right eye. She was juggling a bottle of iced tea and a plate that was piled high with a sandwich and potato salad. She accomplished the buffet waltz with admirable agility. Claven said something that made her laugh and a narrow flash of teeth erupted into a wide smile that lit the room in a way that reminded me of the infectious smile I'd just seen on the snapshot of Tami Franklin.

Lauren was looking toward the woman, too. She said, "Cool patch, don't you think?"

"Definitely," I concurred. "Has to be custom. Can't get one of those at Walgreens."

Without turning back to face me, Lauren said, "You know, I think A. J.'s MS is worse."

"The cane?"

"Sure. Her balance is bad, she's holding on to chairs when she walks. Something else is going on, too. I see it in her eyes."

Both Lauren and A. J. lived with multiple sclerosis. Although we had never discussed it with her, we both suspected that the form of the disease that A. J. struggled with was more virulent than Lauren's version.

I asked, "You're still thinking she may have progressive disease?" I was describing the most dreaded form of the illness, the one that causes rapid deterioration without remission or recovery.

Absently, Lauren caressed a stretch of skin on her shoulder that had recently gone numb. "God, I hope not. But she's lost weight, don't you think?" Without waiting for my reply, she asked, "What do you think about the case?"

I shrugged. "It's interesting. The forensics seem fascinating. I'd be more comfortable with my part of it if it didn't involve my needing to interview Raymond Welle. How well did you know him? Did you and Jake spend much time with him and his wife?"

"You know, we didn't see them very much. Jacob's family wasn't . . . close . . . and Raymond and Gloria were up in Steamboat most of the time we were in Denver. Jacob's father wasn't very tolerant of Raymond, so he and Gloria tended to stay out of the city. Jake and I skied with them once for a long weekend, but I spent more time with Gloria than I did with Raymond."

"What was your impression of him?"

"Raymond? He was as shallow as they come. Always trying to pump himself up so he'd have some stature in the family. Given Jake's family, and all they've accomplished, that wasn't easy. Being around Raymond was painful for me. Gloria was self-absorbed in her own way, but at least there was an underlying generosity about her. She wanted to be kinder than she really was—you know what I mean? But she always did seem to manage to have enough energy to taunt her father. I think Raymond was part of that."

"What are you saying? She married him to spite her dad?"

"Jake's father is a Kennedy Democrat. He always played the family-wealth thing very low-key. Gloria made loud Republican noises at family gatherings and was as visible with her trust fund as she could manage while she was out on the gilded-horse-show circuit. It made her father uncomfortable. I always assumed that was her intent."

"And Raymond?"

"He had a certain charisma, I suppose. Not charm, but charisma. The thing that made it so uncomfortable to be around him was that he was always cooking up some scheme or another to try to look large. With Gloria, he married into the big leagues, Alan. I did, too—by marrying her brother—so I know what it was like to try to function up in that rarefied air. And I can tell you that as unprepared as I was, Raymond certainly didn't have the tools to play at that level."

"Well, he's not underachieving now."

She chuckled. "I don't know about that. Ever take a close look at the current makeup of the House of Representatives? Most of those people wouldn't stand a chance of winning a second day on *Wheel of Fortune*. You have to admit that Congress has fulfilled the founding fathers' dreams and become the ultimate equal-opportunity employer."

"But before he was elected, Raymond Welle had his own nationally syndicated radio show. Not too many people get that far."

"And the ones who do? Whom exactly are we talking about, sweetie? Howard Stern and Don Imus? Rush Limbaugh? Dr. Laura?" She smiled at me in a way that was, at once, both patronizing and enormously affectionate. "Are you going to try to make an argument that the cream has floated to the top of that vat?"

The premise was distasteful. "I'll grant you a point on that. But you do have to admit he's made a name for himself. Raymond."

"Sure he's made a name for himself. What did he call himself on that stupid radio show before he was elected? America's therapist? And his campaign slogan, what was it? 'Colorado needs to get Welle.' But I don't think he did it all by himself. Raymond's where he is because he was smart enough and slimy enough first to marry Gloria, and second, to capitalize on the fact that she was brutally murdered. They used each other while they were alive. He got the last laugh though: he used her after she was dead. The man took his grief and vengeance onto his radio show like he was the one who'd invented the Greek tragedy."

My wife was being unusually reproachful. Typically, she found a way to shadow her criticisms behind a veil of acceptance. "So, can I safely assume that you didn't really like Raymond very much?" I asked.

"No," she replied. "I didn't. And I still don't."

"Is it politics? What?"

I watched her face contort into a yawn. The day of travel and meetings was taking a toll on her energy. "What he spouts off about, that's not politics. I'm sorry, that's dogma."

"What then? Why the negativity?"

Lauren picked some turkey from the side of her sandwich and slid it into her mouth. She chewed and swallowed before she responded to my question. "If you knew him in high school—Raymond, I mean—he would have been the boy who was always between cliques. He was the kid who considered himself too good for the group he was with and he would be doing everything he could to ingratiate himself with the group he wanted to be in. When I met him, he'd already managed to marry into the best clique he'd ever find. I suppose I was as guilty of that sin as he was. What I never liked about him is that he felt that his marriage, and his new status, elevated him to some new exalted level. Raymond actually believed that he was a better person because he'd married Gloria."

Lauren and I had never done a detailed tour of the marital territory she'd left behind with her divorce, so my next question to her was not uncomplicated. I couldn't foresee how she'd reply. I asked, "What was it like for you when you were married to Jake? I mean socially, I guess. You know, in the world of wealth and privilege?"

She sipped through a straw from a bottle of herbal tea

before she replied. "What was it like up there? Well, the food was almost always good. The sheets were always soft. The flowers were always fresh. The lines were short. But the people? The people were the same as they are everywhere else. Some wonderful, some ordinary, some despicable."

"Raymond?"

"He was never ordinary."

After lunch, the group filed out of the theater and descended the wide oak stairs to the main room in Kimber Lister's flat. Chairs were pulled in from the dining-room table. Large pillows were tossed on the wood floor. Lister and Russ Claven wheeled an old-fashioned schoolhouse chalkboard in from another room.

Before everyone was settled down, Lister began to make introductions of the visitors to the proceedings. First he introduced the current chief of the Steamboat Springs Police Department, a barrel-chested man with red hair named Percy Smith was identified as the man responsible for bringing the case of the two dead girls to the attention of Locard. The next introduction was Lauren. Finally, me. The group pretty much ignored us.

Lauren and I had grabbed a small chintz love seat at the back of the room. I sat enthralled as a discussion of the facts about the two dead girls slowly developed into a tornadic debate about whether the case could be closed with help from the group that was assembled. Questions were posed. Some were answered. Some were deflected or deferred. Lister outlined every advance and failure of the debate on the chalkboard with a fine hand that wasted precious little chalk.

The woman with the eye patch, it turned out, was a crime-scene specialist from North Carolina. Her name was Flynn Coe. She quickly became the focus of much of the early discussion, which dealt with the management—or mismanagement—of the crime scenes where the two girls had been found and where the snowmobile had been recovered. I assumed that Flynn had studied the police reports in advance of the meetings, because her comprehension of the problems posed by the collection and contamination of the evidence was so thorough and thoughtful.

Russ Claven, much to my surprise, revealed himself as a forensic pathologist who was on the faculty at Johns Hopkins. I struggled to understand the nuances of the questions that were thrown his way about the initial autopsies, tissue preservation, and the effects of long-term freezing on human cadavers. Most of it, thankfully, was way over my head.

I was also trying to begin to internalize a roster of the other regular members of Locard. At least three or four people in the room were FBI, including a supervisor from the Bureau's crime lab, and a hair-and-fibers specialist whose head was as bald as a baby's butt. I counted two prosecutors besides Lauren, one federal, one Maryland. Two homicide detectives. A faculty member from Northeastern University. A ballistics person who didn't look old enough for full membership in the NRA. A document analyst. A forensic dentist. A forensic anthropologist. A couple of cops whose specialties I couldn't discern. A forensic psychiatrist who looked like a game-show host, and A. J., who was a forensic psychologist. Two or three people never said enough to permit me to make a guess about their professional specialties.

After the focus shifted from Flynn Coe and the crime scene, a number of questions were directed to A. J., who had already completed a search of the FBI VICAP database looking for evidence of similar crimes in other jurisdictions. A few Locard members argued that two murders of young men—one in Arizona the year before, one in Texas the year after—that were accompanied by hand amputations warranted further analysis. To me, A. J. seemed skeptical about the connection. The very fact that she wanted me to assess the premorbid psychology of the two girls argued against her having much faith in the serial-killer theory.

My watch told me that we were almost two hours into

the debate before a sedate woman who sat far off to the side in the gathering took a break from her needlepoint long enough to speak for the first time. I guessed she was in her early sixties. She wore a long denim skirt and a pale green cardigan over an eyelet blouse. Only the top of the cardigan was buttoned. Everyone in the room quieted in response to her clearing her throat. As the room hushed, she lifted her half-glasses from her nose and dropped them gingerly to her ample chest, where they hung on a beaded chain. She said, "Excuse me, please, Kimber. But I have a question. Maybe two."

Kimber softened his booming voice as much as he could, which wasn't much. "Yes, Mary. Of course."

"What consideration was given to the involvement of the brother? Tami Franklin's brother? The one who claims he knew where she was taking the snowmobile that night?"

Percy Smith, the current chief of the Steamboat Springs Police Department, responded. "He was interviewed, but the boy was only fifteen at the time, ma'am."

"Yes?"

Her incredulity was an act intended to place Smith on the defensive. It worked. Smith said, "It is his family, the Franklin family, that requested that I contact Locard, ma'am. The family is underwriting a significant amount of the expenses associated with reopening the investigation."

"Yes?"

The chief hesitated and looked around the room for help. None was forthcoming. "Do you follow golf, ma'am?"

She fielded the non sequitur with aplomb. She said, "No, I'm sorry. Should I?" as she busied herself with picking some errant threads from her needlepoint that had ended up on her sweater.

"Tami Franklin's younger brother is Joey Franklin. The golfer? Perhaps you've heard of him."

"Actually, no, I have not. But that's very nice for him. I hope he enjoys the sport more than I do. But my question remains, what was Joey Franklin, the *golfer,* whose family so wants our help solving these crimes, what was that Joey Franklin doing the night his sister and her friend disappeared?"

Excitement clear in her voice, Lauren whispered. "Alan, you know who that is? I think that's Mary Wright. She's a legend in the Justice Department. She was on the team that prosecuted Noriega. People talk about her sometimes for the Supreme Court."

The name Mary Wright meant nothing to me.

The police chief finally replied to Mary's question. "In his initial interview, Joey stated that he was out riding his horse until sunset. He said that after he brushed his horse down he went inside and was playing video games after that. He maintains he went to bed early."

Mary had returned her half-glasses to her nose and had refocused her attention on her needlepoint. "Were his reports of his activities ever corroborated?"

The chief didn't respond. Kimber said, "No, Mary, to my knowledge his whereabouts have not been independently verified. His parents were out that night. Mr. Franklin wasn't back from a business trip of some kind. Mrs. Franklin was having dinner with a friend. Joey was home alone."

Mary clarified, her voice mildly admonishing. "I'm afraid that is a slightly elastic version of what we know to be true, Kimber. What we know appears to be limited to the reality that, if young Joey was home, he was home without parental supervision, and without a corroborating witness. His solitude cannot be established with anything approaching certainty."

Kimber grinned and proceeded to add a line to the chalkboard that read:

Alibi, Joey Franklin ??? Reinterview.

Lauren gestured at the new line on the board and whispered, "Is Joey Franklin who I think he is? That young golfer who everyone's talking about? The one who had the playoff with Tiger at that tournament?"

That tournament was the recent Masters. Lauren didn't follow sports much. I nodded and said, "It must be him."

"He's cute," she said.

I didn't have an opinion about his cuteness.

Kimber continued his solicitousness toward Mary Wright. "Is there anything else, Mary? Before we move on?"

She smiled warmly, her gaze wholly above the lenses of her glasses. "Perhaps one more thing. The location of the murders? I'm troubled that we haven't talked more about that. The initial investigation? One of the things that we don't know is where these poor girls were murdered. That's correct, isn't it?"

Kimber's strategy all along had been to require that the Steamboat Springs cop take the responsibility for acknowledging the weaknesses in the case. The chief finally admitted, "No. The initial investigation did not reveal the precise location of the actual murders."

Mary faced Flynn Coe. "Flynn, dear? You and Russ have determined that the site of the murder wasn't where the bodies were found, was it?"

"No, Mary. The girls weren't killed there. The bodies had been moved. Possibly on the snowmobile."

Mary said, "It seems to me that it would be very helpful for us to find that girl's hand and the other one's toes now, wouldn't it?"

Kimber wrote:

Tami Franklin, missing hand. Mariko Hamamoto, missing toes. Locate.

"That's all for me," said Mary.

CHAPTER
5

The meeting persisted through two breaks until late afternoon. Lauren was gamely trying to stay awake as the day waned. A. J. looked exhausted, too.

Finally, Kimber Lister called for an end to the debate and then a vote about the formation of a working group. To the visitors, he explained that the creation of a working group, if approved, would indicate that Locard had reached a decision to make resources available for this investigation. The membership of the working group would be composed of those Locard regulars and invited guests whose special skills were considered essential to advance this particular case.

The debate was brief. In short order, the formation of a working group was approved with only one dissenting vote. Kimber moved to appoint Flynn Coe to coordinate the working group, no one demurred, and he quickly listed the initial working-group membership on his chalkboard.

Flynn Coe, crime scene, working-group coordinator
Russell Claven, forensic pathology
Laird Stabler, hair and fibers
A. J. Simes, profiling, psychology
Mary Wright, prosecutor
Percy Smith, guest, detective
Lee Skinner, detective
Lauren Crowder, guest, prosecutor
Alan Gregory, guest, psychologist

Lister asked for recommended additions. None were proffered. He gave a short speech about confidentiality and relations with the media, should they learn of our work. He explained that each guest would be partnered with an active member of Locard. Percy Smith would work with Lee Skinner, Lauren with Mary Wright, I with A. J. Simes.

He thanked us for our time, and the meeting was over.

My watch told me it was 4:36 in Boulder, Colorado. But Lauren's drawn face and rapid-fire yawns told me it was much too late in the day for her. She'd told me more than once that one of the most difficult things about her illness was how it shortened her days. Most people get twelve or fourteen waking hours to work and to play and to love. "Sometimes," she'd said, "I feel like I only get four or six." Whatever allotment she'd had today, she'd severely overdrawn the account. It was absolutely clear to me that she needed to get horizontal and she needed it quickly. I despaired for her and worried about the effects of the fatigue on our baby.

Percy Smith approached the love seat just as I was about to go looking for Russ Claven to see what he could tell me about travel arrangements back to Colorado. Percy smiled at Lauren, whose eyes were closed, her fingers laced across her belly. He said, "Jet lag? Me, too."

I didn't bother to correct him.

He and I introduced ourselves, and managed some small talk about how nice it would be to be working together, before he said, "Listen," in a tone that was unnecessarily abrupt. "The three of us? We're traveling back home to Colorado together on Joey Franklin's jet. Just us. At the last break I phoned the people who coordinate the jet service. They can be ready to fly in about an hour. We'll get a cab from here out to Ronald Reagan. I assume that's okay with the two of you. The jet will drop me off in Steamboat and then take the two of you back down to Denver or wherever."

I glanced at Lauren for some sense of her inclination.

Her eyes didn't open; I suspected she had actually fallen asleep. The alternative to accepting Percy Smith's invitation was finding a hotel room for the night, arranging a commercial trip back to DIA the next day, the getting a cab to Jefferson County Airport, where we'd left our car. Smith's plan sounded better.

"Sounds good, Chief Smith. My wife's pretty tired. She will probably just sack out on the sofa in the plane."

He exhaled in a short burst through his nostrils. A feral snort. "Well, if there's two of them I got dibs on the other," he said. I was about to chuckle at the juvenile humor until I realized that the man was serious. He pointed at my chest and said, "How about you get the cab," then looked down at his watch. "Say, twenty minutes."

The word echoing about inside my head was *asshole*. I tried to smile, but I couldn't. I did manage a nod to his departing back. I promised myself it was the last directive I would take from the man.

A. J. Simes appeared as tired as Lauren as she approached us to say good-bye. She was leaning more heavily on her cane than she had been earlier in the day. She couldn't miss the evidence of Lauren's decline, and smiled sympathetically at me. "I think we may have asked too much of your wife today. Sorry. I will admit that I'm tempted to sack out next to her."

"She'll be fine. I think she's thrilled at the chance to be working with Mary Wright."

"She should be. Mary's a prize. What about you? Are you comfortable with what you heard today, Alan?"

I said, "Reasonably, A. J. I'll admit that I'm not too thrilled about interviewing Raymond Welle. The rest of the case seems interesting—fascinating, actually. But, given the expertise of this group, I feel like a total novice with all this—I'm counting on your guidance to help me through it."

She touched my arm. I couldn't tell whether it was an act of reassurance or whether it offered some protection against her losing her balance. "Don't worry, I'll provide whatever guidance you need. But if I read you right last year, before this is over you'll probably be telling me to get my nose out of your face."

I said, "I doubt that will happen. This work must be very satisfying for all of you in Locard. To be able to go back and offer consolation, or at least closure, to the victims' families on all these old cases."

"Not just old cases. What we revisit are cold cases. The way I look at our work is that our goal is to try to raise the dead. Or the presumed dead. Or the feared dead. If we do our work well, we bring them back long enough to help us solve the crime that took them away. When Kimber and I and a few others started all this a few years ago, I wanted to call the organization Lazarus. No one else liked the name though. But I thought it would be the most fitting label of all."

"I can see how it would be."

A. J. shifted her weight and tried to disguise a grimace. "And it has been very satisfying. For someone like me who isn't able to participate professionally in the Bureau any longer, it provides an opportunity to satisfy a true need. For others on the team, it provides a sense of camaraderie, of collegiality, and a feeling of being able to directly impact justice in a way that their career paths often deny them."

I said, "I don't actually know too much bout Vidocq, your counterpart in Philadelphia, but what I saw today leaves me with the impression that you do things a bit differently than they do."

"We can't match them in reputation, but we have every bit as much expertise. Our profile is lower, by design. Our style is more proactive. Our membership is, well—how should I put it?— less mainstream. We're less hesitant to dive in and investigate where we need to. Lister calls the difference between Vidocq and Locard the difference between cogitation and investigation. But Vidocq has certainly enjoyed its successes."

"What about Lister? Where does he fit?"

My question caused her to smile. "That . . . is another story. A long one. One that will have to wait until a time when your wife and I aren't so tired. I'll phone you tomorrow or the next day in Colorado and we'll begin to map out an initial strategy for how to approach our particular piece of this puzzle. Then we'll get started filling in the holes. I'm grateful, Alan, that you agreed to help. I definitely wanted someone I could trust on this one. Please say good-bye to Lauren for me and express my gratitude to her as well."

She turned to leave. I said, "Before you go, A. J.— the jet that we flew out on? It belongs to Joey Franklin, isn't that right?"

She tightened her eyes. "Yes, he owns a piece of the plane. Apparently, it's a time-share arrangement. He buys an eighth or a quarter interest or something and then he gets to use so many hours a year to fly around to his golf tournaments and things. I recall that your ethical knife has a very sharp blade, so I think I know what you're concerned about. A possible conflict of interest, right? I've mentioned it to Kimber already. We'll have to keep an eye on it and see what develops with the young girl's brother. If money to aid the investigation continues to flow from the Franklin family, we may have something to be worried about."

"You probably already know this, but Lauren and I and Chief Smith are flying back on the jet in an hour."

She shrugged. "My advice? Enjoy the flight. It'll be much easier on Lauren than going commercial." She touched my arm again and nodded at my wife. "When is she due?"

Very little escaped A. J.'s attention. "Beginning of October. Thanks for asking. The pregnancy has gone well so far."

"Is she stable?" From the slight alteration in tone, I discerned that she was asking about Lauren's MS, not her pregnancy.

"The pregnancy has been kind to her as far as her illness is concerned. It's after that has me concerned.

You know? The stress of having a newborn?" Lauren's neurologist had told us that pregnancy was often a period of respite and remission for women with multiple sclerosis. Unfortunately, the protection often ended abruptly with delivery.

"I know," said A. J. "Her role on this case shouldn't be too difficult. If it gets to be too much for her, let me know. Mary and I are friends." She adjusted her weight on her cane. "We'll talk soon."

She held out her hand. I responded by leaning in and giving her a quick hug. Into her ear, I said, "You feeling okay? Honestly."

She pulled back. "Honestly? I can't complain."

I watched her walk away and then went in search of a phone to call for a car to take us to the airport.

Lauren woke to an almost empty loft. She was embarrassed by her fatigue, as I figured she would be.

Kimber Lister saw us toward the elevator. "The car is here. Downstairs, idling at the curb. Chief Smith does not endeavor to travel as lightly as the two of you. His luggage is, believe me, not insubstantial for such an abbreviated visit. He's downstairs now, loading his things." He placed a hand on the small of each of our backs. "These days when we at Locard introduce new cases always turn out to be quite hectic for me. My principal regret is that I usually don't get a chance to acquaint myself with my guests as thoroughly as I would like. Please forgive me if I have not managed to be an attentive host. I pray we will have another opportunity to visit and that on that occasion you will permit me to properly express my gratitude for your participation and your sacrifice on our behalf."

I wondered how he could construct sentences like that after a day as draining as this one had been. I said, "You've been very kind. Your home is quite lovely. And we'd welcome another chance to get to know you better, as well. We're honored to have been asked to participate. And we appreciate your hospitality."

He closed his eyes briefly and nodded his head in some manner of acknowledgment.

Lauren stopped in front of the elevator in the foyer. "The film we saw earlier? Was that your work?"

Lister blushed. "Yes," he said. "I . . . composed that piece. An avocation of mine."

"You have talent, Mr. Lister. I was captivated."

"Kimber, please. You're too kind."

"I'm not being insincere."

"Well. Thank you, then."

"You're quite welcome. Alan and I both hope we're able to provide enough help to warrant A. J.'s faith in us."

Lister laughed. "I do not concern myself with that for even a moment. A. J. Simes does not assess people incorrectly. That is why she's such a valuable member of the Locard team."

The elevator arrived. Lister kissed Lauren on the cheek and told us both to be well.

The taxi waiting downstairs was, fortunately, a huge something from General Motors. Percy Smith was already sitting in the backseat staring at his watch in a manner that I figured was intended to induce our guilt at being tardy. I don't think Lauren noticed. I was irritated by his pettiness.

Apparently Smith had already given the driver directions, for the car lurched from the curb the second I closed the door behind me. I asked the driver to please switch on the air conditioner. Lauren's MS caused her to be intolerant of heat. I assumed her pregnancy would only aggravate her discomfort.

Smith said, "I don't like air-conditioning."

I leaned forward and faced him, Lauren between us. Intentionally forcing civility into my voice, "I'm sorry, Chief Smith. My wife requires the air-conditioning for her health. I hope you can accommodate her for the brief amount of time it will take us to get across town to the airport." As the words came out of my mouth, I felt as though I were talking like Kimber Lister.

Without a word, Smith pressed the button that raised his window. When the glass finally sealed shut, he muttered, "On such a fine day, too."

I began to wonder whether this private jet with ten seats was going to be large enough for the three of us.

The flight attendant on this leg was a gentleman in his fifties named Hans. He was solicitous and professional in getting us settled on board. Lauren noticed, as I did, that the interior of this plane was slightly different than the one on which we'd flown east. I wondered out loud whether Joey Franklin leased an entire fleet.

Chief Smith spoke for the first time since muttering about having to close his window. "Joey actually leases time in the air, not on a specific plane. Any plane in the fleet that's the right size might arrive when he calls for service. He uses them mostly to get to his golf tournaments. Shares the cost with one of his buddies."

Lauren was settling down on one of the leather sofas, fumbling for her seat belt. "It certainly is a pleasant way to fly."

"Can't beat it," said Smith. "Can't beat it. Hans? A cold beer would be great right about now. One of those green ones, from your homeland."

Hans looked right at me and, his face otherwise impassive, raised one reddish blond eyebrow about an eighth of an inch before he said, "I'm from Germany, sir. The beer you are requesting is, I believe, Heineken. It is made in Holland." He turned as a soldier might and retraced his steps to the galley to retrieve Percy's beer. Percy glared at him; Percy didn't care in what country his beer was made, but he didn't like being corrected by the help.

Lauren had apparently decided to put more effort into being cordial to our traveling companion than I had. She asked, "Have you flown on Mr. Franklin's airplane before, Chief Smith?"

"Yep. Came out here for the first Locard meeting."

Lauren asked, "How did it come about that you requested Locard to reopen the investigation of the murder of the two girls?"

He took the beer from Hans, immediately finishing almost half of the contents. "I took over the force in Steamboat almost two years ago. Weren't too many cases left for me to clean up in town. And none anywhere near as serious as this one. Even though it was a sheriff's case and not a city case I was naturally interested—it being a homicide and all—and so I made it a point to familiarize myself with everyone who had been involved back then. It was Mr. Franklin—senior, not Joey—who told me about Locard. I'd never heard of them. He'd seen something in some newspaper about that kidnapping they solved in Texas. That high school boy? You remember? So I asked the sheriff if he minded if I started looking at the stuff he had in his files. Sheriff didn't care. So I reinterviewed some of the witnesses. Inventoried the evidence that hadn't been misplaced. I actually pulled everything together that I could—even put it all together in a new murder book—and Mr. Franklin senior and I came out and met Kimber and three or four others a couple of months back. That's how it all got started."

Lauren asked, "What about the other family? Mariko's family?"

"Long gone. Back in Japan for all I know."

"So they haven't been consulted? You don't know how they feel about the work we are going to be doing?"

Percy shrugged. "Why would they object?"

I was about to press to try and determine whether any effort had been made to contact the Hamamoto family, but the captain was walking to the back of the plane. She was a tall woman with intricate braids that had been pinned up at the sides of her head. She had swimmer's shoulders. She introduced herself to her three passengers and said we'd begin taxiing in about three minutes and that the first hour or so looked to be pretty bumpy. A big wall of thunderstorms was heading north out of the Virginias. "So I want y'all to listen to his safety instructions extra carefully." She waited. I nodded. "Good. Now enjoy your flight. Our first stop today is Yampa Valley Regional Airport, then we'll be heading off on a very short hop to Jefferson County."

Hans had been waiting patiently for the captain to finish speaking. He stepped forward and leaned from his waist toward Lauren. "A refreshment, miss, while we taxi? Perhaps a warm towel for your hands and face?" he inquired.

I leaned down and raised one of Lauren's legs to my lap and removed her shoe. As I began to massage her foot, I decided I was going to do everything in my power to enjoy this flight.

CHAPTER
6

Lauren and Percy quickly fell asleep and Hans covered each of them with a quilted blanket. Lauren stirred each time the plane encountered turbulence, which was frequently, once opening her eyes and gazing at me before rolling onto her side. I reached over and tightened her seat belt a little, briefly resting my hand on the slight swell in her abdomen. Percy Smith didn't move at all. I made a silent bet to myself that he would snore.

The conversation that accompanied dinner was banal, and was mostly focused on Percy's background because Percy displayed absolutely no interest in either Lauren or me. He lost no time in letting us know that he had played football for Tom Osborne at Nebraska—although it turned out he had actually played very little football for Tom Osborne at Nebraska. Lauren stopped him before he launched into a description of the knee rehab he had endured for the ACL he'd torn during his sophomore year. He was equally eager to boast that he had married a beautiful cheerleader named Judy. He lifted a fat wallet from his hip pocket and showed us a worn picture of Judy in her Nebraska cheerleader outfit. Judy Smith *was* quite pretty. Percy explained that his "wife's people are from Routt County. Mining. Cattle. Old-timers."

Lauren asked if he and Judy had any children.

He replied, "Yeah. Two."

O-kay. In Percy's mind, I guessed that covered the topic.

Percy's life didn't fascinate me enough to continue the conversation in the direction it was heading. I changed the subject back to the issue of the two dead girls. "What about the man you replaced in Steamboat? What was his name? Barrett? What did he think about the way his investigation concluded?"

"I didn't replace Barrett. Barrett was Routt County sheriff. And he left in ninety-two or ninety-three. I replaced Tim Whitney."

"So you don't know Sheriff Barrett?"

"Didn't say that. Phil Barrett still works for Congressman Welle—he's some bigwig on his staff—and they both still call Steamboat home. We've crossed paths a few times since I've been in town. Played golf with him once. Man has more slices than a deli. Barrett, not Welle. And he can't putt to save his life."

Lauren asked, "Have you discussed the case with him?"

Percy scratched himself on the back of the neck but didn't reply.

Her fork in midair, Lauren persisted. "I have to wonder how he feels about his work being scrutinized by a bunch of strangers."

I was surprised to observe Percy appear thoughtful. After a moment's contemplation, he said, "Nobody would like this case solved more than Phil Barrett. Well, maybe Mr. Franklin. But after him, Phil Barrett wants the answers the most."

Lauren said, "I've been wondering about something else. Was Mr. Barrett the sheriff when Raymond Welle's wife was killed?"

Percy Smith seemed to find the change in direction curious. His eyebrows jumped up and caused the shape of eyes to change from narrow ovals to nickel-sized circles. "What does that have to do with anything?"

Evenly, Lauren said, "It has nothing to do with anything as far as I know. I knew her, that's all. Gloria Welle. I'm just asking."

Percy nodded in a manner that said "I knew that."

although it was apparent that he hadn't been aware of Lauren's connection to the Welles. "That nastiness happened when Phil Barrett was sheriff. Not a pretty chapter in the congressman's life. Thank goodness I don't have to reopen that one."

I said, "I'm not sure what you mean by that."

Percy gestured at Hans as though the man was a waiter in a diner. When Hans hesitated, Percy stared him down until he approached. Percy didn't look toward either Lauren or me when he continued. "Just that it's solved, that's all. That case had all the pieces this other one doesn't. Witnesses who saw something, forensics that mean something, ballistics that handed us a gun, a motive that made sense—the whole nine yards. I wish we had some of that going for us with the Franklin case."

"And the Hamamoto case," Lauren added.

"Yeah. That, too. Coffee, Hans. I need sugar." Percy reached into a leather carry-on and removed a paperback copy of Tom Clancy's latest. The book appeared to have been through a war that was fought in a humid climate. Percy folded it open, cracking the spine mercilessly. I guessed he was on page 60 or so.

The night was almost moonless when we glided to a stop at the Yampa Valley airport. Hans preceded Percy off the plane and helped him collect his plentiful luggage.

We were airborne again in minutes, the rolling mountaintops of the Routt National Forest quickly yielding to the sharp rock faces and glacial precipices of the Continental Divide. We'd be zooming down the Front Range in minutes, home in bed, I guessed, within the hour.

Adrienne, our neighbor across the lane, heard us drive up and released our dog out her front door. Emily bounded across the dirt and gravel toward our garage with astonishing enthusiasm. She pounced left, she charged right. Before proceeding farther, she lowered her head and scooped up a stick, shaking it with enough intensity to kill it.

From Adrienne's doorway, we heard a little male voice scream. "Emily! Em-i-ly! Come back. Come back!"

Lauren called, "Hi, Jonas. She'll come back and see you tomorrow, okay? It's late. It's time for her to go to bed."

He lowered his arms as though he were a bird preparing to fly. He stomped one foot. "She wants to *play*. She doesn't want to go to bed."

"Tomorrow, honey. Tell your mom thanks for watching her, okay?"

Jonas flapped his arms again and started to cry. Lauren placed the palm of one hand on her belly and looked at the watch on her other wrist. She shook her head and her face looked rueful. She said, "Gosh, sweets, I hope our baby isn't a night person. I don't know what I'll do."

I let our carry-ons fall from my hands and gave her a hug. "We'll do fine. You'll do fine."

She was looking back over my shoulder toward Adrienne's house. "That's not Erin's car, is it?" Erin Rand was Adrienne's girlfriend-partner of quite a few months, and her first same-sex paramour ever.

I looked and said, "No. It's not Erin's. Not unless she won the lottery." Erin was a struggling private detective. The car by Adrienne's front door was a cream-colored Lexus.

Lauren mused, "I haven't seen Erin in a couple of weeks. Do you think she's . . . I don't know. Do you think they broke up?"

"I don't know either. Adrienne hasn't said anything to me about any trouble in their relationship."

Lauren hooked an arm around my back. "It's funny, don't you think, that if that car belongs to some new love interest of Adrienne's, that neither of us really has a clue what the gender of the driver might be?"

"I bet girl," I said without any confidence. "That looks like an estrogen-colored Lexus."

"Estrogen-colored? What the hell does that mean? No. That's an androgynous Lexus. And I bet boy," Lauren countered, holding out her hand for a shake. "Bet? Let's say the loser cooks and cleans up dinners for a week."

"What about take-out or restaurants?"

"No more than twice."

"Why do you think Adrienne's gone back to seeing a guy? Do you know something I don't know?"

She spun me at my shoulders and pointed me toward the front door. "Gosh, Alan, I certainly hope so."

PART TWO

The Two Dead Girls

CHAPTER
7

Monday morning came around just when it was supposed to. After some weekends that simple occurrence surprised me. This was one of those.

I drove across town to my Walnut Street office to see my 8:15 patient. Lauren took her own car into town, heading up Canyon Boulevard to the Justice Center for a meeting with the coroner's chief assistant. Their meeting was to discuss his testimony in a trial scheduled for that afternoon. She was doubtful that the case was going to plead out.

My patients all showed up at their appointed times. None of them threw me any curveballs that I couldn't hit and I was home in time for dinner.

Neither Erin's old Saab nor the cream-colored Lexus had reappeared in front of Adrienne's house across the lane, and neither Lauren nor I had been brave enough to inquire about the current state of fluctuation of our neighbor's sexual orientation. Lauren and I were still sharing dinner chores, our bet unresolved.

For me Tuesday began like Monday. I had four patients to see before lunch, three afterward. I was hoping to get home early enough to indulge in a long bike ride on the country roads that crisscrossed the rapidly disappearing open prairie of eastern Boulder County. Lauren had given the opening statement in her child-abuse-resulting-in-death case on Monday afternoon and was due to call her first witness at 9:30 on Tuesday morning. She thought the trial would last through Wednesday at least but had grown more hopeful about settlement and half expected a plea conference during the lunch recess. She considered the first three witnesses in her case to be lethal to the defense and expected to get them all in before noon. She also suspected that her adversary at the defense table would blink.

I cooked Tuesday's dinner. Grilled halibut and steamed baby bok choy in garlic sauce. The menu was my wife's idea; Lauren was currently religious about omega-3 fish oils, garlic, and iron. On her way home from work she'd picked up a loaf of multigrain from the Breadworks on North Broadway.

She was just about done cleaning up the paltry mess I'd left in the kitchen when the phone rang. I took it in the big open room that ran the length of the west end of the house.

The house was one that I had called home for a long time. I'd lived through two periods of being single there and was now in my second period being married there. Two different wives, the second a much better match than the first. The house, once a shack, now felt new to me. The previous autumn Lauren and I had embarked on an ambitious addition and remodeling project, and the smells and feels of the place were those of a new home.

The views, fortunately, hadn't changed at all.

Our home sits near the top of a western-facing slope in Spanish Hills on the eastern side of the Boulder Valley. On a clear day—and in Colorado most of them are clear enough—our view of the Front Range extends from north of Pikes Peak to north of Longs Peak and from the greenbelt on the east side of the city of Boulder all the way to the Continental Divide. God might have a better view than we did but I wouldn't believe it unless He sent along a postcard to prove it.

As summer threatened, the days were getting longer and the sun was lingering so low in the evening sky that the sharp rays made it impossible to sit facing west without lowering the blinds, which I was loath to do. When the phone rang, I picked up the receiver and sat with

my back to the mountains. I expected to hear my partner's voice. Diane Estevez had left me a message during
our workday that she wanted to talk about a weekend
away that Lauren and I were planning with Diane and
her husband, Raoul. Diane was currently on a Taos kick.
I was guessing that she wanted to lobby us to change
our weekend plans from the Great Sand Dunes to Taos.

I said, "Hello."

"Alan? It's A. J."

My breath caught in my throat. I'd almost forgotten
about the two dead girls. "A. J. How are you?"

Almost forgotten.

"Fine," she said in a manner that precluded further
inquiry about her health. Lauren employed the same
tone sometimes; I had radar for it. "I think we're ready
to get started on our little adventure. I have some information. You have something to write with?"

"No. Hold on." I ran to the new master bedroom and
grabbed a pad of notepaper that I kept by the bed.
"Shoot."

"First, I've made contact with Representative Welle's
office. With remarkably little fuss he's agreed to see you.
That surprises me. His next visit home to Colorado is in
about two weeks. He's flying into Denver a week from
Friday for some meetings and fund-raising appearances
before going up to his place in the mountains for a few
days of R and R. I worked out a tentative time for you
to see him on the Friday that he's in Denver. Can you
make that work? I hope you can make that work."

"I try to keep Fridays pretty clear, A. J. Shouldn't be
any problem. Where does he want to meet?"

"Representative Welle will be attending some fund-
raiser at a place his aide called the Phipps Mansion. Said
it's where the recent Summit of the Eight was held when
it was in Denver. Do you know anything about it? Know
where it is? I can get more details if you need me to."

"That's not necessary. I've been there once before. I'm
sure I can find it again."

"Anyway, Welle wants to meet you there, at that mansion, just before or just after his fund-raising luncheon."

"Either is fine with me."

"Well, you won't get to choose. They'll call you the day before and tell you whether it's going to be before or whether it's going to be after. I think it's a petty little political control thing—keeping you waiting to be beckoned—but who am I to question the motives of the powerful? I was told you'd get a message from a man named Phillip Barrett. He'll—"

"I heard about Barrett from Percy Smith on the plane ride back to Colorado. He's an old friend of Welle's. He was the sheriff in Routt County when Gloria Welle was kidnapped and murdered. And when the two girls were killed."

"I didn't know that. Interesting. Now Barrett's one of Welle's congressional honchos, maybe even chief of staff. I don't know. I don't really care. These staffers are mostly just insulation as far as I can tell. They function like they're just rolls and rolls of that puffy pink stuff—ways to keep regular folks more than a few steps away from their elected representatives. Regardless, Barrett'll call you with the time that Welle chooses for your audience. I gave Barrett both your office number and your beeper number, but not your home."

"Good. I'm grateful that I have a couple of weeks before I meet with Welle. I want to drive up to Steamboat and try to get to know Tami Franklin's family—you know, begin to flesh out a profile on her and learn what I can about her relationship with Mariko. And I need to get permission from Mariko's family to receive information about her psychotherapy with Dr. Welle. Do you by any chance have phone numbers and addresses for them—any way for me to reach the Hamamotos?"

"If I don't have them already, I can get them. I'll fax them to you as soon as I do. You want me to fax it to your home or to your office?"

"Please send everything here, to my house."

"Oh, and you'll get a package from me tomorrow. I

overnighted it to your house. It's copies of all the parts of the original investigation that might be pertinent to what you and I are doing. Statements, interviews, reports. You know. I've highlighted some things that I found interesting. Is there anything else I can do for you tonight?"

I looked west just as the sun was cresting the Divide. The long shadows of dusk were creeping in a relentless advance across the Boulder Valley toward our house. "Just some advice. Do you think I should let Raymond Welle know that I'm married to his ex-sister-in-law?"

A. J. laughed. "No. Absolutely, no. There may come a time when we want to throw that in his face. This isn't it. Hey," she asked, "how's the pregnancy going? Is Lauren feeling okay?"

"Great. No problems so far. She actually seems less tired now that she's pregnant."

"I've heard that happens. Don't think I'll try it, though. Has she gotten a call from Mary Wright yet?"

"Not that I know of. But she's been in a trial both days this week."

"I really envy Lauren's strength. I couldn't do what she does. It's much too draining."

"The disease you two have has many faces, A. J. Your illnesses have the same name, but never the same consequences. Still, sometimes I worry that it's too draining for her, too."

She didn't really want to talk about her illness. She said, "I'm sure Mary will be in touch, soon."

Two seconds after I hung up the phone, it rang again. This time it was my longtime partner, Diane.

Her greeting was, "I've been trying to reach you for hours. Why don't you get call waiting?"

"I've only been on the phone for ten minutes. And I don't like those annoying little clicks in my ears."

"Well, I don't like busy signals."

I shrugged. This argument didn't appear to offer much hope of reward. "What's up?"

She sighed. "Would you guys consider going to Taos

instead of the Sand Dunes? There's this gallery I really, really want to go to. They're holding a piece for me. Please? Pretty please? We'll do the wilderness and buffalo thing some other time."

The fax with addresses and phone numbers for the Hamamotos slithered out of our machine a half an hour after I yielded to Diane about Taos.

Mr. Hamamoto was living in British Columbia. His wife was in Japan. His surviving daughter was a graduate student at Stanford, in California. I phoned the number in British Columbia and left Mr. Hamamoto a message, along with an abbreviated explanation of my involvement in Locard and my interest in his daughter. I asked him to please return my call.

Lauren's case pleaded out on Wednesday morning before court commenced for the day. Since she was only working half-time, she decided that she was free to take the rest of the week off. I would be done with my last patient of the week Thursday afternoon at 3:45. The five-day forecast called for sunny days and cool nights. Afternoon thunderstorms were always a possibility.

Adrienne and Jonas were eager to watch Emily.

It was a perfect time to visit Steamboat Springs. By the time we left for the mountains late on Thursday afternoon I still hadn't heard back from Mr. Hamamoto.

I was tempted to take Highway 40 north through Granby—it was the more scenic route to Steamboat—but it was a longer drive and I didn't really want to be forced to do Rabbit Ears Pass in the darkest of darks, so we opted to stay on Interstate 70 all the way to Silverthorne, and headed north from there. Less than ten minutes after departing the interstate I pulled over to the side of the two-lane road and stopped the car in the dust. I pointed up the hill to the east and said to Lauren, "That's Dead Ed's ranchette." The sign above the gate in front of us read THE NOT SO LAZY SEVEN RANCH.

The previous year, one of my patients, a teenage girl

a little younger than Tami Franklin, had had her life turned upside down in a barn up that dirt road. Although I'd been to the ranchette once before with my friend, Boulder detective Sam Purdy, this was the first time I'd had the opportunity to point it out to Lauren.

She didn't know the psychological details of the tragedy, only the more public, legal ones. Both of her hands were resting on her abdomen as she said, "That's where it happened? Whatever it was with the RV and . . . Merritt? And the shooting? This is where that was, too?"

She knew the answers to her questions. But I responded anyway. "You can't see the barn from here, but yes. On the other side of that stand of aspen is where it is. You can see a little bit of the house from here. The sun is still reflecting off the windows. See? There? To the left?"

"Yes, I think I see it." She had already stopped looking up the hill. Her gaze was focused straight down the highway, as straight as the parallel lines of yellow paint down the center of the road. Her voice was soft, but adamant as she said, "We won't ever let things like that happen to our baby, will we?"

I checked my mirrors for traffic and touched her on the cheek. "No way, sweets. No way." Neither of us was naive enough to believe we actually had the power to protect our baby from life's hurts—big or little—but to embark on this journey as parents we knew we needed whatever talismans bravado could provide. So I conspired with her to parental assurance. Although it was relatively new behavior to me, I found it to be a totally natural act.

I eased the big car from the shoulder back onto the asphalt and pressed hard on the accelerator. The car lurched. Behind us a pair of headlamps was gaining ground too quickly for my comfort.

The sun had already disappeared behind the Gore Range and the narrow valley that hugged the Blue River was quickly losing its luster. The daylight that remained was bruised black and blue. We stopped in Kremmling

and ate at a bakery that sold pizza. The Colorado River
flowed nearby. We'd cross it in the final light of dusk. I
was thinking that it would be swollen with snowmelt.

Over bitter coffee, I became conscious of the images
that this journey along Highway 9 was foisting into my
awareness. *Bruising, swelling, tragedy, tumult.*

Snowmelt.

The reason, I knew, was simple. The next morning
Lauren and I were scheduled to meet with Catherine and
Wendell Franklin to talk with them about their dead
daughter, Tamara.

The drive up County Road 129 into the Elk River
Valley outside Steamboat Springs had taken a little more
than a half hour. The road hugged the river as it climbed
gently through a gorgeous high-country valley that was
blessed with wide expanses of pasture and rolling hillsides that were covered with spruce, fir, and aspen. It
was difficult to believe that we were high in the Rockies.
This didn't even feel like the same mountain system that
spawned the Gore Range, the Maroon Bells, or the
San Juans.

I didn't get lost on my way to the ranch. "Go until
you almost get to Clark. You'll see the ranch on your
left. If you get to Clark, you missed us. The barn has a
new roof," Dell Franklin had explained on the phone.
Lauren spotted the new roof and I pulled off the road.
The Elk River was at least a half mile to the west of us
at that point. The deep meadows between the river and
us rippled as gentle breezes brushed the silky tops of the
alfalfa crop.

I'd been expecting to greet a couple on the verge of
retirement. But the Franklins weren't too many years
older than Lauren and me. I guessed that Cathy must
have been only eighteen or nineteen when she had given
birth to her first child, her daughter, Tamara. Now their
nest was empty while we were only beginning to prepare ours.

"Call us Dell and Cathy, please." The order came from

Dell Franklin. "Sit down, sit down. Have some coffee and cake."

Dell collapsed heavily on his chair and his breathing was labored. He was portly and wore his hair in a buzz cut that has recently become fashionable again. I doubt that Dell knew much about fashion, though. To meet with us, he had dressed in a long-sleeve blue polo shirt with a Cadillac insignia over one breast, and new blue Wranglers. The sleeves of the polo shirt were pushed up halfway over his thick forearms. He wore boots that were reserved for indoor use. Even this early in the summer his skin was brown and weathered and the ladder of wrinkles on each of his temples was deeply furrowed from many hours, probably too many hours, in the high-country sunshine.

Cathy's gaze seemed to burn and her eyes filled me with sorrow. Over the years I'd met with dozens of parents who displayed their pain in their eyes the way Cathy did—mothers who were desperate for whatever psychological help, or salve, I could provide to aid their childen. Mothers who had placed all their hope in me after they'd concluded that I was their last best chance for salvation, but were preparing themselves for the possibility or even the likelihood, that their hope would again be burned at the pyre of disappointment.

The big book that Cathy Franklin held in her lap was a photo album.

She wore a pair of old Lee jeans that she'd cherished so long the cotton was now as soft as chenille. They still fit her as they did the day she bought them. Her blouse was rayon or silk, and she wore it with the top four buttons loose. Underneath was a faded yellow chemise.

We were sitting in what Dell had called the "sitting room." I would call it a family room. A massive stone fireplace filled half of a long wall above a hearth fashioned from thick pine logs and topped with stone. The mantel above the firebox was crowded with trophies topped with brass golfers and silver golf balls. A coffee service was set up before us on a low table.

Cathy had been anxious for our arrival.

CHAPTER
8

She'd be twenty-eight today. She'd have babies by now.
I think she'd have . . . two babies. I'd be a grand-
mother." Cathy sighed and flipped open the photo album
on her lap and stared at a picture that I suspected had
not been chosen at random. Tamara, upside down from
my point of view across the coffee table, appeared to
have been eight or nine when the picture was taken. She
was standing on cross-country skis in front of a teepee.
The psychologist in me wondered why her mother had
chosen a photograph of her daughter during the quies-
cence of latency. It might have meant nothing of course,
but Cathy Franklin hadn't locked on to an oedipal Tami,
or a preadolescent, pubertal one. She hadn't chosen a
picture of Tami just before her death, either.

Cathy said, "Her smile—Tami's? It was so bright—it
would make you glad that you're alive." She fidgeted
and stared at her hands as she spoke to us about her
dead daughter. I was thinking that the absence of a
daughter's smile could probably leave a mother wishing
she were dead. My thoughts leapt to the life growing in
Lauren's belly. I pried my attention away and my stomach flipped.

Cathy continued. "It's been over ten years," she said
as she lifted one hand and scratched behind her ear.
"Well more than ten." Her voice was disbelieving. I
couldn't tell whether she was disbelieving because the
tragedy still felt like yesterday, or whether she was disbelieving because she felt as though she'd already cried
away enough tears to lubricate a few lifetimes.

Wendell—Dell—reached over and touched his wife on the knee. He was a bear of a man and the act seemed all the more gentle because of his mass. His breathing grew less labored as he made contact with her. He said, to his wife as much as to us, "It's still hard sometimes. You know—it's hard to remember . . . and . . . it's hard to forget." Cathy clenched her husband's thick fingers and lifted her face to us. She manufactured a smile that brought tears to my eyes.

"We're so grateful you've agreed to help," she said.

I was fighting therapist proclivities. Cathy's arrested grief was fertile ground. But I reminded myself that this field wasn't mine to furrow. Not here. Not now.

Lauren jumped in and explained our role in Locard. That we were consultants. And that our participation in the investigation was limited to specific tasks that had been delineated by the permanent members of the Locard team. She explained her role as a local prosecuting attorney.

When she was finished, I spoke. "As you know, I'm a psychologist. One of my most important tasks is to get to know your daughter," I said, moving my gaze from Dell to Cathy and back. "When I'm done with my work, I'd like to feel that I've come to know who Tami was on that day that she died."

Dell raised an eyebrow and asked, "Don't get it. How will that help you find her killer?"

I took a moment to compose a response. "The more I know about Tami—the better I know Tami—the better chance I have of being able to figure out what caused her to . . ."—I struggled to find the right word—". . . to collide with whoever it was who murdered her."

Dell appeared to be on the verge of responding when Cathy said, "She was a sweetheart. No one who knew her would ever want to kill her. It had to be a stranger."

"Tami . . ." He shook his head a tiny bit and smiled lovingly. "She could be kind of ornery," added Dell. "But she was our girl. We loved her from sunrise to sunset. God, how we loved her."

Over a decade had passed and they were both still crying over Tami's death. I noticed that Lauren's hands, which had been folded on her lap, were now spread palms down, the fingers nesting protectively around her womb.

Lauren and I didn't have a plan. As things developed she spent much of the next hour sitting with Cathy at a game table in an alcove on one side of the sitting room, poring through photo albums, listening to Cathy reminisce about a daughter she had never imagined living without.

As soon as the wives retreated to the photo albums Dell invited me outside to show me some of his ranch and, it was apparent, to talk about his living child and not just his dead one. I waited while he changed his boots in a big mudroom before he led me away from the house. He had already surprised me with his openness and his sensitivity in discussing his daughter. Anticipating the visit to the ranch I'd unfairly pigeonholed him as a taciturn old cowboy. It was neither a fair nor an accurate assessment. I was beginning to see Dell as an emotionally resourceful man who didn't run from either his own pain or Cathy's.

The ranch was "a lot of acres," according to Dell. "My father assembled almost all the land. I've added a couple of small patches over the years. Some new buildings. The technology of course, though Dad would have been the first to have that if it was available to him. But mostly I've been a caretaker of what my father imagined. I consider this place a kind of trust, you know?"

I said, "I think I understand." My focus was on the expansive high prairies and the vaulting peaks of the wilderness below Mount Zirkel. Those aspen groves would sparkle like gold dust in the fall. "Trust" felt like a good enough word.

"My part's been the animals. My addition to my father's vision. I do well with them. With the animals. I especially love just about everything that's involved with breeding. You know much about ranching?" I was a step behind him, following him down a wide asphalt lane that led from the family home to the barn with the shiny new roof.

"Not much," I admitted. "Almost as much as I know about the economy of Serbia."

He laughed. "Most don't. Some think they do; they think any brain-dead cowboy can run a ranch. Some pretend they know. But most don't understand. Tami did. She loved it out here. Really understood what it was we were up to. What it takes to feed this monster. What it takes to tame it. We hoped—me and Cathy—we hoped Tami'd stay, marry somebody who would want to take over the ranch with her."

"Joey's not interested, Dell? In the ranch?" I assumed he wasn't but wanted to hear Dell's response.

"In this? Nah. He's got his golf. It's all he seems to need. Never seen anyone who's been so completed by one activity." Dell shook his head, apparently perplexed by his own son. "We're blessed in Routt County. You know you can play golf up here almost as long as you can in Denver? In a good year you can play all the way from May through October. We're not as high up in the mountains as people think. Where we're standing right this minute, we're only a little above seven thousand feet. You're surprised, right? Still, don't know how Joey got so darn good at it. Golf, I mean. Some people just click with some things. You ever notice that?"

I said I had noticed that.

The first two stalls on the inside of the huge barn had been rebuilt as an indoor golf driving range. An elevated tee. A huge net to catch balls. A computer to analyze and measure something. Distance? I didn't golf. I couldn't tell.

"I play a little. Been a member for years at the little golf club that's out on 40. Started as an excuse to hang out with some friends, really. I hack. It's a nine-hole and if I'm lucky, I break fifty maybe twice a summer. Never really have time to play eighteen. Lose more balls than

I care to count. Joey used to like to come with me to the range when he was little, you know, like five or six. He'd hit some balls. Had a real sweet swing, right from the start. Soon enough, he wanted to play in the winter, too. Only kid I knew who would rather hit golf balls than go skiing, so one year I built this for him." Dell waved at the indoor golf setup. "It wasn't always this fancy. At first it was just a piece of Astroturf I nailed to the floor and a net I hung to keep him from killing the animals. I added stuff to it as he got better and better during high school. After . . . you know . . . he's been . . . well, a kind of salvation for me. Whenever I hated life because of what had been done to Tami, I had Joey to be thankful for. I can't tell you how much it helped. Church helped, too, of course. But when life got especially rough, Joey helped me keep the ball on the fairway."

I didn't know how my next words were going to be received. I said them anyway. "You more than Cathy though, Dell?"

He didn't flinch at all. "Oh, you betcha. You . . . betcha." He scuffed the toe of his boot into the floor. Did it again. "Cathy was Tami's best friend. And Tami was hers. Cathy loves Joey, don't misunderstand me. But . . . he was never the right shape to fill the hole that Tami left when she was . . ."

Dell couldn't bring himself to say "murdered" or "butchered" or "ravaged" or whatever word his unconscious mind had used to pigeonhole the horror that had been inflicted on his only daughter.

I tried to remember why I was there. Despite my instincts, I steered south of Dell's pain. "Mariko wasn't Tami's best friend?"

"Miko was new. For Tami, for us. And she was . . . what's the word? Exotic, you know, Oriental like that and all? I think that Tami was intrigued by the foreignness. Tami spent her whole life up here. Other than occasionally family trips, I mean. Until the Japanese bought the ski area we never saw too many of them in these parts. I think most of 'em went to Vail and Aspen. Hell, we never saw much of anybody but the American tourists. And most of them were as white as we were. We got some Mexicans for a while before their economy tanked. But they go more for Vail and Aspen, too. That's what I hear anyway. Better shopping over there.

"The girls became good friends, sure. Miko could ski with Tami. Bump for bump. Not too many girls could, or would. Tami liked that. But when I talk about Cathy and Tami and friendship, I'm talking the bigger picture. Confidences and all that. Cathy and Tami shared something special."

I was at a loss as to how to follow him wherever he was heading. It was as though he were leading me through a cave. I should have just shut up. Instead, I asked, "Does Joey still live up here?"

The tone of his voice lightened and I knew I'd let him off a hook with my question. "We see him a lot. But he has a big fancy place near San Diego. On a golf course, of course. We visit. He visits."

"He has that plane. That must make it easier to see him."

Dell shook his head. "Joey has investment advisers. Agents. Managers. The jet was their idea. They want him rested and relaxed while he plays. He's just a kid; he went along. Waste of a lot of money as far as I'm concerned. But it's his now so I try and get him to do some occasional good with it."

I decided to see how Dell would react to my mentioning that Lauren and I had been on the plane. Did he already know? "We were flown to the Locard meeting in D.C. on it. I was grateful for the convenience."

He nodded. He knew. "Yes, I know. I told him it was the least he could do for his sister."

Although the tone harbored no bitterness, the words surprised me. I followed them. Apparently the plane trip was Dell's idea, not Joey's. "What was their relationship like? Joey and Tami?"

"Good. Fine. They got along all right. Typical brother-sister stuff. But it was good."

I waited a long minute for Dell to expound on his impression of his children's lives together. But he just let the silence bob and float on the surface and didn't nibble on it at all.

I tried another cast. "The ranch must feel empty."

Almost instantly, he replied, "I tell her over and over that they'd both be gone now anyway. Tami'd probably have married and moved away. Maybe to Denver. She'd probably live closer to you than she does to us. And Joey would be . . . Joey. No matter what."

"I'm getting the impression that it doesn't help to tell Cathy that. Is that right, Dell?"

He smiled at me. "You seem like a bright guy. You could see it in there, right She's still tethered to Tami. Cathy is, over all these years. I'm hoping you guys can find some answers that will set her free. You know? That's why we're going to all this trouble. That's why I'm willing to scrape the dirt off the top of my daughter's grave. I'm hoping it will set us free."

I thought I knew what he meant and I said so.

We left the barn and I followed Dell. After he plopped down in a four-wheel all-terrain vehicle with big balloon tires I climbed onto the passenger side. "I talk better when I'm moving," he explained with admirable self-awareness.

"Why don't you tell me about her, Dell? About Tami?"

Before he said a word, he started the little cart on a straight line toward some distant fields. The air was as clean as fresh water. The hay smelled sweet. The ride was surprisingly smooth.

Later on, walking through Steamboat Springs looking for a place to have lunch, Lauren and I compared notes.

Lauren started, "Cathy thinks Dell was too hard on her—on Tami—says she thinks that he felt that Tami needed to be broken, like a wild horse. Cathy knew her daughter wasn't a saint but couldn't get behind Dell's program, so she kept a lot from him. Tami was on birth control pills, had been since just before her fifteenth birthday. Cathy said that Dell doesn't know that and that it would have caused a whole lot of trouble if he did."

"Does Cathy know if Tami was sexually active?"

"Cathy says she was. She maintains she never asked with whom, but says she did ask Tami if she knew him—the boy. Tami replied, 'Mom, you know everybody.' And they dropped it. Anyway, that's the story."

"Go on."

"Couple of times at least, Cathy became aware that the kids had been going out and drinking. Tami and her friends. She says that Dell never knew about it. She was working with Tami on her own to try and get her to 'moderate.' That's Cathy's word: 'moderate.' "

"That's all the bad news?"

We were walking down Lincoln Avenue, the long spine of downtown Steamboat. Lauren had stopped to read a menu outside a café called Winona's. The tables on the sidewalk along the main thoroughfare were full, a propitious sign. "Tami had some minor problems at school. Skipped her afternoon classes once with some friends and went skiing. They all got caught. Did some detention time. She got into one fight when she was sticking up for a friend in the lunchroom. Got caught again. Cathy says Dell was proud of her about that one. Freshman year she gave a science teacher a hard time about grades. Felt the guy had been unfair. Principal ended up getting involved. Dell was behind her on that one, too. How does this look?"

Lauren's question was about the menu. Without really assessing the offerings I said, "Looks fine to me."

"Shall we?"

"Do you mind if we walk around town a little longer before we eat? Are you up to it? My memory is that this street is pretty much it for downtown Steamboat. We can circle back this way when you want to eat. Downtown hasn't changed that much, you know? But around the base of the ski area? Mountain Village? Wow, a whole new world in the last few years."

"I'm not sure I like it. The development."

I didn't either but I didn't want to get distracted from Tami and Miko. "Walk some more?"

"I feel great," she said. "Let's go."

We walked. It was my turn to report on Dell. I said, "It's funny, considering what Cathy had to say about Tami and Dell's relationship, but Dell focused on Tami's strengths. Didn't say much about any trouble they had with her. He talked about the day-care work she did at the church during Bible studies, the tutoring she did at school with the younger kids. Dell's mother was still alive then and he says that Tami was devoted to her. She lived here in town and Tami would stop by to see her and read to her and help her out three or four times a week with chores and such. Dell was real proud, too, of the way she handled the animals and skied. Hell, he was proud of her for just about everything she did."

Lauren said, "I got the impression from Cathy that Dell could be real critical of Tami."

"Well, he wasn't when he was with me. That didn't come across at all. Did Cathy say anything about Tami breaking her leg when she was twelve? She was in a cast all spring?"

Lauren said, "No."

"Apparently she was skiing off a cornice on a dare from a boy she wanted to impress. Landed funny and shattered her tibia. Dell called it a 'damn fool thing' but I never got the impression he was mad at her about it. It was just an example he used to show me what an adventurer she was. You know—how her judgment wasn't always that sound? Not that she was a bad kid but that sometimes she didn't think things through. I think he was trying to tell me that she was capable of making bad decisions. Impulsive decisions. That he feared one of them might have had something to do with her murder. Does that make sense?"

"Sure. She was a kid. She was a risk taker."

"Yeah. Like that. Dell was real aware that she was a kid."

Lauren stopped in her tracks and pointed at some birds flying in formation across the valley. "It's interesting now that I hear you talk about Dell and where his memories take him. Because Cathy's memories take her someplace else. She focused mainly on Tami playing around with adult things. Not kid things. Alcohol, sex. Maybe Cathy wasn't comfortable with the child and adolescent part of her daughter."

"Or maybe," I said, "she just needed her to be an adult."

"Maybe."

"Dell describes his daughter as strong-willed. Says Tami demanded an explanation for 'every damn thing' he ever wanted her to do or not do. Said she'd argue about anything. She'd hear the news on TV and she'd bark at the screen arguing with Larry Green about the five-day forecast. But Dell didn't think Tami was out of control. Far from it. In fact, he said that in many ways Joey was a tougher kid for him to raise. I'm left wondering what Cathy felt she was protecting Tami from. You know, why she felt she needed to keep so much from Dell? She say anything about discipline? Any problems?"

"What do you mean?"

"Any issues between Tami and her father?"

"You wondering about abuse?"

"I guess. Mostly I'm just trying to explain to myself why the parents ended up approaching this kid so differently."

"Well, Cathy didn't say anything about any concerns in that area, but I wasn't really asking. Did you hear anything from Dell about Mariko?"

I nodded. "Dell liked her a lot. He called her Miko. Same as Tami did. Said she was polite, friendly, grateful. Full of life. He said if you took away most of Tami's orneriness and stubbornness, you'd end up with Miko Hamamoto."

"That's funny. I got the impression that Cathy wasn't too fond of Mariko. She calls her Mariko, by the way, not Miko. Told me that Mariko was one of Tami's projects."

"Projects?"

Lauren grabbed my wrist. "Yeah, like the friendship was some kind of a charity thing. And I almost forgot. At one point she said that Tami adopted her, Mariko. Said she was like a stray puppy that Tami brought home. Cathy said the friendship wasn't going to last."

CHAPTER
9

After lunch Lauren napped. She didn't want to nap. But she napped. As soon as we got back to the room she kicked off her shoes, took off her bra, and pulled on a T-shirt. She claimed the middle of the queen bed, curled up, and slept. She considered her almost daily afternoon sleep a reluctant sacrifice she offered to the MS gods. The interlude helped to refresh her only slightly more than half the time. The rest of the time, she woke from her nap groggy and disoriented, and the process of reacclimating to the day would debit another hour from her useful life. One hundred percent of the time, the absolutely necessity of the daily interlude infuriated her.

We were staying in a bed-and-breakfast below Howelsen Hill. Our room was small and had big dormers on two walls. Everything that could be plastered with wallpaper was. The paper had an abundance of stripes that seemed to go every which way around the dormers. I found myself tilting my head involuntarily to try to straighten out the lines. The room also had a pleasant balcony that was about the size of an old clawfoot bathtub. While Lauren curled up, I squeezed a chair out to the deck and pecked out notes on my laptop, sipping occasionally on a diet soda I'd claimed from the downstairs refrigerator.

The air in Steamboat was light—almost feathery—and the blue hue of the sky seemed less fierce than it did in the resorts farther south in the Colorado Rockies. The almost inevitable afternoon summer thunderstorms were skirting north of town that day, and the distant thunder that they generated reminded me of the muted booms I would hear as I was trying to fall asleep while a fireworks show was still going on during some past Fourth of July.

I filled five pages with notes before I read them through once. I made some changes and easily typed three more. The excitement I felt at what we'd learned at the Franklins' ranch felt almost visceral. Tami was becoming real to me much faster than I'd anticipated, and the questions I had about her relationships with her parents—and their relationships with each other—felt swollen with possibilities that might lead to further discoveries.

At another level, I was aware that I'd already decided that I needed to talk with Joey Franklin. Not because I couldn't rule him out as a suspect—which, of course, I couldn't—but because I knew that by speaking with him, I would gain even greater perspective on the Franklins as a family. I needed Joey's perspective to try to sort out the discrepancies between Cathy's and Dell's perspectives on their daughter. I assumed that A. J. Simes would have no objection to my expanding the horizon of my piece of the investigation a little.

Lauren walked out on the balcony just before four. She hugged me from behind, one of her breasts heavy on each side of my neck.

I liked the way it felt. I was about to tell her that I liked the way it felt when she said, "Before it gets dark, I want to go see the ranch."

I was surprised. "You want to go back to the Franklins' ranch?"

Her voice was husky in my ears. "No, I want to go see the Silky Road Ranch. The one where Gloria was killed. I don't know why, I just want to see it. It feels like, I don't know, a family thing. It feels unfinished."

I hadn't conjured up any plans for the late afternoon. Another drive in the country sounded fine. "You know where it is?"

"Not really."

I said, "Shouldn't be too hard to find out. I'm sure the owner of the B and B will know."

The owner of the B and B did know.

The Silky Road Ranch was up the same county road along the Elk River as the Franklins' ranch, but much closer to town. The directions she gave us were straightforward. I only got lost once, having to double back to the entrance to the Silky Road after crossing the bridge that ran over Mad Creek.

The ranch abutted the western-facing slope of a wide horseshoe canyon below Hahn's Peak, and most of the ranch's acreage was gently rolling high prairie. How high? I was guessing it was about the same elevation as the base of the ski area at Mount Werner, which was about sixty-nine hundred feet or so. The setting, on this late spring day, was sublime. The southern sun lit green fields, set trees to shimmer, and sparkled off the ice-cold snowmelt in the Elk River. A serene quiet filled the narrow valley, broken only by an occasional gust of wind.

Along with directions, Libby, the owner of the B and B, had provided an abbreviated version of the ranch's recent history. Raymond Welle never sold the Silky Road after Gloria was killed by Brian Sample in 1992. After the murder Raymond lived in a rented condo near the ski area for a year before he felt that he was able to return to the ranch. He continued to practice clinical psychology but was also getting more and more involved in his radio show, which had been picked up by a few dozen small stations and was gaining a regional audience. Within another year the show had gone national.

Ranelle and Jane—the "girls," our hostess called them—stayed on and looked after the big house at the Silky Road while Ray was living in town. But Raymond, who had never shared his wife's great love for horses, sold Gloria's herd and closed up the stable within a month or two of her death. The two cowboys moved on. Libby didn't know where those boys had gone.

Raymond did some minor renovations to the ranch house and moved back in quietly. According to Libby, some said that the first night he slept there as a widower was the first anniversary of the day that his wife was murdered. Our hostess couldn't confirm that. The bunkhouse and stable had fallen into disuse. Raymond had never had any use for them. Eventually, Ranelle and Jane were let go.

Even though she knew that her one-time brother-in-law was still single, Lauren asked if Raymond had ever remarried.

"No, he never showed much interest in the local ladies. If he ever comes back here with a bride, you can bet it'll be some Jane Fonda type. Some society or Hollywood thing. You watch—when we're not looking he'll show up with some city girl and the two of them will go and fill the whole damn Elk River Valley with buffalo and ostriches. Maybe even *emus.*" She made her pronouncement with disappointment and a tiny hiss of venom, as though she was one of the local ladies who had been scorned by Raymond Welle.

I pulled in front of the main gate to the ranch and parked on the dust in the shadows of the trees that lined the Elk River. Traffic on the county road was sparse. After a minute or so, I killed the engine.

The gate was unassuming enough, a couple of long triangles of steel tubing that came together in the center. The structures that supported the gates were less modest, however. They were built of a rich red stone and they were big. Each footprint was at least four by four, and I knew if I stood next to one it would soar above my head.

A brass sign on one of the structures read GLORIA'S SILKY ROAD RANCH—NO VISITORS.

A box recessed into the other structure had a buzzer and a speaker on a stainless-steel plate that was about the size of a microwave oven.

Lauren and I both got out of the car. She pointed

north and said, "I think that's the house Gloria built. Way back there. See? By the woods?"

I saw some structures and nodded. "Were you ever there? At their home?"

"No. Not once."

A gust of wind kicked up a dust devil down the dirt lane that led into the ranch and we were both distracted watching it flourish and die.

I asked, "Do you want to see if we can drive around the perimeter? Doesn't look like we're going to be invited in."

"No, I don't think so. We can leave in a few minutes. I just want to get a feel for it."

I was listening to the wind whisper to me when the speaker in the far gate support blared. "You are on private property. Please leave. Repeat: You are on private property. Please leave immediately."

After my pulse subsided a little I looked around for a lens or an infrared sensor or something. I couldn't find a thing but didn't feel much confidence that we weren't on *Candid Camera*. I asked, "Do you think that was a recording? Or was it a real live person?"

Lauren raised her eyebrows and shook her head incredulously. "Not sure. But I'd guess it was a recording. Just know it was the voice of Big Brother."

The same voice belted out the same tune again.

I said, "Apparently Big Brother would like us to move along."

She turned her back on the ranch and mouthed words to herself that I interpreted to be her thoughts about something Big Brother could just go ahead and do to himself instead.

A minute passed. Maybe two. I wasn't sure what Lauren was up to. She wasn't a pacer. But she was pacing.

"Company's coming," I said, pointing up the dirt road that snaked away from the gate toward the house, the same road that the dust devil had been teasing a few minutes before. In the distance, a fresh cloud of dirt was rising behind a dark speck that I guessed was some kind of pickup truck. It was coming our way.

Lauren watched the vehicle approach for a good ten seconds. I watched her watch it. I didn't really want to have to explain to Raymond Welle's security people why we were hanging out around the entrance to his ranch. Certainly not a few days before I was scheduled to meet with him in Denver about an old murder case. I said, "I don't think I really want to get to know those people, hon. I'd rather have a clean slate when I meet Dr. Welle next week. Do you see anything to gain by hanging around?"

She ran her fingers through her hair and buttoned the top button of her shirt. Finally, she said, "No, nothing to be gained. Let's go then." She climbed into the car and waited till I joined her before she continued. "I want trout for dinner. And a big salad. Spinach. That sound okay to you?"

We stopped back at the B and B and I used the communal phone in the downstairs parlor to check my office voice mail and the answering machine at home. The messages were all mundane except for two. The first unusual call had been from Mary Wright. She asked that Lauren get in touch with her at the Justice Department the following Monday. The second call that drew my attention sounded almost British in its formality. Taro Hamamoto had returned my call from British Columbia. His message informed me that he would be interested in speaking with me further. Would I be so kind as to call him back? He left a number that was different from the one that A. J. had given me for him. The area codes were the same though: 604.

I returned the call right away.

He answered on the fourth ring. "Yes," he said.

"Hello, may I speak to Mr. Hamamoto, please?"

"This is he. Dr. Gregory?"

"Yes, this is Alan Gregory. I want to begin by thanking you for returning my initial call. The circumstances—

a stranger calling about your daughter after so many years—must feel peculiar."

"That's a good word. Yes. It is peculiar. Perhaps you would take a moment and familiarize me, once again, with the organization that you represent. On your message you said it was called . . . ?"

"Locard. It is named after a nineteenth-century French detective. He was an early forensic scientist, a pioneer. The current Locard is a volunteer organization of forensic professional dedicated to solving what are sometimes called cold cases."

"And in your message you said you are revisiting the circumstances of Mariko's murder. That is correct? Her death is the cold case? Yes?"

"Yes. Her death and that of Tami Franklin."

"And you have chosen to focus on my daughter and her friend precisely . . . why?"

"A few months ago Locard was approached by the Franklin family—Tami's parents—and by the new police chief of Steamboat Springs, a man named Percy Smith. They petitioned for Locard's assistance. Obviously, they are hoping that Locard will be able to uncover new information that might lead to the apprehension of whoever is responsible for . . ."

"Killing my daughter."

The words exited his mouth with a facility that was unnerving to me. I replied, "Yes."

"And from me? You wish . . . ?"

"I am a clinical psychologist, Mr. Hamamoto. My role in the investigation is limited. I've been asked to try to get enough of a social and psychological history of Tami and Ma-riko"—I stumbled over his daughter's name, almost calling her Miko—"to understand what might have brought them in contact with their killer, or killers."

Taro Hamamoto was silent for at least half a minute. "You are . . . in the process of dissolving an assumption, Dr. Gregory."

I waited, unsure what he meant.

"Back then, there was an assumption that a stranger,

perhaps a, a . . . drifter was . . . responsible for the murders. You are proceeding as though that hypothesis may lack merit."

"Yes, Mr. Hamamoto, I suppose I am proceeding as though that hypothesis may lack merit."

Again he paused, this time for even longer. "I am intrigued by what you are proposing. I would like an opportunity to meet with you to discuss your idea in more detail. Personal contact is important, I think. Don't you? I will make a decision at that time whether or not I feel it is proper to assist you in your new investigation. Unfortunately, I am unable to leave Vancouver at this time, so you will need to come to Canada. I can arrange to meet with you for two or three hours." I heard him pecking on a keyboard. "There is a United flight into Vancouver from Denver that will have you arrive at twelve-thirty, Monday through Friday." More keyboard tunes. "A return flight departs daily for Denver at fourten. I will meet you in between the two flights in the Air Canada departure lounge. Pick a day next week and leave me a message as to your choice. Tuesday is inconvenient for me. Is that acceptable, Dr. Gregory?"

"Tentatively, yes. But I am required to clear any travel plans through Locard. In advance."

I thought I heard him scoff before he said, "I will be waiting to hear from you with your choice of dates."

I was off the phone in plenty of time to join Lauren for an early dinner at Antares, where my wife, true to her word, ordered trout and spinach salad. We spent the rest of the mild evening driving and then walking the trail that led to the Strawberry Park hot springs, the popular spot that Tami had told her brother was her likely destination the night she disappeared with Mariko.

The last time I'd been in Strawberry Park it was a hippie hangout. Now it was a tourist attraction with a gate and an admission fee. Despite the artificial accoutrements, I still would have been up for a soak in the natural springs, but hanging out in hundred-plus-degree water wasn't an option for either pregnant women or people with MS, so I was content to enjoy the sights and the air and the company.

"Have you decided? Are you going to go to Vancouver?" Lauren asked. During dinner, I'd filled her in on my conversation with Taro Hamamoto.

"If A. J. says yes, I'm going. I need to talk with him."

"And if A. J. says no?"

"I'll probably go to Vancouver anyway."

She said, "We can afford it."

"I know we can. That's not it. I'm beginning to feel some compulsion about all this. I don't know exactly what it is, or why it is, but I can't stop thinking about those two girls."

Lauren laughed gently. "Me neither. This work really hooks you, doesn't it? I feel the same tug that you're feeling. I can't wait to talk to Mary Wright and find out what she wants. I'm ready to dive in headfirst. I think I'm beginning to understand why all these high-powered people donate time they don't really have to organizations like Locard and Vidocq."

I said, "It won't feel so good if we don't figure it out, though."

"You mean who killed the girls?"

"Yes. I mean who killed the girls. I hope I can help, hope we both can help. But my assumption is that Flynn Coe and Russ Claven and the forensic types hold the key to this one. Not us."

CHAPTER
10

We decided to drive home to Boulder late Sunday morning on Highway 40 instead of Highway 9. The route would take us through Granby, past Winter Park, and over Berthoud Pass before it intersected with I-70. For the first hour that we were on the road the traffic was minimal, the air outside was more warm than cool, and the midday sky above us a pale and soothing blue that was the color of glacier ice.

As we neared Silver Creek I asked Lauren, whose nose was buried in the Sunday newspaper, if she could guess what Mary Wright wanted.

She spent the next minute or so folding the newspaper down the spine, then over the fold, then once more in half. She rested the project on her lap, turned my way, and said, "Who knows? Statute of limitations, grand jury rules, trial protocols, special prosecutors. Could be just about anything."

"No guesses?"

"No. No guesses."

We arrived home by about 1:30. Adrienne and Jonas were out somewhere and they'd left Emily in her dog run. I assumed that there had been a protracted argument between mother and son about why Emily couldn't go with them wherever they were going.

I emptied our things out of the car, played with the dog for a few minutes, opened some windows to ventilate the house, and started a load of laundry before I called Diane and told her I was back in town and back on my beeper. She said my patients had been good while I'd been gone. No emergencies. We talked about things friends talk about for a little while before I thanked her for covering, hung up, and checked messages on the home machine.

Our contractor for the renovation project that we'd done the previous year, Dresden Lamb, had returned my call about a leaking downspout and some disintegrating grout in the new shower. He promised that he'd take care of both problems the following week. My friend Sam Purdy had called inviting me to loiter—his word—with him at North Boulder Park during his son Simon's last soccer game of the season.

There were two hang-ups.

The last message was from a woman named Dorothy Levin. Her succinct message wasn't directed toward either Lauren or me. She said, "Hi. My name is Dorothy Levin. I'm with the *Washington Post.*" She left a number with a 202 area code—which I knew from my recent Locard experience was indeed Washington, D.C.—and concluded with, "Please return my call at your earliest convenience."

Lauren heard the message, too. She asked, "Is that for you or for me?"

"I think it must be for you."

"Bull. It's for you."

"I bet it's Locard business. *Washington Post?* It has to be."

"How would a reporter with the *Washington Post* know about us being involved with Locard?"

"How did they know about Monica Lewinsky?"

"I don't want to have that discussion again," Lauren admonished me. "Ken Starr has managed to do for prosecutors what O. J. did for Heisman Trophy winners. Should we return Ms. Levin's call?"

"No, I don't think so. Kimber's instructions were to 'no-comment' the press and to let him know about any contacts we receive. We should just let him or A. J. know she called and not worry about it."

Lauren said, "Until we return her call, we don't actually know whether or not we've been contacted about Locard business, do we?"

Her argument was persuasive, as usual. "Okay," I said, "then you go ahead and call her back."

She was already walking away from the general vicinity of the phone. "No. I think you should. This may just be another JonBenet cold call. I'm tired of them and I don't even want to think about taking another one. You promised you'd field them for me while I was pregnant."

"You haven't had one of those for months."

She leaned over and knocked on the pine table in front of her. "Thank God for small favors."

I *had* promised that I'd shield her from JonBenet calls. "Okay, on the unlikely premise that this might be yet another reporter writing a true-crime book about Jon-Benet, I will return Dorothy Levin's call. But . . . it's only because you're pregnant and beautiful."

"Actually," she said, lowering her T-shirt off one shoulder, "I'm beautiful and I'm pregnant."

"Whatever you say. I'm not about to argue. Pretty soon you'll be bigger than me so I have to be careful." Two seconds later I successfully dodged a pillow that was whizzing past my head.

The number in D.C. was that of Dorothy Levin's home phone. She answered breathlessly after two rings. She said, "Hell-o." The emphasis was harsh and clearly on the "hell."

"Dorothy Levin, please."

"You got her."

"This is Alan Gregory returning your call from Colorado."

"Yeah? Good, good. Great. What a surprise. Hold on a second." I heard background noises as though she was fumbling around for something. "Listen, is it Mister or Doctor?"

What?

"You still there? Is it *Mister* Gregory or *Doctor* Gregory?"

I had enough of my wits about me to ask, "Am I being interviewed about something?"

She sighed. "I didn't say on my message? I'm a reporter with the *Washington Post* and—"

"No, no. You didn't say that you were a reporter. Only that you were with the *Post*."

"Really? That's not like me. I'm an honest person and I'm pretty sure I—"

"I'm happy to play back the message for you. Would you like me to play your message back for you?"

Another sigh. "That won't be necessary." The sarcasm was spread thick, like peanut butter on Wonder bread. "Listen . . . okay, okay. This isn't going like I had planned. I'm not smiling at the moment—you know what I'm saying? I'm just not a happy person when things don't go well at the beginning. Whadya say we start over?" She didn't wait for me to concur with her request. "Here goes. This is my new intro: Hello, Mr. Gregory? I'm Dorothy Levin. I'm a reporter with the *Washington Post*. How are you today?"

She was so out-there that I played right along with her. "I'm fine, Ms. Levin. How are you?"

"Great, great. Hey, what I need—" She caught herself falling back out of character. "Sorry. Sorry. I'm doing well, thank you. I'm so sorry to interrupt your weekend, but I'm doing this story about fund-raising practices in the early congressional campaigns of Representative Raymond Welle. Your name was brought to my attention as someone who—"

"How? How did you get my name?"

She slapped something. Hard. The sound cracked like a steak dropped on the counter. "Oh, damn. And we were doing so much better the second time around. That question really ruins things though. The momentum? It's a fragile thing in interviews. You know I can't tell you how I got your name. There are *rules*. Journalism rules. You ever hear of Watergate? Confidential sources, stuff like that? Deep Throat ring a bell? Let me see—do you want to just back up and pretend you didn't really ask that question? Or do we need to start all over again?"

I laughed. She laughed. I heard her strike a match and light a cigarette. She sucked hard on it before she spoke again.

"You still there? You didn't hang up on me, did you? Can't *stand* it when that happens."

"I don't know anything about Welle's campaign financing."

It sounded like she was trying to spit a speck of to-bacco out of her mouth. Was she really smoking nonfilters? I tried to imagine a Camel hanging from her lips, smoke circling toward the heavens carrying the souls of dead smokers to their reunions with God.

She said, "Go on."

I laughed again. "I'm not going on, Ms. Levin. I don't have anyplace to go on *to*. I don't know anything about Raymond Welle and his campaign financing." She didn't respond immediately. But I thought I could hear the squeaky sounds of someone writing quickly with a felt-tip pen. She was jotting down everything I said.

I decided that it was prudent to either shut up or hang up. But I couldn't decide which. So I waited.

She did, too. Patiently. For about twenty or thirty seconds. Then she said, "Okay? Yeah?"

If this was her best attempt at conducting an interview, I decided that hanging up would make the most sense. Not even trying to hide my incredulity, I said, " 'Okay? Yeah?' That's your next question? Seriously?"

She broke into a mixture of coughing and laughter that caused me to pull the phone away from my ear. At the conclusion of her paroxysm she said, "That *was* kind of lame. I'll do better. I promise. Oh, please give me an-other try. And whatever you do, don't tell my editor. Deal?" She was still laughing.

"What is it that you want, Ms. Levin? As entertaining as this conversation might be, I think we may both be wasting our time."

She had composed herself by the time she spoke again. "I am doing a story . . . about fund-raising practices during Representative Welle's 1990, 1992, and 1994 congressional campaigns. I got your name. I'm calling for information."

"About . . . ?"

"About what you know."

"But I don't know anything."

She sighed before she took a deep drag on her cigarette and hummed a few bars of "Will the Circle Be Unbroken?" She stopped the melody abruptly and asked, "Tell me this, then, Mister or Doctor Gregory. If you're so ignorant about Representative Raymond Welle, then why are you planning on meeting with him before his fund-raiser in Denver on Friday?"

How on earth did this reporter from the Washington Post *know about that?* I stammered, "Excuse me?"

Her voice turned slightly arrogant as she said, "Now please. You're going to have to help out a minute. With a small, small clarification. Was that an 'Excuse me, I didn't hear you'? Or was that an 'Excuse me, I can't believe you know that I'm meeting with him'?"

"No comment."

I thought I heard her muffle a profanity before she said, "Ah jeez. I hate this. Suddenly something doesn't feel kosher to me. We go from 'I don't know anything' to 'No comment' in less time than it takes me to clean my contacts. What's happening with the world?"

I had a temptation to explain to her why I couldn't talk to her about Welle. But I resisted. "I don't have anything to say, Ms. Levin."

"That's a mite different from 'I don't know anything about Raymond Welle, Ms. Levin.' " She mocked me with a whiny rendition of my words.

I shrugged and opened my eyes wide, confident that she couldn't hear me shrug or open my eyes wide. I said, "I'm afraid that's where I'm going to have to leave it."

She made a noise that I didn't really want to know the source of. "You may leave me no choice but to write a piece reporting what I do know. Without any opportunity for your comment."

I laughed again, more nervously this time. "What you know is too boring for the *Washington Post.*"

Her lips popped as she exhaled. I imagined a cloud of pungent smoke around her head. "So be it. We'll talk again. I'm sure."

She hung up.

I used directory assistance to get the number of the main switchboard at the *Washington Post.* I asked for Dorothy Levin and was immediately connected to her voice mail message, which she'd recorded herself. I'd have recognized that voice anywhere. I hung up before the tone.

She was for real.

"Who knows about your appointment with Raymond Welle besides us?" Lauren asked.

"Welle's office. And apparently the *Washington Post.*"

"And A. J. Don't forget A. J. And whomever she might have told."

"You're thinking someone in Locard would intentionally mislead a *Post* reporter about the nature of my meeting with Welle?"

"No, that doesn't make any sense. Then it has to be someone in Welle's office who's been helping Levin with her investigation of his fund-raising practices. She has to have a source inside Welle's congressional office or campaign office. This person must have misinterpreted the reason for the meeting you have scheduled with Welle because it's happening around one of his fund-raising events."

"That explanation makes the most sense. The next question is, do I need to tell A. J. and Kimber Lister about the press contact?"

Lauren considered it for a moment. "No. I don't think so. This doesn't involve Locard. She didn't say anything about Locard, right? Or about the two girls or Steamboat?"

"Right."

"There, then."

I should have had an easier time clearing my conversation with Dorothy Levin from my head than I did. But the fact that a reporter from a big eastern newspaper wanted to talk with me made me nervous. It just did.

When I'm nervous, I do. I get decisive. I get focused.

My first decision was to go ahead and go to Canada. I chose Wednesday to fly to Vancouver. I called United Airlines and booked a round-trip on the flights that had been suggested by Mr. Hamamoto. When I heard the price for the ticket I prayed that A. J. would approve the expense. I left her a message asking for approval.

Next I left a message for Hamamoto confirming our meeting in the Air Canada lounge on Wednesday afternoon.

Five more phone calls later, I'd succeeded in rescheduling the five patients whose day would be inconvenienced by my impulsive decision to fly to Canada to meet with Taro Hamamoto. After the shuffling was over, Tuesday and Thursday were going to closely resemble psychotherapy marathons in my office and I was going to be working on Saturday, too.

Emily needed more attention so I took her over to Adrienne's house to play with Jonas. While dog and child were playing a game that made no sense to me, I asked Adrienne how she and Erin were doing. Erin was Adrienne's last known romantic interest.

Adrienne was cranky. She said, "Why?"

I lied and said I was just curious.

"Yeah. Right. You and the *National Enquirer*."

"Well, I haven't seen her around much lately and I've been, I don't know . . . wondering."

"God, you're such a pathetic liar." She laughed. "The truth is I think I've been dumped."

"Ren, I'm so sorry."

She waved off my sympathy. "Nah, it's okay. We were winding down to the basics, anyway."

"The basics being?"

"The . . . uh . . . gender thing."

"Oh, yeah. The gender thing. Are you having some second thoughts about . . . you know?"

"No. I had second thoughts about that so long ago I can't remember what they were."

I waited for her to move on someplace. We both watched Jonas try to mount Emily as though she were a horse. Emily was pretty cool about it. Jonas stayed on for the better part of ten feet. I thought it might be a new record.

"Are you still gay?"

She smacked me on the shoulder. It hurt. "That's not a question a polite person asks."

"Then how does a polite person find out the answer?"

"A polite person minds his own business."

"So who's the Lexus?" I asked.

She glared at me. "What Lexus?"

"You've been getting visits from a Lexus. Whose carriage is it?"

She made a guttural noise I associated with disgust. "A woman lives alone out in the goddamn wilderness with her kid and still she can't get any privacy? I'm beginning to understand those nuts with guns in Idaho."

"We live in adjoining fishbowls, Ren. We can see into yours. You can see into ours."

"Not fair. Mine's much more interesting. You ever watch your life from a distance? It ain't no *Truman Show*."

She hadn't told me who owned the Lexus.

It should have been enough activity to calm me down about Dorothy Levin. But it wasn't. I was still anxious about the phone call by the time Lauren and I climbed into bed to watch the late news. I told her about my conversation with Adrienne.

"Is she okay?"

"Adrienne's resilient."

"The bet's still on," she concluded. "I'll go talk to her. She'll tell me things she won't tell you. I still say it's a boy Lexus, not a girl Lexus."

Lauren connected with Mary Wright early Monday morning. Mary had a list of questions about Colorado law and procedure that she needed answered. Lauren suggested E-mail, Mary said she preferred paper, and they settled on a correspondence via fax. The first sheet of paper from the Justice Department was sliding from our home machine as I was rinsing out my coffee cup and heading to town to see my first patient on Monday morning.

Lauren thought she could have something drafted for Mary by the end of the week at the latest.

CHAPTER
11

The flight to British Columbia was painless. At least two dozen of the 737's seats were empty, and miraculously, one of them was next to my exit-row aisle. Having the room in front of me to be able to actually cross my legs on an airplane felt decadent. I read a biography for the first couple of hours before allowing my attention to drift outside as the pilot began the descent. As the plane banked to make our approach into Vancouver my eyes followed the linear wake of an early-season cruise ship that was heading north from Canada Place toward the Strait of Georgia and the Inside Passage. In the opposite direction a freighter headed south out to the Pacific through the Strait of Juan de Fuca.

I fantasized about being on one ship and then the other.

After a long winter and spring in Colorado's aridity, the lushness and richness of the northwestern landscape was seductive. The day was clear enough to make out topographic details of the distant face of Vancouver Island. Closer in, the smaller islands and inlets of the San Juans gave my eyes and my imagination a thousand inviting places to hide. There are plenty of cities in North America where it would be just fine to hold a business meeting at the airport. Vancouver isn't one of them. I immediately wished I had made arrangements to stay longer.

Canadian immigration and customs were efficient, and within fifteen minutes of deplaning I had checked back

in with United Airlines and was going through U.S. customs and immigration prior to moving on to the departure area for flights to the U.S. On the U.S. immigration
form I was asked about my length of stay in Canada. I
was tempted to write "fifteen minutes." Officially, I had
left the United States, arrived in Canada, and returned
to the United States without ever leaving the Vancouver airport.

The immigration official who checked my papers, the
customs official who didn't check my carry-on, and the
ticketing agent who gave me my boarding pass were all
of Asian descent. In the ten years or so since my last
visit the city of Vancouver had truly become a gateway
to the Pacific Rim.

Taro Hamamoto had not arrived but he had made
advance arrangements for me at the desk of the Air Canada lounge. The facility was small by U.S. standards but
its comfort and amenities more than made up for its
dimensions. Wonderful local beer on tap, plentiful
snacks, fresh fruit, friendly people. I helped myself to
something to eat and drink and settled into the small
conference room where I had been instructed to wait for
Mr. Hamamoto's arrival.

He stood in the doorway about ten minutes later.

I expected a man of typical Asian stature. But Taro
Hamamoto was almost as tall as I was, nearly six-two. I
expected a man graciously creeping from middle age into
gentility. But Taro Hamamoto appeared to be no older
than his late forties and had the lean, fit look of a distance runner. I expected to see a man wearing the Japanese version of Brooks Brothers. But when I stood to
greet Taro Hamamoto as he walked into the conference
room, he was Polo and Timberland.

We shook hands and he bowed almost imperceptibly
as he introduced himself. Immediately he offered me a
business card. With barely a glance at his, I fumbled in
my wallet for one of my own."

"Dr. Gregory," he said. "I'm pleased to meet you."

"The pleasure is mine, Mr. Hamamoto. I'm grateful for the opportunity to talk with you."

"I hope I wasn't late."

"Not at all. My flight was early. Immigration was a breeze."

He glanced down at the conference table and saw the empty plate and the bottle of water in front of me. He said, "May I offer you anything before we begin?"

"No. I'm great. I helped myself. May I get you something?"

"Indeed not," he said. "Please, let's get started, shall we. I'm . . . anxious to hear more from you. It's not often I get the opportunity to speak about my daughter." His eyes saddened noticeably. "My wife, she . . . well, she would rather forget than remember. Does that make sense?"

"Of course."

He held the tip of his tongue between his teeth for a moment and sat straight, his shoulders squared. He achieved the posture without effort or strain. The polo shirt he wore under a white cotton sweater was the exact same hue as the tip of his tongue. "I have resources—contacts, if you will—in the United States. At my request these individuals have been kind enough to provide me with some research and background into the organization you represent, Dr. Gregory." He smiled the slightest bit. "Locard. It's a fascinating group with an impressive record."

"Yes."

My business card lay on the table in front of him. He lowered his eyes to it before he spoke. "And you . . . are not a permanent member."

Hamamoto's words were not posed as a question. I tried not to sound defensive as I replied. "No. As you can see from my card, I'm a practicing clinical psychologist in Boulder, Colorado. I am not a permanent member of Locard. They consider me 'a guest specialist,' which is a fancy way of saying that I'm an invited volunteer. I was asked to participate only in the current investigation.

The one involving the murder of your daughter, Mariko, and her friend, Tamara Franklin."

"And—please excuse my ignorance—why does Locard feel it needs the assistance of a clinical psychologist in Boulder, Colorado?"

My speech about the necessity of getting to know the two dead girls was beginning to feel rehearsed, even polished. I gave it again with some confidence.

As I finished, Hamamoto's face softened and his lips parted. "You have completed your words, Dr. Gregory. In your eyes, though, I see that you are not done with your explanation of your involvement with me and my family."

Prevaricating with this man felt as though it would be counterproductive. "All right," I said. "Let me share the other reason for my involvement. Sometime shortly before her death your daughter, Mr. Hamamoto, was in psychotherapy in Steamboat Springs with a clinical psychologist like myself. It is an episode in her young life that Locard feels is worthy of more investigation. I concur with that assessment. The forensic psychologist and psychiatrist on Locard thought that I would be the correct person to explore the issues related to that therapy."

"Dr. Welle," he said. "The now famous Dr. Welle." Taro Hamamoto touched the collar of his shirt and swallowed. I expected him to launch into criticism of Raymond Welle. Instead, Hamamoto said, "He helped her. I want you to know that. He helped all of us. Dr. Welle did. Dr. Raymond Welle." His hands clenched into fists before he released the pressure and spread his fingers. "Back then, Mariko was skiing too fast. She was in danger of catching an edge. Dr. Welle helped her get back under control. It was a great service to us."

The skiing metaphor surprised me almost as much as the praise. I said, "I'm glad to hear that he was so helpful to your family."

"Yes."

"It turns out that I am scheduled to meet with Dr. Welle in two days. In Colorado. His office has been gracious enough to set up a meeting to discuss the resumption of the old investigation."

Hamamoto nodded.

"For that meeting to be of any benefit to me I will need to provide Dr. Welle with written authorization from you—or your wife—that he has your permission to speak with me about your daughter's psychotherapy. Without that permission the records of her treatment remain confidential and he is not allowed to share with me any details of his work with Mariko."

"Are you suggesting that Dr. Welle has information that would help identify my daughter's killer?" His jaws tightened as he finished speaking.

"I have no reason to suspect he has direct knowledge," I replied. "But he may know something that might help us reconstruct—with the benefit of hindsight and modern forensics—the circumstances that brought your daughter in contact with her killer."

I didn't know how Hamamoto was going to reply. He said, "My wife is not available. She is . . . living in Japan." These words were clipped, almost unfriendly.

I didn't comment on the tone. "Your signature alone is sufficient, Mr. Hamamoto."

My carry-on bag was a slender satchel that contained a notebook and a case file. I removed the file and from it withdrew a single sheet of paper that I had prepared on my computer the previous evening. I slid it toward him.

"This is all you want from me?" His voice betrayed his disappointment. Was there also contempt? "This paper is all you want from me?"

I softened my voice and leaned closer to him, just an inch or two. "No, Mr. Hamamoto. I need this paper for the next step in my work. But this step"—I touched the table in front of me—"what will happen between us today, must precede it. I want you to help me know Mariko. I want to know your daughter through your eyes. I want to begin to appreciate her the way you did."

He raised the index finger of his left hand to his mouth

and pressed gently on his upper lip until it separated from the lower one.

Symbolically, I thought, he was unsealing them.

"When my company acquired the ski area in Steamboat Springs I was honored to be selected to serve as general manager. My family joined me in Colorado after I was in Steamboat Springs for four months and two weeks. My family then was my wife, Eri, and my two daughters, Mariko and Satoshi. Mariko was sixteen, Satoshi fourteen, then, I think. Yes."

Taro had allowed his posture to soften enough that I no longer felt that I had to impersonate a marine to sit comfortably with him.

"We had, of course, lived abroad before. As a family. The children spoke English well. My wife, not so well. She has always found the language and the culture to be . . . difficult. She often mused to herself while she knew I was close enough to overhear that she hoped our exile in Colorado would be a brief one. It was one of her favorite words." He said something in Japanese. In English, he said, "Exile."

His eyes grew heavy as though he were suddenly too tired to continue. "My wife, it seems, she was granted her wish." His eyes closed for a few moments as he composed himself. "My children loved living in Colorado. Are you familiar with Steamboat Springs, Dr. Gregory?"

I said, "Yes, as a matter of fact I was there last weekend with my wife. It's a lovely town."

"The Mountain Village was small then. The town quiet. Everything was much less congested than it is now. The hillside—it reminded us of the place in Japan where my parents lived—a small village near Nagano. You know Nagano? From the Olympics? I felt safe in Steamboat. So did the girls. There is some irony there, yes? They walked places on their own. Visited with other children, went to school, had a normal life. We were outsiders yes, but we were accustomed to that. The girls were . . . happy.

"Both girls were skiers, of course. Excellent skiers. That helped them—what do you say?—fit in with the local kids in Steamboat. At my urging my wife permitted Mariko and Satoshi freedoms similar to those enjoyed by their new friends. My wife argued against the permissiveness. She felt that it would not serve them well when we returned to Japan."

With apparent sorrow, he said, "My wife . . . it seems . . . has always been someone who is concerned mostly with the past . . . but also some with the future. She worries little about the present . . . except that she worries as to how it will change the future. And how it will be viewed—appraised?—once it has become the past. I am a businessman, the one in the family who concerns himself with the present. A flaw of mine? Perhaps. If it is a defect it is one that Dr. Welle supported. But . . . that came later."

I didn't ask permission to take notes, but simply removed the notepad from my satchel and a pen from my pocket and started keeping a chronology of dates and people as Taro Hamamoto sketched in every minute detail of his family's acculturation in Colorado. If he objected to my keeping a journal of the specifics I couldn't discern it from his demeanor.

We were halfway through the time allotted for our meeting when he mentioned Tamara Franklin for the first time. We both laughed as he said, "I met her father and mother, of course. Her father called Tamara 'a little pistol.' When I got to know her better I thought she was more like a whole big gun." The memories were affectionate, not cross.

He turned serious again immediately. "But she was kind, so kind to my Mariko. I forgave her the impetuousness. I forgave her the occasional disrespect. I forgave it all because she was so kind and generous to my daughter. Tamara was a very good friend to Mariko. I had good friends growing up, so I know about friendship. And Tamara Franklin was a good friend."

I perceived a natural break in his narrative and opened

my mouth to ask a question about Tami and Miko. But
he continued before I had a chance. "I was here, right
here, when I learned she was missing."

Confused, I asked, "In Vancouver?"

"Yes. In Canada. In Vancouver. In this airport. I'd just
completed a business trip to Whistler Mountain. I wasn't
there with my family when she disappeared. My wife,
she is silent, but she blames me I think. For not being
there to help." He shrugged. "What could I have done?
But at the time . . ."

I felt a familiarity with Hamamoto right then. It
calmed me. It was as if our interview had become psychotherapy. I did what I do best. I said nothing and tried
not to get in his way.

"Work. I was here for work. The company? We were
negotiating then to buy Whistler Mountain. You know
Whistler? The ski resort?"

I shrugged. Whether or not I knew Whistler Mountain
wasn't the point. He knew that, too.

"A beautiful resort. It is my assignment, now. Whistler.
For a different company, though, not Japanese. The
economy in Japan in the late nineties was . . . so fragile.
So much of what was gained in the eighties was lost in
the nineties. It has seemed to me that whenever Japan
begins to feel strong that is when Japan is most weak.
That is our history. Are you a student of history, Dr.
Gregory?"

"Personal history."

"Ah." He appraised me warmly. "My Mariko? Her
personal history? Yes, I think I see. From her confidence,
too, perhaps came her vulnerability. But she was never
arrogant, like Japan. Even like Tamara. Mariko was
young, had the self-assurance of the young."

"Her vulnerability?"

"To influence."

"From friends?"

"Yes. From friends."

"Including Tami Franklin?"

"Of course."

He stared at me in a manner that I found disarming. He said, "You know, of course, that my daughter was arrested?"

I did my best to try to not act surprised. I thought I did a pretty good job. But not good enough.

"You didn't know?" Hamamoto said. "I'm disappointed."

"I've read the investigative reports thoroughly, Mr. Hamamoto. That information is not there."

"No?" He shrugged. "Her record was eventually cleared. And now, it doesn't really matter. It is not relevant to finding who killed her. Only to knowing her and her—what did you say?—personal history. It is because of the arrest we came to know Dr. Raymond Welle."

CHAPTER
12

"Marijuana," he explained. "In case you are wondering."

I waited for him to go on. He seemed embarrassed by his admission and was content to allow the word to hang in the air for as long as possible, as though it were a cloud that would dissipate with the wind.

Finally, I asked, "Possession or sale?" I immediately regretted my bluntness; I needed to encourage Hamamoto, not assault him.

As I feared, my question appeared to offend him. "Possession. Mariko and Tamara and two boys . . . men, really. Tourists, skiers. They were from Chicago. They attended Northwestern University. The sheriff arrested them all. This was in March. We were . . . devastated. My wife, she . . ." Hamamoto bowed his head. The hair on his crown was thinning.

"There was much shame. It was my fault. Mariko should not have been granted the . . . the . . . oh, oh . . ." He snapped his fingers twice. ". . . the license . . . the, the . . . freedom. That was my fault. Mariko should not have been free to be there then with those . . . men who we did not know. That was my doing. My responsibility. My error in judgment. As her father, I failed."

He looked up and examined my face, wary. I assumed he was trying to assess whether my infelicitous frankness was likely to continue. "But my daughter was smoking the marijuana. She admitted that to me honestly. And that was Mariko's responsibility. That was her error." He closed his right hand into a fist and struck his chest lightly with the wide where his index finger and thumb united.

I was wondering what was so grave about what I had heard. A sixteen-year-old girl experimenting with dope, hanging out with college boys? Not exactly earth-shattering behavior.

"They were at one of the hot springs. You know about the hot springs in Steamboat? At Strawberry Park?"

"Yes. It's where Tami told her parents that she and Mariko were going the night they disappeared. It's become overrun by tourists. They charge admission now."

"Really? I suppose that I am not surprised that the tourists have discovered it. Your other statement is true as well. Mariko did not tell her mother that she and Tamara were going to the hot springs. Mariko knew she was prohibited from returning there."

"You are concerned that Mariko lied to her mother?"

Taro Hamamoto's face flushed. "When the sheriff arrested my daughter, she was . . ." He averted his eyes. "She was . . . naked." He corrected his posture and touched his collar with the fingers of both hands. "Mariko was in the hot springs without clothing. She was with two young men she had just met that afternoon on the gondola. She was smoking marijuana. And you think that she would not lie to her mother about a plan to return there? The shame."

I considered the facts I was hearing. When I was sixteen I hadn't done what Mariko had been caught doing. But I'd done it when I was a little older. Different hot springs, in the Sangre de Cristo Range above Buena Vista. Older girls, graduate students at Arizona State.

The memory warmed me now as the experience had then.

But the difference was, I hadn't been caught.

"I was at a meeting that night at the resort. I came right home. My wife, Eri, she was in shock, and was not sure how to proceed. I went to the police station and retrieved Mariko. She was released to me without . . ."

He snapped his long fingers. "Bond? Is that the right word?"

"Yes."

"Good. At the police station I saw Mrs. Franklin, Cathy Franklin. Tami's mother. I was upset, more upset than she. I told her I was afraid that Mariko would now need to go home to Japan. The influences, I explained. We, her parents, were failing. We couldn't control her.

"Cathy tried to calm me down. She explained that the kids were just being kids. Experimenting, she said. Spreading their wings, she said. We argued a little about that. We discussed grounding. She said maybe we should keep the girls apart for a while but she thought sending Mariko to Japan was . . . rash? Is that the right word? She gave me a name of someone who could help settle Mariko down."

I said, "Dr. Raymond Welle."

"Yes. That is when I heard for the first time of Dr. Welle."

I remembered Lauren telling me that Cathy Franklin wasn't fond of Mariko. Tami's mother thought the friendship wouldn't last. That she referred to Mariko as one of Tami's projects.

Taro Hamamoto stood and excused himself to the rest room.

The pieces didn't fit together with any grace.

Our time together was running out. I felt it burning away like the wax in a candle. I decided I needed to be more assertive with the remaining minutes available to me. I doubted that I would ever be face-to-face with Taro Hamamoto again. "You went to see Dr. Welle together? As a family?"

"Not right away, no. Eri, my wife—the shame was too much of a burden for her right after the arrest. She felt that everyone in the town was judging her because of what Mariko had done. She begged me—she wanted to take the girls and leave Colorado. Return to Japan. It was, for me, a difficult time."

Taro was silent long enough that I felt it necessary to prod him. "Difficult? How?"

He paused. "Selfishness." The solitary word was spoken as an almost-question. "Not one of my most proud traits. I am vain, and I can be selfish. I was loving my work at the resort. I knew that it would not look good for me in my employer's eyes for my family to leave Steamboat and return to Japan. The company would be . . . unsympathetic to our problems. They would be critical of my inability to control my daughter. And as to that solution?" He shook his head. "My career would be in jeopardy."

"Ultimately, your wife agreed?"

"My wife . . . submitted . . . to my wisdom. A few weeks later, we saw Dr. Raymond Welle for the first time."

"As a family?"

"First he met with Mariko. Alone. Then he met with Eri and myself, alone. Finally, he met with the three of us together. Three different days during one week. He called us all together the following week and offered us a plan. He called it a treatment plan.

"He wanted to meet with Mariko two times each week to help her with her adjustment to . . . being a young woman. To being in America. To being in Steamboat Springs. He wanted to meet with my wife and me once every other week to discuss ways to assist us in managing our daughter during this difficult time in her life. He described Mariko as straddling two cultures and sometimes losing her balance. He also said that she was not ready to relinquish either culture and if we tried to force her to choose one, or if we took one away from her, she would rebel against us further. Our problems would only exacerbate. He was telling us that we could not make our problems go away by returning to Japan."

Given the facts, Welle's treatment approach sounded thoughtful and cogent. I don't know what I'd expected, but given the pontificating nature of his national radio show, I wouldn't have been surprised to hear a plan that consisted of something much more embarrassing to the profession, and much less potentially salutary for the Hamamoto family.

As described by Taro Hamamoto, Dr. Welle's treatment of Mariko sounded like an appropriate method for dealing with an adolescent and her family after a single serious incident of acting out. The intervention with Mr. and Mrs. Hamamoto lasted for six sessions over a period of almost two months. Mariko was seen individually in psychotherapy for slightly longer; her father estimated that she attended psychotherapy sessions twice a week for one month, once a week for two months after that. Maybe sixteen sessions total. He offered to check old financial records if the specific number of visits was important. I told him I'd let him know.

These days her managed-care company would never have approved such a luxurious investment of psychotherapeutic intervention. But her treatment was back in 1988, when health insurance policy provisions were less strict. Psychologists with psychologically unsophisticated clients often took advantage of the system in such circumstances and continued treatment long after it was necessary. It didn't appear to me that Dr. Welle had abused the system, however.

The treatment he provided to Mariko was not too long, not too short. Just right. When I was able to pull it off in my own practice, I liked to think of it as the Goldilocks solution.

Taro noticed me eyeing my watch. "I am aware that our time is almost up. I will try to be brief as I conclude. As I said before, Dr. Welle helped us. He helped my wife and me understand better the pressures that were weighing on our daughters. He taught us ways to help the girls adjust. He was sensitive to the cultural concerns we had. Eri and I did not want to relinquish . . . the Japanese culture. And whatever Dr. Welle said to Mariko, whatever he advised her to do, we never again had problems with her about drugs and boys."

I sensed that he expected me to challenge him about the last point he'd made. I didn't.

He tapped his wristwatch with his fingertip. "You have a flight to catch. I will be pleased, now, to sign your paper before you go." He slid the permission form from the center of the table and aligned it in front of him. "I am grateful for your interest in my . . . family. Please give my greetings to Dr. Raymond Welle when you see him." He fished a pen from the pocket of his chinos and scrawled his signature along the bottom line.

I slid the paper into my satchel.

"Thank you," he said. "What you are doing—it gives me a small measure of hope. For my family, for me, this has been a wave that never breaks."

I thanked him.

"Should we have the opportunity to talk again, we can talk about my other daughter. Satoshi. She is at Stanford, in California. She is studying zoology. She hardly remembers living in Japan, I think. You should consider talking with her as well, you know? She knew her sister in ways that I never would."

"She would be agreeable?"

"Of course. Let me write down her phone number for you. I will tell her you will call."

Ten minutes later I was on board the 737 that would take me back to Denver. Only after I'd walked the length of my jetway did I glance at my boarding pass and notice that my seat had been upgraded to first-class. On board, the flight attendant couldn't tell me why I'd been moved in front of the curtain, and suggested with a crooked smile that I not "question fate that comes in the form of sunshine."

It seemed like good advice. My suspicion, though, was that Taro Hamamoto had pulled a string or two.

After a moment's contemplation I decided I was more grateful than suspicious, and eagerly accepted the champagne I was offered by the flight attendant with the wisdom and the crooked smile.

PART THREE

A Fool's Errand

CHAPTER
13

A few years back, during a late spring when I was between wives, I attended a large, formal wedding reception at the Phipps Tennis House in Denver. I remember arriving at the affair mostly cynical and leaving mostly drunk. The buddy who drove me home afterward accused me of hitting on the maid of honor without success—and without honor, for that matter.

The facility where the event was held remained a bit of a blur in my memory. My recollection was of a huge Quonset hut–like structure with a glass roof. The building itself was constructed of red brick and covered with green ivy—a monument that a family with too much money had erected shortly after the turn of the last century to indulge its interest in court sports and to express its disdain for the vagaries of Colorado weather.

At the wedding reception I'd done most of my drinking in the gardens adjoining the huge tennis house. I remembered the gardens fondly for the abundant shade. I also recalled that a pair of flickers had been using nearby downspouts and gutters to drum a staccato advertisement for mates. Or perhaps they were after sexual partners—gladly, I don't know enough about flickers to make the distinction. I did recall that their insistent percussion had mitigated my enjoyment of the Mumm I was downing at a pace I would later regret.

Although I don't remember many details from the afternoon of the wedding reception, I am pretty certain about two things. One, I never set eyes on the mansion that day. And two, the couple who were married that afternoon years ago are now, sadly, divorced.

It was the Phipps Mansion and not the tennis house that was my destination on the Friday in June after I returned from Vancouver. The mansion and its adjacent play structure had been bequeathed by the Phipps family to the University of Denver. The university routinely made the facilities available for community uses that ranged from weddings and bar mitzvahs all the way to the elegant proceedings of the Summit of the Eight industrialized countries. The spectacular buildings were also used for occasional political gatherings in support of presidents, governors, and sundry state and local politicians.

My instructions from someone named Trish in Representative Welle's office in Washington, D.C., were to arrive at the front door of the mansion at 10:45 and to be sure I was carrying identification. Approaching the mansion in my car, I drove past two black-vested valets who were hijacking vehicles at the entrance to the tennis-house parking lot. I didn't slow, instead continuing up the hill in the general direction that I expected to find the manor.

It wasn't hard to spot. The mansion is a grand Georgian structure that commands a pleasant knoll not too far south of the tennis house. The redbrick home looks down both front and rear—and both literally and figuratively—on an expansive neighborhood that has grown up around it on what the Phipps family probably once called "the grounds." I was deterred from entering a long circular drive up to the mansion by two large men in gray suits who I surmised had not been hired for their facility at traffic control. I smiled at their stern warning to move on and continued around the block, driving a long, looping route that rolled up and to the west before circling back behind the tennis house.

I was in a nice neighborhood. On a street shaded by stately elms I parked across from a brick-and-stucco house that looked like a country hotel designed by Frank Lloyd Wright and in front of a vaulting A-frame that would have done Aspen proud. I decided to forgo the services of the valet because I'm cheap and also because I didn't want my car to be boxed in by the cars of the attendees of the day's fund-raising event. I knew I would be exiting early. Trish had informed me that my meeting with Representative Welle was "preluncheon" only. She had asked me if that was clear.

I told her I thought it probably meant that I wasn't staying for lunch.

Yes. Trish and I had been on the same page.

In that morning's editions the Denver newspapers had reported that political supporters of Dr. Welle were going to pay one thousand dollars each to attend a pre-lunch reception at the tennis house. I could only guess how much the two dozen or so who had been invited to luncheon in the dining room at the mansion afterward would be paying—or, more likely, had already paid—for the privilege of tearing puglia with the congressman.

Some memory fragment from the long-ago nuptials I'd attended suggested that I could cut through the gardens of the tennis house from near the spot where I'd parked my car and thus considerably abbreviate my walk to the mansion. I followed some catering employees past a.red-olent Dumpster, through a ratty wooden gate, and into the familiar tennis-house gardens. I listened for the per-cussive evidence of flickers. None around. From the tennis-house gardens I wandered up some brick stairs and through a charming wrought-iron-and-brick portico into the formal gardens on the north side of the mansion.

Although the flowering plants weren't at their peak, they hinted at what was to come in July and August. The grape arbors offered shade, and the abundant rose gardens were in perfect early-summer form. The cherry and apple trees showed the beginnings of a summer of good fruit. Upright junipers spaced like soldiers at pa-rade rest protected the perimeters of the huge garden.

I wished Lauren were with me. She could tell me what some of the perennials were.

One of the two gray-suited men from the end of the driveway spotted me wandering the paths of the gardens. He apparently didn't think my stroll was a good idea and jogged up the driveway and across the lawn to tell me so.

"I have an appointment with Representative Welle," I said in response to his query about whether he could help me find my way.

"Your name, sir?" He stood between the distant entrance to the mansion and me. "I'd like to see some ID."

I told him my name and handed him my driver's license. When he returned it I asked, "And your name is?" I also held out my hand to shake his. He didn't notice; he was busy repeating my identity into a microphone that was hidden somewhere in his gray suit.

A moment later he said, "They are expecting you, Dr. Gregory. At the front door." He pointed up the hill.

I checked my watch. "I'm a little early."

"That's not a problem. We would prefer that you not be on the grounds unaccompanied, sir. Would you like me to accompany you the rest of the way to the mansion?"

"I don't think that will be necessary."

"I'm glad to hear that."

The man who met me at the door of the big house was built like a double pork chop that had a grape stuck on the meaty end. Thin legs, tiny head, huge trunk. Maybe five-nine. The only way to get by him in an airplane aisle would be to get down on your knees and crawl past those spindly legs.

"Phil *Barrett*," he said in a slightly too loud voice that I could only imagine coming in useful at a high school reunion as he was greeting someone he was afraid didn't remember who he was.

"Alan Gregory," I replied.

He shook my hand. "Of course. Of course. Welcome.

Come in." I imagined that he'd been at Phipps no more than half an hour and he was already acting like he'd just inherited it from some dead aunt.

I looked around. "Nice place."

"Yes," he said. "Ray's an alumni."

I was tempted to correct his Latin. Didn't. "Of?"

"D.U. He was a Chi Phi. President, I think. His undergraduate degree is in economics. Not too many people know that part of Ray's background. Before he became a healer he was quite a student of economic policy and all. Bet you're surprised. Am I right? I know I'm right. We have to do a better job of getting that part of Ray's background out to his public. Ray's been good to his school and the trustees are kind enough to let us use this place once in a while."

"That's nice."

"It's especially appropriate this year, of course. The original Mr. Phipps was a United States senator from Colorado, too. Did you know that? I'm afraid the history of this great state of ours eludes too many of its citizens."

I had indeed been aware that Lawrence Phipps was Senator Phipps but I said that I hadn't. It seemed important to Phil Barrett that I be ignorant.

We'd stepped far enough into the entrance hall so I could see the bustle of activity in the dining room, where the caterers were setting up tables for at least two dozen people. Lunch, apparently, was going to require a lot of silverware.

"Major supporters," Phil Barrett explained. Maybe he'd been thinking the same thing about the silverware.

"Hey," I said, shrugging my shoulders. I wondered if Raoul Estevez, my partner Diane's husband, would be in attendance. Diane had told me that Raoul threw major money at politicians sometimes. Raoul's politics were usually difficult to discern but I felt confident that he threw money at both Democrats and Republicans without revealing his bias about their beliefs. He was practical enough, and honest enough, to admit that he was seeking influence, not ideology.

Barrett led me in the opposite direction from the dining room and we promptly got lost in the huge house.
We backtracked once unsuccessfully and a second time
with more success and he showed me into a library that
was almost as large as the top floor of my house. The
paneling and shelves were of knotty pine that had aged
to a color halfway between honey and bourbon.

I let my eyes wander the room. Walls of books. Comfortable furniture. Nice lights. I decided I could read
there.

"Ray will be just a minute or two. You'll be fine?"

I smiled.

Less than a minute later I was checking titles on the
shelves when a young man dressed as though he was
from the caterer's staff entered the room and asked me
if I would like something to drink.

"Please. A soft drink. Something brown and diet
would be great."

I climbed a rolling library ladder and was perusing
titles on the upper shelves, my back to the door, when I
heard, "Your libation, sir."

I chuckled at the pretension and turned around to see
not the young man from catering, but rather the familiar
face of Dr. Raymond Welle. He was bowling lightly at
the waist, a tray balanced perfectly on his right hand, a
linen napkin folded expertly over his wrist. From my
vantage, I could see that the crown of his head was becoming mostly bald.

I said, "Dr. Welle, Representative Welle, hello."

"Don't bother with all that rigmarole. Ray will do just
fine. May I call you Alan? Or is it Al?"

"Alan." I reached the bottom of the ladder and took
the glass from his tray with my left hand and shook his
hand with my right. "Thank you very much. I'm pretty
sure this is the first drink I've ever had delivered to me
by a member of the United States Congress."

"I like to think we're good for something other than
raising money, spending money, and arguing about everything and nothing. I think that if I could deliver a

cold drink to every one of my constituents we might all be better off. We'd certainly trust each other more."

Over Welle's shoulder I saw Phil Barrett entering the room. He had donned a dirt brown suit jacket over his shirt and tie. I thought of a breaded pork chop. A stuffed breaded pork chop.

"You two have met, right? You don't mind that Phil's going to sit in, do you? Didn't think so. Sit, sit, everyone, please," cajoled Welle. He guided us toward the windows, where we each took a Queen Anne chair.

I didn't want Phil Barrett anywhere near this part of my inquiry. But I already knew what objection I was going to make about his presence and knew it would play better later on than it would at the start.

"Trish tells me you want to take a trip down memory lane, Alan. Back to my roots, so to speak. Clinical psychology. Seems like at least two lifetimes ago that I was doing psychotherapy every day. Some old case of mine, right? That's what you want to talk about? I don't know how much I'll remember after all these years. But I promise to do my best."

"Thank you. That's all we can hope for." I was having trouble finding comfort while addressing Welle by his first name, but I didn't have the luxury of time to figure out why I was stumbling. I assumed it had to do with his congressional status, hoped it didn't have anything to do with his celebrity. I did know I didn't want to enter into this conversation intimidated by this man. I said, "As I'm sure your office was apprised when the request was made for this appointment, it was an unfortunate case that I wish to discuss. That of Mariko Hamamoto."

He raised one eyebrow and glanced at Phil Barrett. Something passed between them that I wasn't privy to.

Welle said, "Although I'm not fond of starting conversations this way, I'm afraid I'll have to be disagreeable right off the bat. Case wasn't unfortunate at all. Textbook intervention. I'm proud of it. I did good work. Fine work. Poor girl's murder sure was unfortunate, though. Obscene."

"I've recently spoken with Mariko's father and—"

"You have? Well, you talk to Taro again you give him my best wishes. I still pray for him and Eri at least once a week. Sometimes more than that. And that little girl of theirs, what was her name?"

I assumed he meant Mariko's little sister. "Satoshi."

"That's right. Satoshi. The whole thing broke her in two. The disappearance. The murders. She was a real sweetheart."

I suspected I was watching the process by which a natural politician transfers a forgotten name into permanent storage. He wouldn't forget Satoshi Hamamoto's identity again.

I reached into my jacket pocket and took out a photocopy of the release-of-information form that Taro had signed in Vancouver. "I'll be sure to pass along your regards. This is for your records, by the way. It's a photocopy of an authorization signed by Taro Hamamoto permitting you to release information about his daughter's psychotherapy to me and to Locard."

Phil Barrett reached for the sheet of paper. I retrieved it from his reach and handed it instead to Welle. To Phil Barrett, I said, "I'm afraid you'll have to excuse us at this point, Mr. Barrett. You don't have permission to hear any confidential information about Mariko Hamamoto's psychotherapy from Dr. Welle. The consent that Mr. Hamamoto signed applies only to me and to the professional members of Locard. You . . . are not covered."

Welle and Barrett again exchanged something nonverbally. While Welle glanced at the document I'd handed to him, he said, "I'm sure Taro wouldn't mind at all Phil's hearing what I have to say about his daughter. Phil was sheriff in Routt County back then. He knows all this anyway."

I thought he was waiting to see if I would react to the news about Phil Barrett's involvement in the earlier investigation. I didn't. I said, "But Taro's not here to give his assent. And I have no doubt that someone in your position would not want to risk violating patient confidentiality. Even on a technicality. Ray." The "Ray" rolled right off my tongue. I smiled. My pulse was getting back to normal.

Welle wet his lips and said, "I'm afraid the man's right, Phillip. He has both ethics and law on his side. Tough combination to fight, even in Washington. So you'll have to excuse us for a few minutes. If we move onto unrelated subjects you can come right on back in."

I tried not to watch Barrett's embarrassing efforts at extricating himself from the wing chair. I failed. The weave of the material of his suit seemed to have a magnetic attraction for the velvet fabric of the upholstery.

Barrett finally departed. Welle said, "So what can I tell you? Mariko's treatment, to my memory, was a total success. Adjustment problems. A little acting out. Basically a good, good kid having trouble being an adolescent and being an American. She worked it out. I helped. Case closed."

I smiled. "That's nice to hear. Taro Hamamoto told me basically the same thing. My dilemma about Mariko is that I'm not sure exactly what I need to know about her, Ray. Would you mind if I take a moment to explain my role with Locard and then perhaps you can help me decide what it is I might need to know about the treatment you did?" I proceeded to give my I-need-to-get-to-know-Mariko-to-try-to-know-her-killer speech.

He listened patiently. When I concluded, he said, "So the thinking now is that it wasn't a stranger who killed those girls."

"I'm not privy to Locard's current hypothesis, Ray. All I know is that this is a base they've asked me to cover."

"I think Phil and his boys investigated this whole thing pretty thoroughly. Back then, of course. Better computers, more technology, better science now, sure. That may help your group with its work. But my memory is that they ruled out that the killer was someone who knew the girls. FBI concurred."

"Locard seems to like to proceed from a point of view where the assumptions are wiped clean."

He nodded. "Like to reinvent the wheel, do they? Can't argue with it. They've had their successes, haven't they? That Texas thing? Wow. Have to admit that was impressive."

"Yes, they have been successful. Why don't we start with the presenting problem? What were the issues that you were helping Mariko with?"

"Let me see." He tightened his eyes as though he was trying to appear pensive. I wasn't convinced by his act when he said, "I think I got it. She'd been caught with some dope. Just enough to smoke, mind you, not to sell. That's my memory. Too bad Phil's not here. He'd remember for sure about the dope part. Mother was overprotective. Father was more reasonable but was kind of absent, you know, very busy at work. He was a big shot at the resort. Mariko was trying to find her way around a new culture, with new friends, new temptations. Adolescent stuff."

"You mentioned her friends. Would you say she was especially susceptible to influence from her friends?"

"Especially? I wouldn't say especially. Had a good friend . . . yes, Tami—Tami Franklin, who was a very strong personality, a natural leader. I must say Tami didn't always lead kids in the direction that their parents wanted them to go. But she was a natural leader. She certainly influenced Mariko."

"Tami was the girl she was murdered with."

He waved his left hand at me. "Of course, of course. I know that. But lots of kids in town were susceptible to Tami's influences, not just Mariko. Tami was that kind of kid. She caused a lot of sleepless nights for a lot of Steamboat Springs parents, that girl did."

"Boyfriend?"

"Tami? Always. Mariko?" He shook his head and made a clicking sound with his tongue. "You know, not that I recall. It's possible, I suppose, but I don't remember her talking about anyone special."

I was immediately curious why Welle knew and re-called so much about Tami Franklin. Had Mariko talked about her friend in therapy that much?

"What about other friends besides Tami?"

"Mariko talked about some other kids, I'm sure. But I couldn't remember their names. We're going back a lot of years. I bet the Franklins could be of some help on that. The kids all hung out in a group."

"School problems?"

"Again, not that I recall. Just being picked up that once with the dope and the, oh yeah—the . . . I almost forgot. Her parents were mortified that when she was picked up by the police she was skinny-dipping in the hot springs out at Strawberry Park with some boys. And there was the lying, of course."

"The lying?"

"Mariko wasn't truthful to her parents about where she was going and who she was going with. That sort of thing. Her parents made a big deal out of it. May have been a cultural thing. Me? I didn't consider it too un-usual for a teenager. Certainly didn't see it as pathologic. Tried to get Taro and Eri to put it in context."

"Did you do any testing?"

"You mean psychological testing? Nope. Wasn't my thing. When necessary, I referred for that."

"Did you refer Mariko for testing?"

He didn't hesitate. "No. There was no need. I told you. This was an adjustment issue, a maturation thing. Pure and simple."

I softened my voice as I asked, "What was she like, Ray? As a person, I mean. Mariko?"

He smiled, it seemed, involuntarily. "She was vibrant. Had a little accent still, sort of a mix of Japanese and British. Pronounced her words, every one of them, as though she'd been practicing. She was a smidgen shy, but she had this brilliance inside her that . . . just shined. Bright as a spotlight. Mariko was a little self-deprecating. Maybe a bit too much. But she was . . . witty . . . caring. And pretty. Oh my, pretty, pretty." I thought I saw his eyes moisten. "You've seen pictures, right? She was a little treasure of a kid. Her death, her *murder* . . ." His fists clenched; his eyes tightened. "My wife's death, my wife's *murder* . . . they are profane, bloody indications of what's so sick about this country. It's why I decided to go on the radio to try to do some healing. It's why I went to Congress to try to force some change. It's why I want to be in the Senate. It's why I put up with these silly fund-raising luncheons." He waved his arm around the library as though the books were to blame.

I was moved, but at the same time, I knew I was being manipulated. I was too aware that Raymond Welle *wanted* me to be moved. It troubled me; I felt as though I'd been leashed and was being taken for a walk. I also wondered why Ray was so eager to alter his own personal history. He had decided to run for Congress for the first time—and had lost the primary—long before his wife was killed. Why was he arguing that her murder was a motivation for him to run for office?

Somewhere about here I lost control of the conversation. Raymond edged me, ever so cleverly, into small talk about Mariko, eventually concluding with "I think it's time to get Phil back in here. See what he can add." He tapped his watch. Before I could object, Welle was on his way to the door.

The first words from Barrett's mouth were, "We're way off schedule, Ray. People are waiting next door at the tennis house." He turned his head to face me. "Doctor, I'm sorry, but we need to wrap this up."

I'd just looked at my watch. The time period I had been promised for the meeting had not been used up. But I didn't protest; I expected the congressman and I would be speaking again and I didn't want to poison the well. I also suspected the final request I planned to make was going to cause him some trouble and I didn't want to antagonize him before I antagonized him.

I needed to get a copy of his case file for the treatment of Mariko. The case materials should have been collected for the initial investigation by Phil Barrett's department at the time of the murders. But I'd searched the materials twice already and they contained no written records from Raymond Welle.

"I understand you have a busy day. I appreciate your time, Congressman. And your candor. One last thing, though. I'll need a copy of your case file. Notes, treatment plan, ancillary contacts. You know what I mean. Locard insists on the written records. It's part of the protocol." I made that part up.

With only a heartbeat's hesitation, Raymond said, "I'm sure I don't have that anymore. I think those old clinical files were all shredded. Years ago. When I moved on in my career."

I didn't hesitate any longer than he had. "I hope not, Ray. State board regulations require that you keep those records available for fifteen years after therapy termination. I wouldn't like to see you reprimanded for violating that kind of thing." I wasn't certain what interval the regs actually specified but I suspected Ray would be more ignorant than I about the regulations of the State Board of Psychologist Examiners.

Ray's cheeks scrunched up and I could hear him force an exhale through his nostrils. "Really? Didn't know that." His face immediately transformed into something more conciliatory. "I'll tell you, the fool laws that legislators pass sometimes . . ." He made a comical face. "I'll have someone look into the record thing, then. Phil, can you have someone show Dr. Gregory to the door? I promised to make a couple more of those damn phone calls." He smiled and waved good-bye.

Barrett escorted me back to the entry hall. A large table in the center was now nearly covered with a neatly arranged pyramid of Dr. Raymond Welle's two-year-old hardcover book, *Toward Healing America: America's Therapist's Prescription for a Better Future.*

Rather snidely, I thought, Barrett said, "Want one? Go ahead. Take one. They're all signed."

I did.

He walked me all the way to the door. He said, "You

people at Locard are wasting your time. You won't solve this case. Those girls are going to stay dead. And the killer's going to stay gone. You, my friend, are on a fool's errand."

Before I could come up with a response, he had turned and walked away and the door was being closed against my back.

CHAPTER
14

One of the men in gray suits was blocking the shortcut that led back to my car through the formal gardens. I waved in his direction as I circled down the long driveway. He didn't wave back.

Since my arrival an hour earlier the streets of the quiet residential neighborhood around the mansion appeared to have been transformed into the parking lot for a convention of limousine drivers. A sound system blared music from the direction of the tennis house. I thought I was hearing a Barbra Streisand ballad. Barbra, I assumed, would not be pleased. I loitered for a while and the music changed to a Garth Brooks number that stopped abruptly as a shrill voice screamed, "I give you the next United States senator from the great state of Colorado . . . ," but clapping and cheers drowned out the final words. I assumed they were "Representative Raymond Welle." The music resumed. Garth had been replaced by some patriotic march that I couldn't name, but that I assumed was by John Philip Sousa.

I reflected on the introducer's comments—*"I give you the next United States senator . . ."*—and decided that allowing for the prices that were being charged for admission to Raymond Welle's fund-raising reception, there might be a whole lot of buying and selling, or at the very least, renting, going on.

But *giving?* Certainly not from Welle's side of the ledger.

I haven't met too many national politicians in my life. Seeing them on the news, especially when they are engaging in their four most public activities—raising campaign funds, making laws, and either accusing their opponents of impropriety or defending themselves against charges of impropriety—does not leave me inclined to socialize with them. But the point of my disinclination is moot: the fact that I'm not prone to donate money to their campaigns seems, somehow, to interfere with their desire to pencil me into their social calendars.

Nevertheless, my meeting with Raymond Welle had not left me running for a disinfectant shower, as I feared it would.

I was not surprised that Welle was as smooth and polished as a river stone. I was surprised that I also found him to be affable, gracious, and personable. He was slippery enough to survive in the treacherous waters of Congress, but he wasn't, well, slimy—and the fact that he could actually talk intelligently about the profession we shared pleased me. The platitude-rich national radio program that had carried him to national prominence on a tide of poorly considered quasi-psychological advice and narrow-minded polemics had not prepared me for the possibility that the man might actually have known what he was doing as a clinician.

This new appraisal gave me caution. If I was viewing him accurately, Welle was an effective chameleon, which made him a more dangerous adversary. And despite the tacit cooperation he had offered during our meeting, Welle and his right-hand man, Phil Barrett, felt like adversaries to me.

I was walking down the road from the manse, skirting a Mercedes limousine that was sporting an American flag from each fender, when I heard my name. Loudly, a female voice called, "Dr. Gregory? Hello-o."

I turned to see a thin woman who appeared to be on the northern side of thirty approaching me from the entrance to the tennis house. I stopped and waited for her. She pulled sunglasses from her eyes and perched them on top of her head.

I decided immediately that she wasn't a native. She was dressed in a chocolate brown gabardine suit that was way too warm for a typical June day at the base of the Rockies. Her skin was so pale it seemed to glow from within her like a pearl. The purse she carried screamed "carry-on luggage" and was so large and heavy it caused her left shoulder to sag a good three inches lower than the right.

I guessed Seattle or Portland.

The wind shifted to the west and a noxious blend of good perfume and stale tobacco wafted my way. The combination smelled like an industrial-strength room deodorizer.

The woman was tall and composed, and as she got closer to me I couldn't steal my attention from her eyes. They were large and the color was the deep green hue of shallow water in the Caribbean. From ten feet away she again said, "Dr. Gregory? It's you, right?"

Damn. I knew that voice. I'd guessed wrong about the Pacific Northwest. This lady was from Washington, D.C.

"I'm Dorothy Levin. We've talked? I'm a reporter with the *Washington Post.* Ring any bells?"

"Oh, yes."

"Good. Niceties are covered. I know you're a doctor. You know I'm a reporter. And you know the story I'm working on." She stretched the collar of her blouse away from her neck with her fingers. "Is it always this hot here? I thought I was going to be in the mountains."

"Common misconception. Summers tend to be quite warm along the Front Range."

"And dry? Shit, I swear the inside of my nose is cracking into a miniature mudflat and my contacts feel like they're made of Saran Wrap."

I was going to go into a relatively lengthy explanation about the value of good hydration in high-desert climes, but decided against it.

"Someplace we can sit and talk? Preferably someplace air-conditioned. I have maybe forty-five minutes till the fund-raiser lets out. They instituted a no-press rule.

Pisses me off. Leaves me standing out here in this convection oven."

"I'm afraid I still don't have anything to tell you."

She smiled in a way that clearly communicated "Don't patronize me." Her smile was pleasant enough but I was still having difficulty getting past her brilliant eyes and the tobacco fumes. "You were just with him, weren't you?"

"Him?" I asked, feeling caught and feeling stupid.

She laughed at my lame attempt at being disingenuous, caught herself, and swallowed. "You know whom I'm talking about. Colorado's next senator—Raymond Welle? Six-two. Handsome enough. Bad five o'clock shadow. Body mass index just this side of obese. You were just meeting with him, I think?"

"I don't . . . I don't have anything to say."

She licked her lips. "I already know about the meeting, Doctor. I'm just trying to be polite, here, generate a little discussion. Tomorrow's editions of the *Post* will report the meeting you just had with Welle. My story won't say what you two discussed because I don't know yet. But the fact that you just had a private tête-à-tête with Ray Welle prior to a major fund-raising luncheon will soon be national news. The local papers here in this thriving metropolis will pick it up off the wires and then—I promise this on my mama's grave—then you'll get lots of calls from reporters who are nowhere near as pleasant to deal with as I am."

"Why on earth would you want to do that? The fact that I met with Welle isn't news."

She shifted the heavy bag from one shoulder to the other. "Of course it's not news—yet. So I'll bury the fact somewhere in the story to smoke you out. Eventually, you'll tell me."

I could hardly believe what I was hearing. "Am I being threatened?"

She scoffed. "You kidding me? You're being *encouraged*. This . . ."—she waved her hand back and forth between us—"is encouragement. I say please, you say no. So I say pretty please. You still say no. So I try pretty-pretty please. That's what this is. This is the pretty-pretty-please phase of encouragement. Can we go somewhere? This laptop I have weighs a ton. I'm trying to get them to buy me one of those little tiny ones. You seen those? Couple of pounds. That's what I need. Color screen, word processing and a modem. I don't need the rest of this shit. What on earth am I going to do with a DVD or a 3-D video card?"

I wasn't press-savvy. I didn't have any way of judging whether or not she was telling me the truth. Would she really print my name in the next day's *Washington Post*? If she did Locard would not be happy with me.

To buy time to think, I said, "Yes, we can go somewhere. My car's around the corner. There's a place a few blocks from here."

"I have to be back by the time this thing lets out." She pointed at the tennis house door.

"I'm not going to kidnap you, Ms. Levin."

"Can I smoke in your car?"

"Not a chance."

"Shit. My friends warned me about coming to this state. And you can call me Dorothy."

I've always had an affinity for smart women with an attitude. By the time we got to the restaurant I already liked Dorothy Levin.

"I bet I can't smoke here either, can I?" she asked as she was pulling off her jacket and settling onto a chair in Cucina Leone in nearby Bonnie Brae.

"I doubt it."

A waiter approached and she ordered coffee and two chocolate chip cookies. I ordered coffee.

She said, "I never get enough calories when I'm on the road. Do you have that problem?"

"Will my answer be in your story?"

She laughed.

I said, "Let me ask you something. A journalism question. What's it called when I tell you something but you agree in advance not to use it."

She lowered her chin and batted her eyes. "I think it's called a cock tease, isn't it?"

It was my turn to laugh.

She said, "What? You mean not attribute it? Not quote you? That's called background."

"No. I mean not use it at all. You'll know it, but you won't print it."

"Ohhh. Deep background. We're getting sophisticated, are we? Sorry, I don't play that game."

The coffee arrived. Dorothy started into her cookies immediately. She ate them by breaking off small pieces and transferring them to the tip of her tongue as though they were communion offerings.

I announced, "Then I'm afraid this meeting is just gong to be coffee." I sat back on my chair and lifted my coffee cup. "Go ahead and write your story and start to smoke me out. I'll just have to live with the consequences." I inserted as much bravado into the words as I could muster.

She sighed and rubbed the back of her neck with the hand that wasn't breaking apart cookies.

"Don't be disappointed, Dorothy. I wasn't lying before. I really don't know anything that will be helpful to you."

"These are good." She pointed to the cookies. "Want a bite?" She broke off a corner and handed it to me. "A peace offering. I lied to you before. About not playing the deep-background game. I'll listen to what you say. If I start having problems, I'll warn you. How's that?'

"You won't print anything?"

"Unless I come upon the same information independently. Then it's fair game. But I still won't quote you."

"Are you trustworthy? You lied to me once."

"*Hello.* You've lied to me more than once. And whom are you going to ask if I'm trustworthy? My cats? My ex-husband? My editor? My shrink? Probably get a lot of different answers."

"You're in therapy?" I asked.

"Don't get me started. So why did you meet with him?"

"This is deep background, right?"

She rolled her tantalizing eyes and nodded.

"Okay. I'm a clinical psychologist, right?"

"Yeah."

"So is he. Welle."

"Yeah. This is news?"

"I met with him because I needed to discuss one of his old psychotherapy cases with him."

"That's it? You're seeing one of his old patients and you wanted to compare notes?"

"Not exactly."

"Oh, here we go again. I smell the acrid odor of obfuscation. No more cookies for you." She slid the cookie plate far out of my reach and guarded it in the crook of her elbow.

"It's not one of my cases. It's a quasi-legal thing, actually. I've been asked to review some old therapy records."

"Ah! Malpractice? Is someone suing Welle? Cool. Not as good as a campaign violation, but cool enough."

"No, not like that. Nothing like that. I'm not sure I can tell you more without breaching confidentiality, but suffice it to say that I've been asked to review one of his old cases with him and he was gracious enough to do it."

"But a lawyer asked you to do it?"

I thought for a moment. The request had actually come from A. J. Simes. "No, another psychologist."

"Why didn't the other psychologist do it himself or herself?"

"The other psychologist isn't local. It wouldn't be . . . convenient."

She chewed on my answer for a moment. "And that's what you did this morning?"

"Yes."

"In person? He met with you to review a case? I'm
sorry, that doesn't make any sense to me. Couldn't that
be done over the phone?"

"Could be, isn't always."

"Welle doesn't give away hours to just anybody. What
he'a doing now at the tennis house—raising money—
that's how he spends his free time."

I made a face to indicate I was offended and shrugged
my shoulders. "I asked for a meeting. I was granted a
meeting."

"No." She shook her head. "No. Uh-uh. It's not that
simple." She checked her watch. "Time to go back to
my stakeout. Have a couple more people to talk to at
the old fund-raiser."

"What do they do in there for all this time?"

"Never been to one? It's basically a meeting of rich
white guys over forty-five. Some of them bring wives or
dates but over eighty percent of the donors are rich men
with an agenda. It goes something like this: Welle gives
his stump speech about economic freedom and moral
decay and the necessity for America to heal itself—blah,
blah, blah—then there's a reception line where people
who forked over enough dough get a formal picture with
the candidate and the American flag. Patriotic music
plays in the background. Backs get slapped. Lunch meetings get set."

"That's it?"

"Yessiree. That's our election process. What's so ap-
palling isn't just that it's corrupt. It's also unimaginative.
In my mind, there's no excuse for that. None."

Her cell phone went off as soon as she got into the
car. Neither of us could do anything to keep me from
eavesdropping.

"Ohhh, Jesus. Whadya mean, where am I? I don't
think I have to tell you that anymore, remember. Wasn't
that the point of my asking you to leave? . . . No, you
can't go checking the file cabinet for those papers. Your
keys don't work in the apartment anymore, anyway.

You'll have to wait until I get back. . . . Not long, no. It's business. Business . . . Whadya mean am I sure? Of course I'm by myself. . . . I'm not doing anything to you. . . . Douglas, I'm sorry, it's just going to have to wait. . . . I don't care; it'll have to wait until I'm back . . . You should have remembered about it when you packed the rest of your things. . . . Not my problem . . . No. I'll leave you a message when I get home. Later."

She folded up her phone. I said, "Sorry."

"Not your fault. That was the aforementioned ex. Actually that's wishful thinking on my part. We're separated, not divorced. He's not happy with me. Apparently I'm not as sweet with everybody as I have been with you."

"Hard to believe," I said.

"We've been separated three months and I feel much better about it when I'm out of the District. For a while I was pretty sure he was following me. I'd go to a bar, he'd show up there. I'd be out with a friend, we'd see him." She shivered.

"Is he a possessive guy?"

"You bet. Jealous. Waste of emotional energy as far as I'm concerned. As if I have any interest in other men. Any."

"Is he violent?"

"Douglas? We're both kind of hotheads. You know? Him no more than me, though. Maybe less. Stuff gets said. Occasionally things were thrown around. You know." She smiled but didn't look my way. "He never actually hit me. And you—you're starting to sound like a goddamn shrink."

"Sorry, it's a reflex. Possessive exes worry me. It's an occupational hazard, I'm afraid."

"Is the air conditioner on high?"

"Yes."

She tugged at her collar and raised her chin. "I have to admit that he worries me sometimes, too."

"Have you thought about changing your cell phone number so he can't track you down so easily?"

"My life? I need to change a lot of things." She looked out the window. "And you know what? I think I've just decided what's going to be first." She undid her seat belt, raised her butt in the air, reached under her skirt, and started tugging down her panty hose. A moment later, the act completed, her bare toes wiggling on the dash- board, she said, "Dearest God, that feels good. Don't you wish it was all that easy?"

CHAPTER
15

The Bonnie Brae neighborhood is a maze of little curving streets. I got lost on the way back to Phipps from the restaurant. Dorothy Levin had no patience for my directional impairment.

"I can't be late, Doctor."

"I'm trying, Dorothy. This isn't my neighborhood."

On my third attempt at finding my way to the mansion, I chanced on the shingled round roof of the tennis house from the rear. I said, "Voilà."

Dorothy said, *"Merde. Finalement."* She had finished stuffing her panty hose into the big shoulder bag along with God knows what else. I pulled around to the edge of the driveway that led to a small parking area in front of the building. She climbed out of the car, leaned over, and asked, "You're being straight with me, right?"

I should have just said, "Yes." Instead, occasionally forthright to a fault, I said, "I answered all your questions honestly."

She reacted as though I was intentionally screwing around with her. Which, in a way, I was. "Oh no you don't. What does that mean? How is that different from being straight with me?"

The door to the tennis house flew open. Grateful for the diversion, I said, "I think your prey is about to enter the meadow. A herd of rich white guys over forty-five is approaching downwind."

She didn't even look in that direction. "They won't bring Welle out that door. Certainly not first. Not when there's all that money still inside waiting to be caressed.

Don't change the subject on me. What are you not telling me about Welle?"

"That's not Welle, right there?" I asked, looking over her shoulder. The man I was pointing at was Welle's size and coloring but his back was turned to us. The man was speaking to someone still standing in the doorway. I looked around for Phil Barrett, assuming he was never far from Raymond Welle's side. I didn't see a single pork chop in sight.

She turned away from me for a split second, then back. A cigarette had materialized in her hand. "Where? That guy? It's just some dude in a dark gray suit. They all wear dark gray suits. I don't know . . . no, that can't be him. The candidate never comes out of these things first. He still has the damn luncheon to go to."

"Looks like him."

She banged an open hand on the edge of the door and slammed it. "I have to go. We'll talk. You and me. We'll talk, count on it."

She was no more than ten feet into the driveway when I saw the first puff of smoke floating up around her head.

Of course, I thought the smoke was from her cigarette.

But the loud crack of a gunshot that immediately followed the puff of smoke caused me to rethink its source. I was sure it came from behind me. I screamed, "Dorothy, get down!"

She spun 180 degrees, bewildered, her hair flying. I yelled, "Someone has a gun. Get down!" She stared at me as though I were a lunatic. Her eyes shined even brighter than before.

Only a total of five or six people had made their way out of the door of the tennis house by the time the shot rang out. They reacted to the blast by pushing and shoving at each other, scrambling to get back inside the building. Two of them fell beside the concrete landing as they tried to force their way back in. I couldn't tell whether the man who I thought was Welle was still outside.

Closer to me, Dorothy finally dropped to a crouch, the damn cigarette glued to her lips.

Another shot cracked the quiet, the slug hitting directly over the top of the door to the tennis house. I saw splintered brick flying. People started screaming, covering their heads.

A man in a distinctive green suit standing near the door yelled, "There!" and pointed right at me.

Behind me, I heard a car engine accelerate gently. I lowered myself farther onto my seat and turned to see a white Ford van pull away from the curb. The vehicle was unadorned and was heading in the opposite direction from mine. The driver was wearing a baseball cap of some kind, left elbow on the sill of the door, a raised hand spread casually in front of his or her face. Before I had the presence of mind to look at the license plate, the car was around the corner and gone.

I waited for another shot. Nothing.

I spun back toward the tennis house. Three large men in gray suits with weapons in their hands were sprinting at my car.

I heard ravens cawing.

I wondered, *Had I just seen the shooter?*

Any plans I might have had for the rest of the day were put on hold by the arrival of a diverse group of law enforcement authorities who made it clear that my short-term freedom was dependent on my cooperation with their investigation. More cops of more stripes than I'd ever seen in one place in my life. I met Denver police detectives, FBI agents, CBI agents, and some Secret Service people who had apparently stopped by just to offer their assistance.

News helicopters started hovering overhead. Microwave trucks from the local TV stations lined the distant perimeter of the neighborhood.

I kept asking everyone who approached me whether anyone had been hit by the bullets. I didn't get a straight answer. Two ambulances arrived, one with sirens and lights, the other traveling more incognito.

I watched two men and a woman wearing FBI baseball caps examine the sewer drain that was closest to my car. I was asked if I would volunteer to allow my vehicle to be searched. I signed a piece of paper that said I would, and a platoon of forensic investigators descended on the car. I was asked if I would volunteer to allow my hands to be tested for trace metals to determine whether or not I'd recently fired a gun. I signed a piece of paper that said I would, and I was swabbed and sprayed for evidence of gunshot residue.

After about an hour, I was escorted from the gardens adjacent to the tennis house to a location in the mansion for more formal questioning. The formal dining room would have been an appropriate setting but it was still set for lunch. No one was dining. I was led to the back of the house to a sunny room overlooking the rear yard. In other circumstances the setting would have been serene.

I kept telling myself that I was a witness. That was all. But from the queries being tossed my way over the course of about forty-five minutes, my best guess was that the cops were hypothesizing that I might actually have fired the gun before handing it off like a relay runner to the driver of the white Ford van. As the questions became more insistent I started moving with some rapidity toward a decision to demand to call an attorney. The attorney I planned to call would be my wife, an assistant district attorney. Lauren would know what to do, and would know whom to call next.

That's when they told me I was free to go.

Dorothy Levin was waiting for me on the long circular driveway of the mansion. I asked if she was okay. She assured me that she was but didn't reciprocate by inquiring about my well-being—instead she pumped me for details about my interview with the cops and feds. Before

I would tell her anything, I demanded that our conversation be on background.

She took a step back from me and glared at me as though I'd just spit on her. "What? Background? You're just a witness to what happened. Same as me. Jesus, give me a break. A quote or two isn't going to kill you."

"I don't want my name in the paper."

With an incredibly irritating whine, she said, "Poor baby, you don't want to get involved."

"Apparently I am involved. So are you. I just don't especially want the world to know it."

"Somebody else will find out your name."

The man who had escorted me from the gardens earlier spotted Dorothy flipping open her notebook, a mechanical pencil between her teeth. He walked over briskly and said, "No press in here, ma'am. You're both going to have to exit the grounds."

She wasn't the least bit intimidated. She said, "Today, I'm a witness. Thanks so much for your help."

He pressed. "Are you a reporter?"

"I said I'm a witness. What's your name? You have ID? Who are you with? Are you legal or rental? Let me get my camera, get a snapshot of you. My camera's in here someplace." She lowered her head to her big bag and started a search-and-rescue mission trying to locate the camera inside. I watched her push the jumble of panty hose out of the way.

The man turned and walked away.

Dorothy stopped her subterfuge. "I don't actually have a camera. But God almighty I love being a reporter. Okay, you win. We're on background. What happened in there?"

I told her.

She was disappointed, as I assumed she would be. "That's it?"

"That's it. Except I did hear one FBI agent whispering to another FBI agent that they thought they found the white van that drove away in the King Soopers lot up the street."

"The what?"

"The white van that drove away behind me? They think they found it in a grocery-store parking lot not far from here."

She was scribbling. "King what?"

"King Soopers—two o's—it's a supermarket chain."

"Guy must have switched cars in the lot. Smart. I gotta go." She stuffed her pencil back into her bag. "I'm staying at the Giorgio. You know where that is?"

"No."

She shrugged and laughed. "Me neither. I hope there's somebody around here who can give me directions."

Near sunset, Lauren sat down beside me on the deck outside our bedroom. There are two decks that face the mountains on our house. One is outside the living room/ dining room; the other is off our new master bedroom. She had already made me dinner and cleaned up the kitchen. Now she handed me a cognac on ice. I was being pampered. We waited until the sun finished its lazy decline behind the Continental Divide, enjoying the show. She said, "Pretty sunset." For a hundred miles to the north and to the south the clouds were lighting up like coral.

"Gorgeous," I agreed.

"Hon?"

"Yes."

"You should have asked for an attorney. Right away." The tone employed was less scolding than her words.

"If you were questioning me, you wouldn't have wanted me asking for an attorney."

"My point exactly."

"I didn't do anything."

"I wish that mattered more often than it does." She started rubbing my neck with her left hand. "I'm just glad you're okay. Were you scared?"

"Terrified. More for that reporter from the *Post* than for myself, though. She was right in the line of fire." I sneezed suddenly, which startled both of us.

She blessed me.

I said, "Right after? You know what was going through my mind? I was thinking about the baby. As soon as that van drove away, my first thought was of the baby. I don't want anything bad to happen to any of us. You know? You have those feelings sometimes?"

She touched my arm. "I know. Yes, I do. Frequently."

I was startled again as one of the French doors that led to the deck outside the living room opened. We weren't expecting any guests. Reflexively I jumped up and shielded Lauren's abdomen with my body.

"You guys out here? Hey, there you are." Sam Purdy stepped out on the deck. "Didn't hear Emily barking, was afraid you weren't home. You really should lock your doors."

"Hi, Sam," I said. "You scared me."

"I knocked. I said 'yoo-hoo.' Hi, Lauren. How's the baby? You're feeling just fine, I hope."

"Good, Sam. Thanks. How're Simon and Sherry?"

"Simon's Simon. Kid just breezes through life. Sherry's working too hard. People die, people want flowers. People get married, people want flowers. Economy's good, people want flowers. And it's Boulder, so she can't get good help. Hey, where's the dog?"

"Over visiting Jonas across the way. They're becoming pretty tight with each other."

Sam eyed the four-foot expanse that separated the two decks. "Tell Jonas he has to learn to share. I'm not giving up any claims to Emily." He pointed at the deck we were on. "So how do I get from here to there?"

Lauren was afraid Sam was going to climb, or worse, try to jump. "How about we join you over there. That deck's larger. Get you a brandy, Sam?"

"You got beer? Last time I was here you gave me one with a trout on the label. I liked that."

"Of course."

Sam Purdy was a detective with the Boulder Police Department. Years ago we met over a case, as adversaries. It had taken a while, but he'd become one of my best friends. We saw eye to eye on almost nothing in life, but it didn't seem to matter. He liked guns, rodeos, fishing, porterhouse steaks, the Milwaukee Brewers, and hockey. I could live with hockey. But I was an advocate of gun control and American Humane, didn't understand piercing fish cheeks with metal spikes for recreation, was trying not to eat much beef, and could never remember what sport the Brewers played.

Still, I'd trust Sam Purdy to help deliver my baby.

Lauren walked to the kitchen to get Sam his Odell's porter. After I had woven through the house to the living room, I found my friend still standing at the rail on the deck. He said, "Heard through the grapevine that you were out dodging bullets today."

Hearing it said out loud, I shivered. "You heard right. As a recreational activity, all I can say for it is that it ranks well ahead of needing to dodge bullets and not quite pulling it off. I've been thinking about what Winston Churchill said—'Nothing in life is so exhilarating as to be shot at without result.' "

"I like that—there's definitely some truth in that. Case you're wondering, I made a call for you. The two victims are going to be fine. Both just lacerations from the ricochets. One's already been released from the hospital. The other one got a fragment in the eye. Nothing serious."

"That's good. Neither of them was Welle, right? Nobody at the scene would tell me."

"No, Welle wasn't even in the vicinity. He was still inside the building. So what were you doing there? At Welle's fund-raiser? You turning over a new political leaf? Something I might actually endorse?"

Politics was another one of those areas where Sam and I didn't exactly see eye to eye.

"Hardly. I needed to talk with Raymond Welle about an old case of his. I had an appointment to meet with him before the reception that he was at when everything went crazy."

"What? You were talking to him about a psychology thing?"

I vacillated for a fraction of a second before I said, "Yeah," and knew that my brief hesitation wouldn't escape Sam's scrutiny.

"But not just a psychology thing?" he asked.

I said, "Remember A. J. Simes?" I knew he did. Sam had been intimately involved in helping Lauren and me sort out the mess with A. J. and her partner the previous year.

"Sure."

"She called me recently and asked for my help investigating an old case she's working on. My role involves talking to Welle."

He lowered his elbows to the deck railing, leaned over, and cupped his chin in his palms. "Is it Locard business?"

I exhaled audibly and shook my head a little before turning to face him. "How the hell do you know about Locard?"

He laughed, and I felt the day's tension begin to tumble from my musculature. "I checked her out for you last fall, if you recall. A. J.? You wanted some background research."

"Oh yeah."

"When I turn over rocks, I'm thorough. So is it Locard business that you're helping her with?"

I nodded. He asked, "What's the case?"

"Two teenage girls were murdered up near Steamboat Springs in 1988. Place called the Elk River Valley. Their bodies stayed hidden all winter. Were found during the spring thaw."

It obviously rang a bell. "I think I remember that. The snowmobile thing? That one?"

"Yes."

"I do remember it. Weren't they mutilated or something? What's the connection to Raymond Welle?"

Again, Sam noticed my hesitation. He said, "A. J. asked you not to talk to me about all this, didn't she?"

"Not in so many words, Sam." I decided right then that I wasn't going to keep him in the dark. "Welle used to be a psychologist in Steamboat. You knew that?" He nodded. "When Welle was still in practice he treated one of the two murder victims in psychotherapy. This was back when he was just a clinician, before his radio fame and political fortune."

I guessed that Sam was still working on trying to figure out two things. One, why A. J. didn't want him to know about me being involved in Locard. Two, why the hell A. J. thought I could be of any help.

Sam asked, "So, did you have your meeting? With Welle?"

"Yes. We talked before all the fireworks."

He examined his fingernails and half-jokingly he said, "You wouldn't want to tell me what he said."

"Sorry," I said.

"Why were you still hanging around? You said your meeting with Welle was before this campaign thing."

"A reporter kind of hijacked me. Thought I might know something about illegal fund-raising practices she's investigating."

"Regarding Welle?"

"Yes."

His eyebrows elevated a smidgen. "Do you?"

"Nope."

Sam cracked the knuckles on the little finger of his left hand. Then he did the right.

His silence made me nervous. I said, "Lauren's helping out, too. With Locard. She's the local legal connection."

The French door opened behind us and Emily barked once until she recognized our guest. The dog loved Sam Purdy and almost knocked him over while displaying her affection. Lauren told her to get off of him and said, "Here's your beer, Sam," and handed him a bottle with a cutthroat trout on the label.

He gazed at the bottle with some curiosity. He shook his head and mused, "Never thought I'd prefer one of

your froufrou beers to a Bud. Wonder what's happening
to me."

I said, "I was just telling Sam about Locard."

We were still standing at the rail of the deck. The
pastels had totally dissolved from the clouds and the
western parts of the valley were starting to be soaked in
dusty black. Behind us, Lauren lowered herself to the
end of a weathered teak chaise. She said, "Ah."

CHAPTER
16

Lauren had made an angel food cake before dinner. She excused herself and went inside to whip up a fresh strawberry sauce for it.

I asked, "When you made your calls today, Sam, did you hear anything about threats? Against Raymond Welle? There seemed to be a lot of security around when I was there."

He shook his head. "Nobody said anything to me about any threats. But a lot of security doesn't mean much. Controversial politicians travel with plenty of muscle these days. They need to. And Welle's a controversial politician. You know something specific about that? About threats?"

"No."

He sipped some beer. "Do you wonder about a connection? Between what you're doing for Locard and the shooting?"

I was surprised at the question. "No. Of course not. Not at all."

"Why not?"

"Just don't see any relevance."

He swallowed a yawn. "You have to admit it was a pitiful assassination attempt. I mean—a major amateur act. A nine-millimeter handgun at over a hundred feet? The target not even in clear sight?"

"That's not totally accurate, Sam. There was a guy at the door who looked kind of like Welle. And who's to say it wasn't an amateur? As you just pointed out, Welle is plenty controversial. I'm sure he stirs up some resentment among that segment of the citizenry that is fond of guns and struggles with impulse-control problems."

He tapped his fingernail on the edge of his chair. "And my guess is that reopening old murder investigations tends to stir up resentment among those people who are not only fond of guns but also have old homicide problems. You know what they say about sleeping dogs."

He was being obtuse, making me guess at things. It was his way of telling me what a pain in the ass I was being. "You think somebody was trying to keep Welle from talking to me because of some old murders?"

Sam shrugged. His eyes were locked on the prairie grasses below the deck. It was apparent to me that my arguments were weighing on him with all the gravity of a slight fluctuation in atmospheric pressure. He said, "You're sure this out-of-town reporter you were talking to doesn't know anything about the Locard investigation?"

"Not unless she's lying to me."

He found that denial particularly amusing. "God, that would be a first. A reporter misleading a source. Wow."

I smiled. "She doesn't seem to know anything."

"And Welle wasn't evasive with you?"

I thought back on the interview. "Sure he was, a little. But he's a politician. He's evasive by nature."

Sam's smile was cunning. "That's the facile explanation. It's also possible that he knows something he'd rather you not know he knows. Being linked to an old murder of teenage girls, even tangentially, is not exactly the stuff of a politician's dreams while he's running for the Senate."

I thought about it before responding. "Raymond Welle rode the crest of his wife's murder pretty well, Sam, if you remember. Rode it all the way to national prominence on the radio, then to a seat in Congress. I don't think this investigation would swamp him, even if news about it got out. He'd probably use it to try to prove his point about our degenerate society."

"You done with him? Welle?"

I thought of the case notes I'd requested. "No, probably not. If I had to guess I'd say I'll probably talk with him again."

"Some advice? Keep an eye out when you do. Things may not be what they seem."

"And sometimes," I said, "a cigar is just a cigar."

He shook his head a little to let me know I wasn't really getting it. "These cold cases . . . they aren't really ever very cold, especially not to the people who might get burned by them. The more you stir up the embers, the more dangerous everything becomes. Sleeping dogs," is how he concluded. "Sleeping dogs."

"Are you suggesting you don't like what Locard is doing?"

"No, no. Not at all. What I'm suggesting—no, what I'm guaranteeing—is that whoever murdered those two girls isn't going to like what Locard is doing. Don't forget it."

Lauren arrived with the news that dessert was ready.

Sam finished his beer in one long pull and stood to go inside.

After Sam left to go home, I called A. J. Simes. It was almost eleven on the East Coast. A. J. sounded exhausted. I asked if she was feeling okay.

"Good enough," was her reply.

She'd heard about the shooting at the tennis house, of course; it was one of the lead stories on the national news. She didn't know I'd been a witness at the event. Her curiosity about the ambush was cursory, however. She implied that the FBI members of Locard would funnel any necessary information into the pipeline, information more reliable than my impressions. The questions that were foremost on A. J.'s mind had to do with my interviews with Taro Hamamoto and Raymond Welle and my impressions of the psychotherapy Welle had done with Mariko Hamamoto.

I shared my conclusions, told A. J. that it looked like Welle had done a decent enough job with Mariko and that his story about her presenting problems and the therapy outcome was consistent with Taro Hamamoto's account. "Hamamoto didn't tell me anything about his daughter that we didn't already know. He's still trying to come to terms with it, A. J. With the murder."

"Wouldn't you be?" she replied.

"I'm sure I would." I informed A. J. that I was about to fax her a detailed report about my trip to Vancouver to see Mariko's father. I asked, "Does Locard have any information about a drug arrest in Steamboat Springs involving Mariko and Tami maybe six, eight months prior to their disappearance?"

"No. Absolutely not. What kind of arrest?"

"Possession. According to Taro Hamamoto, the girls were picked up smoking dope with some tourists."

"And?"

"He says the charges were eventually dropped. Why doesn't Locard know about this?"

"I don't know. But I'll look into it."

I then told A. J. about the contacts I'd received from Dorothy Levin. A. J. peppered me for details about Levin's calls and questions, and asked twice for reassurance that Ms. Levin wasn't on to the Locard investigation.

Twice I gave her the reassurance. I also relayed my suspicion that Dorothy had a source inside Welle's Washington, D. C., office. A. J. seemed to concur with that impression.

We discussed strategies for what I should do next. She wanted me to write up what I had so far, then sit tight while some other avenues were being developed.

"What other avenues?" I asked.

"Soon," she said. "And under no circumstances should you contact Welle again without clearing it with me first."

"How about talking with some people who knew the girls? Would that be okay?"

"No one in Welle's camp?"

"No."

"Fine. And Alan? You're doing a great job."

"Oh, A. J.? One last thing."

"Yes."

"I'd like to talk with Hamamoto's other daughter."

"I assumed that would be your next request. You're convinced it will add something?"

"She was old enough when her sister was murdered to be a reliable informant about her sister's lifestyle. And there are no records of interviews with her in the material you sent me."

"None? You're sure."

"I've checked twice."

"Go ahead and plan it. I'll talk to the committee and let you know if there's a problem."

The moment I hung up with Simes the phone rang again.

"It's me, Dorothy. You survive all the excitement?"

"Yes. You find your hotel okay?"

"I did, I did. If you're ever looking for it, it's a black glass box behind a bank. What I'm calling about is . . . I just want to know your impression of what you saw today. Now that things have settled a little bit. No more bullet whizzing past our heads. Was Welle really the target? What do you think?"

I was silent while I thought about how I wanted to answer. Just when I was about to speak, she said, "Don't worry. We're still on background." I heard her take a bite of something. "Room service isn't bad here. It's Italian. I love room service. Don't you love room service?"

"I have a cop friend here in Boulder who thinks that if Welle was the target of an assassination then the target shoot was pure amateur hour. Wrong weapon at the wrong distance fired at the wrong target in the wrong circumstances."

"You agree with your friend?"

"I just know what I saw. Somebody shooting at the doorway of a building where a controversial congressman was raising campaign funds to run for the Senate. It doesn't make sense to rule him out as a target. It doesn't make sense to assume he was the target, either."

"That's what I'm thinking, too. I'm trying to put together a list of the other people who were close to the doorway so I can rule them out as possible targets. I have the names of the two people who were hit by debris and a few others' names, too. Do you know who any of those people were?"

"Sorry. I don't run in the rich-white-guys-over-forty-five circles. But I'll bet the Denver papers and the local TV station shows manage to run most of them down for you."

"Figured you wouldn't know, but thought I'd ask. I've got the Channel 2 news on right now. They're not giving out names. And I can't wait for the Denver papers to fill out my piece. I only have half an hour till deadline." I heard her light a cigarette. "At least they still let you smoke in hotel rooms in this state. That's something, right? I was afraid I'd be out on the roof with coyotes or something."

She sucked hard and exhaled before she continued. "The shooter's escape was well planned today, don't you think? Have you thought about that? The getaway? Not amateurish at all. And you were right about the white van being found at that grocery store close by. King Soopers? What kind of a name is that, anyway? I thought Winn Dixie was a stupid name for a supermarket. But King Soopers? In case you care, the van had been stolen the night before in . . . Aurora. That's like a suburb, right? No witnesses yet who saw anybody switch vehicles in the parking lot. I bet the guy just got out of the van, walked in one door of the store, walked right out another, and got into his second vehicle."

Made sense to me. "Are you heading back to D.C. in the morning?"

"I could. But I have some people to see in Steamboat Springs on Monday about this campaign-finance thing. How far away is that? Looks close enough on the map. I may just spend the weekend there."

"If you drive, it's over three hours by car assuming you don't get lost in the mountains."

"You mean I have an alternative? I can fly there? There's an airport?"

"Yes. Yampa Valley."

The nicotine was invigorating her. "Cool. Maybe I'll do that. That's Yampa spelled how? Y-a-m-p-a? Like it sounds? Bet you it's one of those little planes though, isn't it? I don't really like them. Too . . . tubey. And I like jets more than propellers. I wonder why that is . . ."

I didn't know why it was but I suspected Dorothy didn't need to hear that from me.

She plowed on. "Do you know Ray Welle hasn't done a single interview—broadcast or print—about his wife being murdered since he was elected to Congress? I find that kind of strange, don't you? He wouldn't shut up about it when he was on the radio every day. And do you know her parents—I'm talking about Welle's dead wife, now—you remember about her being taken hostage and executed, right? Her parents live a few blocks away from where we were this morning. Okay, they don't actually live there—people that rich don't actually live in just one place—but they have a house there. She grew up there. Gloria did. Right around the corner from where the Coors kidnapping took place. Bad neighborhood for having your rich kids kidnapped. Oh Christ! There's another one. Hold on."

"Another what?"

"My hotel room has been invaded by these kamikaze moths that buzz around like they're drunk. They dive-bomb right at you, flap all over the place. And they're covered with dirt."

I laughed. "They're miller moths. They're pretty harmless. They're migratory; they'll all be gone in a few weeks."

"Ahhh. Shit. It almost flew in my mouth. Gross. This one will be gone before that, I promise you." I could hear her whacking at it. "Got it! Yes!"

I hadn't known that Gloria's parents—Lauren's ex-in-laws—lived so close to the Phipps Mansion. I also couldn't see how it meant anything significant. "Who are you going to see in Steamboat?"

Her tone switched from conversational to suspicious. She said, "You connected up there?"

"Not at all, no."

"Then why do you want to know who I'm going to talk to? And why do I keep getting the feeling that you're more withholding than my two-year-old niece when she's constipated?"

"I was just asking."

"No you weren't. You weren't just asking. We're going back to class for a minute so pull out your syllabus. Here's lesson number two in Journalism 101. Let me show you how this is done. Okay? I'm actually going to answer your question. This is what it sounds like when somebody actually answers a question. Is your pencil ready? Pay attention. The reason I'm going to Steamboat Springs is to talk with some people who were involved with the ski area a few years ago. I need to talk with them about the campaign-finance irregularities I've been investigating. At the time, a big Japanese company controlled the resort. Does any of that information ring any bells for you?" She gave me two seconds to respond, then said, "Hello? I'm still listening for the peal of those bells."

I swallowed and hoped she didn't hear me.

She said, "Near the end there? A moment ago? That was a question. Now it's your turn to answer." Pause. "You know, you're not very good at this."

I knew I was about to lie to her. I didn't want to tell her I'd been in Steamboat only a week ago and that I'd already interviewed someone who had been one of the local managers of the ski area back in the late eighties. I said, "No. No bells. What? Are you looking for foreign money being shoveled into Welle's campaign? Japanese money?"

"Should I be?"

I didn't answer. She said, "Were you always this bad

in school? How the hell did you ever get a Ph.D.? Let me try an easier one for you. If I do go to Steamboat for the weekend, where should I stay? Keep in mind, there's a possibility this will be my dime."

"Do you want charming or do you want efficiency?"

"I want plumbing. I want to be able to smoke. And I want room service. Not necessarily in that order."

The smoking part would limit her choices considerably. I suggested she call the Sheraton.

My first wife, Merideth, had been a producer with Channel 9 in Denver. I still had some contacts at the station. I called one of them at home, a young man who had been an assistant producer. He had lusted after Merideth for the entire three years that he worked with her. I hoped that fact would make him guilty enough to agree to do me a favor.

It did.

I came home late Saturday morning after a long bike ride to Lyons and back and found that a messenger from Channel 9 had left the package beside the front door, as promised.

Inside were two videotapes. One was a compilation of clips of the disappearance and murder of the two girls in the Elk River Valley. The other was a compilation of clips of the kidnapping and murder of Gloria Welle.

I stripped out of my Lycra and took a shower. Lauren called while I was in the bathroom. She left a message letting me know that since I was seeing patients that afternoon, she and a girlfriend had decided to go shopping in Denver. Maternity things. She thought she'd be home for dinner.

I made a sandwich and carried it into the living room. The first tape I stuck into the VCR was the Gloria Welle footage.

Nineteen ninety-two. Channel 9's talent was a lot younger then. Still, except for some curious hairstyles and some dubious wardrobe choices, Ed and Mike and Paula looked pretty good back in 1992.

On tape, the entrance to the Silky Road Ranch was totally different from the one I'd seen recently in person during my visit with Lauren. The day that Brian Sample went to visit Gloria Welle with retribution and murder in his heart, no gate at all blocked the entrance to the ranch. No imposing stone pillars marked the spot where the dirt lane broke off the county road. No video cameras checked on the arrival of visitors. No speakers announced curt warnings; no microphones eavesdropped on conversations. In those days before the murder, the sign that hung above the rough-cut pine logs that marked the entrance to the spread was carved of wood and read SILKY ROAD RANCH. It wasn't engraved on a stainless-steel plate that read GLORIA'S SILKY ROAD RANCH—NO VISITORS.

The Silky Road wasn't a memorial to Gloria back then. It was just Gloria and Raymond Welle's horse ranch.

It didn't surprise me that few of the actual details of the murder had stuck in my memory. The television stories about the crime referred to the victim of the murder as a "Denver debutante," "a wealthy socialite," or "the daughter of railroad billionaire Horace Tambor." None of the reports identified Gloria as a successful horse breeder, or even as Mrs. Raymond Welle. Ray's radio fame was barely starting to percolate; and his first term in Congress wouldn't start until 1994.

I was curious about having my memory tweaked. What had transpired on the ranch that day?

According to the television news reports, the whole affair had lasted only ninety minutes. During that brief window of time, Brian Sample had somehow entered the ranch house, joined Gloria for tea, forced her to make a telephone call in an effort to lure Raymond Welle home from his office, locked Gloria in a guest-room closet, and then shot her to death right through the wooden door. Shortly thereafter, Brian had fired a few rounds at the arriving law enforcement authorities. The police had gunned him down as he made a dash to the woods to try to escape.

A follow-up story the day after Gloria's murder reported that authorities had learned that the suspect in the killing, Brian Sample, had been a patient of Gloria Welle's husband, psychologist Dr. Raymond Welle. Sample was, it was assumed, bent on revenge when he invaded the Welle home. Although the exact motive for seeking revenge upon his psychotherapist wasn't revealed in the report, the reason that Sample had sought mental-health treatment was already apparently the stuff of local lore. No one in town had any questions at all about what the precipitant was for the almost yearlong decline in Sample's emotional state.

Brian Sample had owned a local saloon called The Livery. On a Tuesday night eleven months before he killed Gloria Welle, Brian had been behind the bar of that saloon, pouring drinks. One of his customers that evening was a regular, a not-certified public accountant named Grant Wortham who played catcher on Brian's softball team. Wortham had come into the bar after work for a cheeseburger and a beer, and had left the establishment three hours later after consuming eight beers and two shots of Cuervo Gold. When he left to go home, Wortham climbed behind the wheel of his big old Dodge Ram pickup truck.

Wortham had managed to maneuver the vehicle only three blocks before he ran a stop sign at the edge of town while going almost fifty miles an hour. In the intersection, the big truck demolished a bright red Subaru. The driver of the Subaru didn't leave an inch of skid mark on the road. The driver of the Subaru never saw the big truck coming.

The driver of the Subaru was killed instantly.

The driver of the Subaru was Brian Sample's son, Dennis. He had been on his way home from a Drama Club meeting at the high school.

By delivering those beers and pouring those shots of tequila for Grant Wortham, Brian Sample had effectively handed a loaded gun to the man who would soon become his son's executioner.

On the ides of March, Sample sold the bar for less than he owed the bank. Weeks after that Brian attempted suicide, overdosing intentionally on Jack Daniel's, Valium, and penicillin. When he got out of the hospital, his wife, Leigh, kicked him out of the house.

Not too many more days passed before Brian Sample killed Gloria Welle.

The last clip on the videotape was a montage of scenes from Gloria's Denver funeral. A massive procession from the synagogue to the cemetery had tied up the metro area's streets for most of an hour.

CHAPTER
17

To get my mind off the tragedy of Brian Sample's family, I stuffed the second of the two videotapes into the VCR.

This one would tell the story of the two dead girls.

I'd already crossed whatever line of psychological defense it required to think of them—deceased—as the "two dead girls," not as Tami and Miko. And, from the detailed presentation at the Locard briefing and from all the reading I'd done of the case documents, I already knew the details of the story that the television journalists were about to tell me, so little about the video anthology surprised me. My interest in reviewing the news reports was limited. I had, in fact, only one goal. I wanted to discover the identity of the local residents who had been interviewed by the surprisingly tenacious reporter that Channel 9 had sent to Steamboat Springs to report on the developing story. I was hoping to uncover the names of some locals who seemed to have been well acquainted with Tami and Miko.

The first few reports had been taped in the late autumn days right after the girls had disappeared. The sheriff in Routt County, Phil Barrett, was a much smaller pork chop back then. He certainly gave a lot of interviews, and appeared to enjoy acting constipated around the media. One of his first impromptu press gatherings took place in front of the snowmobile trailer that had been discovered the day after the girls disappeared. The trailer had been found in the parking lot of a condominium near the gondola at the base of the ski resort. The base area of Mount Werner was far from the Strawberry Park hot springs and even farther from the upper reaches of the Elk River Valley.

The mayor of Steamboat spoke on camera twice without revealing a thing. I assumed that her discretion soon caused her to be removed from a list of locals deserving airtime. Mr. and Mrs. Franklin made three different televised pleas for help and mercy, young Joey a silent witness in the background each time. The Hamamotos, in contrast, never appeared on any of Channel 9's broadcasts.

One of the television reports had been taped at the high school. It piqued my interest. As I watched I wrote down the principal's name, those of two teachers who knew both girls, and the names of three classmates who identified themselves as good friends.

It was a start.

I glanced at my watch and noted that the first of my appointments with my rescheduled patients began in twenty minutes in my downtown office. Emily needed fresh water. I filled her bowl and hustled out the door.

Our home is at the end of a dirt and gravel lane that Lauren and I share with only two other residents—our neighbor across the way, Adrienne, and her son, Jonas. By default, any traffic on the lane is either heading to one of our homes—or more likely the case—the driver is lost. Vehicles almost never park on our lane. Not only is there no reason, but there is also no room. The lane is barely wide enough for two small cars, and the shoulders are as soft as cotton candy.

So I was perplexed by the white Nissan Pathfinder that I saw parked on the west shoulder of the lane when I climbed into my car to go to my office after lunch. I was sure the car hadn't been there when I'd ridden my bike home an hour or so earlier. I slowed my own car to a crawl as I edged past it.

I didn't see a driver at first, so I stopped just opposite

the car. A man suddenly sat up on the front seat. He appeared to be as startled as I was.

I waved hello and lowered my window. So did he.

"Hi," he said through a mouthful of food. He was listening to a country station on his radio.

I wasn't. "Hello," I said. "Can I help you?"

He swallowed and smiled. "No. No. Don't think so."

The man was young, mid-twenties at the most. Wide shoulders, crew cut, small silver earring in his left ear. He held a drink cup from Wendy's in his right hand and a single French fry in the other. The French fry was long, laden with ketchup, and was drooping in the middle.

Farther down the lane Jonas was home alone with his nanny. I wasn't comfortable having this stranger parked down the road from their house when I wasn't around. I said, "This is private property."

"Really?" he said. "I didn't know that. I'll just go, I guess." Although he wouldn't look me in the eye, he could hardly have been more polite.

I wrote the license-plate number of his SUV in the dust on my dashboard as I pulled away. I waited down near South Boulder Road until I saw his car leave the neighborhood.

I was late for my one-thirty patient.

I saw two patients in succession, after which I had a half-hour break—which barely gave me time to walk over to the Downtown Boulder Mall to pick up a part I'd ordered for my bike and grab something to eat to hold me over until dinner.

I rushed out the back door of my office and down the driveway to the street. In my rush I almost missed notic- ing the white Nissan Pathfinder that was parked at the curb in front of the building. When I saw it I stopped in my tracks and looked over my shoulder. My heart rate jumped as I walked up to the car. No driver was sitting inside. I looked for a Wendy's bag on the seat. The car was tidy.

I walked to the front bumper and checked the license

plate. It matched the one I'd scribbled in my dashboard dust earlier that afternoon.

I immediately accepted the obvious: that the presence of this vehicle first near my home and next in front of my office was not a coincidence. The echo of yesterday's gunplay hadn't quieted in my head, so I spun on my heels to go back inside to call Sam Purdy and ask him to check out the license-plate number for me. That's when I saw the young man who had been sitting in the car on the lane earlier in the day. He was perched on the rickety porch swing on the rickety front porch of the little Victorian house that contained my psychology office. He was reading the *Boulder Planet*.

I hustled up the concrete walk. He didn't notice my approach. He was engrossed in the newspaper, humming something. Something country.

I stood on one of the steps and said, "Hello again. I think you may be looking for me."

"What? Oh. Darn. It's you again. Hello." He made a mess of folding the newspaper and stood up. He towered over me by at least ten or eleven inches. Subtracting for the stair tread I was on, that made him six six or so.

Involuntarily I took a sideways step away from him. I said, "Yes. It's me."

"I didn't see you coming. I saw your car in back and expected you would come out this other door, here." He pointed at the front door of the building, then proceeded to wipe his palms on the thighs of his khakis. Before he spoke, he swallowed. "Hello, then. I'm, I'm Kevin." He held out his hand for me to shake.

I stepped up to the porch and we shook hands. His was huge and soft. He offered almost no resistance during the greeting, as though he was afraid to hurt me with his grip. Shaking his hand was like sticking my hand into a warm loaf of Wonder bread. My tone more tempered, I said, "I'm Alan Gregory. But I think you already know that."

"Well, I do now, I guess. If I had known who you were before I would have said hello up on the road earlier. Where you live, you know? You kind of caught me by surprise up there. Embarrassing. I'm Kevin, by the way, Kevin Sample." He smiled in a manner I found quite affecting. "I hear you've been asking around about some stuff that has to do with my dad."

Picking up my new crank at the bike shop would have to wait until tomorrow or the next day. I said, "Yes, Kevin. As a matter of fact, I have," and I invited Brian Sample's son into my office.

Kevin Sample was a veterinary student up the road in Fort Collins at Colorado State University. I didn't ask but I assumed that he was planning to specialize in treating large animals.

Most of the strangers I'd met recently had been either new therapy patients—with all their inherent defenses—or people associated with the lives and deaths of Tami and Miko—with all their invisible agendas. Kevin presented himself so differently from either category that I was briefly taken aback by his manner.

The young man appeared to lack guile. Absolutely.

"You stayed at a B and B in Steamboat recently. The owner, Libby, is an old friend of our family. She phoned my mom and said you were asking questions about Gloria Welle's death. My mom told me about the call. I've been waiting a long time for someone to care enough to ask some questions about what my father did that day. I thought I'd come down and talk to you about him. Who knows, might help us both."

I was trying to decide whether or not to admit to Kevin that my queries during my recent visit to Steamboat were actually directed not at learning more about his father, but rather at learning more about Raymond Welle. I postponed the decision and asked, "Help you how, Kevin?"

"Dennis was my twin brother. Did you know that?"

His reply felt like a non sequitur. I said, "No, I didn't know that."

"Fraternal twins, not identical. But we were tight." I

watched Kevin smile again, then watched the smile vanish. "In less than a year I lost the two most important people in my life. I lost my brother first and then I lost my father. And because of what Dad did on his last day on earth, I lost all sense of my family. I lost all my friends. Eventually I lost my school. Mom and I left Steamboat a few years after what happened up at the Silky Road. We had to, I guess. It's been just me and Mom since then. To be honest, she never got over Dennis's dying. And she certainly never got over what happened at the Silky Road."

I was still waiting to hear how talking with me about his father was going to help Kevin Sample. The tone of his words had caused me to begin to wonder whether he was perceiving me as a poténtial therapist.

"Can you imagine what it was like for him after Dennis died? For my dad?" he asked, and shook his head. "You know that my father poured the drinks to the man who ended up killing Dennis? My dad felt that it was exactly the same as if he ended up killing his own son. Well, when you imagine what it was like in our house, imagine the worst. Because that's how it was. The guilt. The shame. The recriminations. The anger. The anger was vicious. It was all there in our house after the accident."

Honestly, I said, "I can't really imagine. It's too horrible."

"The truth is I lost my father and my brother on the same night. Dad was never the same after Dennis died."

I needed a clarification. "The anger? It was his?"

"No. Mom's. She could be . . . mean. Still can be. She had a mean streak even before the accident. But after? Especially after Dad decided he was going to sell the bar and she saw the writing on the wall. She knew they were going to lose the business and then we were probably going to lose the house. She was cruel to him after that. And he just took it from her. It was like a penance for him."

"But it took its toll?"

"You know about the suicide attempt?"

I nodded. "Not much. Just what I saw on the news." I didn't mention the fact that I'd seen videotapes of the news earlier that day.

"He took an overdose. Pills and alcohol. She found him in the basement. Mom did. Made me drive him to the hospital. She wouldn't call an ambulance. She didn't want the neighbors to know what he'd done. She didn't want anything to do with him. Didn't visit him in the hospital. She called him 'the coward' after that. To me. To his face. To any friends the two of them had left. He didn't have a name anymore. To her, he was just 'the coward.' She wouldn't let him come back home after he got out of the hospital. He stayed with some people in town. Eventually he got a little apartment."

Every day in my practice I saw men and women who had crumbled in the face of psychological stresses that didn't begin to compare to the pressures that this young man had endured as an adolescent. Yet he appeared emotionally intact. I wondered about things I couldn't assess so readily, about his relationship with women, and his relationships with mentors in the veterinary school.

Still, I marveled.

Kevin interrupted my reverie. "That's when Dad went to see Dr. Welle. After the suicide attempt."

I nodded knowingly.

Kevin spotted my arrogance and corrected me, gently. "No, you don't understand. This is the part that people get confused about. Dad *liked* Dr. Welle. He liked him a lot. He wouldn't have done anything to hurt him. *Anything.*"

I was perplexed. This young man seemed way too intelligent to discount, so cavalierly, the evidence of his father's crime. "You don't believe that your father shot Gloria Welle, Kevin?"

The young man's face tightened. I saw wrinkles around his eyes where there had been none before. "Of course he shot her. There's no other explanation for what happened at the Silky Road that day. But it wasn't because he was angry at Dr. Welle. That's the part that everyone has wrong. And that's the part that I want to help everybody clear up."

"And you know that how?" My voice was soft. He was out on a limb and I wanted to offer him a cushioned place to fall.

"Because I had breakfast with him that morning. With Dad. He was pretty upbeat. Not happy, not like that. He wasn't capable of being happy anymore. But he was up enough that we could actually have a conversation, you know? That hadn't happened a lot recently. He told me that Dr. Welle was a man he could trust. A man who was going to save him from himself." Kevin pulled a battered little notebook from his shirt pocket and slapped it on his thigh. "I'm not making all this up. I kept a journal in those days. Like a diary? That's how I know."

"So why do you think it, um . . . happened?"

"At first I thought maybe he just snapped. I'd been worried about him losing it—you know, going crazy?—for a while."

"But you rejected that?"

"Yes sir, I did. I didn't think he could go from being reasonable at breakfast to being psychopathic and homicidal midmorning. Now maybe that's possible with some people. But not with my dad. And then there's the gun he used."

"Yes."

"It was his. When Dennis and I were, oh, twelve or thirteen, he'd showed us where it was at home and taught us how to use it. He also told me that he could never use it himself—could never point it at another human being—unless the family was in danger. He wanted us to feel the exact same way. He meant what he said that day. I know it. I knew him."

I wanted to believe Kevin was correct in the same way I often wanted to believe the veracity of my patients as they constructed and polished a version of reality that would shine more brightly than the tarnished one that often stains the truth. Kevin's view of his father was part of his ego's defenses against the enormous weight of his pain. I decided to say nothing that might interfere with the integrity of those defenses. He needed them.

I said, "It must be hard making sense of what happened, then."

"Yeah," he acknowledged. "Hard."

I watched a tear form in the corner of his eye. Kevin didn't react to it until it had migrated halfway down his nose. "There is one way that you might be able to discover . . . some information that might help you answer the questions you have about your father's frame of mind."

He swallowed. "How?"

"Talk with Dr. Welle."

Kevin laughed bitterly. "My mom tried. Years ago. He wouldn't talk to her. Said he didn't have the right to tell anyone what my father said to him during therapy. Confidentiality."

"Technically, that's true. But after your father died the rights to control the record of what happened in his treatment with Dr. Welle passed to the person who controlled your father's estate. If that person asked Dr. Welle about your father's treatment, Dr. Welle would have to respond. He'd have no choice."

"That would be my uncle Larry. My dad's brother. He handled Dad's estate."

"If your uncle Larry sends Dr. Welle a letter identifying himself as the personal representative of your father's estate—if I were him, I'd have the letter notarized—and authorizing the release of confidential records, Dr. Welle should be happy to cooperate with the request."

"That's it?"

"That should be all it takes."

"Will you write that down for me? How to do it?"

"Of course." Across the room I spotted a tiny red dot light up beside the door. The light was a sign that my next patient had arrived. I said, "Kevin, I have an appointment now. Just one more today. I'll be done in about forty-five minutes. Would you like to get together again when I'm done and talk some more about all this? Maybe go have a beer or something? I'll go over the instructions on how to approach Dr. Welle again then."

He smiled. "That would be great. But maybe coffee or something to eat. I don't drink."

I felt foolish.

CHAPTER
18

I was late getting home after meeting with Kevin Sample.

Once my last patient had left my office I'd walked Kevin over to the mall and offered to buy him something to eat. He wavered for a moment on the sidewalk between Juanita's and Tom's Tavern on Pearl Street, finally choosing Tom's and ordering a cheeseburger, salad, fries, and onion rings. He drank lemonade. He devoured the food and afterward talked almost nonstop for another hour.

I walked him back to his car and watched him drive away, hoping he felt more contentment than he had when he decided to come to Boulder and look me up. On the way out of town I stopped at the police station to leave the videotape of the news coverage of Gloria Welle's murder for Sam. Despite the errand, I made it home before Lauren returned from her shopping excursion to Denver.

After her friend dropped her off, Lauren and I took Emily for a walk before dinner. Lauren was wearing a new maternity top that, to my eye, had enough gussets sewn into the front to permit her to carry quintuplets to term. On the way out the lane I told her about Kevin's arrival on our doorstep that afternoon and replayed his impressions of his brother's death and his reluctance to believe the theories about his father's motives the last day at the Silky Road Ranch.

Her assessment of Kevin's protest about his father's intentions when he shot Gloria Welle was about the same as mine had been. She said, "He sounds like a kid who's trying to make sense of the unfathomable. You like this?" She fingered the hem of the new top she was wearing.

"Yes. Of course. It's um, nice." My praise was so weak I didn't even believe me.

She punched me on the arm. "Get used to it. I got some jeans and some shorts with elastic waists, too."

"I can't wait to see them."

She hit me again.

As we climbed a ridge to the east to watch the shadows edge into the valley, I moved on to the next part of Kevin's story. "There's more that I learned from Kevin. I should have made this connection on my own, but I didn't. It turns out that Kevin and his brother were the exact same age as Tami and Miko. They were in the same year at school. Kevin knew both of the girls."

Lauren looked my way, raised her eyebrows, and asked, "The plot thickens. So were they friends?"

"Kevin says his brother was actually closer to Tami and Miko than he was. Kevin says that Dennis, his brother, was the better skier. This group of kids who hung out together—apparently they were all pretty great skiers. Only the best of them could ski with Tami and Miko, though. That wasn't Kevin—but he knew the girls well enough. They had classes together, hung out together after school. You know. It was a pretty small town then."

"Still is," she said, pointing out a big bird soaring high above Highway 36. "Especially if you leave out the tourists."

"Is that a hawk?" I asked.

"Don't know. Maybe. Did he date either of them?"

"Says not."

"And? What does he remember about what happened to them? What does he think?"

"Mostly he just remembers it as the beginning of the tragedies. That's what he calls that time in his life. 'The tragedies.' "

The hawk, or whatever it was, swooped behind a ridge top. Above the grasses on the crest of the hill the sky had turned thick and black. A massive thunderstorm was building in the foothills near Golden. Lauren said, "I'm glad that's not coming our way. Bet it's full of hail."

We started back toward our house just in case Lauren's meteorological forecasting abilities were flawed. Emily ran into the thick grass along the lane and pawed frantically at something in the dirt. We waited for her to finish whatever she was doing. She dawdled until a crisp crack of thunder in the distance spooked her out of the meadow, her ears as plastered down as a Bouvier's cropped ears can be. If she had possessed more than a nub of a tail it would have been between her legs. Emily despised thunder and lightning. Lauren asked, "Did Kevin and his friends have theories about the girls? About their disappearance? About the murders?"

"Sure. At first—for a few days, he said—everybody thought that the girls had run away. He describes Tami the same way everyone else does. Heart of gold, a lot of fun, but a bit of a wild child. She was always talking about wanting to see the world, to go places. To get away. Her friends thought she may have had a fight with her parents about something and just taken off."

"Did she argue a lot with her parents?"

"The impression I got is that it was a love-hate thing. She and her mom would be real tight and then Tami would push her away for a while."

Lauren chewed on my impression. "And Kevin and his buddies—they thought that Miko would just go along with Tami if she ran?"

"I asked the same thing. He was evasive about that. Said Miko wasn't really like that. Wasn't really a follower. But he didn't elaborate."

Lauren knelt down to comfort Emily after another explosive clap of thunder. "And after? After the bodies were found? What did he and his friends think then?"

"Kevin said that he and his buddies all bought into the stranger theory. None of them wanted to believe that anyone they knew in town could do what had been done to their friends. He said that none of them really considered that it might have been a local. But . . ."

"But?"

"But . . . he also told me that there was a rumor going around that Miko was seeing an older guy. Somebody in town."

"But they didn't know who?"

"No, they didn't."

"Did they speculate?" She stood back up.

"Yeah. And this is where it gets really interesting. Kevin and his friends thought it might be Raymond Welle. Some of the kids had seen the two of them together a couple of times. Going for a walk. Having coffee. Things like that."

"Did Kevin know that Miko was in psychotherapy with Welle?"

"It didn't sound like he knew. I didn't tell him. Couldn't figure out a way to ask directly without spilling the beans."

She threaded her fingers through mine and pulled my hand over her abdomen. The tight bulge made my heart jump every time I felt it. I desperately hoped to feel a kick from her womb.

No.

She asked, "Could that be benign? Mariko and Welle being out together? Could that have been part of her psychotherapy?"

I thought about it. "Could have been. Would have been unusual, but not unheard-of. Sometimes with kids, you find they talk more openly outside the office. I've done it with a couple of adolescents. It could have been that. At this point you have to give Welle the benefit of the doubt about the therapy. I keep reminding myself that Miko's parents thought he worked wonders with their daughter."

Lauren stopped and picked up a stick. She shook it in Emily's face and threw it deep into the meadow. My wife has a good arm, and the stick covered a lot of territory before it fell to the ground. Emily stared at her as though she were a moron. She laughed at the dog and said, "Take all the speculation to its most toxic conclusion, sweets, and it gives Welle a pretty darn good motive."

It was exactly what I'd been thinking since I'd waved good-bye to Kevin an hour earlier in downtown Boulder. "You mean if we accept the proposition that he was involved with Mariko?"

"Yes. Absolutely. What if—I'm speculating here, so cut me some slack—what if Tami found out somehow that her friend was involved with Raymond Welle? Or what if Miko told Tami that she was screwing around with Welle and Welle suddenly saw some threat to this wonderful life he was building for himself? You know, his practice, his little radio show up there, his marriage even. It gives him a motive for the murders."

"That's a lot of ifs. But you're right. If he was sexually involved with Mariko, and if Tami knew about it, it would give Welle a motive."

"No one in Locard has discovered anything that gives anyone else a motive, have they?"

I shook my head. "They haven't told us anything. But that doesn't mean they don't know something."

"So?"

I pressed. "Who could corroborate what might have been going on with Miko and Welle?"

"Welle could."

"Yeah, and he's going to admit it. Right."

"I don't know who else would know. You have to assume that he would have been smart enough to keep it a secret."

"You know, none of this is in the records we got from Locard. None of it. The original investigation should have uncovered some of this information, even if it was just categorized as rumor. Phil Barrett and his detectives should have talked to all the girls' friends. All of them. One of them should have mentioned to the police the possibility that she had an older lover."

"Makes you wonder all over again, doesn't it? About the thoroughness of the initial investigation?"

"To tell you the truth, it makes me wonder more about Phil Barrett. And whether he was already in bed with Raymond Welle back then."

We heard a car approaching from behind us and moved off to the shoulder. I called Emily to my side while Adrienne plowed by in her Suburban. She honked. We waved. I heard Jonas yell, "Emily, you want to come over and play?"

The dust settled around us, on us. "You knew him back then—Raymond," I said to Lauren. "And you've known a lot of violent criminals, right? Do you think he could have done it?"

"What? Screwed one of his patients? Or murdered two high school girls?"

"I don't know. Take your pick."

We walked a good ten paces before she responded again. "My answer is that . . . he wouldn't have suffered a single night of guilt for being unfaithful to Gloria. Would he have done it with a sixteen-year-old? I really hope not. And murder? That's something else. I don't know." We walked a few more steps. "And the very fact that I don't know is incredibly troubling."

"Was the marriage, Gloria and Ray's . . . I don't know . . . stable?"

She shrugged. "I didn't know them that well as a couple. Gloria was a flirt, but that was just her nature. She may have said something to Jake about problems, but I think he would have told me. If they kept their problems up in Steamboat with them I'm not sure any of the family down here would have known."

The fax machine had been busy while we were out on our walk.

"Look at this," Lauren said, handing me three sheets, keeping one for herself. "It appears that your reporter friend did exactly what she said she was going to do."

I was busy throwing together some lo mein with

shrimp and bok choy. Dark, leafy greens had become as much of a staple in our diet as kibble was in Emily's. I dried my hands and examined the first page of the fax.

It was an article from that day's *Washington Post.* The byline was Dorothy Levin's. The headline was "Trail of Questions Dogs Candidate's Finances." The focus of the piece was Raymond Welle. I read quickly and skimmed the continuation on the next page.

In the margin of the first sheet Dorothy had scribbled, "*Et voilà.* Steamboat is breathtaking. Literally. There is no air up here."

I flipped a page and said, "I wonder what this means?" I was reading another note from Dorothy, this one in the margin of my last sheet. It read, "Met with a guy today who couldn't help me with my stuff but seemed to know a lot about Gloria's death. Interesting . . . I'm going to follow up. Planning on seeing someone else, too."

Lauren asked, "What?"

I pointed out Dorothy's margin note. Lauren shrugged. "I bet there are a lot of people in Steamboat with a lot of opinions about Gloria Welle's murder."

"You're right." I smacked the paper. "But at least Dorothy kept her word. I don't think my name is in the article," I said, smiling.

"You're much happier after reading that article than Raymond Welle is going to be." She read the fine print on the leading edge of the fax. "This was sent from Steamboat. She's still in Colorado?"

"The last time I talked with her she told me she had some interviews to do at the ski area on Monday. She was trying to decide whether to stay over or go back east for the weekend. I guess she stayed over." I shook the pages in my hand. "How serious are these allegations she's making? Can you tell?"

"I don't really know the federal election laws very well, but if what the *Post* found is actually true, it will make Ray pretty uncomfortable. Especially the allegations about the Japanese contributions being funneled through employees of the ski company. He won't want to deal with this so close to the election. Not after what Clinton and Gore and Reno went through with those Buddhist nuns. Remember that? And especially after he was one of the House members who was so instrumental in killing the latest campaign-reform bill."

My mind was still consumed by the possibility that Raymond Welle's biggest problem was an old murder investigation, not a new campaign-finance probe. I pointed to the sheet of paper Lauren still held in her left hand. "What's on that last page? That's not from Dorothy?"

"No. This one's from Russ Claven. Remember our chauffeur to the Locard meeting in Washington? He and Flynn Coe are flying in tomorrow. They want to see us before they go up to Steamboat."

I spent a moment trying to remember some of the people I'd met at the meeting in Washington. "Flynn's the one with the eye patch?"

"Yes. And the great smile. She's the forensics-crime scene expert. Our case coordinator."

"What time do they get in?"

"Their flight gets in at eleven-thirty. According to this, they want directions here. To our house."

"Here? Where are they staying?"

"Doesn't say."

"Let me see that." She handed me the fax. The stationery was from Johns Hopkins Medical School. That meant Claven. "Do you think they want to stay here, with us?"

"Doesn't say."

"We only have one guest room. Are they a couple?"

She pointed at the sheet in my hand and laughed. "Doesn't say."

Lauren's day had fatigued her. While she went to bed early, I plopped in front of the word processor and typed a report for A. J. Simes. I wanted to bring her up to speed on my meeting with Kevin Sample and to relay his suspicions that Mariko Hamamoto might have been having an affair with an older man and that Mariko's adolescent peers considered Raymond Welle to be a likely suspect.

I printed it and faxed it on its way before I climbed into bed beside my sleeping wife.

Russ and Flynn arrived the next afternoon a few minutes before one. The trunk of their rental car was packed full of heavy nylon duffel bags.

Among other things, Russ had come to Colorado to do some rock climbing.

CHAPTER
19

Russ Claven, it turned out, was blessed and burdened with more energy than even my friend Adrienne. And Adrienne was occasionally so hypomanic I considered her in need of medication.

After popping the trunk open and saying a cursory hello to Lauren and me, Russ patted a frantically barking Emily on the head, found his way inside to the bathroom to pee and change clothes, to the kitchen to examine the contents of our refrigerator and swipe an apple, and then back outside. Lauren and I were still standing near the car renewing our brief acquaintance with Flynn Coe.

Flynn's eye patch that day was a rusty satin stripe. The stripes were horizontal and the patch went well with her hair.

Russ interrupted and asked for directions to Eldorado Canyon. I drew him a crude map on the back of his airline-ticket envelope. His eyes brightened; he couldn't believe he was only ten minutes away from the rock-climbing equivalent of Disneyland. He asked Flynn if she was cool hanging out by herself for a while. She said she was. He asked me whether I wanted to go climbing with him. I declined. I think he was relieved that I'd declined. Russ jumped into the car and took off west toward Eldorado.

We invited Flynn inside. She excused herself to the bathroom after suggesting that traveling cross-country in the airplane seat beside Russ Claven did not make for a particularly restful journey. But I thought she offered the assessment with humor and at least a trace of affection.

*   *   *

Flynn wasn't as good a pool player as Lauren was, but at least she could give her a competitive game, which was something I'd never managed to do. Considering how much her eye patch must have compromised her depth perception, Flynn's playing was all the more remarkable. I could tell that she wasn't accustomed to running into players with Lauren's skill, but she handled the competition, and the repeated losses, with grace.

I parked myself on a nearby chair while I watched the women demonstrate their talents, and actually had the feeling they forgot I was there.

Once Lauren managed to get Flynn talking, she spoke of herself with little self-consciousness.

Flynn Coe had been a protégée of Henry Lee's in the Connecticut State Police crime lab. She had worked with him for over three years before she was recruited away by the North Carolina authorities to run their crime lab facilities, the job she still held at the age of thirty-three. She'd been married once at twenty-four, divorced at twenty-six, and had a nine-year-old daughter named Jennifer.

Flynn had known Kimber Lister for years, had actually met him when she was attending a training seminar at the FBI Academy on a fellowship when she was still a graduate student at Northwestern. Years later, when he'd started to discuss his ideas for Locard with her, she'd volunteered her services before he got around to asking her to join.

After almost ninety minutes of pool Lauren excused herself to go rest. I asked Flynn if she was tired from her trip, if she wanted someplace to lie down. She said she didn't and followed me into the kitchen, where I began to prepare some food.

"Will you and Russ stay for dinner?" I asked.

"Sounds great to me but I think we need to wait for Russ. He may have other ideas about tonight."

"Are you two on your way to Steamboat Springs?"

She nodded. "Eventually. I need to interview the people who worked the initial crime scenes and I want to examine the physical evidence that's still in storage. It helps me sometimes. And Russ wants to talk to the doc who did the autopsies on the girls and check on the storage of some blood and tissue and fluid samples that he wants to retest."

My head was mostly inside the refrigerator as I said, "I don't really know how to ask this, but, are you and Russ, you know, a couple?"

I looked back and watched her smile, suppressing a giggle. "God no. But I have to admit that we tried once a few years back. Neither of us could do it. Even long-distance we couldn't make it work. I spent the whole time feeling like Captain Ahab. Always trying to reel him in, always feeling that he was too big, too strong, too indefatigable for me. So . . . it didn't work romantically. But I've learned to love him anyway. He's a good man."

After a few minutes of small talk, I asked, "So—if you don't mind my asking—what happened to your eye, Flynn?"

She smiled. "Most people don't ask."

"I'm sorry if I offended you. But you seem pretty comfortable with it, whatever it is."

"Comfortable? I don't know about that. You must be reading something into the patches, though. When it was clear to me that I had to start wearing one, I decided that I could either think of the patch as a medical device or think of it as jewelry. I decided that I liked the idea of jewelry better. I design them myself, and my sister makes them for me. Now, when people look at me funny—you know, don't look me in the eye—I can allow myself to believe that they're distracted by the patch, not by my disability. It's a nice rationalization, a little advantage."

I finished washing some tiny round carrots that I had

picked in Adrienne's garden. I handed Flynn a couple. "So what happened?"

"I got . . . fooled . . . by a booby trap at a crime scene. A serial rapist left me a present. An explosion. My eye got mangled in the blast. The vision couldn't be saved. I can still perceive light with it, but it's distracting—it interferes with the vision in the good eye. And the scarring is . . . well . . . it's butt ugly. So I wear the patch."

"I'm sorry."

She bit off a piece of carrot and shook her head. "Don't be. It was my own damn fault. I was careless. Good carrots."

We talked about the two dead girls and about Locard until Flynn said, "You're a believer now, aren't you?"

I asked what she meant.

"The work we do. Investigating old crimes. Reopening wounds. Examining scars. Finding answers. You like it, don't you?"

I admitted that I did.

She smiled. Her eyebrow arched so that the narrow end peeked out from below the patch. "By the time I get to see these old cases, everyone is always discouraged. The bodies are always buried, the crime-scene tape is always down, the blood is always dry. *Always.* When I arrive, what I try to bring along with me is some hope, some enthusiasm, and some science. I try to bring fresh blood to an investigation that is often as forlorn as the victim. I try to be . . . that fresh blood. I try to be a . . . transfusion."

"And you see that in me?" I asked.

"It seems that the work is most infectious for those of us in Locard who actually get to meet the families. If you do enough of this you'll see the variety of their responses. Some of them—I'm talking about the loved ones—are . . . almost numb to our arrival. The resumption of the investigation doesn't cut deeply for them at all; it's almost as though they're anesthetized to us. But that's rare. More often we watch the parents or the wives or the children come alive with hope . . . or grief . . . or even rage. Sometimes in the end, we see gratitude. Even though we're always investigating something that has to do with death, the process somehow is incredibly invigorating for me. Others too." She smiled warmly at me. "Yes, I'm seeing some of that in you," she said. "You're fresh blood, too."

Russ and Flynn agreed to stay for dinner, so they were still at our house when Phil Barrett called that evening. I excused myself from the table when the phone rang and took the call in the bedroom.

Barrett was summoning me back to Steamboat to retrieve Mariko Hamamoto's case file from Raymond Welle. Welle would be departing for Washington at four-thirty the next afternoon. I'd need to be at his ranch by three at the latest. I explained to Barrett that I had patients scheduled on Monday and requested that he overnight the material to me at my expense.

"Representative Welle didn't offer any latitude when I received my instructions, Dr. Gregory. He said if you want to see these records, you're going to have to meet with him again. He wants to go over them with you in person. It's not negotiable. Because of his schedule, it's either tomorrow in Steamboat or sometime much later on in Washington."

Welle's request was not out of the ordinary. Clinicians often asked for, and usually were granted as a matter of courtesy, an opportunity to review case records face-to-face before making the copies available to other clinicians.

Although I suspected that Welle's case notes would reveal little or nothing novel about his treatment of Mariko, I knew I couldn't risk not examining them. I suspected that Welle knew it, too.

"I need to make some calls, try to get in touch with tomorrow's appointments and try to reschedule them. Where can I reach you later tonight, Mr. Barrett?"

He dictated a number and said, "Confirm by ten."

I started making the calls.

*   *   *

By the time I rejoined Lauren and our guests at the table, the dinner plates had been cleared and the rest of the wine had been consumed. Lauren frowned and asked me if everything was okay. I think she was assuming that I'd had an emergency in my practice.

I replied, "That phone call earlier? That was Phil Barrett. Raymond Welle's chief of staff. Welle wants me to drive up to Steamboat tomorrow to meet with him about Mariko Hamamoto's treatment file. I've been busy rescheduling patients so I can go up there and do it. What a pain."

Flynn identified the issue instantly. "Welle doesn't want to send the records to you—he wants to go over them with you in person."

"Exactly."

Russ said, "Which means he's concerned that there's something in there that might be misinterpreted."

"I'm not sure I'm willing to jump to that conclusion," I said. "It could be something more benign; it may just be that the treatment file is really thin and he wants a chance to explain why he takes such sparse notes."

Flynn again: "He couldn't do that over the phone?"

"He obviously didn't want to."

Flynn told me, "Try to get the original file. I can get a documents guy to look at them and see if anything's been forged or tampered with."

"I doubt if he'll give me the originals. I wouldn't if I was in his shoes."

"Never hurts to ask."

Lauren asked, "So it sounds like you're going to go?"

I said, "I'm not sure I have much choice. You working tomorrow? Can you come with me?"

"Sorry, I'm too busy."

"Well, if I have to go, I'm going to go up early. I want to be back before dark." I looked at Russ, then Flynn. "You want to ride up there with me, or do you want to take your own car?"

Russ looked at Flynn and said, "We'll caravan. I do best when I have my own wheels."

"He does," Flynn agreed, smiling at him.

I went back to the bedroom and phoned Phil Barrett to confirm an eleven A.M. meeting with Raymond Welle. Barrett offered directions to the Silky Road Ranch. I accepted the directions; I didn't want to admit that I already knew my way around the Elk River Valley. My final telephone call of the evening was to the Sheraton in Steamboat Springs. Dorothy Levin didn't answer her phone. I left a message on her voice mail and asked her to meet me in the lobby for lunch at one o'clock.

Flynn and Russ accepted an invitation to spend the night at our house. They somehow negotiated a way to share the double bed in the downstairs guest room. I admit I was curious about the details. But neither of them offered any clues. Our little convoy was on its way into the mountains by seven the next morning.

We arrived in Steamboat at 10:05. Flynn and Russ drove straight to the police station to find Percy Smith. I continued on to the Sheraton to try to confirm my lunch with Dorothy Levin.

The base-area village for the ski resort is a couple of miles from the town of Steamboat, and the Sheraton is the dominant structure in the village. Even I didn't get lost. I tried Dorothy's room from the house phone in the lobby. She didn't answer. As I left yet another message on her voice mail I noticed a freshly printed sign hung on a banner above the entrance to the bar off the lobby. It read WELCOME HOME, JOEY. WAY TO GO IN AUGUSTA. I returned to my car, and made my way out of town to the Silky Road Ranch. Over the course of the drive I went back and forth a half dozen times about whether or not I should try to interview Joey Franklin while I was in town.

Despite the fact that Welle was in temporary residence at the ranch, there was no visible change in appearance at the entry gate. I left the engine of my car running as I walked up to the microphone and identified myself. A voice told me to stand back five feet. I did. Thirty seconds later, the voice told me to get in my car and wait for the gate to open. I did that, too.

My mind wandered as I slowly drove the dirt lane into the heart of the ranch. My only real context for this huge property had been through the lenses of the news cameras that had recorded the aftermath of the brutal deaths of Gloria Welle and Brian Sample years earlier. As I approached the big ranch house, my eye sought the landmarks that I associated with that day. I identified the spot where the sheriff's vehicles had circled together like pioneer wagons. I decided which window it was that Brian Sample had busted out in order to fire at the deputies. I spotted the cedar deck that led from the master bedroom to the woods. I knew which garage bay Gloria Welle had used to park her green Range Rover.

Pork chop Phil Barrett was waiting for my arrival. He almost filled an Adirondack chair on the front porch. I didn't consider it auspicious that the mug of coffee in his hand was adorned with the smiling face of Rush Limbaugh.

"Doctor," he boomed, calling to me as though I might have somehow missed the fact that he was sitting there.

I waved.

"You're early," he said.

"Didn't know how long it would take me to find you," I said as I stepped up onto the porch.

"That's a lie, Doctor." Phil smiled broadly as he accused me. "I think you've been out this way before. Matter of fact, I know you have."

I immediately decided that I would neither confirm the earlier visit nor defend my untruth. "If I arrived at an inconvenient time, I'm happy to wait in the car. Or even go back out to the road."

"No. No. Sit right down here next to me. I have some coffee coming for you. How do you take it?"

"Black."

"I guessed that right. Look at this day." He opened his arms to the expanse of the valley. "Now aren't you glad you decided to come up here and spend another day in all this beauty?"

The horseshoe of peaks surrounding the ranch was stunning in its summer splendor. The green trees played off the distant granite, and the pastures and cultivated fields glistened in the light breeze. "It is beautiful," I acknowledged. "But the reason I came is because I had to. You know that. My being up here has inconvenienced a lot of people."

He shrugged; he wasn't moved. Inconveniencing strangers cost Phil Barrett no sleep whatsoever.

I sat next to him on a chair identical to his. An athletic young woman ¯in jeans and a pale green polo shirt brought coffee. She smiled at me with a look that I interpreted as sympathy. I thanked her while trying to convey the same sentiment back to her. I was relieved that my mug wasn't adorned with Russ Limbaugh's face. It was decorated with Dilbert's.

I decided to try some small talk. "Until now, I've only seen this house on the news."

Barrett immediately knew what I was referring to. "That was a day. Let me tell you. I was here, you know. I was the commanding officer who gave the order to fire on the rascal."

The *rascal?* "Yes," I said. "I do recall that."

"Only three rounds were fired by the guys in the white hats that morning. First two of them hit him. Either of the two would have been kill shots. My boys did good work. I only have one regret, one wish. Only wish we'd made it out here before he got to Gloria."

"Yes." I paused. "He didn't really give you a chance though, did he? Didn't he shoot her before you got here?"

"Actually, right after we pulled up is when we heard the three shots come from inside the house. Didn't know he was shooting Gloria right then, but the possibility certainly crossed my mind at the time." He turned his mug upside down and let the last few drops of his coffee drip onto the porch. "Been over that day a thousand times. I wouldn't play it any different if it happened here today. You know, I mean, now. All in all, though, quite a shame. Quite a shame."

I couldn't think of a way to respond. "Yes, a tragedy."

"Crazy men do crazy things."

I nodded, but quickly decided that I didn't want to discuss Brian Sample's mental health with Phil Barrett. I asked, "Where's the original house, Phil?"

He pointed down the hill. "Can't see it from here."

"And the stable and bunkhouse? I understand Gloria built some truly special buildings. Where are they?"

He'd been sliding his coffee mug on the wooden arm of the Adirondack chair. He stopped the motion and said, "Huh?"

"I heard that Gloria had a pretty impressive bunk-house. Nice digs for her ranch hands. That's not ex-actly true?"

"Oh, oh. Those? Ray doesn't use them except for some storage. I don't think about them much." He stood and pointed toward the southeast. I had to stand, too, just to gaze past him to look where he was pointing. "Follow that dirt lane with your eyes. You can see the stable and part of the corral poking out from behind that stand of aspen. See it?"

I did. "Ray's not fond of horses?"

Phil laughed his response. "Nope. That was Gloria's thing. Ray isn't exactly here at the Silky Road very often, anyway. Most of our time we're in Washington or on the road in the district. This is a big district. Spend a lot of days taking the pulse of the constituents, you know. One good thing—I'm glad Gloria never had to see that stable empty. That would've broken her heart."

"I'm sure that's true," I said, making conversation.

"Tell you what, though, I think Ray has some plans for all that space after he retires from public life. I wouldn't be surprised if he sets up a recording studio out there, gets back into radio."

"Really? Back into radio?"

"Sure. He calls it the pulpit of the new millennium. Ray's a preacher at heart. Don't you think?"

I hadn't thought about it, of course, but at first blush it didn't seem too far off the mark. I decided to consider the thought further. First I said, "This is all a major change for you, Phil. Do you miss what you were doing before? Miss being in law enforcement, I mean."

He sat back down before he answered. "You know, sometimes I do. But in a small town like this, being sheriff can get pretty routine. Which is something I can't say about being in Washington. I like my life now just fine, thanks."

I nodded as though I were being agreeable though I wasn't feeling particularly agreeable. "I saw a sign in town that seemed to indicate that Joey Franklin is in Steamboat today. Do you know him? Do you ever get to play golf with him? I would think that would be a thrill."

Phil stretched his neck and made a valiant effort to touch his chin to his chest. Wasn't going to happen. "Golf is not my game. But the congressman plays. As a matter of fact, he and Joey are playing nine as we speak."

Hadn't Percy Smith told me he'd played golf with Phil? Why the lie? I glanced at my watch so that Phil couldn't see how perplexed I was. He saw me check the time. "Don't worry. They teed off at eight-thirty at the course at the Sheraton. He should be back out here any minute."

"Good," I said. I was aware that Barrett hadn't answered my question about being acquainted with Joey Franklin. I decided that pressing the issue would be too obvious. Instead I asked, "Do you stay out here when the congressman is in town, Phil? On the ranch, I mean?"

He nodded. "I still have my old place in town, rent it out. Good location, do pretty well with it actually. But it's more convenient for everybody if I'm out here close

by trying to keep messes from oozing under the congressman's door. That's my job, protecting him from blind-
sides. I think of him as the quarterback of the team. And
I like to think of myself as the offensive line. Unheralded
but essential. That's me. I keep Ray Welle from getting
sacked."

I thought, *Well, you certainly have the size to play the
position.* I kept the thought to myself. What I said was,
"It's ironic, don't you think, that you ended up living out
here? After what happened?"

He shrugged. Apparently he didn't see the irony.

I snapped my fingers as though I'd just remembered
something I wanted to ask him. "I knew there was something important I was meaning to talk to you about, Phil.
The two girls—Mariko and Tami? I heard that they got
into a little trouble with your office just a few months
before they disappeared. Something about some skinny-
dipping and some dope up at Strawberry Park?"

"Let me think," he said.

He thought for half a minute. I assumed he knew exactly what I was asking about, which meant that he required half a minute to choose and polish a falsehood to
serve me on a dish. "You know, I do remember them
coming in for something like that. My memory is that
that's why the Oriental girl ended up seeing Ray for
mental help. You know? Of course you know—you're
here to see Ray about the mental help he provided for
the Oriental girl, right?"

I was trying hard not to be disagreeable. But I couldn't
keep myself from giving the "Oriental" girl a name.
"Mariko Hamamoto. Tami Franklin's friend. What's surprising is that there's nothing in the murder book that
refers to the girls' being arrested at all. I've read the
reports quite carefully. Does that, I don't know, concern
or surprise you—that the incident wasn't part of the initial investigation?"

He harrumphed. "No, can't say that it does."

"Do you mind telling me why?"

"Do I mind? Or will I tell you anyway?" He slapped his knee, thought his comeback was pretty amusing.

"Will you tell me anyway?"

"Sure. The reason there was no report is that they were never arrested. They were never charged. I met with the parents myself after the girls were brought in. Came to a reasonable disposition with the parents. I promised to throw the book at the two of them if it ever happened again. Didn't ever have any more trouble with those girls until . . . well, you know."

I said, "I know."

But I remained skeptical. Taro Hamamoto was certainly still under the impression that his daughter had been arrested and charged with a crime after the police had picked her up. I supposed that his cultural unfamiliarity with our legal system could have left him confused about what had actually happened. Or I supposed Phil Barrett could have been lying to my face at that very moment.

"As sheriff I was, mostly, a compassionate man," Phil Barrett explained. "They were good kids who made a mistake. I decided not to make them pay for it the rest of their lives. That's all."

CHAPTER
20

The scene that began unfolding below the horizon in front of me felt a little like an old western movie. A plume of dust had kicked up down the trail, and over my shoulder the sun was riding high in the sky above the distant peaks.

Pointing in the direction that the dust cloud was rising, Phil said, "I bet that's the congressman now."

Distances on the ranch were deceiving. Although the gate to the Silky Road was visible from the porch, the dirt lane that ran from the entrance soon descended and meandered alongside a dry creek bed, where it temporarily disappeared from view from the house. The road curled around for quite a ways in a pattern that roughly followed the confusing path of the creek before climbing back up toward the house.

Phil and I sat silently watching the progress of the cloud of dust that was Raymond Welle's vehicle as it tracked slowly through the dry bottoms near the creek bed and then through the wide expanse of high prairie that carpeted the dirt all the way up to the house.

"He loves this ranch," Phil told me. "He was born and raised in Manitou Springs, of course, but he calls this place home."

I sipped bitter coffee from my Dilbert mug. I hadn't known that Ray was from Manitou, but I didn't see that it was relevant to much. I said, "I think it would be pretty easy to love this ranch."

Phil shot a glare my way. I guessed that he was wondering if I had been sarcastic with my comment about the ranch. To put him at ease I said, "Most of us can only dream of having a spread like this, right, Phil?"

"Amen," he said. I suspected that it was a word that rarely crossed Phil Barrett's lips on any given Sunday.

Raymond Welle's vehicle was finally pulling up to the house. The car, if you could call it that, was actually a snow-white Humvee. I should have been more surprised than I was. Welle was driving the huge thing himself. The young woman in the jeans and polo shirt who had delivered my coffee rushed out the front door to meet him. I wondered if that was part of her job description. Ray jumped out with the motor still running. A light breeze was to his back, and it carried his crisp radio voice to the porch. I heard him say, "My clubs are in the back, Sylvie. They'll need to come back to Washington with me this time. Pack 'em up careful, okay? I don't want to see any scratches on that new driver."

I didn't hear him say "please."

Phil Barrett stood, and I decided I should, too.

Still twenty yards from the porch, Raymond said, "Joey let me beat him on a par three, Phil. The fourth, you know that one? The one with the green by the creek? After I got a lucky tee-shot that left me a three-footer for a birdie, I think he intentionally put his in the sand so that I could say I beat him on a hole. Had witnesses for it, too. Good kid. Jesus, Mary, and Joseph. Nice of him. Nice gesture. Only wished I had time to play eighteen with him. Who knows, I might have gotten lucky a second time." He reached into his pocket, pulled out a golf ball, and held it high in the air. "I kept the ball I used, too. He even initialed it for me. When Joey goes and finally wins one of the majors, this will be a sweet memory for me."

He stuffed the ball back in his pocket.

"Alan, Alan. Welcome to Gloria's Silky Road. I can't tell you how grateful I am to you for pulverizing your schedule to accommodate my need to return to Washington. So kind of you. So kind. Please offer my personal apologies to all of your patients for the inconvenience

I've caused them." He hopped up the two steps to the porch and held out his hand to me.

"I'll be sure to do that, Ray." *Yeah, right after I distribute copies of my driving record and income tax returns to each of them.*

"The only good news for me is that it's real likely that they're all living outside my district. Don't have to worry much about voter backlash." He laughed and moved toward the front door. "Come on inside, now. It's starting to get warm enough to cook oatmeal out here." We walked inside and stood in a bright entryway. The walls were papered in rich red paisley and the floor was made of octagonal limestone tiles. To my left I saw the huge post-and-beam space where Gloria Welle and Brian Sample had shared tea and Girl Scout Cookies. Ray said, "Phil, go find those files for me and bring them to us in the study."

I followed Welle down a narrow hall to a pine-paneled study. The room was large, but warm. One wall was covered with bookcases. I've learned that my eyes are as magnetically attracted to a wall of books as they are to a woman's cleavage. I had to remind myself not to be distracted, and I tried to stay focused on my conversation with Welle.

"Sit, sit."

I did, in a leather club chair beside a low table that had been built on a frame fashioned from an old wagon wheel. The wheel caused me to recall the photograph that Kimber Lister had used to begin his film about the two dead girls. Tami and Miko against a background of an old wagon wheel.

I expected Ray to take his place behind the monstrous desk halfway across the room. He didn't. He chose another one of the club chairs. As he sat down, his trousers rode up, and he spent a few moments trying to free his boxers or his briefs from the confines of his crotch. He yanked and tugged at his underwear as though I weren't even in the room.

Finally he said, "I don't know about you and the way

you practice. But I've never been comfortable just hand-ing over case files. I actually like to review them, ex-plain them."

"Sometimes I feel the same way, Ray."

"Good!" he said much too jubilantly. "Glad to know we're on the same page. Phil should be in here any sec-ond with those files. Phil! Hey!"

Phil chose that second to waddle through the door shaking two manila folders. "Sylvie had these in the lock-box of papers that were packed to go back to the Dis-trict. I had to dig them out." He handed the files to Raymond. I could tell he was dying to be invited to take a chair.

Without looking up Ray said, "This will be one of those clinical talks you're not allowed to listen to, Phil. Sorry. We won't be long."

Phil looked hurt. "Oh. Sure. Sure. I'll be, uh, following up with Senator Specter's office about that highway mat-ter, Ray. I'd like to have that whole thing settled before we get on the plane." To me, Phil said, "The congress-man is trying to get funding for two additional lanes on I-25 south out of Denver."

"That's great," I said, trying to sound like a grateful constituent though I was neither grateful nor Ray's con-stituent. And I-25 south of Denver wasn't even in his district.

"Yeah." Ray's attention was already on the case file.

The label on the tab of the manila folder was handwrit-ten but I couldn't read it from where I was sitting. I said, "That was scary the other day. What happened at the tennis house."

Ray shrugged, seemed nonplussed. "You know, I didn't even hear the shots. Saw some people runnin' around crazy over by the door. Then Phil flattens me to the floor. Next thing I know I'm being hustled into a side room by a bunch of security types. I wasn't so much scared as I was . . . puzzled."

"Do your people think you were the target, though? The thought of someone coming after you with a gun has to be frightening regardless of the amount of security you might have."

"My people?" He chuckled and seemed to find the concept amusing. "It's risky, being in public life. But the danger comes with the territory—that's what I think. We all have to come to terms with it. Those two Capitol policemen killed by that crazy guy? No more than sixty feet from my office. Who can predict those things?" He shook his head, and his voice changed an octave or two with that sentence. For a moment I thought he might have reminded himself of his wife's murder. When he continued, though, his tone had modulated again. "I'm an outspoken advocate of some unpopular ideas. I always have been. And that, my friend, raises ire." Listening to him, the thought that crossed my mind was *stump speech,* and I prepared myself for a long oration, but he quickly returned to the matter of the two dead girls.

"Here we go"—he opened the file and his face softened a little as he continued—"one of my absolutely favorite clients of all time."

Ire? I repeated to myself while he silently perused the top sheet in Mariko Hamamoto's record. Had he really said, "raises ire"? I tried to steal a look at the rest of the file on his lap. The collection was as thin as an anorexic gymnast. If it had held as many as six sheets of paper, I would have been surprised.

Fifteen minutes later we had accomplished our review. To say the case file added anything to my understanding of Miko's psychotherapy would have been a generous assessment. The first page in the folder was a typical doctor's-waiting-room information form. The second was Colorado's mandatory disclosure statement for psychologists. Welle had asked both Mariko and her parents to sign it. The third page was a request for information about Mariko from the local high school. I didn't see any indication that he'd ever received anything back in writing. The next page was a photocopy of a billing record.

The ledger form had been kept by hand. In 1988, Welle charged fifty bucks an hour.

Only on the last two pages did I see any useful information. Welle had scribbled a half a page of notes after his intake meetings with Mariko and had repeated the process after his first meeting with Mr. and Mrs. Hamamoto. Nowhere in those intake musings did Welle offer opinions or perceptions different from those we'd discussed in Denver the previous week.

The last page in the file was the only page that surprised me at all. It was typed. The other pages were either printed forms that had been filled out in handwriting, or notes in Ray's handwriting.

The top of the last sheet was a five-point treatment plan listing outcome goals. The bottom of the sheet was a termination summary that specified the accomplishment of the stated outcome goals. Basic stuff.

I immediately suspected that this last sheet was a relatively recent addition to Mariko Hamamoto's case file.

On the long drive up from Boulder I'd already decided that I wasn't going to critique the contents of the file in Welle's presence. As he handed me each page and I read it, Ray seemed relieved that I appeared to peruse his work with acceptance and equanimity. So I pondered my choice of words for a moment before I held up the last sheet and asked, "Did you type these last notes yourself, Ray, or did you dictate them for a secretary?" I handed him back that last sheet.

"Um, I don't know—both. Could have been either, I suppose. Sometimes I'd do it myself, type the notes. Sometimes I'd dictate it—you know, put it on tape, and turn it in to a service for transcribing. Couldn't tell you with this one specifically. It's been a long time. A long time."

I suspected he was lying to me, and I was impressed, but not particularly surprised, by how facile he was. "This one you must have done yourself though, right? Since her name is typed right on it, I mean. You wouldn't

give that kind of personal information to an outside sec-
retarial service, would you? Small town like Steamboat?
I use initials or case numbers on my dictations."

He looked at the page again. "Course you're right. I
must have done this one myself."

I asked a couple of mindless questions about the treatment plan so he wouldn't be wondering about my interest in that last sheet of paper. I concluded with, "I
appreciate your continuing candor about all this, Ray.
As we discussed last time, I'll need to take these with
me." I retained the slimmest of hopes that Welle would
allow me to keep the original file. It couldn't hurt to ask.
I was already wondering what forensic magic Flynn could
bring to bear on the question of the authenticity and age
of that last page.

Ray didn't smile as he told me, "I anticipated your
request and I've had copies prepared for you." He
handed me the second of the two files that he'd been
given earlier by Phil Barrett. "I'm sure you'll find this
complete. You understand that I can no longer guarantee
the sanctity of these records after I turn them over to
you?"

Sanctity?

I nodded and opened the file containing the copies
he'd given me and glanced at the patient-information
form that was on top. Next to the space marked "Referred By" someone had written "Cathy Franklin." The
information wasn't new to me; I'd already been told by
Taro Hamamoto that the Franklins had recommended
Raymond Welle to them. Seeing it here in writing gave
me pause, however.

I wondered about something else. Nonchalantly I
asked, "Did you treat Tami Franklin too, Ray? I've been
thinking how hard it would have been to be in your
shoes and have one patient murdered. Didn't even cross
my mind that you might have treated both girls at one
time or another."

He shook his head. "Tami? You want to know if I
treated her?" He squirmed on his chair. It could have

been the underwear riding up again, of course, but I
thought he was squirming from my question. "Course
I couldn't tell you if I did treat her, now could I? But I
suppose I can tell you that I didn't."

It was a good answer. Ethical and barbed simultaneously. Ray was a favorite on the weekend morning news
shows. I was beginning to understand why. He could
think on his feet.

"What about Cathy? You help her out with anything?
Before or after the shooting?"

"I think you're fishing now, Doctor. And I'm afraid
this is private land that you're trespassing on."

"You're right. I apologize. One last thing, Ray, and
I'll get out of your hair. The most important piece to me
is still something that I'm uncertain about. And that's
the relationship between you and Mariko. How would
you characterize it?"

He sat back and looked as though he wished he had
something in his hands, a prop of some kind, maybe a
cigar. He'd be good with a cigar. I judged him to have
failed the nonchalance test as he asked, "Why do you
ask?"

"Just curious. What I'm really trying to discover—what
I really need—is some sense of how she related to people. You know, specifically, to men. The assumption has
always been that she was killed by a man, perhaps a
stranger. I'd like to know what style she might have
brought to the table when she came in contact with that
man for the first time."

His tone sharpened. "You talking interpersonal style
or are you wondering about the nature of the transference?"

"Both." I wasn't sure how much Ray Welle was going
to like talking about the transferential aspects of his
treatment of Mariko. But he had kicked the door open,
so I was happy to walk on in.

For a moment it seemed he couldn't find a comfortable
place to rest his eyes. They finally settled on mine. "She
idolized me. Almost right from the start. She seemed to

think of me as a sage. I had never before had a patient who made me feel wiser or more . . . I don't know. I don't know. She treated me as though I knew the secrets of the universe."

I allowed his words to hang, hoping he would pick up on them himself. He didn't seem eager to continue though.

I decided to be empathetic. "It's my experience that that kind of reverence can be quite a therapeutic burden."

My words surprised him. "What do you mean?"

"An idealizing transference. It aggravates the power you would have over her just being her therapist. Requires additional delicacy. You have to be especially conscious of everything you do and say. Don't you think?"

"I don't know. I found it delightful to work with her. That she thought I was more perfect than Buddha caused me no problems. I can live with that transference." He laughed at the image. "It's when patients thought I was more evil than Satan that I didn't like it so much."

"Did that happen much?"

"That was a joke, Alan."

"What was Mariko's style with you?" I asked.

"What do you mean?"

"Interpersonally. How was she when she was with you? Was she reticent? Assertive? Coy? What?"

His eyes narrowed. "You want to know if she flirted with me, don't you? If she came on to me. You want to know if I played Bill to her Monica."

I was taken aback not only by his bluntness but also by how much he'd revealed with his question. I said, "Only if you did."

He stared me down, then finally said, "Next question."

"I'm trying to discover how she might have interacted with her killer."

"She did flirt with me. Almost from the start. No need to pretend it was any different."

"And?"

"I dealt with it."

"Which means what exactly?"

The easygoing camaraderie that had characterized our earlier interaction was now completely gone. The tension between us was thick. We were two boxers just before we raised our gloves. For the first time, I felt that he was now on the defensive. I kind of liked it.

"Which means I handled it appropriately. Kept her on her side of the room, so to speak. Keep in mind, I wasn't doing psychoanalysis with the kid. I was helping her find her way through adolescence. I pointed out the transference that I saw. I interpreted it. We worked with it. And . . . I'm proud to say . . . she got better."

"Did she ever act inappropriately with you?"

He crossed his legs and his voice sharpened again. I heard anger. "You trying to blame the victim here? Insinuate that she might have acted inappropriately and seduced her own killer?"

"No. I'm just trying to know the victim. Did she ever act inappropriately with you?"

"For instance?"

I shrugged. "Patients cross the line sometimes. I had a young woman start disrobing in my office once."

He snarled. "And what did you do?"

"After I asked her to stop and she didn't I left the room and sent a female colleague in to talk with her."

"Nothing like that with Mariko."

I looked him in the eyes and smiled as ingratiatingly as I could. "You know, Ray, you and I have something else in common besides this case. Something that's probably been even more difficult for you than it was for me."

"And what's that?" I could tell he found it almost preposterous that we might have something significant in common.

"A few years back, I had an irate patient act out some transference and try to kill the woman who's now my wife. The outcome was more fortunate for me than it was for you and Gloria. Unlike you, I got there in time to interfere. She survived."

He crossed and uncrossed his legs before he said, "I

admit that I find that interesting. You know, I didn't know that about you. Don't get a chance to meet too many folks who have walked in these shoes of mine." He slapped one of his cowboy boots. I thought he seemed uncomfortable.

What was my reaction to his discomfort? I watered the weed that was growing up through the crack in Raymond Welle's demeanor. "I didn't see it coming clearly enough. Did you see it coming with Brian Sample? I mean, I knew my patient was angry. I knew he was threatening. But I didn't actually believe he would do anything, you know? Certainly not to this woman I loved. Was it like that for you?"

He wasn't looking at me as he shook his head. "Totally different. Totally. I didn't see it coming at all. I thought my patient and I were doing fine. I'm still at a total loss. Right to this day."

I opened my mouth to ask another question but stopped as the door opened across the room. I actually suspected that Welle had hit some concealed button to signal for an interruption. Phil Barrett, now dressed for travel in a suit and tie, burst in. "Sorry to disturb, Ray. We have a call for Dr. Gregory. Urgent, so they say." His tone communicated his disbelief that anything in my life could be urgent enough to interrupt a meeting with Raymond Welle.

Welle smiled at me, suddenly the gracious host again. "Take it right here, Alan." He pointed at his desk. "What line, Phil?"

"The one lit up there. I think it's line two."

Instantly, I feared for Lauren and our baby. Trying to retain my composure, I stepped across the room, lifted the receiver and touched the button below the light on the phone. "Hello."

"Alan? It's Flynn. I'm in town at the Sheraton. It appears that your reporter friend from the *Post* has been involved in something serious. She may have been injured in some way. There's blood in her room, which is a mess, and she's nowhere to be found. Do you mind finishing up out there and getting back here as soon as possible? Chief Smith has some questions for you—given that you know her."

I swallowed and turned my back to Welle and Barrett. Dorothy Levin, injured? Dorothy Levin, missing? "I, um, appreciate the update. Are there any other details I should know?"

"You're with Welle right now, aren't you?"

"That's right."

"You're doing the right thing. Keep this quiet for now. Russ and I will fill you in as soon as you get back here. We're up on the fifth floor of the Sheraton. Tell whatever officer you run into that Chief Smith is expecting you."

"I will take care of that as soon as I can," I said.

"We'll be here. And Alan?"

"Yes."

"If this turns out the way I'm afraid it looks, I'm sorry."

"Me, too." I hung up the phone. Out the window, I stared at the ragged horizon between the mountaintops and the high clouds. My eyes locked on the line with some desperation, as though I were using its stillness to quell motion sickness.

Ray Welle said, "Nothing serious, I hope."

Without facing him, I said, "Nothing I can't handle, Ray. Some colleagues need my consultation on something that's just come up. I apologize for the interruption." I looked at my watch and spun to face him. "Listen, I've taken too much of your time already. I'm sure you have plenty to do to get ready for your trip back to Washington. If any other questions come up about Miko's case I'll get in touch with Phil."

"Now, you also be sure to let me know if you guys get lucky and find the monster who killed those girls. I want to be the first to know."

I nodded. "Of course," I said.

As I drove away from the ranch house I realized I'd started my visit on the Silky Road with a lie and now I'd ended it with one.

I quickly decided that politicians didn't bring out the best in me.

CHAPTER
21

R uss Claven spotted me arguing with a police officer who was acting as a sentry at the top of the fire stairs that led to the fifth floor of the Sheraton. Russ walked up behind the officer, placed a hand on his shoulder, and said, "Please go ahead and sign him in to me. I'm Dr. Claven, remember? The coroner's consultant for Chief Smith? The chief's been waiting for this man to arrive."

I offered ID to the cop and was soon under the yellow tape. Except for a cluster of men and women loitering together halfway down the hall, the corridor of the hotel looked like the corridor of a hotel.

"Sorry about all this," Russ said. "It's always harder when it's somebody you know."

"Thanks." Russ Claven seemed like a changed man. The hypomanic abruptness I'd become accustomed to in his manner was absent. He was calm, thoughtful, and centered. The task at hand focused him.

We stopped in the hallway at least four rooms away from the cluster of authorities. "Before we go any farther, here's what I know: Flynn and I were with Chief Smith this morning at his office at the police department when a call comes in about a bloody mess in a hotel room here at the Sheraton. Not surprisingly, Smith was kind of flustered by the news. Tells us that there hasn't been anything like a homicide since he's been chief. He invites Flynn and me to come along with him while he checks things out.

"By the time we get here, three different hotel staff

had already been in the room, which means at least three different hotel staff had already potentially contaminated the scene prior to us protecting it. Front desk records show that Ms. Levin checked in on Saturday. Reservations said they expected her to check out today. With me?"

"Yes, that fits with what I know."

"Worse news is that the local ship isn't really set up to handle this kind of crime scene. Better news is that they know that they're not equipped to handle this kind of crime scene. Flynn observed as a couple of detectives secured the scene. She said their work was fine. Then they went and got a warrant, which took like no time, and we've all been waiting around ever since for help to arrive from the mobile unit from the Colorado Bureau of Investigation. Flynn asked for and received permission from the chief to look things over, though. From a distance.

"If it turns out we need him, the local coroner is an M.D., but not a forensic pathologist. He's out of town on a family thing of some kind. They reached him on his pager. He's coming back into town tonight, late. Percy Smith asked him, hypothetically, if they found a body was it all right with him if I took a look at it. Coroner said it was cool.

"Anyway, Flynn goes in and does her thing for a while. She—"

"She's separated from her husband, Russ. Dorothy is. She was fearful he was stalking her. When she described his behavior to me, I worried about his potential for being violent."

"Really? That may fit what we see in there. Know his name?"

"Douglas. She called him Douglas."

"Great. See? This is exactly why we wanted you to join us here. We figured you might know something that would help. Anything else?"

I was speechless.

Russ filled the void. "Turns out that what we have

looks like a crime of passion. There was almost certainly a struggle. There was a knife, or something equally sharp. I think Flynn sees it the same way. For now."

"But? I hear a 'but' lurking in there."

"But . . . Dorothy's also a nationally known reporter who has just published a highly critical piece about a well-known local politician who's prominent enough that his problems are beginning to show up on national radar. And then it turns out her hotel room is trashed and streaked with blood. Can't ignore those facts either."

I was having trouble riding along with Russ as he was doing his problem solving. I said, "She's funny. Witty, too. Dorothy." I was beginning to digest the idea of her being dead.

He touched me on the shoulder again. "Like I said, it's always harder—always—when it's someone you know. No sign of forced entry into her room, by the way. She let whoever it was in. Which means Smith can't rule out hotel personnel. That's a lot of people to interview."

I got the sense that his mind was wandering away from the conversation we were having. He cupped my elbow in his hand and eased me down the hall closer to room 505. The hotel was configured in a T; room 505 was near the center of the intersecting hallway. We stood against the wall on the far side of the corridor. A second perimeter of yellow crime-scene tape blocked any closer access to the scene. "This is her room. You can't go in, of course."

I didn't want to. I didn't tell him that.

Close by, between the two perimeters of tape, detectives and cops huddled together in separate clusters, their voices hushed to reverent whispers. None of them faced the door to the room; most of them were no more comfortable around violence than I was.

The door to 505 was open. From where I stood across the hall I could see part of the bedspread on the floor at the foot of the near side of the king bed. The sheets and blankets were ripped and torn from the end of the bed. The mattress was exposed. At the far end of the room a side chair lay on its side on the floor next to an overturned telephone. Above the chair a smear of blood as wide as a wrist ran at least eighteen inches across the glass panes of the doors that led from Dorothy's room out to a small wooden balcony.

In the distance, through the glass, I could see the ski runs decked out for summer. A steady stream of mountain bikers flowed down the mountain trails. Today, from my vantage, the green grass of the runs appeared smeared with blood. *Dorothy's blood?* Likely.

The gondola continued carrying tourists to the top of the mountain.

As I narrowed my focus back to the room, I became aware that I was breathing through my mouth. That's when I saw Flynn Coe leaning into my field of vision. Her hair was covered by a surgeon's cap and her gloved hands were clasped behind her back. She seemed to be examining the carpeting beside Dorothy's bed.

Percy Smith startled me by opening the door directly behind where I was standing. "Got a little command post set up in there." He pointed toward the room behind me. "My idea."

I ignored his bluster and told him without being asked what I had told Russ Claven about Dorothy's marital problems. Smith jotted down everything I said in great detail. He asked a few questions. I answered them.

"And this story she's been working on? The one about Ray Welle. What can you tell me about that?"

"Don't know anything more than I read in yesterday's *Washington Post.* She faxed me a copy of the article at my home in Boulder on Saturday. Campaign irregularities that go back a few years."

"You wouldn't happen to have the article with you?"

"No."

"But it's about Ray Welle and the fund-raising rumors?"

"Yes. Something like that. Also, she handwrote a note on it about having met with somebody who wasn't helpful with the campaign thing but who seemed to know a lot about Gloria Welle's murder."

"This person have a name?"

"It's a man. She didn't give a name. She's a reporter. That makes him a source. She wouldn't give out his name. She also said she had another meeting planned. Didn't say with whom."

Russ' said, "Flynn hasn't searched carefully, but she didn't see a laptop in the hotel room. Did Ms. Levin use one?"

I tried to remember. "Yes. She mentioned one at one point. She said hers was too heavy. Could this have been . . . I don't know, a burglary?" Oddly, I found the possibility soothing. I wanted to think that this had been a greed-based, random attack. I directed the question at Russ.

Percy Smith raised his voice to a patiently pious tone that reminded me of Charlton Heston sermonizing about the Second Amendment. Smith said, "I'm of the opinion that . . . we have a lot of ground to cover before we arrive in the territory of the coulda's and the shoulda's."

Russ waited patiently for Smith to cease pontificating, then responded more directly to my question. "Anything's possible. It's even possible . . . that maybe someone really didn't want her to work on her story anymore."

"Theory," complained Smith. "Just theory. Right now we need to collect evidence. We'll build a theory around the evidence we collect. We're not going to collect evidence to fit a theory. That's not how we do things around here."

Russ Claven was standing slightly back from Percy Smith. I watched a small smile creep onto Russ's face as he papered himself back against the wall. He said, "Hey, Flynn, Alan's here."

Flynn pulled the paper cap from her hair and leaned across the tape to kiss me on the cheek. Her unpatched eye captured both of mine and she said, "I'm so sorry. I got the impression you're fond of her."

Flynn's tones told me that she thought that Dorothy Levin was dead. I swallowed back a tear and said, "I am." I was thinking, *I was.*

Percy Smith interrupted. "ETA on the crime van is about ninety minutes. Anything else we should do before then, Flynn?" I thought I heard some smugness in his words.

She said, "I've done what I can in there without compromising the scene for them."

Russ interjected, "If a body shows up I'll need a physician with a Colorado license—something I happen to lack—to come with me. He or she can supervise me while I work up the body. The sooner we get somebody on deck the better, Chief. If circumstances arise I'd like to get started as soon as possible."

"I'll get somebody on call. Anybody with a license will do?"

"That's right. As long as they'll leave me alone to do my work."

Flynn took me by the hand and said, "Come on. Why don't we go somewhere and get something to drink?"

Smith said, "Room service set up a canteen for me down in 533. You go help yourselves."

Flynn replied, "I think we'll get some distance from all this and go downstairs. Thanks, Percy."

We settled into a booth in the restaurant off the lobby. The view was up the ski slopes and was almost identical to that in Dorothy's room. Each of us ordered iced tea. As soon as the waitress departed Flynn said, "He's all right, you know. Percy. You get past his narcissism and he's reasonably competent."

The eye patch she was wearing that afternoon was of bronze satin stitched in concentric circles with burgundy thread. I found that it was distracting me as I said, "Maybe I'm not as generous as you are, Flynn. I find Percy Smith's narcissism to be a major impediment to perceiving his underlying strengths."

She shrugged, and contemplated my face for several

seconds. "You know what it is I do for a living? I mean really? What I do for a living is . . . I work other people's crime scenes. On every job I do, I'm an outsider. On every job I do, I'm a woman. On every job I do, I have only one eye. On every job I do, I'm a threat. Butting up against inflated egos comes with the territory. I would think you've seen your share of them along the way, too."

"Maybe I'm more tolerant when I'm in my office."

"And maybe you're more tolerant when you haven't just learned that someone you cared for may have been murdered?"

"That too. You think she's dead?"

She shrugged. "A lot of blood in there. A bad struggle. Let's say I'm afraid that she's dead."

"Me too."

"You haven't asked, but do you want my impression of what happened upstairs?"

"Absolutely."

"I could be wrong. These are first impressions, okay?"

"Okay."

"The evidence of struggle is clear. The room is trashed. It appears that the fight she put up was protracted and . . . valiant."

"Help me with something, then. Why didn't anybody hear her? Why didn't she scream for help?"

"Room on one side of hers is vacant. According to housekeeping, the neighbors in the other adjoining room haven't been around much. Dawn-to-dusk tourists. Why didn't she scream? Maybe she couldn't. She might have been gagged before she started resisting. One possibility of the order of events is that the offender entered her room and had her under control long enough to get a gag on her face. Probably at knifepoint. At that point she broke free and started to fight."

"Someone she knew?"

Flynn chose not to answer me directly. "I think one of two things happened in that hotel room. Either what happened in there was, plain and simple, a crime of passion committed by someone with reason to be passionate enough to commit it. Or what happened in there was disguised to look like a crime of passion."

"But not a burglary?"

She touched my hand. "No. That would surprise me."

"Russ said her computer was missing."

"I only did a quick visual. I didn't see it. But we can't be sure that it's actually missing until the criminalists look around carefully."

I repeated my concerns about Dorothy's estranged husband, Douglas, and about her recent meeting in Steamboat with someone who wanted to talk about Gloria Welle's murder and her planned meeting with someone else.

She didn't comment at all about the mystery man with the interest in Gloria Welle, but she looked relieved at the news about Douglas Levin—pleased that the crime scene might be a simple domestic scene gone bad. She said, "There you go then. If I were Douglas Levin I'd be getting my alibi on real straight right now. Real straight."

Hearing Flynn comment about Douglas Levin's need for an alibi caused me to recall the day I met Dorothy and left me concerned that I'd missed something important already. "I wonder if it was him in Denver on Friday, too?"

"What do you mean? What happened on Friday?"

"Those shots that were taken at Welle's fund-raiser on Friday? You read about them?"

"Yes."

Dorothy was the *Post* reporter covering the event. She was directly in the line of fire. She and I had been talking until seconds before the shots rang out. Until right this second I didn't even consider that she might have been the target and not just a bystander."

"She was literally in the line of fire?"

"Yes."

"Then, so . . . so were you."

"I was in my car. The shots were way too high to be

aimed at me. Dorothy was between my car and the door. She was a potential target. I wasn't."

"The possibility that this is the second attempt on her life in a few days is something that has to be blended into the mix. I'll run it by Percy when we're done here."

I finished my iced tea and watched the clear cubes tumble together as I placed the glass back on the table. My mind retreated from the horror of Dorothy Levin's hotel room, and I recalled my meeting with Ray Welle that morning and the suspicious last page of his treatment record. "Flynn, can you do anything magical with a photocopy of a piece of paper? Basically I want to know if you can help date it."

"Date the copy or date the original?"

"Date the original."

"Possibly. If it's a forgery, it will depend on how sophisticated the forgery was. If they used time-period-appropriate devices and materials to generate the document, it would be hard to pick up discrepancies on a photocopy. We're talking a machine copy? That kind of copy, right?"

"Right. Assuming the forgers weren't that good—that they might have made a mistake—what could you pick up?"

"I'm not a documents specialist, so this is an educated guess, but let's say they used a computer printer that generated a typeface that's common now but wasn't common then. That sort of thing would help date the document. Or, I don't know, maybe a reflection of the watermark on the paper came through on the copy. With a watermark the documents people can sometimes date the paper of the original. There are ways. What do you have for me to look at?"

I explained my suspicion about the last page of the file that I'd received from Raymond Welle that morning.

"Let me take the first-generation copy with me. I'll see what our documents examiner can do with it. Why would Welle forge something like that?"

"I don't know, Flynn. It's down in my car. Want to walk out with me? I'll get it for you."

She paid for the tea and followed me out of the hotel lobby and over to my car. "Did you learn anything else from Welle this morning?"

I shook my head. "No, the file is as thin as it could be. I'm still working under the impression that his psychotherapy of Mariko Hamamoto was relatively skillful. I did discover that Welle drives a Humvee. And that he was out playing golf with Joey Franklin this morning."

She raised her eyebrows. The patch moved provocatively. "Really?"

"Raymond seems quite fond of Joey."

"Does he?" she asked.

"You have any gut feelings that this guy Dorothy met with about Gloria Welle might be connected somehow to her disappearance?"

Flynn shook her head. "Why would that be connected? Gloria Welle's murder was solved, wasn't it?"

She must've seen something in my face as I conjured a response to her question.

"Isn't it?" she repeated.

"I guess," I said. "I guess."

CHAPTER
22

I drove back to Boulder later that afternoon without having learned anything new about Dorothy's disappearance and without having learned anything that I could use to fashion a cushion that might soften the blow of seeing her bloody hotel room.

By the time I'd traveled most of the way down the Divide and cut off onto Highway 6, the route into Golden was jammed with gambling traffic generated by the casinos of Central City and Blackhawk. I managed to pass one giant motor coach that was belching diesel fumes into my face only to end up smack behind another. At that point I gave up fighting the traffic and tried to get lost in the radio broadcast of a Rockies game at Shea Stadium in New York. After losing four in a row, the Rocks were up by three runs. The best thing about baseball is the constant opportunity for redemption. Almost every day the players and the teams get another chance to try to set things right. I wished life were like that. There were so many nights that I felt as though I were climbing into bed after going 0 for 4.

The ivory Lexus was in front of Adrienne's house again, but I was too distraught over Dorothy's disappearance to grant the solution to that puzzle much of my attention. Lauren was at a dinner meeting with a committee that was organizing a benefit for the Rocky Mountain MS Center, so the house was quiet when I got inside. I took care of Emily's pressing needs—food, water, exercise.

A. J. Simes called while I was outside with the dog.

She left a terse message approving my request to fly to California to interview Satoshi Hamamoto. The approval felt like a small victory. I started throwing together a sandwich for myself for dinner while I mentally plotted when I could squeeze an abbreviated trip to Palo Alto into my schedule.

Sam interrupted my plans with a phone call and an invitation to go out for a beer to talk about the videotape of news clips about the murder at the Silky Road Ranch that I'd dropped off at the police department. My impulse was to stay home and pout about my rotten day, but I reminded myself he had done me a favor by looking at the tape, and I agreed to meet him at a barbecue place close to his house on North Broadway in twenty minutes.

Sam was in a good mood. That helped.

The first beer helped, too. But not as much as the second.

I'd already decided that I wouldn't tell Sam about Dorothy's disappearance in Steamboat until we were done talking about the murder at the Silky Road Ranch. I didn't want to distract him.

It turned out that Sam had been so troubled by two aspects of the news coverage of Gloria Welle's death that he'd made some calls himself to learn what he could about the details of the crime. It turned out that the two parts that had bothered him were things to which I hadn't given a second thought.

I told him that.

"That's why I'm the cop," he explained.

"So the first problem, the problem with the shooting, what's that? I don't understand."

"Like I said, the first thing I don't like is that the offender shot her right through the closet door. I've never heard of such a thing. This guy—this Brian Sample—he supposedly went there wanting vengeance, right?"

He waited for me to reply. I said, "Yeah, that's the assumption."

"So he's furious, right You're the psychologist—people wanting vengeance tend to be your angry people, right?"

"Yeah."

"You could say murderous, even?"

"Yes. Apparently so in Brian's case."

"So what does he do with all his murderous vengeance? He kidnaps his shrink's wife, has tea with her, locks her in a closet, gives her a chair, and then shoots at her through a locked door? *Huh?* Why?" His tone had grown way too sarcastic for my comfort.

"I don't know, Sam. I guess he didn't want to watch her while he, you know, killed her."

"*He didn't want to watch? Are you kidding me? Think about it. This guy is eager to inflict pain. He wants to torment her.* I mean, if I know him right, he'd pay extra to watch her head explode. He's bought his ticket and he wants to watch her *die.* If you put it on tape for him he'll play it back a hundred times in slow motion and freeze-frame. He's rageful enough to kidnap her, and he's rageful enough to kill her, but you're telling me that when push comes to shove his sensibilities are offended and he doesn't actually want to watch her die Sorry, buddy, but it does not compute."

I was tempted to order another beer, but I'm a cheap drunk and I thought it might take me over the threshold of inebriation and didn't want to have to take a cab home. I passed. "What you're saying makes sense, Sam. I have to think about it some more, but it makes some intuitive sense. Now go back to the second problem you found again. I don't get that either."

"This ranch house of theirs? It's a big house, all on one level. From the news footage, I counted at least twelve doors to the outside. That includes the garage doors, patio doors, all the doors. Okay?"

"Okay."

"What are the odds that these two cops with their scopes and high-powered rifles are going to be set up in exactly the right place to shoot this guy when he makes his break from the bedroom deck? How the heck do these geniuses know that he's coming out that door?"

I was playing with the cocktail napkins on the table, making patterns of diamonds and squares. "Sam, why do I get the sense that you already know the answer to your own question?"

He laughed. " 'Cause I do. I tracked one of 'em down. One of the two shooters. I got his name, found out where he lives, and gave him a call at home. He's a welder in Lamar now. You know where Lamar is? He says that it was all deduction. That they guessed that the guy had ditched his car in the woods near those bedroom doors by that deck. So they figured that's where he would run out to make his escape. He and the other deputy had already taken up position. Had their weapons ready. The guy I talked to, he called it a duck shoot."

Sam's voice was still singing a melody of suspicion. I said, "But? You're not satisfied. I can tell you're not satisfied."

"But? But do you know who did the deducing? Raymond Welle and Phil Barrett, that's who."

I shrugged. My own conclusion was that this second argument Sam was making wasn't anywhere near as compelling as the first had been. I said, "Somebody had to do the deducing. And it sounds like they did it well."

He sat back on his chair. "No, you're not getting it. With a hostage inside a house, cops don't put all their eggs in one basket like that. The reason is that kidnappers don't usually make a run for it in hostage situations the way Sample did.

"Strategically, if you only have a few deputies you certainly don't set up snipers waiting for a kidnapper to scoot. The kidnapper is in there for a reason. Before you commit resources you have to know what that reason is. The kidnappers barricade themselves in and hunker down or they make demands or they take pot shots at the cops. Sometimes they set fires. They ask for a helicopter and a zillion dollars. They want to talk to reporters or they want to talk to their mother. But they're there for *something.* I've never seen anybody in Sample's circumstances just run for it when he knows that there's a couple of cops with rifles aimed right at his intended escape route."

"Sample knew they were there? He could see them from the bedroom where he was?"

"Clear line of sight, according to the videotape you gave me. The cops' vehicles were out in the open. One of the bedroom windows faces the front of the ranch. He could've seen them. Have to assume he did see them."

I considered the circumstances Sam was describing. Tried to conjure up Brian Sample's state of mind and tried to imagine his tortured decision-making process. It wasn't easy. I said, "Brian Sample underestimated them, I guess."

"I . . . guess." He raised an eyebrow. "Fatal damn error."

I decided to try another argument. "Maybe he just didn't care. He was a very depressed man."

Sam scowled and flagged down our waitress to order another beer. Before it arrived, I decided it was time to start to tell him about the visit I'd received from Brian Sample's son Kevin the previous weekend.

When I finished the story Sam's beer was gone and he had an evil little smile on his lips. He said, "See? What'd I tell ya. The kid is making a variation of the same argument that I'm making. The story doesn't make sense. What his father did when he was in that house—hey, the whole thing is too goofy for words."

"What's the alternative explanation?"

"Don't have one. It's not my job. But it was that sheriff's job. Barrett took the easy way out. He had an obvious crime with an obvious perp. He closed his case even though his solution doesn't make a whole lot of sense."

"Even though Barrett couldn't really explain what really happened inside, or why. That's your point?"

"That's my point."

"Interesting," I said, still unconvinced by Sam's argument. I excused myself to the bathroom, and stopped at a nearby pay phone to make sure Lauren was home safely. I got the answering machine. My watch told me it was only 8:30. I decided to forgo panic until at least 9:30.

Back at the table, without preamble, I said, "That reporter from the *Washington Post?* The one I told you about who wanted to talk with me about Raymond Welle's fund-raising?"

"Yeah?" I could tell he was disinterested in the new topic. I also knew that his disinterest would evaporate as I leaked out more details.

"I was up in Steamboat earlier today on that Locard thing. I was actually up there with two other Locard people. A forensic specialist and a pathologist. While we were there, Dorothy Levin—the reporter—disappeared from her hotel room. The room showed evidence of a major struggle. I saw it; there was a lot of blood."

"Was she murdered? I didn't hear there was a homicide up there."

"They haven't found a body."

"Witnesses?"

"Not really."

"Suspect?"

"They're looking at her husband. They're separated. He's a jerk. Some violence in the history."

"But the local cops aren't sure?"

"No," I said. "They're not sure."

"She's the one who was in the line of fire with you at the Welle fund-raiser, wasn't she?"

"Yes."

"Nothing new on that, though?"

"I've been checking the papers, haven't seen anything."

"But this reporter friend of yours? She's been both shot at and kidnapped within a forty-eight-hour period?"

"I guess."

He slowly moved his eyes away from the two young women who had just been seated at the next table and froze me with his glare. "What the hell are you messed up in this time, Alan?"

*   *   *

Nine o'clock had come and gone by the time I'd finished regaling Sam with the details of my visit to Steamboat to be a supplicant in Ray Welle's regal court at the
Silky Road Ranch. Nine-thirty had finally rolled around
when I was done adding the fine points to the story of
Dorothy Levin's disappearance. I traipsed back to the
pay phone, where I had to wait in line while a drunken
man named Lou—"Come on, babe, it's me, Lou"—tried
to lure a recalcitrant woman named Jessica to join him
for a pitcher of beer and a game of pool. Jessica wisely
wanted none of it. Lou finally hung up, or at least gave
up. The receiver never quite made it back into the cradle.

I called home and got the machine again. Worried, I
tried Lauren's cell phone and heard an out-of-service
recording. I walked back to the dining room with as
much calm as I could muster.

"I can't reach Lauren, Sam."

He spotted the concern in my eyes, wisely searching
the edges for telltale signs of paranoia. "She should be
home?"

"She should have been home over an hour ago. She
was at some committee meeting."

"It wouldn't have run late?"

"Unlikely. If it did she would have called."

I watched as his mind ticked through some mental
checklist. Calmly he asked, "Is she on call for the DA
tonight?"

"You know, I didn't even think about that. I don't
have her call schedule with me."

"But it's possible?"

"Sure."

"Do you know the number of the pager she carries
when she's on call?"

"No, I don't have it memorized. It's in my appointment book."

"Which you don't have with you, right?"

"Right."

He successfully refrained from criticizing me. I was

grateful for the effort. "I can get it from the department dispatchers. I'll be back in a minute. Do you have any quarters?"

I handed him all my change and watched him stride from the room. I waited at the table for about three minutes before my anxiety rose to a level that my false patience couldn't arrest. I followed Sam's trail to the pay phone and ran into him outside the men's room.

He held up his hand like a traffic cop controlling an intersection. "It's cool. She got called in on a rape. She's right down the street at Community. Said she just left you a message on the home machine. She's fine. Said to tell you she loves you but that she'll probably be a while." Sam showed absolutely no discomfort passing along the message about my wife's affection.

"Thank God. Thanks."

He put his arm around my shoulder and said, "Let's you and me go home. You haven't had a very good day."

Better than Dorothy's, I thought.

I wasn't ready to sleep when I got home, so I parked myself in front of the computer and continued my narrative report to A. J. Simes. I wrote about my summons to Steamboat. My meeting with Ray Welle at his ranch about his treatment records. Dorothy Levin's disappearance.

By the time I printed the report and faxed it to D.C. the clock told me it was almost eleven-thirty. I waited up until after midnight for Lauren to get home. We had both witnessed a lot of misery that day and talked for at least another hour before we fell asleep.

The phone woke me up at 6:45 the next morning. After I identified the noise as emanating from the telephone, my first thought was that they had found Dorothy Levin's body. I managed a pasty-mouthed "Hello."

A wrong number. Someone wanted to speak to Patricia.

PART FOUR

Satoshi

CHAPTER
23

Her father had surprised me so much during my brief visit to see him in Vancouver that I cautioned myself not to have preconceptions about what Satoshi Hamamoto would be like. I was certain I would fail to imagine her correctly.

On the congested drive south down the Peninsula from the San Francisco airport my mind, despite my intentions, continued to conjure images of her. The portraits I composed were mosaics of fragments of the various photographs I'd seen of Satoshi's dead sister, Mariko. Without ever having met her, I was unable to picture Satoshi as anything more than a composite of her sister. My mind insisted on perceiving Satoshi as Mariko was at sixteen—her skin tawny, her smile alluring. For some reason, my imagination would not allow Satoshi to have an identity separate from her sister. I concluded that I was so eager to actually know Mariko that I was desperate for her sister to be her twin. I wanted Satoshi to be a window into her sister's life, and I wanted to gaze through that glass and see what had led Mariko to walk with her killer.

In 1988, when Tami and Miko disappeared, the two friends were sixteen years old. Satoshi was younger, thirteen or so—a girl. But the person I was about to meet in Palo Alto was somewhere around twenty-five, a woman.

She'd asked me to meet her on campus at Stanford.

I found the building where we were to meet without too much trouble. Locating the specific room was not so simple. The room numbers made little sense and the building was chockablock with culs-de-sac and dead ends. I begged for directions at least three times. The students I asked for help seemed to be as clueless to their surroundings as I was.

My watch told me that I had found the appointed room with only a few minutes to spare. The door was open and I stepped in after a cursory knock. Satoshi wasn't there. No one was.

I suspected from my own days in graduate school that this room functioned as a group office that was shared by at least four grad students. Desks and tables were crammed against three walls. The fourth was lined with shelves and file cabinets. Computer equipment, some new and some old enough to be considered quaint, littered every horizontal surface.

"Dr. Gregory?"

The voice came from behind me. It was light and friendly and almost without accent.

I turned and saw a young woman standing on the far side of the hallway outside the door. In one hand she held a can of Coke. The other hand gripped a laptop that she was pressing tightly against her chest.

The woman was certainly of Japanese ancestry. I said, "Satoshi Hamamoto?"

She said, "I've been thinking that it's too nice a day to stay in here. Would you mind if we go outside to the courtyard? Is that okay?"

I said, "I'll follow you."

As I walked toward her she stepped back from me. First one step, then quickly, two more.

She said, "This is awkward, but . . . ." Satoshi's black hair was pulled back and it mostly disappeared beneath a floppy beret the color of dying bluegrass. Her head swayed slightly from side to side as she asked, "May I see some ID? Maybe your . . . driver's license?"

The request puzzled me but I didn't have a reason not to comply. I tugged my wallet from my pocket and fished out my Colorado license.

She juggled the can and her computer and examined my ID for half a minute before she handed it back to me. "I'm sorry that was necessary. But thank you."

This time she didn't shy away as I moved closer to her. Satoshi was tall and thin, like her father. Her face was narrower than Mariko's had been, though her cheeks were full, the bones below taking on definition only when she smiled. Her manner displayed more confidence than I imagined Mariko had ever managed to accumulate in her limited years on the planet.

She asked about my flight and my drive from the airport and if I'd had any trouble finding her office. When I admitted I'd gotten lost inside the building she laughed along with me.

Outside we settled on a stone bench beneath a tree that she told me was a laurel. "This is my bench. I come here every day. Almost." She placed her laptop and a shoulder bag on the grass at the base of the bench and faced me. "Thanks for this," she said. "For coming all the way here. And even more for caring about what happened to Mariko." The moment was poignant but she met it head-on. Her gaze stayed locked on mine. I watched as the corners of her mouth turned down infinitesimally, hinting at some lingering sadness about her loss. Her dark eyes glowed from within like black pearls.

I said, "I'm grateful that you'll meet with me. It's not easy, or pleasant, to dig up painful memories."

She placed her hands behind her on the stone and leaned away. She was wearing a loose top that was cropped near the waistband of khaki cargo pants. The top rode back onto her abdomen, exposing a band of caramel flesh at her naval. I tried not to look. I failed. She appeared not to notice. She said, "That sounds suspiciously like a platitude. My father didn't prepare me for that about you. He said to expect you to be forthright."

I don't know what it was that I had expected from Satoshi. But it wasn't confrontation. I fought surprise as I said, "Despite the circumstances, I enjoyed meeting your father. And I hope you won't be disappointed and end up disagreeing with his assessment of me. I can only assure you that my comment wasn't intended as a platitude. I believe what I said before. The territory we need to cover is painful. I have trouble with it, and I never knew your sister or Tami Franklin."

Her eyes closed briefly and she said, "I think that you are trying to be kind. It's not necessary. You don't know—you can't know—the agony, Doctor. No matter how hard you've looked, how many people you've talked to about what happened, I promise you that you don't know the half of it."

When her eyes opened again she was looking away from me, her lips dry and parted. I noticed her breathing had changed; she was exhaling through her open mouth. I followed her gaze to the distance. The sky on the western horizon was hazy. The rolling hills of the coastal range appeared as ghosts. It was as though I were peering at the edge of the world through gauze.

"Before I begin with my story," she said, "there is something to which you must agree."

I waited. I couldn't begin to guess what she wanted now. The driver's license request had seemed odd enough.

She leaned forward from her waist and folded her hands on her lap in a way that left her palms open and cupped to the sky. "You must agree not to divulge the information that I am about to provide to anyone beyond the membership of your committee. Your group—I believe it's called Locard. Is that correct? And your committee must agree never to divulge the information to anyone else. Simply, this story I will tell you must not become public. Specifically, my parents cannot ever— ever—learn this information. If it does become public— or if my parents learn the details—I will not only deny that I told you this story but I will also deny that it is true. I guarantee you that you will find no independent source for the information I plan to give you today. If it turns out that what I say is useful, I hope your organization will be able to exploit it to guide your inquiry into my sister's murder. But you must develop your own proof. Do you understand?''

I tried to keep my voice level. I failed. "No. I don't understand. You have information that you feel is so potentially helpful that you invited me all the way to California to hear it—and yet, you forbid me to use it? I don't pretend to understand. I don't."

She reacted physically to my words. Her neck tightened; her kneecaps came together. She composed herself—allowing her shoulders to sag back down half an inch—before she replied. "Neither of us—neither you nor I—knows the value of what I'm about to tell you. If I knew with any certainty that this information would help you find the person who killed Mariko, I would have told this story to someone long ago. I'm willing to divulge it now only because my father is convinced that the organization you work for is sincere in attempting to find my sister's killer."

"We are."

"Good. Unfortunately, my story is not an answer for you in that quest. It is not proof of anything. I don't know who killed Mariko and Tami. With my story, I am able to do nothing more than to point my finger at a trail the killer might have walked. No more than that, I'm afraid."

She was examining me as closely as I was examining her. I knew she could feel my reticence to accept her proposal.

She said, "If you don't agree I will try to understand your rationale for refusing my request. Then I will thank you for your journey and for your efforts and I will show you back to your car."

I weighed my alternatives and concluded I had little to lose. Any direction she could provide would be welcome. I contemplated how to respond to her for a moment before I said, "I could give you my word, Satoshi. But I would be misleading you by pretending to have authority that I don't really have. I don't have control of the information once I report it to Locard. To provide you with the guarantees you are requesting I need to run your request by someone much higher up in the organization than myself."

She tilted her head slightly, tucking her chin closer to her shoulder. "Thank you for your honesty. You can do that by phone? Get that permission? You could do that now?"

"Yes."

"This way," she said. Before standing, she looked behind her, scanning the courtyard for something or someone whom she didn't appear to find. Finally she led me back to her office and sat me at her desk. I used my phone card to call A. J. Simes in Washington.

A. J. insisted on speaking with Satoshi before she reluctantly assented to Satoshi's demand for discretion. During the negotiation Satoshi was diplomatic but determined in pressing her case. After she was convinced she had the promise she needed from Simes she left her things in the office and removed the beret. I followed her from the classroom building to something like a student union. She bought a container of vanilla yogurt and carried it to a quiet table in a deserted corner of the cafeteria. She chose a seat that placed her back against a wall and began eating by lifting a tiny amount of yogurt on the tip of the spoon and placing it between her lips.

She repeated the act mechanically, taking baby bites over and over for a minute or two. I waited.

The table between us was laminated. The chairs we sat on were molded plastic. My stomach growled and I considered getting up and buying myself something to eat, but I didn't want to fracture her mood.

Before she finally spoke Satoshi stood her spoon in the half-eaten yogurt and brushed a flurry of crumbs to the floor from the edge of the table. She arranged the salt and pepper shakers behind a grimy bottle of French's mustard. A thick golden yoke had hardened around the squeeze top of the mustard bottle. The three containers, once aligned, stood like soldiers at attention behind the chrome napkin holder.

Satoshi crossed her arms across her body, the fingertips of her hands gripping the big tendons between her neck and shoulders. The setting was so antiseptic that I found myself totally unprepared for what she had to say. Finally, she spoke. "Joey Franklin You know about Joey? Well, this is about Joey Franklin, Tami's. younger brother. Do you know what became of him? He's become a big-shot golfer." The words "big-shot" sounded especially foreign coming from her mouth.

I said, "I know who he is."

She'd apparently worked through her hesitation. Her words began pouring forth in a strong voice. "Joey . . . forced me to have sex with him one day shortly after school started in 1988. He was fifteen I think, maybe fourteen. I was thirteen." She took a deep breath before she continued. "The only person I ever told what happened that day . . . was Mariko. No one else. I told her what Joey did to me three days before she disappeared. Three days before . . . she was murdered.

"That is my story."

I was stunned but, for some reason, not surprised. I wanted to comfort her, but she appeared composed and tranquil. I forced myself to refrain from reaching out to touch her hand. I said, "I'm so sorry."

She shook her head. "Don't. Don't misunderstand. I'm not seeking your compassion. This isn't about me. This is about Mariko. And about whoever killed her. Obviously, I have reason to fear it might have been Joey."

"You said that Joey forced you to have sex with him. You didn't say he raped you."

My reply seemed to please her. She said, "A curious distinction, right? This vantage that I have now, today— that of a grown woman—provides perspectives I didn't have when I was thirteen. At thirteen, I felt I had done something wrong. That I had failed, somehow. That perhaps I had lured him into assaulting me. Or that I should have been more, I don't know, aggressive in repelling his advances. At thirteen, I was ashamed of what happened. You can appreciate that, I hope."

I hoped my face reflected the fact that I could appreciate it.

"Now? Now I'm older, maybe wiser. I feel that Joey took advantage of me. Was I raped? I'm not sure. Did he threaten me? No. Did he overpower me? Yes. Was I terrified? Absolutely."

"It sounds to me as though you were raped."

She lowered her chin and placed her hands on the table, her fingers spread, her eyes locked to her fingertips. "Is it that easy for you? To listen to a few words someone says about something painful in her past and proceed to cast judgments about the motives and lives of others? People you have never met? Is it really that easy for you? I've lived with the consequences of what happened that day for almost half my life now and still it seems that the judgments I make about what occurred are no more constant than the clouds."

I considered my words for half a minute before I spoke. "I don't mean to trivialize that struggle, Satoshi. I'm only reflecting back the reality of what you're saying Joey did to you."

She wasn't mollified. "You and your organization are out looking for villains, Dr. Gregory. I've handed you one. Joey Franklin may indeed be an evil man. I know he did an evil thing to me when we were both children. Be careful with that knowledge. For you, Joey Franklin may be a villain and he may be the right villain. But he may also be the wrong villain."

Her anger was so tempered, so measured, that I didn't quite know how to understand it. "Why now, Satoshi? Why bring this to light now?"

"Because you, and Locard, seem to care about what happened to my sister. That's why. I can offer you no proof of anything. If pressed, I couldn't even prove that Joey did to me what I am accusing him of doing. The only person I ever told about the . . ." She shook her head. "The only person I ever told was Mariko. She's not here. All I can do now is say, 'Look over there.' So that's what I'm saying. Go and look over there. I don't know what you'll find."

The line she was drawing may have connected two points, but it didn't feel straight. It was bent, as a beam of light is refracted by water. "You've obviously given this a lot of thought, Satoshi. How do you figure it? Why would Joey kill your sister and his own sister?"

She crossed her arms across her chest. "I don't know the answer to that. I wonder, of course, if Mariko confronted him after I told her what he did to me. Perhaps Mariko told Tami first and they confronted Joey together. The reality is that I'm as lost in the dark as you are." She paused and examined the fingers on her hands as though they were foreign objects. "What happens . . . in the darkest places . . . what happens in the black space between confrontation and rage . . . is something I don't profess to be familiar with."

"You never told your parents what you suspected?"

She looked up and almost smiled. "I spoke once . . . of what happened . . . and my sister and her friend died within days. Why would I speak of it again?" Somehow her question was void of sarcasm.

"You feared for your parents' safety?"

"I was a child. I was in a strange country. I was in a new town. I'd been molested by a boy twice my size. My sister had disappeared. You wonder if I feared for my parents' safety? I feared everything—I feared that the sky would fall to the earth, that the oxygen would disappear from the air."

"Do you still fear for their safety? Is that why you insist on not telling anyone what you've told me?"

She looked around the room, her eyes jumping. "Just as there are many kinds of safety, there are many ways to inflict pain. For my parents, this would be a novel one. I have no desire to hurt them any more. I have lived too many years with the lingering suspicion that they already suffer the consequences of what happened to me, even though they don't even know it occurred. I don't wish to impale them on that sword and draw fresh blood." She shook her head. "No. My parents won't learn of this."

A group of four students took a table across the room. They were loud as they settled. I watched Satoshi watch them. Within moments three of them were reading. The fourth was busy constructing a perfect cheeseburger. I leaned forward and whispered, "You seem to have already come to the conclusion that Joey was capable of killing your sister and Tami Franklin."

"Capable?" She shrugged and momentarily appeared puzzled by the word. "The question isn't one that I've ever struggled with. He forced himself on me. What I know is that he was capable of that."

I lowered my voice again. "But whoever murdered your sister and Tami also mutilated their bodies. If you are indirectly accusing Joey, then he has to be capable of that as well."

She nodded slowly. "Is that the larger sin, Dr. Gregory? The mutilation? Is that where everyone is still getting lost? Give me back my sister absent her toes—I'll take her gladly. *Gladly.* Tami with only one hand? I would welcome her in a second and every day I would caress her stump with lotion. And what about me, losing my virginity at thirteen? Rather irrelevant now, don't you think? The mutilations were distractions back then. And apparently the mutilations are distractions now. It's your responsibility not to be distracted."

"You said 'everyone is still getting lost.' What did you mean?"

"The amputations. Tami's hand and Mariko's toes. It distracted everyone back then. It convinced them that a stranger was at work. Someone more evil than any of us could ever be. The mutilations cracked the mirror that they needed. The mutilations blackened the glass so the town couldn't look at itself, at its own reflection. Instead, they began sweeping back the brush, searching for psychopathic strangers and . . . we took comfort there. All of us."

I thought about the meaning of her words and the truth that was so near that surface.

I pushed my chair back from the table, maybe six inches, just to stretch my legs. Without reflecting long enough, I asked, "What about now, Satoshi? Have you been able to move on, too?"

Her eyes narrowed before they softened. Her chin rose a centimeter or so. She shook her head.

I didn't know how to interpret her expression or her refusal. Had she told me no, she wasn't able to move on, that perhaps she still wasn't able to trust or to love? Or was she telling me that no, she wasn't going to visit that territory with a stranger? I guessed the former, then in the next second, the latter.

Before I left Stanford to return to the airport, I asked Satoshi if she was frightened about something.

She touched her hair with her left hand, looked at me quickly, then away. She replied, "Is it that obvious?"

"While I've been here, you've seemed . . . I don't know . . . spooked. I'm not sure how obvious it is."

She smiled at me and said, "Spooked? Is that a polite way of saying paranoid?"

I smiled back at her.

"I've been edgy since my father called and told me about you and what you were doing. I've been imagining all kinds of things. Phone calls with no one on the line. Strangers I think are following me around campus. Cars I don't recognize parked outside our apartment. Things like that. What I know—about Joey—it must be dangerous to someone, right?"

I said, "Yes," and recalled what Sam had told me about sleeping dogs.

As we spoke we were walking in a circuitous route that would lead back to my car. For a few steps she even held my arm. I suspected that despite her reluctance, she needed to tell me the story about Joey.

She'd only met Joey Franklin twice before he raped her. Both times he had been with Tami and Mariko. Once in town at a store. Once at the Hamamoto residence. Each contact had lasted only moments. Satoshi admitted that she found Joey to be attractive and charming.

The third time she saw Joey he had gone out of his way to find her. He'd been waiting for Satoshi after school, had offered to walk her home. When she explained that her mother would be waiting in the car, Joey had quickly said good-bye, said he'd see her around.

Joey Franklin was the first boy in Steamboat Springs who had shown any interest in the new Japanese girl in town. Satoshi thought he was handsome. She thought his attention was flattering. She not only wasn't alarmed when he joined her on her almost daily run later that afternoon, she welcomed his company.

"The first time we'd met I was just coming back from a run. He must have learned that I ran frequently. He must have known that I ran alone," she said. "Joey was not a runner. He soon grew tired running with me. I slowed down but he couldn't keep up. He asked if we could stop to rest. We did. After a moment or two—it was awkward—he took my hand—gently—and he led me down a trail into the woods. I thought it was a pretty place where we stopped. It reminded me of the hills in Japan where my grandparents live. Finally, we stopped to rest."

They sat on the ground, side by side, leaning back against a rounded boulder. Above her, through the trees, the sky was beginning to lose its luster.

Satoshi was frightened—not of Joey Franklin, but in the way that a young girl is frightened the first time she is alone with a boy whom she likes. She felt that she was violating her parents' admonitions. She promised herself that she would sit with him for only a moment.

He told her she was pretty. She remembered that clearly. He told her that she was prettier than her sister. She remembered that, too. She'd never felt better than her big sister at anything.

Joey kissed her then. He was gentle with her. She remembered finding it difficult to breathe afterward, her excitement at the contact was so intense. And she allowed him to kiss her again.

He touched her bare leg, her thigh, his fingers edging below her running shorts. She was horrified and pulled away from him. She stood. He stood, too, towering over her. He took her by the hands and told her again how pretty she was. His voice was not so kind.

Joey Franklin leaned down and, once more, kissed her. As soon as their lips touched this time, she felt his tongue prodding into her mouth, and she turned her head away, surprised. He clamped down on her wrists with his strong hands. She thought that she said, "No."

He said, "Shhhh." The sound hissed.

"Five minutes later," Satoshi Hamamoto said, "I was no longer a little girl."

CHAPTER
24

I didn't recall the drive north from Palo Alto to the San Francisco airport and didn't know how I managed to go through the machinations of turning in my rental car without remembering a single step of the process. But I had returned the car. I had a receipt to prove it.

At least fifty people were lined up at the podium in the terminal to check in for their flights. I shuffled my feet along patiently until my turn came, hardly noticing the delay. I didn't get upset when the apologetic agent began a laborious explanation that concluded with the punch line that my electronically ticketed reservation had disappeared into some hard-drive version of hell. Not only that, but the agent also informed me that the flight I had been scheduled on was now full. The agent plucked away at the keyboard in front of him for what seemed like an eternity before he smiled at me and said, "Good." I shrugged my shoulders, thanked him, and accepted the offer he made of a front-row window seat on the next departure.

All I had in my carry-on was a book, a magazine, Lauren's laptop, and a bottle of water. Spotting an electrical outlet on the wall near my departure gate, I lowered myself to the carpet, leaned against the wall, and plugged in the laptop. I had a lot I wanted to write about my interview with Satoshi Hamamoto and needed to conserve the battery for the flight back to Denver.

Once I'd booted up the computer and rested my fingers on the keys I was almost surprised when they didn't start flying across the keyboard on their own. But they didn't. I didn't write anything at first.

Where I was initially lost was in understanding Satoshi's adaptation to her own trauma. I wanted to go back and sit with her for many more hours. I wanted to be quiet and perch beside her until she was ready to descend into whatever cavern held her fears, and I wanted to guide her fingertips as she explored the contours of the fissures in her defenses. I wanted to perceive for myself the psychological accommodations she'd had to make to deal with the back-to-back blows of being raped and having her sister murdered.

I wouldn't have that chance, though.

I was left with what I had observed that afternoon. What was it that I had seen? Satoshi was a smart, savvy, disarmingly honest young woman who was functioning at a high level at a university that demanded exemplary performance.

Freud said mental health was the capacity to love and the ability to work.

Apparently, Satoshi could work.

In our brief afternoon together she had demonstrated empathy, compassion, humor, and assertiveness. Important pieces, but I still didn't know whether or not she could love.

I had seen something else, too. I had seen a woman who was wary. Not just of me and whatever I, and Locard, represented. She was not just fearful of the consequences of telling me her story. Satoshi was frightened of something she felt might harm her imminently.

What was it?

I made no progress in answering my own question. And without having typed a word, I recognized that I had never asked her one of the most important things I had flown to California to learn. I folded up the computer, stuffed it in my shoulder bag, and rushed to the nearest pay phone. I glanced at my watch and decided to try her apartment.

The phone was answered on the first ring. I asked for Satoshi.

"No, she's um . . . not here. May I take a message?"

"Is she still at school? I have that number. Should I try her there?"

"Um. No. Do you want to leave a message?"

"Please. My name is Alan Gregory. I just met with her on campus and need to talk with her again as soon as possible."

"You're that guy from Colorado?"

"Yes."

"Where are you now? What's your number?"

"I'm at a pay phone. I don't think it will ring through. Wait, I have a cell phone with me."

"Give me that number? I may be able to have her call you right back."

"Can't you just give me her number?"

"She wouldn't be pleased if I did that."

More paranoia? I wondered. I dictated the number of my cell phone.

The woman on the other end of the line said, "Wait there five minutes. I'll try and find her and have her call. I'm Satoshi's roommate by the way. I'm Roz."

"Roz, is Satoshi okay?"

"What do you mean?"

"She seemed . . . worried about something today."

"She's not herself. Let's leave it at that."

I left it at that and said, "Thank you, Roz."

A few minutes later the phone rang and startled me, despite the fact that I was waiting for it to do just that. I answered it after half a ring, saying, "Satoshi?"

"Yes?"

"It's Alan Gregory. I'm at the airport. I forgot to ask you about something that I need to know. Do you mind?"

"I don't mind. It's all right. I only have a few minutes before I need to T.A. a class, though. I hope it won't take long."

"It shouldn't. I'll be . . . blunt. I'm trying to determine if your sister was involved in a relationship around the time she disappeared."

"You mean a romantic relationship? Are you asking about a boyfriend?"

"Yes."

"Not that I know of, no. She hung around with a group of kids, mostly Tami's friends. But she wasn't dating anyone. I would have known about that. She and I were close. We talked a lot."

Despite my promise of frankness, I had hoped to approach the rumor indirectly. That attempt had failed. So I decided to confront the innuendo straight on. "I've heard, but have not been able to substantiate, that she might have been involved with . . . an older man. Someone in town. Do you know anything about that?"

"You're kidding."

"No."

"Who?"

"I don't know."

"But you suspect someone specific, don't you? I can hear it in your voice that you are . . . I don't know, casting for a . . . a certain fish."

"I don't suspect someone in particular. But—at that time—there were people in Steamboat who suspected that the relationship between your sister and Raymond Welle might have been . . . less than professional. Improper, even."

"What? Raymond Welle? Dr. Welle? You think that my sister was involved with Dr. Welle?"

"Perhaps."

Her voice became hard and all remnants of her accent evaporated. "No way. She idolized him."

I didn't find that argument persuasive. "If she felt so positive about him, why would you rule out a more—"

"It's not possible. That's all."

"Satoshi, please help me to understand why. If the rumors are false, I need to be able to put them to rest."

"It's simple. Mariko would not have taken me to see him if he was being inappropriate with her."

"You *saw* Dr. Welle? You mean professionally?"

"You didn't know? I understood that you'd spoken with Dr. Welle already. My father said he gave you permission. I assumed Dr. Welle had told you that he'd met with me."

"But you didn't think he would have told me about the rape?"

"No. He wouldn't be allowed to, would he? Wouldn't he be forbidden to breach confidentiality?"

"Yes, he would have been prohibited, but the reality is that I didn't know you had seen him professionally. Your father didn't mention it to me. And Dr. Welle certainly didn't."

"My father didn't know. I only saw Dr. Welle once. It was Mariko's idea. It was right after I told her about . . . that time with Joey. She thought he could help me like he helped her."

I tried to keep the dates straight. "I thought you said that no one knew about what Joey did to you except for Mariko."

"I'm sorry. When I said that, I thought you already knew about my meeting with Dr. Welle."

"You saw Welle—what?—a day or two before your sister and Tami disappeared?"

"I saw him that same afternoon. After school with Mariko. She came with me. She took me to see him."

"To his office?"

"No. We met him at his ranch."

At his ranch? "Why did you meet him at his ranch?"

She seemed perplexed at my question. "That's where Mariko took me. I never asked why."

"Was he . . . helpful?"

She was suddenly hesitant. "He was kind. He listened to me. But he said he couldn't see me again without my parents' permission. And, of course, I couldn't ask them for permission. They would want to know why I needed

his help. I couldn't tell them that. Then Mariko disappeared and . . ."

"You never saw him again?"

"Never. Maybe around town once or twice, but not
professionally. Is that it? I really have to go."

"One more thing. Did he send you to someone else
for help? To a colleague, maybe?"

"No."

"Did he arrange for you to see a physician after the
rape?"

"No."

"Did he encourage you to report the assault to the
police?"

"No."

"To your parents?"

"I really do have to go. No. He didn't do any of those
things. He was . . . compassionate. That's all. I really
have to go."

I thanked her.

She said good-bye.

I had to give Welle credit for refusing to see Satoshi
for more than one psychotherapeutic intervention. There
were many reasons for him to refuse. Treating two sib-
lings in the same family was risky business in any circum-
stance. Although it was always a difficult choice to refuse
to see someone in crisis, it was the ethical decision when
the patient was a thirteen-year-old who was lacking parental permission for psychological treatment. But why
hadn't Welle made subsequent arrangements for Satoshi
to see a physician? And why hadn't he referred her on
to someone else in town for further evaluation and psychotherapy? I didn't understand that.

Perhaps Satoshi's memory of the events was clouded
by the trauma she had suffered.

Satoshi's conclusion that Mariko would not have taken
her younger sister to see a man with whom she was romantically involved was logically flawed. If the transference in Mariko's therapy permitted her to view Welle

positively enough to become involved with him romantically herself, she wouldn't have refused to involve her younger sister with him, either.

I was also troubled by the very fact that Mariko even know where Raymond Welle lived.

And why had Welle not told me he had seen Satoshi for a crisis visit? That puzzle wasn't so hard. I quickly determined that there were lots of reasons why he might not have been more forthcoming.

One, I hadn't asked.

Two, he didn't have permission from anyone to discuss Satoshi's visit with me or with anyone else.

Three, he actually didn't have the legal right to see Satoshi at all. She'd been thirteen, below the age where she is permitted in Colorado to consent to her own treatment.

Four, when he did agree to see her, he saw her at the Silky Road Ranch. Not at his office. A questionable decision, for sure.

I concluded that if I were in Raymond Welle's shoes, I'd probably keep Satoshi's visit to myself as well.

But with the information that Satoshi had given me about her visit to the Silky Road Ranch I was in a position to view Raymond Welle differently. I now knew that Welle knew that Joey Franklin was a rapist, which was something that Raymond Welle didn't know I knew.

I typed furiously from moments after takeoff until moments before landing, trying to capture the essence of what I'd learned from Satoshi Hamamoto. It seemed that the more I learned about the case of the two dead girls, the longer my task list grew.

At the top of the list: talking with Joey Franklin. Meeting the famous young golfer no longer felt at all like an option.

CHAPTER
25

Once back home I faxed my report to A. J. and spent a couple of hours puzzling through the new information with Lauren. She had as much difficulty as I did deciding what any of it actually meant.

While we started getting ready for bed, she spelled it out. "Let's pretend that it's all true. Right? Raymond Welle now has two possible motives for killing those girls, or at least being involved in their deaths. We were concerned when we thought he might have been covering up for being sexually involved with Mariko, correct?" I nodded. "Well, now he might also have been mixed up in order to cover up for whatever Joey Franklin had done to Satoshi."

I'd already traversed the same ground. "Sorry, that doesn't work for me. Why would he cover up what Joey had done? He kills Tami to protect Joey? Why? It doesn't make sense."

She was getting frustrated. "I don't know why. I don't think we know enough yet to know why. But every road we get on in this case seems to take us straight to Raymond Welle."

"And to the Silky Road Ranch."

"And to the Silky Road Ranch."

I said, "We're neglecting Dorothy Levin's disappearance. Can it be connected to Welle, too?"

"You haven't heard anything new on that, have you?"

I shook my head. "I'm scouring the news. Nothing either on her disappearance or on the shooting at the tennis house. And apparently the police in D.C. still can't find her husband."

My wife didn't hesitate for long. She said, "Sure, the disappearance can be tied in. She was accusing him of campaign improprieties. She was in the line of fire when someone took some shots at his campaign rally. She disappeared while she was interviewing witnesses in his hometown. Circumstances alone tie her to Ray Welle. Is there anything really there? I don't know. No one knows."

I was suddenly troubled by something Lauren had just said. But I wanted to think about it for a moment, so to keep her talking I said, "Pretend it's all related. What's the connection? What could it be?"

She thought about it while she disappeared into the bathroom to brush her teeth. She was still holding the toothbrush in her hand when she stuck her head back into the bedroom and said, "There's only one way that I can see for Welle to be connected to Dorothy's disappearance. Dorothy's disappearance and Tami's and Miko's deaths have to be related somehow. The investigation must overlap. Someone Dorothy was investigating for her article would have to have been involved—somehow—in Tami's and Miko's murders."

"Are you suggesting someone other than Welle? He's the constant in all this, obviously."

"I'm not sure. I think someone other than Welle, or in addition to Welle. I'd guess it would need to be someone who was involved in whatever campaign-finance irregularities Dorothy was investigating for the *Post*. Someone who also has a link to the murders of the two girls."

"That should be a relatively short list of people. Dorothy's article in the *Post* names names, doesn't it?"

"But it doesn't list her sources. I wonder if her editor would help us out."

"Her editor won't give up sources."

It was my turn to brush my teeth and pee. When I stepped back out of the bathroom Lauren was propped up in bed, rereading the fax of Dorothy's last *Post* article and making a list of all the names that had been mentioned.

I said, "I don't think I even bothered to mention this to you before, but Joey Franklin was in Steamboat the day that Dorothy was murdered. I saw signs welcoming him to town."

She stopped writing and glanced at me sideways. "He was?"

"Yeah, he played golf with Raymond Welle that morning. Welle was coming from the golf course while I was waiting at the ranch."

She said, "More circumstances I don't like." Emily waddled up and placed her head in Lauren's lap. She scratched the dog's ears. "Is Joey still up in Steamboat Springs?"

"I don't know. What are you thinking?"

"We could go talk to him."

"Just like that? I haven't cleared it with A. J."

"Do you think she'd mind?"

"No. As a matter of fact, I think she'd be pleased. But what do we ask him? If he remembers raping Satoshi Hamamoto? I don't know why, but I sort of suspect he'd deny it."

"No. We ask him things he has no reason to deny and see what he does. Did he know Tami's friends? Did he know Miko's friends? How much does he contribute to Welle's campaigns? And oh, by the way, did he know Satoshi?"

"You really want to do it?"

"We both have tomorrow off. It's hot down here. It's cool up there. And I'd really like to see what Joey has to say for himself."

"He doesn't have to talk with us."

"Nobody does. Why would he refuse, though?"

"Maybe because he's a rapist?"

"There is that." She raised the tablet she was writing on. "You know, I don't recognize any of these names. The gist of Dorothy's article is that when Welle was financing his first run at the House seat in 1990, and again during his second run in 1992, Japanese money was funneled into his campaign through local business interests that supported the ski area. The names in the article are mostly the Japanese who were involved."

"Not Taro Hamamoto, though?"

"No. Not him."

I tried to recall the details of Ray Welle's political career. "Welle wasn't elected in ninety, was he?"

"No. He didn't even get his party's nomination until ninety-two. And he won for the first time in ninety-four."

"His first nomination? That was after his wife was murdered?"

"Yes. Gloria actually died during the second campaign."

"A lot of death around that man."

I climbed into bed. "More than his share."

We decided to drive up to the mountains early and make a cold call on Joey Franklin. Either he'd be in town or he wouldn't. Either he'd agree to see us or he wouldn't.

The sky above us was still dark when we left the house. The sun finally cracked the lip of the horizon over the eastern plains as we were climbing Floyd Hill on I-70. I watched the show in my mirrors and Lauren spun on her seat to gaze as the sky transformed itself from the colors of morning coffee to the pastels of cotton candy.

We actually talked about baby names for most of the rest of the journey to Steamboat. So far our lists of favorites shared no common ground and the effort felt to me like a parlor game. Lauren compared it to jury selection. She argued that we were still at the stage where we both felt as though our preemptory challenges were infinite. Later, she assured me, push would come to shove and our discussions would get more contentious.

Twice we stopped so that Lauren could use restaurant bathrooms. She was developing a thing about fetal health and gas-station facilities.

* * *

Steamboat Springs' golfing choices are finite. There's the new Haymaker course and the proletarian Steamboat Golf Club, and there's the Robert Trent Jones–designed course at the Sheraton. Not surprisingly, the morning I'd been cooling my heels at the Silky Road, Joey and the congressman had been playing at the lovely Yampa River Valley course at the Sheraton. Lauren and I decided to try there first.

We arrived in the shadows of Mount Werner shortly after nine and tracked down the course starter at the pro-shop desk. He was busy copying names onto a log sheet. I asked if he knew where we could find Joey Franklin. Without hesitation, the starter told us that Joey's foursome wasn't due to tee off until almost ten. He thought Joey might be having breakfast upstairs on the deck and suggested we look out there for him.

"Who might he be with?" I asked.

"I thought he was meeting you." The starter finally glanced up from his paperwork. He looked at me suspiciously and smiled at Lauren, who took a half step forward.

She said, "Oh . . . he is, a little later." She didn't bother to mention the fact that Joey didn't know it yet.

The starter leaned over the counter, and his eyes traveled the length of Lauren's legs until arriving down at her feet. She was wearing open-toed sandals and had painted her toes the color of the grass on the greens. "You're not planning on playing in those, are you?"

She shook her head. "No. Not that it would make much difference to my score, I'm afraid." Lauren, to my knowledge, had never swung a golf club in her life.

He laughed. "I feel like that some days, too. Might as well play in flip-flops, you know? Pretty sure that Joey's meeting with Tony and Gary and . . . Larson. His sponsors. You know them?"

She shook her head and widened her eyes. "Haven't had the pleasure. But I'm certainly looking forward to it."

We headed up the stairs toward the deck. I said, "You're quite the flirt."

She replied, "Whatever." After a few more steps, she asked, "What did he mean by 'sponsors'? Like golf club companies? Nike and Reebok? Endorsements? That sort of thing?"

"I'm sure that Joey has plenty of endorsement contracts, but no. I think he meant the kind of sponsor who provides seed money for young golfers. When he was first starting out as a pro, Joey probably accepted financial backing for tour and living expenses from individuals or groups of individuals in exchange for a percentage of his future earnings on the tour. The people who bought in to provide that support are his sponsors."

She looked at me with raised eyebrows. "So these guys he's having breakfast with own a piece of him? Is it a big piece?"

"I don't know how the deals are structured. But when he makes money, they make money."

"And he's doing well, right?"

"Very well. I think he's in the top ten in earnings on this year's tour. His earnings could be in the millions."

"So these sponsors wouldn't be too happy to see their cash cow accused of an old rape?"

"Or a new one, for that matter. No, I'd imagine not."

Joey Franklin was indeed on the deck of the clubhouse having breakfast with three men his father's age. Joey drank cola with his breakfast. From my vantage he appeared bored with the company.

Lauren said, "We shouldn't walk over there together. I think that he'll view me as less threatening than he views you. Let me see if I can get him to talk with us."

I demurred happily. I wasn't looking forward to the confrontation anyway. From the doorway I watched Lauren approach the table and introduce herself to the four men. Two of them stood. Not Joey. She said something that made them all laugh and then leaned over and whispered something in Joey Franklin's ear. He whipped his head around so fast his face almost collided with hers. I couldn't hear what he said to her. But she corrected her posture, smiled, and nodded to him once before rejoining me near the entrance to the pro shop.

"He'll be over in a minute or two."

"What did you say to him?"

"Not much. I said I thought he was in a position to help us find his sister's murderer."

"That's it? You didn't mention Satoshi?"

She shook her head. Joey was coming our way.

He was my height, around six-two, and lanky. I thought he walked as though he had too many joints, almost like a rodeo cowboy who's been thrown from two or three too many bulls. His eyes were the lightest amber imaginable, almost golden, and he had his sister Tami's brilliant blond hair. He appeared younger than the images I'd seen of him on the news and in the sports pages. As he crossed the room toward us, his left hand flexed and unflexed repeatedly. I wondered if he was even aware that he was doing it.

I could understand women finding him attractive. My wife, I knew, was one of the ones who did.

Lauren said, "Joey Franklin, Dr. Alan Gregory."

We shook hands. His shake was unenthusiastic. He scratched behind his ear and said, "I tee off soon."

I replied, "This shouldn't take long. Where would you like to talk? Is there someplace we can go?"

He looked around as though it was the first time he'd ever been in the room. "Yeah. Follow me."

We did, and he led us up some stairs to a room with a gorgeous down-valley view. The Yampa was still swollen with snowmelt and it flowed laconically, like an overstuffed hog, toward its distant marriage with the Green River. We took chairs in front of big windows that left me facing Rabbit Ears Pass. On this gorgeous summer morning all the other golfers were enjoying the practice greens or the deck. We were alone inside. Which was good.

"You guys are what? Are you from that group that my dad hired to find who killed Tami?"

Lauren answered, "Not exactly hired. How about enlisted? Does that work? But yes, we're from Locard. We've been looking into your sister's murder and that of Mariko Hamamoto."

"I already talked to somebody. Some detective from the East Coast. He caught up with me in Florida."

"This is a different part of the investigation."

He rolled his eyes. "So you know who did it yet?" Joey was restless, and his posture on the chair left him in a position that was more horizontal than vertical. I estimated that he was around twenty-seven years old, but he seemed to have an inordinate amount of adolescent still wrestling around inside of him.

Lauren said, "Sadly, no," and gestured at me. "Tell him your role in the investigation, Doctor."

I used my best doctor-voice and gave my we-need-to-know-Tami-to-know-her-killer speech.

Joey was unmoved. "Yeah. What do you want from me?"

"What was your sister like?"

His left fist stayed clenched. "She was my sister. She was okay. I don't remember her that well. It was a long time ago."

Don't remember her that well? He was fourteen when she died. I'd bet good money he remembered every scratch on his first snowboard.

"Was she someone who would be likely to be particularly friendly to strangers, someone who—"

"Tami? She'd talk to anybody. Sometimes she wouldn't shut up." From his lips it wasn't a compliment.

"How'd she get along with your parents?"

"What does that have to do with anything?"

"I'm just trying to understand her frame of mind at the time she died. See if she might have been upset. Whatever."

"She and Dad argued sometimes. But she gave as good as she got with him. Mom was more annoying to her, though. Always wanted to be part of her life, you know?" He shivered. I wondered if it was an act.

I said, "No. I don't know."

Joey shrugged. His face said "tough shit." I hoped for more. I didn't get it.

Lauren asked, "Did you ever . . . I don't know . . . develop any theories about what happened?"

He made a noise with his lips. "Sure. Tami and Miko somehow managed to run into the wrong dude. What else could it have been?" He was remarkably lacking in curiosity about his sister's death.

The three of us went on in this unproductive vein for almost five minutes before I ran out of questions and Lauren took over. She asked about Tami's friends. Joey told us nothing new. He tapped his watch.

Lauren said, "Tell us about Satoshi. Miko's sister."

He said, "Who?" His expression didn't change at all. I couldn't tell if he was lying. If he was lying, he was good. I set my antennae for sociopathy.

"Satoshi Hamamoto."

He frowned. "Doesn't ring a bell. Sorry. You say she was Miko's sister? I didn't even know Miko had a sister."

"You didn't know a girl named Satoshi? A Japanese girl?"

"Should I?"

"You never went out with her?"

"I went out with lots of girls."

He smiled. I wanted to slap him.

Joey made his tee time.

"Wasted trip," was Lauren's conclusion about the visit. We were back in Boulder in time for dinner.

I volunteered to cook, so I was standing right next to the phone in the kitchen when Satoshi called.

CHAPTER
26

Although I would have been reluctant to admit it, the truth was that from the moment I'd first stepped into Joey Franklin's time-share jet for the trip to Washington to be introduced to Locard, I'd been enjoying myself playing forensic sleuth. I'd already begun to anticipate the sense of loss I would experience when Locard put this investigation to rest and my role with the organization ended.

The daily life of most workers is routine. That is as true for a psychotherapist as it is for a bus driver. For me, the opportunity to delve into the lives of Tami and Miko had provided a drastic alteration to my routine. Although I was using the same skills I typically employed every day in my office—clinical skills, interviewing skills, interpretive skills—I was using them in ways that enriched and intrigued me in an unanticipated manner.

In my daily work I resented the days or, more frequently, the nights that would come around when I wasn't able to shove intrusive thoughts about one of my patient's lives from my consciousness. But I discovered that I actually welcomed uninvited visits from the ghosts of Tami and Mariko and often allowed myself to lapse into reverie about the two girls and their lives. Sitting on the bedroom deck watching the sun set, walking the prairie trails with Emily, pedaling repetitively during long rides on my road bike, I encouraged the events and the people and the interviews and the history to tumble together in my mind as though they were gems requiring polish.

The events of 1988—the disappearance of the girls, their murder—felt distant to me, like history, even at times like fiction. The atrocity I was examining felt sanitized, safe. It was long ago that they died, and as much as I was trying to know them, I hadn't yet approached a spot where I could know them enough to grieve their deaths with any emotional honesty. The few tears I had shed for Tami and Miko were tears that sprang from the same small reservoir that supplies the almost artificial tears that are tugged by a movie or a novel that digs unabashedly for pathos.

But this was a story I was living and it was different from a book or a movie in that it was interactive and seductive. Each day I found that I could leave the pages and step into the story and find pieces unavailable to others. I could talk to the characters. I could follow Flynn Coe and Russ Claven to Steamboat. I could walk out my door and find Kevin Sample eating hamburgers on the lane. I could get off a plane in California and find Satoshi Hamamoto strolling the shady paths of the Stanford campus, looking over her shoulder. I could drive to Steamboat and get an audience with a hot young golfer who just happened to also be a rapist.

Even Dorothy Levin's disappearance hadn't impeded my enthusiasm for this quest I was on.

Each day as I awoke, I could hardly wait to turn the next page.

That all began to change with Satoshi's phone call.

"I got a telephone call today," she said without prelude. "At my apartment."

"Yes?" I was aware that I was trying to act as though getting mysterious calls from Satoshi happened all the time. I wasn't aware why I was trying to act that way.

"The person asked for me. I identified myself. Then . . . the person said that some things are best left forgotten."

"That's all?"

"That was it. The voice was soft but I think it was a man. After he said that, he hung up."

"You didn't recognize the voice?"

"No."

"And he didn't make an overt threat?"

"No, just said that some things are best left forgotten."

"Are you frightened?"

"Terrified."

"I can understand that. How can I be of help, Satoshi?"

She didn't hesitate. "I haven't decided that yet, but I don't think I can stay here right now. Things feel too creepy. There are plenty of places I could go. I have lots of friends. Family. I could even go to Japan and see my mother." She paused.

I wondered about school, but all I said was, "Yes?"

"But I've decided that I want to try to help with your . . . investigation. It's what Mariko would have done. So I'm thinking of coming to Colorado . . . to talk some more . . . maybe even go back to Steamboat to see if it helps me remember more about what happened. What do you think?"

"I think your help would be welcome by everyone at Locard."

"But you don't think I should come to Colorado?" She'd read the subtext in my words perfectly.

I chose my response with care. "This is the epicenter right now, Satoshi. Given the phone call you just described, I can't imagine it's the safest place for you to be."

She paused, too, but not for as long as I had. "But if my goal is to study aftershocks it's the only place to be. Right?"

I didn't know how to respond. I should have known better than to use an earthquake metaphor with a transplanted Californian.

"If I come," she asked, "will you help me?"

Maybe it was a mistake, but I asked, "How?"

Satoshi had two requests. They were both mundane.

If she came, she would want a place to stay. I offered our guest room, but she declined. "What if they're watching you, too?" she argued.

I thought next of Sam and told her that I thought I had a friend she could stay with.

Her other request was for enough cash for a one-way ticket to Japan, just in case she felt so unsafe she wanted to leave the U.S. She would pay me back, of course, but she didn't want to use her credit card and didn't want to involve her father, for obvious reasons.

I said that the money wouldn't be a problem.

She thanked me, said she'd let me know when she'd made a decision about coming to Colorado, and hung up.

CHAPTER
27

The next day was Saturday. Sam called around three o'clock in the afternoon and invited me to join him and his son, Simon, for a couple of hours of fun at the indoor climbing wall at the Boulder Rock Club on Mapleton. Although I didn't really enjoy rock climbing, I was tempted to meet them there purely for the distraction value. Watching Sam get all harnessed up while trying to prove Newton wrong about the laws of gravity sounded to me like the essence of entertainment.

But I declined, reminding myself I had responsibilities to attend to first. I wanted to consult with A. J. about my meetings with Satoshi and Joey. A. J.'s machine picked up my call and her recorded greeting referred all Locard business to Kimber. I left a cryptic message asking that she call me as soon as possible.

Next I called Kimber at his elegant loft in D.C. "Kimber? It's Alan Gregory in Colorado."

"Alan? I'm afraid you caught me in the theater looking at rushes from the second *Star Wars* prequel. George sent them over by messenger. Fascinating work, truly evolutionary. I don't know how he ever manages to decide to leave some of this footage on the floor." I thought Kimber sounded surprised to hear from me. Not exactly pleased. Not particularly displeased. I decided that what I was hearing in his voice was a slight swell of curiosity.

George *Lucas?* Kimber certainly had an interesting roster of friends. "What a treat to be able to see those."

"A privilege, actually. George has his secretive side, to be certain. But with friends who like movies, love movies . . . it's often like Christmas or . . . well, Halloween."

"Well, I'm sorry to bother you on a weekend, Kimber, but there've been some troublesome developments regarding the case, and A. J.'s answering machine refers calls to you. Is she okay?"

His reply came after a slight pause. "The purpose of your call to her was . . . ?"

"Lauren and I just met with Joey Franklin and I thought I should let someone on the committee know what was happening."

"Yes?" He made the solitary word feel like a meal. His voice was that rich and full.

"I assume that A. J. has kept you up-to-date on my recent interview with Satoshi Hamamoto? Mariko's sister?"

"We haven't spoken about it, but yes, I have a copy of your report."

"You're aware of the rape accusation she made against Joey Franklin?"

"Yes. Proceed, please. Go on."

We did go on this way for almost ten minutes as I reiterated the details of my trip to California and the frustrations of meeting with Joey Franklin. Kimber's manner encouraged me to do almost all the talking. I ended up feeling as though I had been a patient in an initial psychotherapy session. By the conclusion of our conversation I'd learned virtually nothing that was helpful and certainly didn't feel any better.

His last line wasn't, "I'll see you next week." It was, "Please keep me informed as things progress on your end. And Alan?"

"Yes?"

"A. J. is . . . not well. In fact, she is in the hospital. Please don't trouble her with any of this. I will take responsibility for communicating with her and I will be your contact at Locard for the time being."

"What's wrong with her?" I suspected that her MS

had flared. Given that she was hospitalized, that it had flared seriously.

"She would prefer that I be discreet about the details. I'll send along your best wishes. Will that suffice for now? If any of these developments require your continued attention someone will be in touch."

He paused briefly. I thanked him.

"And your sweet wife? I hope she is well. Mary is full of nothing but praise for her efforts and her legal acumen."

"Lauren is fine, Kimber. I'll pass along the kind words from Mary and tell her that you said hello."

Satoshi's subtle paranoia was infectious.

Just in case someone—who?—had a way of monitoring Lauren's or my bank accounts—how?—it didn't feel prudent to give Satoshi the money she wanted from our savings at the credit union. Where would I go if I needed a large quantity of cash in a hurry? Easy. I walked across the lane and interrupted Adrienne as she was plucking slimy green bugs off the tomato plants in her garden. In the same tone of voice I would have used to borrow a cup of sugar, I asked if she would withdraw two thousand dollars from her bank for me. I promised to pay her back.

She, of course, demanded details. Adrienne trusted me; I knew she wasn't especially worried about her money being returned. Anyway, Adrienne had more money than just about any human being needed. She just liked having leverage. I spoon-fed her about half of the facts before she agreed to get me the cash. I had expected to have to tell her much more. She ran upstairs without bothering to kick off her garden shoes. While she was gone I played catch with Jonas with a pink-and-gray Nerf football. My mouth dropped open when Adrienne came back down to the family room with a stack of hundreds and fifties.

"That's eighteen hundred. I'll get you the rest tomorrow."

"You keep this kind of money in the house?"

"What other kind of money is there? I don't have time to be running to the bank every other day for petty cash."

Petty cash? The pile of money in my hand actually had heft. "You have a safe up there?"

"If I did, would I want to advertise it? Stop poking at me and remember your manners. Say 'Thank you, Adrienne.' "

"Thanks, Adrienne. You're great."

"Yes, I am." She turned her back to walk away before she added with a devious smile, "And in lieu of interest, I want updates."

When my patients need to inform me of an emergency, the message on my voice mail instructs them that they must leave a verbal message before dialing my pager number and punching in the phone number of the location where I can reach them. The system serves a myriad of purposes, one of which is to ensure that my patients think twice before categorizing a situation as an emergency.

Monday, at almost 3:30, my pager vibrated. I was in the process of concluding a session that had started at 2:45, so I waited a few minutes until my patient was out the door before I checked my beeper. The screen read an unfamiliar number. I tried my voice mail to look for a corresponding message that might explain the emergency. There wasn't one.

I picked up the phone and punched in the number on my pager screen. After half a ring a voice said, "Yes."

"This is Dr. Gregory. I'm returning a page to this number."

"Hi, it's me."

With those words, Satoshi Hamamoto let me know she had indeed decided to come to Boulder.

"Satoshi? You're in town?"

"I drove straight through. I'm so tired I'm shaking.

But I'm all right. I decided I wanted to help. Did you keep your promise about . . . not telling my story?"

"Pretty much. My wife is part of Locard, so she knows what you told me. And to get you someplace to stay I had to tell the person I described to you the last time you called. Besides the two of them, yes, I kept my promise. I don't feel I have much choice. If I talk about the rape, you'll deny whatever I say, right?"

"Sorry. Right."

"How does my friend get in touch with you?"

"Does your friend have a pager?"

"Yes."

"I'll take that number."

I gave it to her.

"Would you please tell your friend to expect a call."

"He already does. And I'll get the money to him. I have eighteen hundred so far. More is available."

I heard her yawn. "That's probably enough for now, thanks. It's just a net; I'm not planning on needing it."

"Anything else I can do?"

She didn't answer my question. Instead, she said, "I hardly know you, yet I'm trusting you. That's not like me." She made it sound almost like an accusation.

"I know. And I'm doing my best to deserve it. There's another side to this, though. I'm trusting you, too."

She laughed. "Funny, I hadn't thought about that. Yes, you are. That's good. I like that."

"Satoshi, do you really think Joey is sending somebody after you?"

"No. From what I've been able to learn about him over the Internet, I don't think he has the balls. I'm sure he has money people—agents, managers, people like that who are living off of him. They're more likely to come after me than he is."

"It could be one of his sponsors."

"What do you mean 'sponsors'?"

I explained about the financial relationship between sponsors and young touring golf pros.

"I didn't know about that part of the business. So these sponsors have a lot to lose if Joey's career tanks?"

"Absolutely. They might even have more to lose than Joey does."

"You have their names?"

"No."

"Shouldn't be hard to find out. I'll look into it. I have some other ideas, too. Some long shots. I've done nothing but think about this all night long. Do you have any idea how much empty space there is between San Francisco and Denver?"

Sam paged me a few minutes after six. I was packing up to go home for the day.

He said, "She's sleeping. She's safe. Neat kid. I like her. You? You're lucky I like her."

"Thank God. I've been worried. Where is she?"

"Just in case she has a reason to be worried, I don't think I should tell you that. Certainly not over the phone. Know what I mean?"

"Yes. I'm sorry I asked. I'm not used to this." I sighed. "At least Sa—she's . . . safe. Listen, I need to get you that money. Should I drop it by the police department?"

"I don't think that's the best idea. Here's what we'll do instead."

I hadn't seen Sherry, Sam's wife, for months. She looked harried when, twenty minutes later, I walked in the door to her flower shop on the west end of Pearl Street, only a few blocks from my office.

I embraced her and commented that she was staying open late on a Monday evening.

"Spousal request. You know about those? It's been a hell of a day. My employee had an emergency root canal this morning so I've been by myself since eleven. Anybody ever tries to tell you that retail's a fun way to make a living, don't believe them. Listen, you have something to give me for Sammy? I'm sorry to be so rushed with you, but I have to run and get Simon at child care. I'm already so late they're going to scream." She tapped her watch.

I handed Sherry the envelope. She stuffed it into her shoulder bag and offered me a bouquet of lilies to give to Lauren. "Sam insisted," she said. I was about to say it wasn't necessary when I realized that Sam probably didn't want me to be observed leaving the shop empty-handed. I thanked Sherry for the flowers and stayed at her side while she locked the door.

Traffic was a bitch going home. Every decision I made was the wrong one. Broadway was gridlocked by a car-bike accident on the Hill. The left turn signal at Table Mesa was short cycling. An old Mercedes in front of me on South Boulder Road was belching enough diesel exhaust to choke a herd of bison.

I knew I should have taken Ninth to Baseline and cut across on Fifty-fifth. I just knew it.

Lauren had been concerned about my late arrival home. She expressed her concern verbally when I walked in the door, yet the whole time her eyes were darting between my hands and my face. Her expression clearly communicated her disappointment that I'd apparently forgotten to bring home the spinach pizza I'd promised her for dinner.

I looked down at my hands, too. As though it were their fault. I said, "I'm so sorry."

She said, "That's all right." She didn't mean it.

"I'll take you out, okay? We'll go someplace nearby."

"There's no place good that's nearby." She was coming perilously close to pouting.

"Then I'll go back out. I'll get the pizza you want. The one I promised. You were really looking forward to it."

"That's silly. You'd have to go back downtown. I don't know, maybe I'll just fix something here. Open a can of soup." Even a dolt would know that she didn't really want to eat canned soup.

"I'll make you an omelette. Tarragon? You like those."

"I don't know if I want an omelette." She didn't.

It appeared that she wasn't predisposed to let me off the hook easily. I tried a different tack. "Satoshi's in town."

"No!"

Despite a horrendous serve, the point was mine.

I made her an omelette with spinach and tarragon and gave her a foot massage for dessert.

Lauren complained of fatigue shortly after eating and carried a book with her to bed. I plugged her laptop into an outlet near the couch in the living room so I could review all my notes about the two dead girls. I had a nagging feeling that I was missing something important about the case.

Whatever it was that I might be missing wasn't apparently after forty-five minutes of looking. I could find only one item that had remained unaccomplished: I'd promised myself that I would make contact with the high school teachers whose names I had culled from the TV news stories that had been broadcast after the girls disappeared.

I checked the time: 9:15. Not too late to make a phone call—especially to a graduate student. I punched in Kevin Sample's number in Fort Collins. He sounded pleased to hear from me. "I was going to call you tomorrow or the next day," he said. "About that thing with my uncle Larry."

I drew a blank. What thing with his uncle Larry? Oh yeah, the release so that Kevin could talk to Raymond Welle about Brian Sample's psychotherapy. I had hoped Kevin had forgotten about it.

I stammered, "So your uncle agreed to write the letter?"

"Not exactly. He's still protective of me. He said he'd do it but he wants someone else to screen the information first—you know, he didn't want me to be the one to hear things about my dad directly from Dr. Welle. So he wrote a letter that authorizes you to talk to Dr. Welle about my dad. And he wrote you a letter saying it's okay for you to talk to me about whatever you think is relevant. I hope that covers everything and that it's all right with you."

If I agreed, I would have to schedule yet another meeting with Raymond Welle to talk about one of his patients. This particular patient happened to be the one who had executed Welle's wife. I thought I'd rather schedule a sigmoidoscopy. I said, "Sure, I guess, um, Kevin. I'll do that. I mean, I'll consult with Dr. Welle. When he and I can fit it in."

"Thanks. I told my uncle I thought you would. He's already sent the letter to Dr. Welle. I'll have him send you copies. But you called me. Now what can I do for you after I've monopolized the whole darn conversation?"

I explained that I wanted to talk with some faculty at the high school who might have known Tami and Miko and ran the names I'd gleaned from the video footage by him. Did he remember any of them? After tossing the names back and forth for a minute, he suggested I start with two: Stuart Bird, the former principal, and Ellen Leff, who had taught English at the high school. Before I hung up, I nonchalantly inquired whether Kevin knew Mariko's little sister, Satoshi.

If it was possible to blush over the phone, Kevin managed. He said, "Yes, yes. She was . . . around some. She was a couple of years younger than us, I think. Maybe— what?—three? I'm not sure. She liked to run. I did, too."

"Have you stayed in touch with her over the years? Know what happened to her after . . . ?"

"Her family left Steamboat right around the same time we did, which was 1990 or so. I tried to . . . you know, help her . . . after her sister was . . . killed. But . . . she wasn't that interested."

I prodded, but couldn't get him to say anything more.

"You must have been able to be a support for Joey Franklin as well. I mean for the same reason."

"No," he said. "I wasn't much help to Joey."

*   *   *

I couldn't track down a number for Stuart Bird through directory assistance, but Ellen Leff answered her phone on the first ring.

As obtusely as I could, I explained my role in the investigation of Tami and Mariko's murder and asked if I might pose a few questions.

Ellen seemed thrilled at the prospect. She said, "Let me turn down the tube. I'm ready and waiting."

Ellen liked to chat. It took me almost thirty minutes to confirm that she wasn't going to tell me anything that might shake my existing portrait of Tami Franklin. She acknowledged that she didn't know Mariko well. Her apology about that ran for well over a minute.

I thanked her for her time.

She said, "Oh, you don't have to thank me. I still pray for those two girls every Sunday. Worst thing I ever saw in this town. We had those murders and then we had what happened to Gloria Welle—Lord, Lord. And then there was that skiing accident with Doak Walker? Such a nice, nice man. Awful! But Tami and Mariko. That was the worst. Absolutely.

"And still you know it's funny—ironic funny—how things turned out. I mean how crucial those two Franklin kids have been to this town. Tami's murderer is still running loose out there—and I swear her death is like a wound that won't heal for anybody. And now the whole world seems to be in love with our little Joey. I would have guessed it was going to be the other way around. That Tami would be Steamboat's angel. And Joey would be the one causing us to pull out our hair. And it's not just me who'd think that way, everybody would have guessed it wrong."

I woke up. I sat up. "Really, Ellen?" I didn't have to put any effort into sounding surprised. "What do you mean?"

"Excuse me "

"Why would you have expected that Joey would have everyone pulling out their hair?"

"My good friend, Jackie Crandall? She taught Joey

history in junior high. Always thought he was a dark one. In fact, she's the one whose idea it was to send him to Dr. Welle for professional help. And now look what Joey's accomplished. I swear that Ray Welle worked miracles with him. He truly did. I was sure that Franklin boy was heading for serious trouble."

"What did your friend mean by that? By calling Joey 'dark'? Why did she refer him for therapy?"

She tsked me. "Are we just gossiping now, Dr. Gregory? I don't mind talking during recess, but I don't want to—"

"Believe me, Ellen, this is important. I have no reason to gossip with you. I'm trying to know Tami's whole . . . family."

She lowered her voice to a whisper. I had to strain to hear her. "For Jackie, that incident in the girls' bathroom did it. That was the last straw."

I waited for her to go on. She didn't. I said, "The one where, uh—"

"He and the Lopes boy drilled that hole in the wall so they could watch the girls doing their business. That one, mmm-hmm. Doesn't get much sicker than that, does it?"

Her question was rhetorical. I didn't contradict her.

CHAPTER
28

I hit myself so hard on the forehead with the heel of my hand that I startled myself into yelling, "Ouch!"

Lauren called from the bedroom. "Are you okay?"

I yelled back that I was fine. I couldn't believe it. *Of course.* It wasn't Tami Franklin or Cathy Franklin who had been in therapy with Ray Welle. It was Joey Franklin.

That's why Ray Welle had looked so smug while he was denying to me that he ever treated Tami or Cathy. And that's yet another reason why Ray Welle refused to see Satoshi for psychotherapy after she accused Joey of raping her.

My mental to-do list grew a little longer. I wanted to try to discover the dates of Joey's treatment with Welle. I wondered if Welle was still treating Joey when he raped Satoshi.

I'd often wondered what it would be like to be a psychotherapist in a small town like Steamboat Springs. Even in a town the size of Boulder, with over 100,000 people, lives sometimes overlapped so that the boundaries between patients' histories became blurred. In a smaller town like Steamboat, the lines would inevitably intersect like the cross-stitched threads in a piece of fabric. Patient A would talk about patient B, who would be dating patient C, whose father would be patient A's accountant, or the therapist's own golfing buddy. And the psychologist would be alone in the middle of the mesh, entrusted with the responsibility to keep everyone's secrets from everyone else. And entrusted with the mandate not to allow what he or she might learn from one patient to influence how another is treated.

I found myself getting a headache as I tried to imagine the complications that would ensue for the small-town psychologist if patient A wasn't just talking about patient B.

What if patient A was guilty of raping her?

I made a logical leap that seemed reasonable. I concluded that Raymond Welle's treatment of Joey Franklin was either ongoing or had recently been terminated when Mariko took Satoshi to see Welle after the rape. I then decided that it didn't make any difference which version was true.

In Welle's circumstances—with Satoshi literally on his doorstep accusing one of his patients, or recent ex-patients, of rape—what would I do? What ethical and legal obligations would I have as a psychologist?

Like Welle, I probably would have refused to offer Satoshi any ongoing therapeutic intervention after the emergency visit. The number of potential conflicts that would be inherent in simultaneously treating a possible rapist *and* his accuser was too astronomical for me to calculate. But, unlike Welle, I would have encouraged Satoshi to seek other help. At the very least, a physician should have promptly examined her. Pregnancy was an obvious concern. Sexually transmitted disease had to be considered. And I would have referred Satoshi to a colleague for further psychological evaluation and, if necessary, treatment for the psychological consequences of the assault.

The legal issues Welle confronted were less murky than the ethical ones. Welle couldn't divulge the information he had learned from Satoshi to anyone else without her permission unless Satoshi had threatened further retribution against Joey. That was Colorado law. Without threat of future harm to some individual, Welle was sworn to maintain Satoshi's confidentiality. So Welle had been under no legal mandate to report Joey's crime to anyone.

I also considered whether Welle could have used the child-abuse exception to doctor-patient privilege to divulge the rape to the police. If Welle reasonably suspected that Satoshi had been the victim of child abuse, he was obligated to report it to authorities, confidentiality be damned. The problem with that argument was that at the time of the rape Joey Franklin was—legally, at least—a child, too. The age difference between him and Satoshi was not great enough to permit the act of sex between them to be classified either as statutory rape or as child abuse.

I tried to guess what Welle's motives might have been for not referring Satoshi to either a physician or another psychologist. It was difficult to imagine that he had concluded that such a referral wasn't warranted. By her own report, penetration had occurred during the rape, so a physical examination should have been pro forma. Satoshi also admitted being quite traumatized emotionally. So why would Welle not refer her on for further assessment or treatment? The most cogent explanation I could come up with was that he wished to contain the circle of people who were aware that the rape had occurred. Perhaps Welle didn't want his colleagues in town to become aware that Joey Franklin had been accused of rape. Or perhaps he didn't want his colleagues to know that he was treating an accused rapist.

The possibility also existed that Joey had revealed his intentions about assaulting Satoshi while in psychotherapy with Welle. If that had occurred, Welle's failure to alert the police or to warn Satoshi would make him legally vulnerable.

Was Welle protecting Joey? Was he protecting himself? Was he protecting someone else?

I didn't know answers to any of the questions. And I doubted that Ray Welle would be inclined to enlighten me.

The events themselves felt jumbled. I pecked out a

chronology on the laptop in an attempt to order them.
I wrote:

> *Sometime prior to the autumn of 1988, Raymond Welle
> began treating Joey Franklin in psychotherapy after an
> incident where Joey was accused of voyeurism in a girls'
> bathroom at his middle school. Had there been other inci-
> dents involving Joey? It appears likely.*
>
> *Three days before Tami and Miko disappear in the late
> fall of 1988, Joey Franklin rapes Satoshi Hamamoto.*
>
> *That night, Satoshi tells her sister, Mariko, about the
> rape.*
>
> *Did Mariko then confide Satoshi's secret to Tami Frank-
> lin? It would have been an awkward disclosure, since the
> accused was Tami's sibling. But I can't rule it out.*
>
> *Two days later, Miko accompanies Satoshi on a visit to
> Raymond Welle's Steamboat Springs ranch.*
>
> *That night—only a few hours later—Miko and Tami
> disappear on their way to the hot springs at Strawberry
> Park.*
>
> *Months later, the girls' bodies are discovered near
> Tami's wrecked snowmobile. The discovery takes place
> not anywhere close to Strawberry Park, but rather farther
> up the same scenic Elk River Valley that is home to the
> ranches of both the Welles and the Franklins.*

No matter how I looked at it, Raymond Welle was
right in the middle of everything and everybody. He had
treated Mariko in psychotherapy. He was, or had just
concluded, treating Joey Franklin, which meant he'd had
professional contact with at least one of Joey's parents.
Probably both of Joey's parents. At Mariko's urging, he
had just completed an emergency session with Satoshi.
In fact, Welle seemed to have an established relationship
with everyone involved in the conundrum with the possible exception of Tami Franklin.

What else was going on in Steamboat during that
three-day period in the late autumn of 1988?

In 1988, Phil Barrett was sheriff of Routt County.

Gloria Welle was raising her horses.

Raymond Welle was running a successful small town psychology practice and toying with starting a radio show. Maybe he was already dreaming of running for Congress.

And something else. What? I didn't know. But something else must have been going on, too.

And now, years later? Satoshi Hamomoto feared that someone might try to silence her. Why?

I could think of only one answer. Someone wanted to keep her from accusing Joey Franklin of a very old rape. Was that enough of a motive?

To me, it didn't seem sufficient.

If Satoshi ever went public with her accusation, which seemed unlikely, Joey could just deny the story. If the national media picked up the allegation, Joey might suffer some temporary damage to his reputation, but he would survive it. Professional athletes are routinely accused of criminal activities and their careers seem to proceed unhindered by the charges. In fact, their careers often proceed unhindered by a subsequent conviction.

If the threat of disclosure of the rape wasn't the motivation for the danger Satoshi was in, then what was it? The timeline I'd just typed suggested that there had to be a link to whatever originally motivated the murders of Tami and Miko. Something that tied Satoshi to Tami's and Miko's deaths. Perhaps something that Satoshi wasn't even aware of.

What was it?

I didn't know. But I knew whom I wanted to ask.

I called Sam and asked if his guest was awake and available. While he and I were negotiating a safe place to rendezvous in town, the fax machine started spitting out a two-page memo to Lauren from Mary Wright in Washington.

The gist of the memo was that Mary was asking Lauren for advice about two things. First, she wanted a review of Colorado statutes and procedures relating to search warrants. And second, she wanted to know the circumstances under which a Colorado governor could usurp the power of a local district attorney and appoint a special prosecutor for a criminal investigation.

I momentarily stopped breathing when I read that the suspect property for the search warrant was Raymond Welle's home, the Silky Road Ranch. Mary informed Lauren that inquiries were being made of Representative Welle to determine whether he would voluntarily grant Locard investigators access to his property. Should he refuse, Wright seemed prepared to recommend approaching the local district attorney in Routt County to petition a judge to obtain a search warrant. Should the DA refuse to proceed, Mary Wright was devising a strategy for an end around.

It was obvious to me that Mary Wright thought she had grounds for probable cause. Given her reputation, I didn't doubt that she was right.

I wondered what Flynn and Russ had discovered that pointed them toward the Silky Road.

Lauren was asleep. I left her a note that I was going to town to meet with Sam and Satoshi, and headed to Sherry Purdy's flower shop. I spent the time driving across the Boulder Valley trying to imagine what life was like right now in Raymond Welle's camp.

He was in the midst of a senatorial campaign that had necessitated his choosing not to run for reelection to his relatively secure seat in the House of Representatives. The *Washington Post* was investigating him for campaign-finance irregularities dating back ten years or more. With the bloody disappearance of the *Post* reporter who had broken the campaign-finance story, the rest of the national media had sharpened their focus on the accusations that had initially been front-page news only in the *Washington Post* and in the Denver papers.

In addition, Locard had shown up in Raymond Welle's universe and started actively investigating the possibility that he'd had a role in the murder of two young girls a dozen years before. Satoshi Hamamoto, who Welle knew had accused one of Welle's ex-patients of rape, had become a loose cannon. And now Locard's investigation had apparently proceeded to a point where the Locard forensic team felt that it was reasonable to consider asking the local prosecutor in Routt County to petition a judge for permission to search Welle's ranch for physical evidence that might be related to the murders of Tami and Mariko.

Indeed, Mary Wright felt strongly enough about the evidence she had before her to inquire about procedures that would bypass the local prosecutor should he or she turn out to be reluctant to ask a judge for a search warrant.

Raymond Welle was not having a very good month. Given the circumstances, I assumed he had little choice but to agree to a voluntary search of his property. Should he deny Locard permission to search, they were inclined to present whatever new evidence they had accumulated to the local prosecutor and to a local judge. That maneuver would greatly increase the risk of leaks to the media. And that was something that Welle could ill afford.

Sam hadn't turned on any lights, and the interior of his wife's flower shop was streaked with shadows from the streetlights along Pearl. The sweetness of the perfume from the blossoms felt especially cloying in the dark. I followed Sam past a wall of coolers to a crowded back room where Sherry did the paperwork associated with her business. Satoshi was there waiting for us.

She stood and embraced me, kissing me quickly on one cheek. I found myself surprised by the intimacy of the greeting. She smiled warmly at Sam—she had obviously developed a quick affection for him.

Sam wasted no time. He asked me, "What's up?"

I looked at Satoshi as I answered. "I just learned that Raymond Welle was treating Joey Franklin in psychotherapy when he raped you, Satoshi."

She lowered her chin and exhaled in a rush through

her nose. It was as though I had hit her in the gut. It took her half a minute to process the information and to regain her composure.

"For what?" she asked. "Why was Dr. Welle seeing him?" I'd expected her to be full of venom. I found the question curious.

"His assault on you apparently wasn't the first time he'd . . . taken advantage of young girls."

"So Dr. Welle knew about Joey. And he knew . . . what Joey was . . . capable of doing."

"Possibly, yes."

Sam asked how I knew, and I explained about my call to Ellen Leff, Tami's old English teacher, and about her story regarding Joey and his trouble at school. Satoshi's expression was tight as I spoke, but her eyes were unfocused. I guessed that her agile mind was navigating the waters I'd stirred up.

"It's not enough," she said. "It still isn't adequate to explain why someone would threaten me. I can't prove what Joey did to me. If he denies it, and especially if Dr. Welle denies knowing about it, my accusation would be meaningless." Without even having heard Joey's denial that he even remembered Satoshi, and without even considering the fact that confidentiality would prevent Welle from commenting on the case, Satoshi had reached the same conclusion that I had.

I said, "I agree. It leaves me thinking that you must know something else, Satoshi. Perhaps something that felt inconsequential at the time. But something that's crucial to someone today. Something that puts someone at enough risk that they are willing to try to scare you into silence."

She raised her eyebrows and they disappeared beneath her thin bangs. "What?" she asked.

Sam nodded his big head twice and shifted on his chair. He said, "Let's see if we can figure that out." He leaned close to Satoshi and his voice softened. "What I'd like to do now, tonight—what we're going to do now—is we're going to talk about those few days back then and see if we can help you remember some things that you might have forgotten. Or maybe see if there're some things that you remember that have never seemed particularly important until now. How does that sound? You ready to get started? I'm going to be asking you a lot of questions. I'll probably be a little redundant. And I'm going to ask for a lot of detail."

"I'm ready."

He turned and faced me. "Alan, go get us all some coffee. I'm afraid we could be here for a while. I'm sure something's open on Pearl. Get me a Danish or something, too. I really like bear claws."

Satoshi said, "I'll have tea. A plain bagel maybe, if you don't mind."

Sam said, "She'd prefer tea. Get her some tea."

I stepped out of the room and ventured out onto Pearl Street. The night was warm, and the sidewalk was pocked with raindrops that had fallen since we'd been inside. I guessed it had been a thunderstorm cell about the size of a city block. The air was heavy. For an hour or so Boulder would pretend that it had humidity.

I hesitated outside Peaberry's but decided to buy our provisions across the street at the Trident. Something about the place always took me back to the Boulder I'd fallen in love with in the seventies. The Trident was careless and cluttered and autocratic and democratic all at once. The coffee was reliably good. The pastry case was usually overflowing.

Sam got his cherished bear claw. Actually, I bought him two. They were out of plain bagels. Satoshi was going to have to settle for poppy. I went back and forth over the selection of teas. After a mental toss of the coin I chose Darjeeling.

She accepted the pebbled bagel and the cup of tea with grace.

CHAPTER
29

I thought it resembled a pas de deux between an elephant and a doe.

Over the years, Sam had often surprised me with his physical agility. In fact, a time or two, when I'd seen him dance with his wife, Sherry, he had struck me as peculiarly light on his big feet. But I'd rarely seen him dart and probe with the sensitivity and delicate touch that he demonstrated as he interviewed Satoshi about the ancient rape and the tragic days that followed.

The most glaring difference between a psychologist-interviewer and a cop-interviewer is that the cop treasures the facts more than the psychologist does. Facts for me, as a psychologist, are the smooth rocks I step on as I follow my patient across a riverbed. They are the treads I use to ascend a staircase behind her as she climbs toward a destination I cannot imagine. I try never to succumb to the trap of allowing the facts to masquerade for truth, for truth is a commodity that sometimes bears little resemblance to my patients' recall of the facts. But for a cop, like Sam, the facts are everything. They are the gilded riches in the hold of the sunken galleon. When Sam is in full cop mode, the facts are what he's diving for.

As he proceeded with Satoshi—guiding, prodding, probing—I spotted at least a dozen instances where I would have followed different paths from the ones that Sam chose to pursue. A spark of anger that flared in the corners of Satoshi's mouth would have warranted a diversion to explore the source of the detonation. The fingernails that she dug into the flesh of her thigh would have earned a soft "What is that about?" But Sam wasn't interested in reading the signs that were flashing about eruptions in Satoshi's underlying affect; his eyes were focused on the hard details of the ancient wreckage.

In the end—and the end didn't come until the clock in Sherry's office read 2:18—I was pretty certain Sam had learned a story different from the one that I would have learned.

The story of the rape itself didn't change much in the retelling.

Sam insisted on hearing much more than I would have about the setting where the rape occurred. He pestered Satoshi for detail after detail about possible witnesses who might have been nearby. Where were the closest houses? What was Joey wearing that afternoon? Did he remove any of his clothing? What color was it? Sam wanted to know exactly what she did after she returned home. When had she showered? What had she done with her own clothing? At one point he asked if she knew whether Joey had ejaculated during the assault. Satoshi tightened her lips and nodded in response before she turned away from him and faced me. I felt a plea in her eyes, as though she wished that I would rescue her from his onslaught of queries. I wanted to.

I didn't.

A moment later she turned back to Sam and said, "When it dripped down my thigh, I didn't know what it was. There was blood, too. Mariko explained to me what it was."

I couldn't imagine that those prurient facts or the innumerable mundane ones were actually important to Sam. His purpose, I guessed, was to try to goad Satoshi's memory to do some yoga. He wanted her to begin to stretch her mental muscles and find recollections that had disappeared under the weight of the dual pressures of time and suppression. Sam needed Satoshi to be limber for what was to come.

What was to come? At Sam's insistence, Satoshi recalled the details of the conversation she'd had with her sister, Mariko. Satoshi's memory of this event was quite vivid, as though it were a relic she had refused to bury along with her sister. She recalled that telling Mariko what Joey had done to her took only about as long as the rape had taken—a matter of only a few minutes. Satoshi guessed three or four. In Sam's hands, though, the retelling of the conversation took most of an hour. What had Mariko wanted to do after she learned about the rape? Was she going to tell someone else? Would she break a confidence and tell their parents what she had learned? Did she want to go and confront Joey and cut off his nuts? What?

Satoshi's patience with Sam was admirable. She answered the questions, one after another, the best she could. Some she couldn't respond to because she couldn't find the memories; others she remembered like that morning's breakfast.

Sam permitted a few tangents. One was especially poignant to me. Satoshi wanted to talk about the friendship between Tami and Miko.

Her words were halting. She wasn't comfortable with the territory. "She was Mariko's first American girlfriend. Tami was. Before coming to Colorado, our family had been in Switzerland for, I think, two years. And before that, of course, we were in Japan. Tami was something new for her. For both of us. I remember feeling jealous. Tami would lie for Mariko and they would go off on their own after school. At night, at home, they would whisper secrets on the telephone for hours and hours. I felt as though I was no longer the sister. Tami was more important to Mariko than I was—that's how it felt to me. For a long time, I tried to follow along. To be with them. To ski with them. To hang out with them in town.

"I wanted a friend like Tami. That was part of it. But I also wanted my sister back."

Sam stayed in her footsteps, always behind her, always filling her shadows with his mass. Occasionally he asked for a clarification. When she stopped speaking at the end of a long response to another in a series of questions about what she had told Mariko the night of the rape, Sam said, "Good, good. That's great." I mistakenly assumed he had concluded his questioning.

But he soon continued. He rubbed his hands together and rested his elbows on his knees. "Let's do it again," he said. "This time, though, we'll do it from some new angles."

The new questions came in sets, like ocean waves. *Where were you sitting when you told Mariko about the rape? Where was she sitting? Or—maybe—she was standing? How did you bring it up? What were your first words? Did she believe you? What did she say?*

Satoshi found answers for almost all of Sam's questions, surprising herself with the wealth of information that she could remember. Sam tried to stay impassive, but his eyes betrayed his enthusiasm. His subject, he knew, was warming up to her task. I was stifling yawns. I would have gone back out for more coffee but I didn't want to miss what might come next.

Sam said, "Okay, okay. Now we move on to the day that Mariko took you to see Dr. Welle. Do you remember that day?"

"Yes."

"What was the weather?"

For the first time Satoshi's voice betrayed some irritation. "What? Why does that matter?"

"It does. Humor me."

She thought for a moment. "It was a beautiful day. A storm was coming. The day had been warm and the sky was high. No clouds. Not even a thread. You know what it's like in the Rockies just before a big blizzard comes? It was one of those days. A September day in November."

"I love those days before a storm," said Sam. "One time—must've been Thanksgiving a couple of years ago—I was wearing shorts and a T-shirt when I was going into Ideal to get some groceries. I come out with maybe fifty dollars' worth of stuff and the air's suddenly freezing cold and the wind's howling and there's half an inch of snow on my windshield. Don't know why, but I love those days when that happens. It's like weather chaos."

I loved those days, too. But I kept quiet.

Sam had an annoying little buzzer on his wristwatch that beeped on the hour. It tolled at two A.M., causing me to check my watch. Satoshi had just said, "You know what? There was a car there when we left Dr. Welle's house. It was down near the stable. We drove by it on our way out. I remember because Mariko mentioned it. She said she liked it—the car." Neither Sam nor I had reacted to her words as though they were particularly meaningful.

Satoshi continued, and a change sang in her voice, indicating that she was surprised by the memories she was having. "You know what else? I saw it again on the news a few days later. Tami's mom was driving it. It was a . . . I don't know what kind. But it was white. A white car. That was the one that Mariko had said that she liked. It belonged to Mrs. Franklin." She smiled to herself and added, "I haven't thought of any of this stuff in years."

"You saw what?" Sam and I asked simultaneously.

"The Franklins' car was parked down by the stable. I guess Mrs. Franklin had come out to the ranch while we were inside with Dr. Welle."

Sam pressed. "Was Gloria there? Mrs. Welle? When you were at the ranch, before or after meeting with Dr. Welle, did you see Mrs. Welle?"

Satoshi shook her head. "No, we didn't see anyone else while we were there. But I never knew Mrs. Welle. She's the one who was murdered in that house, right? She was the one who was shot?"

I interjected, "Yes, she's the one who was killed there. Satoshi, there were housekeepers at Dr. Welle's ranch—two of them. Women. Did you see either of them that day?"

"No." She didn't hesitate.

"What about cowboys? There were two hands who worked at the ranch full-time. Did you see either of them?"

"No. No one else. Only Dr. Welle." She pursed her lips. "What are you two thinking? Are you thinking that Dr. Welle had called Mrs. Franklin and told her what Joey had done to me and that's why she came over to the ranch? I don't think that's possible; Dr. Welle was with me the whole time. I don't recall him leaving the room at all. I didn't see him call anyone."

I said, "No, that's not what I was thinking."

Satoshi moved her tongue between her teeth for a moment. She cocked her head to one side. "Are you suggesting Dr. Welle and Joey's mom were— No. Is that what you're thinking? That they were having an affair? That that's why she was at the ranch?"

Sam shrugged. I said, "I don't know that they were having an affair. But I guess that would explain some things."

"Like?" Satoshi was tired. She should have been able to answer this question herself.

I said, "Like why Dr. Welle never encouraged you to report what Joey did to the police."

Satoshi wanted to use the bathroom before we locked up the flower shop. As soon as I heard the door close behind her, I said to Sam, "Every time I blink my eyes, it appears that Raymond Welle is deeper and deeper into this mess."

"Go on."

"If he's screwing Joey's mother, he's going to have a difficult time being objective about her kid raping someone."

Sam shrugged. "Sure. But so what? It still doesn't tell me why that would have led him to kill the two girls."

"What if Mrs. Franklin and Welle were having an affair and the two girls found out about it?"

"Yeah? So? You think they put their heads together and decided it would be easier to cover up a double murder than to cover up an affair? You think parents go around murdering their children after the kids discover that the parents have been sneaking around doing a Lewinsky? I don't think so—there'd be dead kids everywhere." I stifled another yawn and suppressed an argument that the number of dead kids in the world was way too high for my comfort level already. Sam appraised me critically before he said, "You know, I'm beginning to get the impression that you don't think too well after midnight. You're sounding kind of goofy."

I was feeling a little bit defensive. "You have to admit it's a mess. The whole situation."

"Of course it's a mess. But what does that tell us? Nothing. You're out looking for suspects, Alan. It doesn't work that way. Look for evidence. We found some evidence tonight—evidence that Mrs. Franklin was at the ranch. That may help lead to a suspect. It may not. It may be Welle. It may not."

Satoshi walked back into the room. She'd apparently been listening to the argument. She said, "I told him pretty much the same thing about Joey, Sam." She faced me. "You know, Alan, you've already told me that you've been suspicious that Raymond Welle might have been sleeping with my sister, right?"

"It wasn't exactly my accusation. But yes."

"And now you're considering the possibility that he was having an affair with Joey's mom. Right?"

I wanted Satoshi to sit down, but she remained standing. I said, "Yes. That's one conclusion."

"So are both suppositions true? Or only one? And which one? His motivation would change, depending on who he was sleeping with, right?"

"Right." Sam had been correct. I wasn't thinking well. "Maybe he was sleeping with both of them. I don't know."

"And maybe neither?"

"I suppose that's possible, too."

Sam and Satoshi walked down Pearl toward the mall and, I guessed, toward Sam's old Jeep Cherokee. The downtown bars had just emptied out and there were a few dozen pedestrians still loitering as though something interesting was about to happen. I had parked on Ninth in front of where Treats used to be. The building that housed the bakery was now history. I still missed the wonderful breakfast rolls and muffins at Treats.

And I missed the trifle at Southern Exposure. And the grits at the original Dot's Diner. And the omelettes at the Aristocrat. The Irish stew at Shannon's. Fred's wonderful pie. And the brats on brown bread at Don's Cheese and Sausage.

When I was finished reminiscing about the Boulder that existed before Subway and Starbucks, and before the Gap and Banana Republic, I realized I wasn't as convinced as Sam that Welle wasn't implicated in at least five different ways in the murder of the two dead girls. But I was also exhausted. I had to force myself to concentrate to remember the final part of Satoshi's story—the part when she described to Sam and me what had happened after Mariko had driven her home from her visit to see Raymond Welle at the Silky Road Ranch.

Satoshi said that Mariko had folded her into the front seat of the car as though she were a small child. She took her home and she did what she could to offer comfort. She brought her tea and she smuggled some American candy into her room. Satoshi thought it had been a Three Musketeers bar. Satoshi remembered that she had really liked them when she was young.

Sam, I could tell, was pleased at the detail of her recollection.

Mariko had plans to see Tami that night. Satoshi said that at some point her sister left her alone in her room and went to get ready to go see her friend. Satoshi watched out the window as Mariko walked away to meet Tami. Satoshi didn't know where the two friends were supposed to meet.

She never saw her sister again.

CHAPTER
30

I sucked down coffee the next morning while Lauren stood at the sink with her back to me and grumbled that she wished she could do what I was doing. I growled back, "What? Stay out till three o'clock and feel terrible in the morning?"

She showed no sympathy as she said, "No. Have real coffee for breakfast. With caffeine."

After my second cup I offered an apology for my intemperance and gave her a quick we-both-have-to-get-to-work rendition of the previous night's marathon with Sam and Satoshi. She found the possibility of a romantic liaison between her ex-brother-in-law and Cathy Franklin intriguing. But she didn't have time to discuss it; she had to get to a breakfast meeting.

Her purse in one hand, her briefcase in the other, she said, "Oh, I almost forgot, Flynn Coe called after you left last night. She said she had a present for you. The mystery man? The one Dorothy Levin mentioned in the note she scribbled on the fax? They managed to identify him through hotel phone records. His name is Winston McGarrity. His phone number is by the phone in the bedroom. Bye. Love you. Oh, and something big is breaking with the forensics on the case. She couldn't say what, but said that they've been reexamining some of the previously unidentified materials from the autopsy and the crime scene and think they have something solid. That's why they're ready to proceed with a search of the ranch. She said we'll hear about it soon enough." With that, Lauren walked out to her car.

Late that morning, between patients, I phoned Winston McGarrity. The telephone prefix was for a Steamboat Springs number. The line was answered by a woman whose voice reminded me of Lauren's mother. She said, "McGarrity Associates."

"Winston McGarrity, please."

"May I tell him who's calling?"

"It's Dr. Alan Gregory."

She paused. I imagined her lips pursing. "Is this about a claim for one of your patients, Dr. Gregory? Because Win—Mr. McGarrity senior—doesn't actually do claims anymore." Her voice resonated with an endearing little chuckle at the thought of Win McGarrity actually doing claims.

"No, this isn't about a claim."

She was silent, waiting for me to elaborate and dig myself a hole so deep that I couldn't climb out of it. I waited along with her. Finally she asked, "It's about . . . what then? If you would be so kind."

I wasn't sure how to respond. I said, "McGarrity Associates is an . . . insurance company? Is that correct?" I don't know why I was surprised to realize the nature of the business I'd called, but I was.

"Agency. We're the largest independent in Routt County. Serving our clients since 1982."

"What kind of insurance do you sell?"

"Home, auto, health, life, disability—you name it, we sell it. Soup to nuts. Are you looking for malpractice? Because if you are, I'm afraid we don't do that." I heard a second line ringing in the background. Her voice jumped an octave as she said, "Oh my, but things are starting to hop around here. Now may I please tell Win what this is all about?"

I wasn't sure I was ever going to get past this woman who was guarding the door and actually speak with Winston McGarrity. I decided to use what I assumed would function as the verbal equivalent of a skeleton key. I said, "Please tell him I'm calling about Gloria Welle."

She said, "Gloria? Really? Oh my! Just a moment. Oh my!"

"Hi," he said, "this is Win." His voice was softer than mine, which made it as soft as a whisper.

"Mr. McGarrity, my name is—" I began. Before I could say another word, he interrupted.

"Win. Mr. McGarrity is my father. You're Doctor . . . ?"

"Gregory. Call me Alan."

"Alan, what can I do for you? I already understand from Louise that you're not buying anything, you're not selling anything, and you're not complaining about anything. So right off the bat—just from the point of view of complete novelty—you have my undivided attention."

I smiled. "I'll try to be brief. I'm calling about a recent meeting that you had with a *Washington Post* reporter by the name of—"

"Dorothy Levin—Dorothy. What a shame what happened to her. What a complete and utter shame. I liked her. She talked a bit fast for my taste. And she smoked like my brother-in-law's John Deere. I tried to tell her that her premiums would be much lower if she just stopped smoking. Health, life, everything. She wouldn't listen; they never do, the smokers. But I liked her. Know what else? Tragedy is that at the time she disappeared she was severely underinsured. Young ones often are."

Actual tragedy was, I thought, that it mattered that she was underinsured. I said, "I'm fond of her, too, Win. The meeting I was talking about? I understand that you spoke with her the day before she—"

"Actually, didn't just speak with her, I had dinner with her. Nice place in town called Antares? You ever been there?"

Before I had a chance to acknowledge that I had, he said, "Well, try it next time you're up here. Use my name if you like, may get you a kick in the rear." He laughed. I sensed that his self-deprecation was not exactly genuine. "I recommend the mixed grill. Dorothy had it on my advice. And I think she enjoyed it just fine. That's my memory anyway."

"Do you mind if I ask what you talked about? Why she—"

"Why she thought I might know something that might interest the *Washington Post?*" The interruptions were becoming less jarring. I was actually beginning to expect him to finish my sentences for me. And I had to admire he was doing a pretty fair job of anticipating my drift.

"Don't exactly know. Somebody probably gave her the name of some local citizens who might have been considered movers and shakers in this town back in the eighties and early nineties. You collect enough lists like that, my name would probably show up on one or two. I've been here awhile. I've made some friends over the years. I've been lucky enough to own some land in some of the right places. And unlucky enough to own in a few of the wrong ones, too." He chuckled. "But nobody ever really wants to talk about the mistakes I made. Dorothy never would say exactly how my name came up. Turned out, though, that what she wanted to talk about was Ray Welle's campaign finances for the primary elections he lost ten years or so ago. The first couple of elections. It was a short conversation cause I didn't have much to say. I didn't run with Ray Welle's herd back then." He laughed self-consciously. "Truth is that I don't run with Ray's herd now."

I tried to keep my tone conversational as I said, "And after you were done talking about Ray, that's when you and Dorothy started discussing Gloria Welle's murder?"

He hadn't been able to anticipate the end of that question. When he spoke again his voice was suddenly a little raspy, as though his throat had dried considerably. He asked, "Now how did you know that?"

I considered lying but didn't. "Dorothy sent me a note the night before she disappeared. Said she'd had an interesting dinner with someone who had some unusual theories about Gloria's death. She knew that the whole episode out at the Silky Road is an interest of mine."

"Why's that? Curious interest for someone."

I'd anticipated the question and told him that I'd recently befriended Kevin Sample.

He said, "Oh." His voice grew even fainter at the mention of the Sample name. I pressed the phone hard against my ear in a vain attempt to increase the volume. Win asked, "How is that boy?"

"He's in veterinary school in Fort Collins. He's doing better than you would expect."

"Good. Good. I'm relieved to hear that. Life like that boy had when he was young—could have ended up with all kinds of tragic outcomes. Hey, I'm sure you don't want to play guessing games with me, so I'll just tell you what I told Dorothy about Gloria's death. No harm there. Curious thing is, only a week or so before he killed Gloria, Brian called me and asked about buying some additional life insurance."

Really? "For himself?"

"For himself, that's right. Well, I knew of course what had been happening to the Samples—everyone in town did. I knew about his son's terrible accident. And Brian's suicide attempt, too. But I heard him out, polite and professional as can be. When he was all done, I told him the honest-to-God truth, which was that, if he insisted, I'd take his application right then over the phone. But I explained that there wasn't much likelihood that any of the companies that I represent were going to be too eager to underwrite a life insurance policy on him after looking at his recent medical history."

"You were referring to the suicide attempt?"

"Yes, that's right, I was."

"And?"

"And nothing. He asked me a few questions about the way the policies worked, the underwriting and all, and after I explained, he said he understood. He hadn't even known that the policy he had already bought from me just before his son's car accident—that one was for two hundred and fifty thou—he didn't even understand that if he had died from his recent suicide attempt, it wouldn't have paid death benefits."

"And that's because . . . ?"

"There's a grace period, a waiting period if you will, on life insurance policies so that someone can't just buy one and then kill himself the next day. The waiting period on Brian's existing policy wasn't up. He didn't remember that. Anyway, I answered all his questions and he thanked me for my time. Brian had always been a gentleman and he was that day as well. He was a gentleman right up until the very end, I would say."

"Do you think he was thinking that he might die while he was doing whatever he was planning to do at the Welles' ranch? Do you think that's why he wanted the additional life insurance?"

"Don't see any other possible conclusion. Do you?"

"No sir," I said, "I don't."

It all made more sense than it had before.

At least a week before he made his way out to the Silky Road Ranch, Brian Sample had already decided to seek his revenge on Raymond Welle. He assumed that his plan for vengeance might result in his death. In fact, he judged it to be enough of a risk that he endeavored to increase the insurance on his own life prior to kidnapping Gloria Welle.

In our recent meeting, Kevin Sample had been eager to view his father's optimism and relative ebullience the morning he died as a sign that his depression had abated. The exact opposite might have been true. The reality is that the mood of a suicidal individual often brightens after he has decided on a plan that will end his life. Many families and many psychotherapists are fooled by the improvement in mood and lulled into believing that self-destructive danger has ameliorated. It appeared likely that the morning Kevin Sample had breakfast with his father, Brian Sample was more talkative because he had already settled on a plan that was likely to end his life.

Kevin, ever hopeful, wanted to believe that what he

saw that morning was evidence that his father was getting better.

But that morning over a breakfast of pancakes and sausages with his surviving son, Brian Sample wasn't less depressed because he had found a solution to his grief. Nor was he brighter because he had discovered a way to escape from his depression. Brian Sample was simply relieved.

He knew that his pain was almost over because he had arranged a standby seat on the next flight off the planet.

The only thing I didn't understand was why he wanted to take Gloria Welle on the ride along with him. I was assuming I would never know the answer to that question. Then I recalled that the night before I'd promised Kevin Sample that I would review his father's psychotherapy history with Raymond Welle.

Maybe I would learn something about Brian Sample's motives after all.

PART FIVE

The Houseguest

CHAPTER
31

I wasn't too surprised that Kimber Lister didn't immediately return my call after I'd left him a message asking for an update about A. J.'s health. I knew from experience how reticent she was to discuss her illness, and Kimber had already informed me that she wanted the facts of her current condition handled with discretion.

When Kimber finally did phone, he didn't mention A. J. at all. The purpose of his call was to inform me that he was coming to Colorado to coordinate Locard's search of Gloria's Silky Road Ranch. He understood that we had a pleasant guest room and wondered if he could impose upon Lauren and me to stay in our home for one night before he headed into the mountains.

Initially, I was surprised by his request. After a moment's contemplation, I was shocked by it. Kimber Lister did not strike me as the guest-room-of-an-almost-complete-stranger type of traveler. I would have suspected him to be someone who assiduously counted guidebook stars prior to choosing his hotels.

I stammered out an invitation and told him we would be delighted to have him as our guest.

He thanked me, said he would be arriving late in the afternoon on Thursday, and asked that I send him directions to our house. I promised I would and wondered aloud if anyone else from the team would be coming to Colorado.

"Yes," he said. "Others will be arriving. Given the political ramifications of our next move, we are proceeding with utmost caution."

"Because of the potential involvement of Dr. Welle?"
"Yes, because of the potential involvement of Dr.
Welle."

Kimber arrived via Lincoln Town Car about a half
hour after I got home from my office. The car was a
deep navy in color and the windows were tinted as dark
as the law allowed. A driver in a polo shirt and khakis
deposited Kimber's luggage—two small honey-leather
cases—on our tiny front porch. No money exchanged
hands. The Lincoln kicked up a lot of dust as it exited
the lane.

I'd prepared for Kimber's arrival by depositing Emily
at Adrienne and Jonas's house. The sounds of her determined barking nevertheless pierced the quiet lane. I concluded that I had been wise in deciding to introduce the
dog to our guest later in the evening.

Kimber's handshake was meaty and moist. I noticed
that he was sweating; tiny beads of moisture dotted his
upper lip and his brow. He kept raising his chin into the
air as though his collar were too tight. It wasn't. The top
button of his denim shirt wasn't even closed. I worried
that he was having an acute reaction to the altitude
change.

"Do you mind if . . . ?" he asked, swallowing. "Maybe
we . . . can—would it be all right if we moved inside
your home?" He forced a smile. His usually sonorous
voice was oddly hollow.

"Of course," I said. "Please come in." I led him to
the western side of the house and settled him onto a chair
in the living room. The weather was putting on a show
that afternoon. The sky directly to the west was a brilliant blue, but immense thunderheads had flared near the
Continental Divide and were flanking Boulder to both
the north and the south. Lightning jumped up from the
mountainsides and lit the gray walls of the storms as the
rumble of thunder shook the house.

Kimber didn't seem to notice any of it. He actually
rotated on his chair so that his back faced the glass. I

excused myself to get him a big glass of water. Dehydration is often a major factor inhibiting altitude adjustment. By the time I returned to the living room Kimber was breathing through his open mouth, his chest rising noticeably with every inhale. One of his eyelids seemed to twitch as he blinked.

I sat down across from him and placed the water close by. "Kimber," I said softly in my office voice," are you all right?"

He raised his eyebrows and shook his head. "No. Not really." He swallowed again. "I'm wondering, although I hate to impose further . . . but . . . do you have a room where I can rest for a . . . few minutes. Someplace that's maybe . . . oh . . . not quite so bright? Darker would be great. Ideal even."

I stood and asked him to follow me. I led him downstairs to the guest room, where I pulled the curtains across the windows. His bedroom was now cool and dark. I could almost feel his sense of relief as the room fell into shadows.

"This will be fine. I think I'll, um, I'll just rest for a little bit. The travel? I'm not accustomed anymore."

"I'll be upstairs, Kimber. No rush. Please rest as long as you would like. Later we'll discuss dinner."

"You're so kind," he said. As I pulled the door closed I saw that he was already flat on his back on the bed, a pillow plopped over his face.

I wondered about migraines.

As Lauren arrived home from work, her car was being tailed by a Ford Taurus driven by Russ Claven. His front-seat passenger was Flynn Coe. The patch on Flynn's eye that day was egg-yolk yellow. From a distance I thought it looked like corduroy.

I'd been outside on the lane playing a game with the dog and Jonas that involved my alternately throwing tennis balls for Emily to run after and not retrieve and for Jonas to jump at and not catch. At the sound of the cars I scrambled to corral both the child and the dog.

Lauren was out of her car before Russ and Flynn got out of theirs. She hugged me quickly and asked, "Were we expecting Flynn and Russ?"

I whispered back, "No. And Kimber's already arrived. He's downstairs resting. He looked terrible when he got here. I'm afraid he's not well."

"Okay," she said, and hustled over to give Jonas a kiss and help restrain Emily, who was not pleased at the arrival of strangers on her home turf.

Flynn picked up the vibes before Lauren and I had a chance to explain. "Russ just admitted to me that he never got around to calling you to let you know we were coming. I'm so sorry to burst in on you like this. Just point us to a motel. We'll be fine."

I said, "We'd love to have you stay with us, Flynn, but Kimber Lister is already here. He's resting down in the guest room."

"What?"

Flynn's reaction surprised me. "Lauren and I didn't know you and Russ were coming, Flynn. When Kimber asked, we agreed to let him stay with us."

She spun and said to Russ, "Get this: Kimber's here, Russ. Right now. As we speak."

Russ was leaning down in the driver's seat, fumbling with levers that he hoped would pop the latch on the trunk. He stopped what he was doing and said, "What? You're kidding. Colorado, here? Or here, here?" He pointed at the dirt by his feet.

"Both."

"No shit? I never thought I'd see it."

Flynn turned back to me. "I never thought I'd see it, either."

"See what?" Lauren and I asked in unison.

"See him leave the neighborhood where he lives in Adams Morgan. He hasn't been outside—what would you say, Russ?—a three-block radius of that place of his since he moved in."

"No more than three blocks. Maybe only two," Russ agreed.

Lauren said, "You have to be kidding."

I recalled the sweating, the nervousness, the agitation, the change in his breathing. I realized that I hadn't been witnessing altitude sickness or an incipient migraine headache. I'd been witnessing a panic attack.

I asked, "Agoraphobia?"

Russ said, "Bingo."

Jonas and I consumed a few minutes in a heated negotiation over custody of Emily. I wanted to take her home with me right then. Jonas wanted to keep her at his house forever and ever. Our compromise? Jonas could have the dog until dinnertime.

After I turned Jonas back over to his nanny, Lauren, Flynn, Russ, and I moved inside to the living room. "That's why Kimber founded Locard?" I asked. "Because he has agoraphobia?"

Russ answered my question. "After Kimber's illness progressed—I mean after it got severe enough that he was a virtual prisoner to it—he obviously couldn't continue working in the field, so—"

"Working in the field as what?" Lauren asked. "What's his specialty?"

"Kimber was the head of the FBI division that uses computers to assist investigations. He's considered the top forensic-database guy in the country, maybe the world. He's also a wizard on the Internet."

I was impressed.

"Anyway, he wanted to continue his work after he got sick. Because of his reputation in the field he had already been invited to be a member of Vidocq, in Philadelphia. You know Vidocq, right? After he went on medical leave he went ahead and joined, became a full-fledged VSM— that's a Vidocq Society Member. But soon enough he discovered that the train trips from D.C. to Philly for the Vidocq luncheons were impossible for him to manage— again, because of his phobias—and he was forced to re-sign his membership. That's when he and A. J. and a couple of others began to develop the concept of Locard."

"Which," Lauren said, "always meets in Washington. In Adams Morgan. In Kimber's loft."

"Right," said Flynn. "And to my knowledge Kimber hasn't done a day of fieldwork since the organization started assisting on cases in the mid-nineties. Until today. Which says something about how seriously he views the progress of this particular investigation."

Russ agreed. "He knows that Locard can't afford to be wrong if we're about to accuse Raymond Welle of complicity in the murder of two teenage girls. If we blow this one, we're toast. Kimber knows that."

Flynn raised her bottle of beer. "To Kimber, I guess. And us. I hope we don't screw this up."

We toasted Kimber. And not screwing up.

The sound of the downstairs toilet flushing alerted me that Kimber might be joining us soon. But then the clarion call of the plumbing let us know that he had started using the downstairs shower. By the time he'd climbed upstairs a pizza delivery had just arrived and I was setting out beer and opening a bottle of wine. The sun was completely obscured by the mountains and the end-of-the-day thunder-and-lightning show had changed venues and was illuminating the eastern plains and not the foothills. Kimber appeared rejuvenated, the tension in his manner greatly diminished. But the confidence he'd displayed in Washington was absent—in our house he was obviously awkward and out of his element.

I walked the western perimeter of the living room and, one by one, lowered the window shades that we occasionally employed to block the searing rays of the late-afternoon sun. The big room upstairs quickly grew even duskier.

At Kimber's urging, Flynn, as case manager, reviewed the progress of the investigation of the two dead girls for Lauren and me, highlighting the forensic findings that had focused attention on the Silky Road. The key pieces

of evidence, it turned out, were eight minute grains of
rock that had been removed from the skull wound of
Tami Franklin. "That was the first wound she suffered
that night," Russ said. "It would not have been fatal on
its own, not immediately, though it was a bad injury. It
crushed bone"—he stood between Lauren and me and
placed his fingers on a spot about three inches behind
our right ears—"right about here. The wound was eight
centimeters by eleven centimeters. The grains were recovered during the initial autopsy. They'd been examined
back in 1989, but no progress was made on identification
at the time."

Flynn took over again. "But we enlisted a geologist—
actually, a petrologist—and he's been able to confirm
that that the grains were from a relatively unusual form
of imported limestone. There were, in addition to the
rock fragments, grains of a man-made mortar. We assumed we were looking for a rock wall made out of
limestone. So we began looking for commercial and residential installations that might have used that specific
rock for ornamental walls in Routt County. The building
department records in Routt County weren't much help.
Chief Smith began checking with local contractors and
masons. He finally found a place that recalled using some
of this imported limestone for a series of rock knee
walls."

Lauren said, "The Silky Road Ranch."

Kimber pursed his lips and nodded. "Right. But even
that information wasn't enough to justify a search. Not
when the target happens to be the private property of a
prominent member of Congress."

Flynn looked at me. "We'd been hoping that the case
file you got from Welle—Mariko's?—might offer some
support for Welle's involvement, but so far the results
from the documents examiner have been inconclusive.
Still, the fruit of your interviews, Alan—especially the
information about Joey and Mariko's sister, Satoshi—
kept leading us back to the Silky Road. Eventually, with
Satoshi's testimony that her sister took her to see Welle,

we could even place Mariko at the ranch the night she disappeared."

"But not Tami," I said.

"Right. Not Tami. And it was Tami's skull that produced the rock fragments. Reluctantly, we concluded that we needed more evidence to justify asking for permission to search the ranch. We wanted to have enough evidence to proceed to the district attorney if Welle denied us access on a voluntary basis."

Flynn said, "When Russ and I came out here to visit a couple of weeks back, we reviewed all the lab samples that were taken back in 1989. We went back over the girls' clothes looking for trace. Russ looked at the original autopsy photos and reexamined the wounds from the amputations. We used techniques that were unavailable back then to look for latents on all the physical evidence."

Russ made a noise with his lips and said, "Nada."

"Until we got to the splinter."

"What splinter?"

"A postmortem splinter in Mariko's left arm, just below her elbow. The splinter was large—over a centimeter—and was totally embedded beneath her skin. Like the rock fragments removed from Tami's skull wound, the splinter was removed and cataloged during the original autopsy, but its significance was never appreciated."

"The splinter is of a hardwood with a polyurethane finish. It's sanded flat on one side. We assumed it had come from a hardwood floor or a finished piece of furniture, like a tabletop."

The phone rang. Lauren jumped up to answer it in the kitchen.

Flynn took over the story. "I sent it out for more analysis. Turns out the wood is ebony. An unusual wood for furniture, a highly unusual wood for flooring. For us, that's good. We went back to the contractor who built the new buildings at the Silky Road and asked him if the flooring sub used any ebony."

"The doorways," I said. "There's a dark border on

each side of all the entry-door thresholds. Is that ebony?"

Flynn nodded. "That's right. According to the contractor, that wood bordering each door is ebony," Flynn said. "We've concluded that there's a high degree of probability that the girls were killed at the Silky Road."

Two minutes later Lauren rejoined us in the living room and said, "Excuse me. Everybody? Percy Smith is on the phone. There's a fire burning at the Silky Road Ranch. He wants to talk to Flynn."

Before he'd called my house trying to track down Flynn Coe, Percy Smith had already interviewed Sylvie Amato.

Sylvie had first smelled smoke while she was watching ESPN, hoping for some late coverage of women's tennis, which was her main summer thing. Skiing was her main winter thing. Sylvie had been killing time while waiting for her boyfriend, Jeff, to get home from his bartending gig in town. They rented the old frame house that the two lesbian housekeepers had occupied when Gloria Welle was still alive. Sylvie also earned a few extra bucks by working as resident caretaker on the ranch and by acting as loyal gofer for Welle and his entourage during their infrequent visits to the Elk River Valley. I recalled that Sylvie was the one who had fetched me coffee in the Dilbert mug while I was cooling my heels with Phil Barrett waiting for Ray Welle to return from hitting nine with Joey Franklin. I imagined that her two jobs left Sylvie plenty of time to play tennis in the summer and to ski in the winter.

The smell of smoke on a warm early-summer night had been sufficient to yank Sylvie's attention away from the tube. She lifted her strong body from the floor in front of the TV to an open north-facing window and sniffed enough dry mountain air to conclude that the source of the smoke was probably an illegal campfire. She guessed the trespassers were somewhere down by the river or maybe even farther east, along the banks of Mad Creek. God, she hoped that nobody was camping on the ranch. She'd catch hell from Phil Barrett if he discovered that the perimeter of the Silky Road was being violated.

Sylvie pulled on some shoes and stepped from the kitchen out onto the covered porch that wrapped around three sides of the old ranch house. She was hoping to see the flicker of campfire flames someplace down-valley to reassure herself that whoever had pitched a tent had done so well outside the fences of the Silky Road.

She scanned the western sky and searched the wooded banks of the Elk River. She didn't see any sign of a fire down there, but the smell of smoke was even stronger than it had been before. As she turned the corner of the porch to check in another direction she couldn't miss the fact that the sky to the southwest was lit up like a carnival midway. Sylvie was certain that she was looking at a forest fire that was burning dangerously close by.

She ran inside and called 911.

The volunteer fire department from the tiny up-valley town of Clark arrived at the Silky Road Ranch minutes before the professional firefighters made it up the hill from Steamboat Springs. Both companies had steeled themselves for the grueling task of trying to contain an incipient forest fire that would immediately threaten life, property, and some of the most beautiful wilderness in the state. But what they discovered instead was a building fire that had fully engulfed the bunkhouse at the Silky Road Ranch. The roof of the adjacent stable was just starting to smolder. The closest woods were at least two hundred yards away though, and so far, no embers had drifted over to ignite the trees.

Since the bunkhouse was unoccupied, the firefighters sacrificed it and concentrated their attention on the stable, which they saved. They also managed to keep embers from igniting the drying grasses or the nearby trees.

Percy Smith harbored no doubts that the cause of the fire had been arson.

CHAPTER
32

L auren decided to stay in Boulder.
  I could tell that she was eager to go to Steamboat with Kimber, Flynn, Russ, and me, and I assumed that she was staying behind in order to conserve her strength for the baby. It was one of the first of countless sacrifices she and I would make for someone we had not yet met.

Kimber and I drove up to Steamboat in my car, with Flynn and Russ following in the rented Taurus. Kimber donned dark sunglasses and stretched out in the backseat with headphones from a CD player over his ears and a big felt hat resting on his face. Every twenty minutes or so he said something reassuring like, "I know you're worried about me and I'm fine." I was worried and I appreciated the reassurance, but the three-hour-plus drive passed slowly. With him in back acting dead, I thought it was kind of like driving a hearse.

Kimber had been dreading checking into a big hotel in Steamboat, and when I described the B and B Lauren and I had stayed at near Howelsen Hill he seemed enamored of it. I used my portable phone to call Libby, the owner of the bed-and-breakfast, and reserved the last three rooms she had available. Once again, it appeared that Flynn and Russ were going to need to come to some sleeping accommodations. I told Libby not to expect any of us until midafternoon. She wouldn't let me off the phone until she had told me everything she knew about the fire at Gloria's Silky Road. The whole town was apparently already talking about the arson. She said word was that the accelerant had been gasoline. Everyone was still working to come up with a satisfactory motive. She was pretty certain she'd hear something good by the afternoon.

The midday sun burned through a cloudless sky. Tourists packed the sidewalks along Lincoln Avenue in Steamboat Springs, wandering aimlessly from shop to shop. Traffic crawled stoplight to stoplight behind an endless parade of construction trucks. The combination of the heat and the mindless tourism was discouraging to me. I was grateful to make it the entire way through town and begin the gentle climb up into the valley that ran along the banks of the Elk River.

I told Kimber we were entering some beautiful country that he might want to see. I had to yell to be heard above his music. He groaned back, equally loudly, "Don't worry about me. I'm fine." He remained supine on the seat with the hat still planted over his face. I knew at that moment that if my clinical practice fell apart I wasn't likely to make it as a chauffeur.

Russ and Flynn had passed us at a light in town and were waiting at the closed gate of the Silky Road. "We haven't buzzed anyone yet," Russ said. "Figured you would be along soon. Where's Kimber? In the trunk?"

"Kimber's right here," Kimber said, raising himself to a sitting position in the backseat. He fumbled with his headphones. "Of course there is no way that Beethoven could have imagined it, but his symphonies provide a remarkable accompaniment to a long automobile ride. I wonder why that is."

Flynn pressed a button on the stainless-steel panel that was recessed in the stone pillar supporting the gate. Nothing happened. To no one in particular she said, "Percy said he'd meet us here. I hope he wasn't kidding."

A voice projected loudly from the speaker. Someone wanted Flynn to identify herself. She did. The gates began to swing open as though they didn't know a thing about hurrying.

Kimber stuck his hands on his hips, spun on his heels,

gazed to the north and then to the east, smiled broadly, and said, "This is an incredibly pleasant valley."

I bit my tongue.

We climbed back into the cars. Kimber once again chose the backseat. But this time he didn't lie down.

I preceded Russ and Flynn through the gate. Near the ridge that climbs up from the creek bed toward the house I turned right onto a dirt track that I guessed would lead across the meadow to the stable and bunkhouse. Russ followed right behind me.

As soon as we cleared the ridge it was apparent that the bunkhouse was a total loss. The structure was little more than a blackened framework of toasted timbers. The glass had burst from the window frames. Waves of sticky ash had oozed through the busted-out doorways, carried along by rivers of water from the firefighters' hoses. A three-foot-high stone wall that supported the exterior walls acted like a dike, containing the rest of the muck inside. The adjacent stable stood intact, mocking the ruined bunkhouse like a prizefighter who has just vanquished an opponent.

Flynn jumped out of the car and took long strides toward the ruins. Without hesitation she dropped into a catcher's crouch and began to finger the sooty stone knee wall that had once supported the post-and-beam walls of the cowboys' living quarters.

Kimber, Russ, and I congregated around her. She said, "I need to get some of the samples of this stone and mortar to the petrologist so she can put them under a microscope, but I would guess that this rock wall might be what we're looking for. Although I'm no expert, I think this is limestone, and the petrologist said we're looking for limestone. For now we certainly can't rule it out."

I gazed inside the building. A section of the floor structure had collapsed into the crawl space below. The top of an incinerated refrigerator poked back up into what had been a kitchen. The beam structure was blackened and blistered into huge reptilian scales. I asked, "But

what about the wood we're trying to find—the ebony?
Maybe someone knew about the splinter and they were
trying to hide evidence of the ebony by doing this."

Flynn said, "Whatever it was they were hoping to destroy might still be here. We'll get plenty of wood samples. Fire doesn't destroy evidence as well as most
people think."

Kimber spoke, his voice suddenly rich enough to fill
the horseshoe canyon. "We need to remain cautious. The
fire may indeed have been intended to destroy evidence.
It may also have been intended to mislead us into believing that this was the site where we should be focusing
our attention. We must proceed with our search as originally planned. Agreed? Sheriff Smith is waiting for us
at Dr. Welle's home, correct? Why don't we join him
there now?"

Percy Smith was waiting on the front porch. He was
perched on the arm of one of the two Adirondack chairs.
Pork chop Phil Barrett completely filled the other chair.
As we got out of the cars Flynn whispered to Russ,
"Look. They used the exact same stone to build the knee
walls and chimney trim for the house up here. Damn—
that will make our job more complicated."

Phil said, "Hi, Alan. See you already stopped to check
on last night's fire. When I first saw it, it reminded me
a little of the hash browns I made the last time I tried
to cook myself breakfast." He laughed at his own joke.
No one else thought he was funny.

I nodded. "Hello, Phil. Percy. Yeah, we just saw the
ruins—I'm learning my way around the ranch pretty well.
Surprised to see you here so early, Phil—I got the impression from Percy that no one was at the house last
night."

"I sure wasn't. I've been visiting with my mama at the
old folks' home she lives in down in Hayden. Drove up
to the ranch with Percy this morning after I heard about
the fire." He smiled at Flynn. "Want to introduce me
around?"

I didn't like the fact that Phil and Percy seemed so chummy. But I proceeded with the introductions. Phil was definitely distracted by Flynn and her eye patch du jour. This one was hand painted to look exactly like her other eyeball. It was my favorite one of her patches so far. Phil sneaked his attention away from Flynn long enough to acknowledge Russ and to pander to Kimber. "The famous Mr. Lister. It's a pleasure. My friends on the Hill speak highly of you, sir. I'm sure you know that Congressman Welle sits on the committee that oversees the FBI. You are quite a legend in those halls, sir. Quite a legend."

"The pleasure is mine, Mr. Barrett. We at Locard are grateful for your assistance with our work. I'm sure it was an inconvenience to fly here from Washington just to supervise our search. We are also appreciative of all that the congressman has done to help us to keep this inquiry from the eyes of the press."

Kimber was warning Phil about the stakes that had already been anted up in the investigation.

Phil hesitated long enough to capture everyone's attention. "One thing I've learned over the years is that Ray Welle protects those who promote justice the way a mama bear protects her cubs. Which is to say, whole-heartedly."

Phil was saying, Don't screw around with me.

So far I was enjoying myself. I wished Lauren had come along. She would have enjoyed this, too.

Kimber asked, "Is it possible that we could move this meeting inside?" His voice wavered a little, and I noticed that a couple of dozen tiny beads of sweat were dotting his upper lip.

Flynn noticed, too. "Yes, let's go in," she said.

Phil said, "Doesn't get any prettier than this porch. I'll get us some more chairs and have the girl bring us all some iced tea. Maybe some sandwiches." *The girl?* I wondered whether Phil had learned about Kimber's discomfort in wide-open spaces and was trying to take advantage of it.

Flynn pressed. "You know, Phil, this light—it's so bright—it's kind of hard on my eye. Sunglasses aren't really an option with the patch. I'd be grateful if we could meet indoors."

Phil stared at Kimber and pulled himself from the confines of the Adirondack chair. "Done," he said. I thought I saw him swallow a chuckle.

We moved into the massive living room with its post-and-beam framing. I grabbed a leather side chair close to a sofa that was as big as a car and wondered if I was sitting precisely where Brian Sample had sat as he sipped tea with Gloria Welle. I said a silent prayer that Sylvie didn't serve Girl Scout Cookies.

A knock on the front door brought a plainclothes investigator from the Routt County sheriff's office into the mix. Her name was Cecilia Daruwalla—I guessed that she was of Pakistani or Indian heritage—and I assumed she was there to ensure the chain of evidence of everything that would be collected. Kimber and Phil Barrett retreated with her to the dining room to review the written agreement that authorized the search of Gloria's Silky Road Ranch and stipulated the ground rules under which the search would be conducted. The search would not include the right for Locard to view or retrieve any documents or personal belongings other than those in plain view. The agreement was intended to allow Flynn to retrieve samples of soil, rock, brick, mortar, paint, lumber, carpet, flooring, cabinetry, countertops, and other materials used in the construction and maintenance of the primary and secondary structures of the ranch. The details of the agreement had already been hammered out via fax and E-mail. The jousting at the big dining-room table was pro forma.

As Kimber preceded Phil back into the living room, he said, "Alan, remember, you're here only as an observer. Russ will assist Flynn with the collection of samples. Flynn, where would you like to begin?"

"Right here is a great place to start, Kimber. I need

to collect my evidence kit from the car and then I'll get started."

Kimber said, "I have some work to do, Phil. Is there a room with a phone I might use? Someplace private, perhaps?" *And dark, and small,* I thought.

"How about Ray's study?"

"I'm certain that would do quite nicely. If you would be so kind as to show me the way." He displayed the case that held his laptop computer. "I'll be on-line much of the time. That won't cause any inconvenience, I hope."

Phil Barrett said, "Shouldn't. The house has plenty of phone lines. Before I help get Mr. Lister settled, just a word for you, Ms. Coe. Per the agreement between Dr. Welle and Mr. Lister, I'll be videotaping everything you do."

She cocked her head and smiled coquettishly right at him. The expression of her painted eye refused to flirt along with the rest of her. The effect was totally disconcerting. "The camera loves me, Phil. Please go right ahead."

I spent the next ninety minutes with my hands in my pockets doing what the sheriff's investigator was doing: following Flynn Coe as she methodically collected samples of the various materials that had been used to construct the house. Flynn began by photographing each room and then plotting the dimensions. Russ charted the progression of the photographs and sketched the rooms while Flynn proceeded to collect the approved samples. Russ assumed the role of forensic assistant with remarkable aplomb. Phil Barrett hung back, his tripod-mounted video camera recording Flynn's every move.

I quickly grew bored and found myself using my time in Raymond Welle's home to familiarize myself with the key places in the drama that had occurred between Brian Sample and Gloria Welle in 1992. I imagined Gloria greeting Brian at the front door and I made a guess as to which telephone Gloria might have used to call her husband and warn him that one of his patients had invaded their home. I guessed she would have used the kitchen phone.

I examined the small window that Brian had busted out with the butt of his gun so that he could shoot at the assembled sheriff's vehicles. The window was an eighteen-inch square mounted above pecan cabinets in the butler's pantry. In order to reach it to shoot out the window Brian would have had to kneel on the countertop. I considered the selection of that particular window an odd choice in a house that had enough glass to construct a commercial greenhouse. I also thought that I recalled reading news reports that Brian had broken out the laundry-room window. I walked from the butler's pantry to the adjacent laundry room to check it out. Sure enough, Brian would have had a much easier shot from there. But the window in the laundry room was a narrow double-hung. It was not the one that Brian had chosen to bust out.

I couldn't resist a ghoulish peek into the guest-room closet where Gloria had been murdered, so I followed Flynn and Russ into that room with interest. The guest suite was decorated in the ruggedly stylish manner that Ralph Lauren and Robert Redford were eager for the world to accept as the authentic portrayal of American western design. Tasteful? I wasn't sure, but probably. Expensive? Without a doubt.

Flynn photographed and measured the room, and I waited impatiently until she finally got around to opening the closet door to take photographs in there. I peered over her shoulder into a closet that was quite a bit larger than the one that Kimber was using downstairs in the guest room of our house in Boulder. The closet at the Silky Road was a U-shaped walk-in with shelves outfitted like a fine haberdasher's display cases. The open center area of the closet was only about three feet square—just enough room for the chair that Brian carried in for Gloria to sit on. The day of the Locard search there was no wine stored on the closet shelves. I checked. Nor was there evidence of Gloria Welle's blood or Robert Mondavi's red wine on the floor. I checked for those, too.

Besides the master and guest suites, the house had two other bedrooms. One, apparently, was set aside for Phil

Barrett's occasional stays at the ranch. Although the bed in that room was made—I assumed by Sylvie—it was clear that Phil was a slob. Although he'd only arrived at the ranch that morning, his suitcase spilled clothes as though an inconsiderate thief had ransacked it after breakfast.

The second of the spare bedrooms had never been decorated. The windows lacked coverings and the floor space was used for file storage. I saw one box marked "Demo Tapes." At least a dozen boxes held copies of *Toward Healing America: America's Therapist's Prescription for a Better Future.*

The architectural layout convinced me that when Gloria Welle was designing this house she was planning for a family with at least two children. The knowledge saddened me.

The master bedroom was at the eastern end of the house at the end of a long hallway that was lit with a clerestory. By the time Brian Sample had walked this hall, I thought, Gloria Welle was already dead or dying in the closet in the guest suite. The master bedroom at the end of the hall was vast, with a sitting area as large as most people's living rooms and a four-poster bed the size of an uninhabited island. An alcove near the bathroom contained a compact desk topped with a laptop computer. The far wall, the one that would catch the morning sun after it had cleared the Continental Divide and then lifted itself over the tops of the fir and aspen groves, was nothing but a series of wide glass doors. I counted six of them.

The deck outside the bedroom windows stepped down twice from the house until it ended above two final stairs that led down to a narrow lawn that abutted the forest. A redwood railing, alternately carved and straight in two-foot sections, lined the north and south sides of the deck.

By all reports I'd read and seen, Brian Sample had leapt that rail on the way to his death.

I wondered why he hadn't just taken the stairs.

CHAPTER
33

Sylvie showed up around two o'clock with a couple of six-packs of soft drinks and a big bag of deli sandwiches from the general store up the hill in Clark. She was dressed in tennis clothes. Flynn and Russ immediately cornered her to question her about the fire in the bunkhouse. I was ready for a break, so I carried a pretty good ham sandwich on sourdough outside to my car and used the cell phone to call Sam Purdy in Boulder. I wanted to talk about Gloria Welle's murder, and he was the only one I could think of who I thought would share my interest in the subject. I found him at his desk at the police department.

I told him why I was at the Silky Road Ranch. He listened patiently to my explanation before he said, "Raymond Welle's no fool, Alan. If he was guilty of something he certainly wouldn't give a world-class forensic investigator the run of his place. Your search is going to be a dead end. Nice try, though."

"Flynn already seems confident that she has reason to hope for a match."

"We'll see. If you're right, I'll buy you a beer. Hell, if you're wrong I'll buy you a beer. But don't get your hopes up."

"Sam, the reason I called isn't because of the two dead girls. While the Locard forensic people have been doing their things here, I've spent my time walking through the house trying to re-create exactly what happened the day that Gloria Welle was murdered. You remember that you thought that the whole story was goofy, at least the way the police presented it?"

"Yeah, I remember I thought that. It *was* goofy. Still is goofy."

"Well, I have two more goofy things for you." I reminded him about the window Brian had busted out to shoot at the sheriff's vehicles and explained what an odd choice of windows it had been. That earned me a bored "hmm" from Sam. I said, "Well? What do you think?"

"I think it's been a lot of years since she died, maybe the landscaping outside the windows has changed. Maybe there was a big bush in front of that laundry-room window back then. Maybe Welle changed the cabinetry in that other room—what did you call it, a butler's pantry? Who knows?"

It was possible. I'd go back and look at the news footage again to see if there was a bush in front of the laundry room back in 1992. "What about this, then? You remember the television news reports said that when Brian was trying to escape from the master bedroom he leaped over the deck railing and started running toward the woods? That's when he shot at the cops the second time. Remember that?"

"Yeah."

"Well, I was just out there, on that deck. The center section of the deck—the part closest to those woods—doesn't even have a railing. It steps right down onto the lawn. I'm wondering why Brian Sample didn't just take those two stairs down to the grass and head straight for the woods. Why did he jump the railing, run toward the cops, and fire at them first?"

Sam was silent for a moment before he responded. "That's a decent question. I'm thinking . . . that . . . who knows? Maybe . . . maybe he wanted the cops to kill him. It happens sometimes. We call it suicide by cop. There's this story—happened recently—of one guy who led this cop on a high-speed chase, and after he was pulled over he got out of his car holding a handgun. He slowly raised it up and pointed it right at the cop.

Wouldn't drop it. The cop took cover and warned him. Guy still wouldn't drop it, so the cop fired till his pistol was empty. The guy died. Turns out the handgun the guy was carrying was a toy and there was a suicide note on the front seat of his car apologizing to the cop. Guy said he was too much of a coward to kill himself."

"Psychologists have a name for that, too."

"Which is what?"

"Victim-precipitated homicide."

Sam digested the awkward phrase. "I think I like 'suicide by cop' better. There's no homicide involved when somebody does this to himself. The guy just uses the cop as a loaded gun."

The theory that Sam was offering about the shooting was relatively cogent but didn't cover all the facts. I asked, "Then why not the front door? Why didn't Brian Sample charge the cops directly?"

"Why didn't he wear blue jeans instead of corduroys? I don't know."

Nor did he sound particularly interested. "You're not being very helpful, Sam. I thought you would find this stuff fascinating."

"Sorry. These new inconsistencies of yours all have possible explanations. Simple enough things. Me? I still mostly want to know why he shot Gloria Welle through the closed closet door. And I want to know how the cops knew he was going to be running off that deck and not out the front door. Those are still the most interesting parts to me."

"I don't have anything to add to those questions."

"Well, then," he said, laughing. "I gotta run. If you can believe it, I actually have some new crimes to solve."

After we hung up I hesitated for a moment while I considered Sam's theory about suicide by cop and then called Winston McGarrity at his insurance agency. I got past Louise, his gatekeeper, in record time. "Winston, are you allowed to tell me if the insurance company paid death benefits on the life insurance policy that Brian

Sample bought from your agency? I'm talking about the first policy, the one for two hundred and fifty thousand."

"Yes, I can tell you. That claim was settled. There was some contention at the time that Brian's acts that day were the acts of a suicidal man and that the policy shouldn't pay because his death was really suicide and the waiting period hadn't ended. But the coroner ended up ruling the death to be a homicide—that basically means death at the hands of somebody else, in this case a cop—so the company paid the death benefit."

"Do you know how the coroner came to that conclusion?"

"It was mostly, I think, because of Dr. Welle. He sent a letter certifying that the day of the shooting Brian Sample was no longer suicidal."

"Really?"

"I thought it was a gracious act on Ray's part. He could have been venomous, could've said that Brian was still suicidal even if he wasn't. Ray could've done that. I'm no fan of Ray Welle, but I thought he showed a lot of class during that time. Said in the letter, if I remember correctly, that he'd seen Brian for treatment just the day before and that he assessed his suicide potential at that time and it was negligible. I thought the gesture was especially kind to Brian's wife and to his boy."

"Kevin and his mother got a quarter of a million dollars?"

"They did."

I thanked Winston and turned my attention to the rest of my sandwich. It left a better taste in my mouth than did the story of Gloria Welle's murder.

Kimber didn't emerge from Ray Welle's study all day. Once during the morning I saw Russ go in to talk with him. The visit lasted about five minutes. Later, Flynn carried lunch into the study.

After the midday meal the search at Gloria's Silky Road moved from the big ranch house to the old frame house where Sylvie lived with her boyfriend. The routine employed by Flynn with Russ assisting her was becoming so familiar it was almost mind numbing. She photographed, measured, collected. He sketched, noted, and labeled. Phil Barrett videotaped every step without complaint. Cecilia Daruwalla stood silently, observing.

The day dragged toward dusk. Flynn was indefatigable and pressed Russ to agree to take samples from the stable and burnt bunkhouse before they stopped for the day. Russ held up his hands in abject surrender. "Tomorrow, Flynn. I'm so tired I'm afraid I'm going to start making mistakes."

She eyed him compassionately and agreed to finish the job the next day. Her last task of the afternoon was to assemble all the evidence they had already collected and organize it in a single large cardboard box. She sealed the box with tape, labeled it, and handed it over to Percy Smith, who signed something and turned the box over to Daruwalla.

Kimber was the last of the Locard group to get in a car to leave the ranch. When he finally emerged from the front door, he walked quickly from the house, his head down, his hands in his pockets, and slid beside me on the front seat. He avoided eye contact as he smiled. "A productive day," he said, tapping his laptop case.

"Really?" I said as I began to ease the car onto the lane.

His voice filled the car. "I've been trying for two weeks to find a data trail for the two housekeepers who were working at the ranch the day the girls disappeared. Dr. Welle terminated their employment, with a generous severance, approximately one month after the death of his wife. Available database records permitted me to track them only through early 1996. I've been assuming that their romantic relationship terminated at that time and they went their separate ways. Today, at last, I succeeded in finding where they have been."

"Ranelle and Jane," I said.

"Very good. Yes. Ranelle Foster Smith and Jane Liebowitz. Today I think that I have found them both."

I said, "Congratulations." But I was confused as to why the news was important. "When I interviewed Satoshi, she said she didn't see the housekeepers the afternoon her sister and Tami disappeared."

"True. But that is . . . only half the story. I would like to know if the housekeepers saw Satoshi. Or Mariko. Or anyone else."

I hadn't considered the possibility that Ranelle and Jane might have had a different perspective on the events of that day than Satoshi did. Which goes a long way toward explaining why Kimber Lister was a world-class forensic expert and I was a clinical psychologist in a college town.

We were approaching the gate at the bottom of the hill. It remained open from the previous car. I asked, "Did you reach them today? Ranelle and Jane."

"No, no, I did not. Sadly, Jane Liebowitz died in an abortion clinic bombing in North Carolina in 1997. Ranelle Foster Smith, fortunately, is still alive, and is residing in Sitka, Alaska. She runs a local art gallery and has apparently become quite renowned for her native basketry. It turns out that she is part Inuit."

"Will you go see her?"

He swallowed before he answered. "Actually, I've presumed upon an old colleague of mine to do that for me. She is already on her way up from Seattle to pose a few questions to Ms. Smith on our behalf. It's apparently not a convenient trip. Getting to Sitka, I mean. From anywhere. It involves . . . seaplanes." I could feel the seat shiver as Kimber Lister shuddered at the thought of being confined in a seaplane.

I pulled left onto the country road to head toward town. The shadows of the big trees close to the river provided a cool canopy. "What about the two cowboys, Kimber? The hands who took care of Gloria's horses?"

"Actually haven't put too much energy into finding them. They were out of town the day the girls disappeared. We've already confirmed that. But . . . I suppose there is something to be gained from talking with them, too. Just in case."

I thought more about the cowboys. "I wonder who watched the horses when the two cowboys were out of town. Maybe someone else was on the ranch that day—another possible witness."

For the first time since he joined me in the front seat, Kimber looked at me. "I hadn't thought of that possibility. I'll have to inquire. Would Gloria have taken care of the horses herself on those days when her ranch hands were gone? I'm afraid I'm rather ignorant about ranching and things. Would it be likely that the chores are something she might just do herself? Or would she bring someone in to help from the outside? I just don't know. That's another question that I can have my friend pose to Ranelle during their meeting."

He scribbled a note on an index card that he pulled from his breast pocket. He replaced it.

I changed the tone of my voice and asked, "How are you doing, Kimber? This has to be difficult for you. Leaving your routine like this."

"I'm doing better than I expected, thank you. So far I've been anxious, but I haven't had an actual panic attack, though I will admit that last night at your house was less than pleasant. Mostly I think I've been anxious about having a panic attack. Does that make sense?"

"Of course it does."

"The day has been long. I'm looking forward to having some time to myself at the B and B to refresh myself before tomorrow. I'm afraid it might be another grueling day. The stable and bunkhouse may turn out to be crucial sources of evidence. Need I say that I won't be joining you and Russ and Flynn for dinner this evening? I'm hoping there's a pizza place in town that delivers. I'm sure you will understand."

"Do you have energy for one more question?"

"Yes?"

"Are you confident about what we're doing here? The forensics? Will this be enough to end the investigation?"

"Once we're on someone's trail, Alan, Locard is like the big bad wolf. We'll huff and we'll puff until we blow the house down. If these forensics don't pan out, something else will." With that pronouncement he pulled his hat down over his eyes and slunk low on his seat.

Once in Steamboat, I checked in to the bed-and-breakfast for both Kimber and myself and gave him his key. Flynn and Russ had already settled into their room without any apparent consternation about the sleeping arrangements. I walked down the hall and inquired about their dinner plans. Flynn wanted to go to an early movie before she ate. Russ wanted to visit the hot springs in Strawberry Park.

I wanted to do neither.

I wanted to be home in Boulder with my pregnant wife. My presence in Steamboat, it had turned out, was superfluous. I was sorry I'd come. I was considering leaving for home first thing in the morning.

CHAPTER
34

Kimber knocked on my door a few minutes after I'd settled into bed for the night. I thought it was around eleven o'clock. I was sleeping naked and the B and B didn't provide robes for its guests, so I answered the door dressed as though I were attending a toga party on a cheap cruise line.

Kimber said, "So sorry to disturb you. May I impose for just a moment? Flynn and Russ haven't returned from their excursions yet." He stepped past me into the room without waiting for my assent. Kimber was someone accustomed to getting his way. He sat in a small club chair beneath the room's only window, which was a double-hung in a narrow gable. Paisley engulfed him from all directions—wallpaper, upholstery, pillows. I noticed that he hadn't changed his clothes from earlier in the day.

I sat back against the headboard of the bed and pulled the comforter over my legs. "Sure, why not?" I said.

While he spoke I assessed him for signs of incipient panic. I didn't see any symptoms. "My friend made it to Sitka at dinnertime in Alaska and phoned me right after speaking with Ranelle. Ranelle has no recollection of ever seeing Mariko or Satoshi at the ranch that night or any other night. Tami? She's not sure about her. Maybe, she says. Ranelle says that Mrs. Franklin was a frequent visitor of Mrs. Welle's and thinks that perhaps Tami may have accompanied her once or twice."

I said, "So we now have confirmation about Mrs. Franklin's visits to the ranch?" I was wondering what about this information warranted invading my room after I had gone to bed.

"That's correct. In addition, Ranelle was able to provide my friend with some more information about the two men who took care of the horses on the ranch."

"Great," I said, without any enthusiasm. I wanted to go back to sleep. My suspicion was that Kimber had stopped by just for company.

He was trying to keep his robust voice down, but seemed physically incapable of whispering. "Both men, Frank Jobe and Thomas Charles Charles—Ranelle said they called him Double Chuck—are living on a ranch outside Austin, Texas. I've been searching databases all evening. They continued working together after they left the Silky Road in 1992. They worked briefly at a ranch near Dallas until 1993."

I pulled the comforter all the way to my waist. "There's more, isn't there?"

Kimber's posture was atrocious. The round-backed club chair made it appear that both his clavicles had collapsed forward. "Yes, there's more. The man who covered for Frank Jobe and Thomas Charles when they were out of town? I located him, too. He still lives close by here. Place called Oak Creek. I found it on the map. Do you know where it is?"

"Yes. I've driven through it a few times. Stopped there once to use the bathroom at the Total station. It's not exactly a metropolis."

"How long would it take us to get there?"

I shrugged. "Guessing? Twenty minutes. Maybe a little more."

Kimber moved toward the door. "I'll wait for you downstairs." He grabbed the doorknob. "I almost forgot. Ranelle said that she and Jane did some major scrubbing of one of the bunkhouse rooms the week after the girls disappeared. Made some extra money by agreeing to paint it all themselves, too."

I tried to control my breathing. "Whose room? Frank's or Chuck's?"

"Neither. The common room, she called it. Ranelle says that there were three little bedrooms, the common room, and a kitchen in the bunkhouse. She was sorry to hear it had burned down. She and Jane and the two cowboys apparently had some good times there."

"Does she remember any blood?"

"She surely does not."

The man who lived in Oak Creek was named Robbie Talbot. Robbie Albert Talbot. Because of the hour I half expected him to greet us with a twelve-gauge at the ready, but he invited us into his home as though he'd been expecting all along for us to show up during the appearance of Jay Leno's last guest of the evening. When Kimber called him Mr. Talbot he told us his nickname was Rat and asked us to call him Rat.

Rat lived in a log cabin a block and a half from where Highway 131 knifed through what constituted downtown Oak Creek. The cabin was a solitary room, maybe twenty-five feet square, and was impeccably maintained. The linoleum floor was spotless, the curtains appeared to have just been ironed, and the split oak logs next to the enameled stove were piled with great care. I assumed there must have been a Mrs. Rat around somewhere, but couldn't see any other evidence of her presence.

Rat offered us a glass of water. We declined. He offered to light the stove to warm the room. We said we were fine. Finally, he asked what brought us to his door.

Kimber said, "If you would be so kind, we would like to ask you a few questions about the work you did for Gloria Welle out at the Silky Road before she died. Would that be all right?"

Rat shrugged as though it didn't make any difference to him. He was a small man, maybe five seven, with a narrow waist and wide shoulders. I guessed that he wasn't forced to shave very often, but his eyebrows, which grew together at the bridge of his nose, were as thick as hedgerows. "I loved that ranch," he said, smiling broadly at memories of the Silky Road, his grin revealing that his teeth were stained brown from tobacco. "Used to always be bugging Frank and Double Chuck, trying to get them to take me on there permanent. But there weren't ever enough horses for three hands at the Silky. Heck, there weren't even enough horses for Frank and Chuck, but those two stuck together and Miss Welle knew that if she wanted one of those cowboys she had to take both of those cowboys. Ain't nobody I ever met took better care of her horses or her cowboys than Miss Gloria. Would've been a dream to work there. 'Cept for how things turned out for Miss Gloria, of course."

Kimber asked, "You covered their jobs on the ranch when Frank and Chuck were out of town? Is that right?"

"Yep. Moved right in. Took right over. Did the routine chores and whatever else Miss Gloria asked."

"Moved in . . . where?"

"Into the bunkhouse Hilton. That's what I called it. Nice place. Had a spare room I could use when I was working. Nice big porch looking down-valley toward the river. Cupboard full of food. Always some beer in the fridge. Didn't mind those days much at all. Sometimes Frank and Chuck'd be gone for a week or more buying or selling horses or whatever." He shrugged. "Just fine with me."

"We're particularly interested in a night you may remember back in eighty-eight. Two girls disappeared from town that night. One was named Mariko Hamamoto. The other was—"

"Tami Franklin. I knew Tami from her daddy's ranch. I hired out there sometimes, too, back in those days. Remember that night real good. The next mornin' I got up and started to feed the horses—heck, must've been about five. Soon enough—couldn't have been much past six—the sheriff came by asking me if I'd join a search for the two girls. Miss Gloria told me to go ahead and go. I spend most of the next two days trying to find those two kids in the snow. Sure do remember."

"The night before the search? The night the two girls

disappeared? Do you remember seeing anyone at the Silky Road beside the Welles?"

Rat looked at Kimber with an honestly perplexed face. "Saw the sheriff that night. Saw Mrs. Franklin. Didn't see the girls, if that's what you're wondering."

"You saw the sheriff and Mrs. Franklin at the ranch? What time do you think that was?"

"Miss Gloria sent me to town on an errand late that afternoon. She needed something shipped somewhere is how I remember it, offered me some money to catch a movie or something while I was down the hill. I saw Mrs. Franklin's truck at the house when I stopped there on my way off the ranch to pick up the package. Passed the sheriff's vehicle down near the gate. I'd say it was dusk, maybe a little later."

"And you got back to the Silky Road when, Rat?"

"Not till late. After the movie I had a few beers with my buddies in town."

Kimber asked, "That night, when you got back, did you sleep in the same room at the bunkhouse or did you move to a new room?"

Rat asked, "How did you know about that? Miss Gloria had moved all my things that same evening. Said that a problem had developed with the plumbing in the bunkhouse. I don't recall exactly what. I slept in the guest room at the Welles' house that night. Fanciest bed I've ever been in my whole life."

Kimber asked a few more questions but Rat had told us all he knew. We thanked him and stood up to leave. I thought Rat might like to know what had happened to the two cowboys from the Silky Road. I said, "In case you've been curious, we learned that Frank and Chuck are still working together. They're on a ranch near Austin, Texas."

Rat stuffed his hands in his pockets and lowered his head. He toed the floor of the cabin with his boot. "Texas? Huh."

"For a while they were at a different ranch near Dallas."

"You know," he said, "those two cowboys are queers." There was a good-sized smile on his face when he looked back up.

"What do we know?" Kimber asked as we climbed back into my car.

"That there was an awful lot of activity at the Silky Road the night the girls disappeared."

"Which means that if the girls were murdered at the ranch, then we have quite a list of suspects and a wonderfully long list of potential witnesses."

I added, "The bunkhouse certainly got a lot of attention during that time. Extra work for the housekeepers. Rat being asked to sleep elsewhere that night."

"It did."

"Flynn and Russ seem to think they can tie that wound on Tami's head to the stones used to build those walls at the ranch. And if the samples from the floor are really ebony . . . well . . ."

Kimber sighed. Before he was done, he erupted into a huge yawn. "I don't know how much longer we can keep this from the press. But I am certain of one thing: I'd like to conclude our work at that ranch before they get a chance to begin theirs."

We drove in silence from Oak Creek and didn't pass another vehicle until we were on the outskirts of Steamboat Springs. Kimber never covered his face during the drive; he stared out the passenger-side window at the high prairies and the distant peaks, thinking I don't know what.

When we got back, the front door of the bed-and-breakfast was locked. My room key allowed us inside. An envelope addressed to Mr. Kimber Lister waited for him on the polished mahogany table in the foyer. I thought I heard Kimber mutter, "Shit," but I wasn't sure.

He slid his finger under the flap of the envelope and carefully released the adhesive. The sheet of paper inside had been folded over only once. Kimber read what was on it, folded it closed, reopened it, and read it again.

He turned to face me. "It's from Russ and Flynn. They think they know where the reporter is. The one from the *Washington Post?* They'd like us to meet them at the general store in Clark. Do you know where that is?"

I nodded. "Clark makes Oak Creek look like Las Vegas. It's up the valley past the Silky Road Ranch. You can spit across the whole town; the general store won't be hard to find. They want us to meet them now?"

"I'm afraid so. We're supposed to page Russ when we're leaving here. They'll meet us at the store."

"Does it say whether Dorothy is alive or dead?"

"I'm afraid not."

"Are we going?"

"Do we have much choice?"

I thought, *Sure,* but didn't say anything.

PART SIX

Blowdown

CHAPTER
35

Kimber had depleted most of his reserves coping with his illness during the long day at the Silky Road. He had apparently consumed the rest during the early evening that he'd spent scouring databases and traveling with me to Oak Creek to interview Rat. On the drive up the Elk River Valley to Clark he chose to return to his familiar pose in the backseat. In a voice that dripped anxiety he asked me to play music—anything—and play it loudly. I flipped through a stack of tapes I had in the car and offered him one of Lauren's favorites, Van Morrison's *Tupelo Honey*. "Ideal," he declared.

I was a reluctant chauffeur. I held no illusions that Dorothy Levin was still alive and didn't really want to be around when her body was discovered after so many days in the wilderness. And I felt relatively certain that her body would be somewhere in the wilderness. Because, other than a few working ranches, including the one owned by the Franklins, and a couple of dude ranches for tourists, pretty much all there is around Clark is wilderness. I wanted to remember Dorothy for her insouciance and her wit. I didn't want a picture of her decomposing flesh etched in my memory. I hoped that Flynn and Russ didn't expect me to identify her.

As we drove past the gate to Gloria's Silky Road Ranch I decided that I would deliver Kimber to the general store in Clark and announce to Flynn and Russ that my errands were over for the evening. I would drive back down to my cozy bed in Steamboat, sleep as late as I could, and enjoy a big breakfast the next morning. I didn't see any reason to change my plans to return to Boulder.

A sign along the right side of the county road welcomes visitors to Clark, Colorado. The sign states that the town was established on September 16, 1889, that its elevation is 7271 feet above sea level, and that its population is "?" A quick glance at the tiny village convinced me that when Flynn, Russ, Kimber, and I rendezvoused at the general store we would temporarily elevate the population of Clark from the single to the double digits.

When Kimber and I arrived, the parking area outside the store was empty except for a pair of old analog gas pumps and a white Ford Econoline that appeared to have been parked in the same spot for many more days than Dorothy had been missing from her hotel room. A moment after I stopped the car Kimber sat up on the backseat. His complexion was pasty, his face was dotted with beads of sweat, and he was on the verge of hyperventilating. "I'm not doing real well," he announced.

My clinical appraisal was that Kimber's assessment was an understatement. I asked, "How's your pulse?"

"Too fast."

"Chest pains?"

"Not yet." *Great.*

"Do you take any medication for this?" I'd wanted to ask that question since I'd learned about the panic disorder, but I'd been hesitant to relate to Kimber as a clinician. Many sufferers have their symptoms largely controlled by medication.

"I've tried them all. I either can't tolerate them or they don't help."

Wonderful.

"Don't worry, I'll be okay. Are they here yet?" He didn't bother to look for himself.

Panic disorder is a physical ailment more than a psychological one. In the face of no apparent danger, the body begins to prepare the organism for a potentially cataclysmic confrontation. It prepares for the coming fight by releasing adrenaline, increasing respiration, changing blood-flow patterns, and sharpening the senses. I could talk to Kimber until he and I were both blue in the face—I wasn't going to do anything to readjust his raging hormone secretion. In fact, the stimulation of my efforts might aggravate his condition even further.

I answered, "No, they're not here. We must have made good time. What would be helpful to you right now, Kimber?"

"I think I'll lie back down until they get here. Close my eyes. The dark is good for me usually. And the music helps, if you don't mind."

I didn't mind. I set the ignition so that the accessories had power and stepped out of the car. The sky was cloudless and most of the stars in the universe seemed to have chosen that night for a convention above the Mount Zirkel Wilderness. The air at seven thousand plus feet was cool, and I wished I'd grabbed a sweater from my room before leaving Steamboat.

Van Morrison crooned at me from inside the closed car.

What did I wish right then? I wished I were in a cozy cabin somewhere on the outskirts of Clark reclining in front of a warm fire with an arm around my wife. What did I have instead? Beneath a canopy of stars I was standing sentry for an agoraphobic forensic genius who was having a panic attack in the backseat of my car while I was waiting for a guided tour to the site of the decomposing body of a woman who I wished had never died.

Either I was fresh out of wishes or my genie was on vacation.

I walked far enough from the car that I couldn't hear the music that was comforting Kimber in the backseat. Three dozen steps away I was blanketed in a quiet that was absolutely surreal. The air was still and it was as though the trees were holding their collective breath, trying not to rustle a single leaf. I strained to hear the water rushing over stones in the Elk River a quarter mile distant, but couldn't. Even the crickets had paused from their incessant chirping. The loudest sound in the universe was the blood rushing through blood vessels near my ears. That sound seemed to roar.

I spotted headlights weaving up-valley through Clark before I sensed the hum of an approaching engine. The headlights moved toward me patiently, deliberately. As the car slowed and began to forge a slow turn into the dirt lot in front of the Clark general store, I'd already come to the conclusion that the person driving the car couldn't possibly be Russ Claven.

The vehicle, an early Ford Explorer, approached mine in the lot. I stayed put outside the arc of lights from the store and watched as the car stopped not alongside, but rather directly behind mine. I didn't think Kimber could hear its approach above the lyrical strains of *Tupelo Honey*. The door of the Explorer opened. Using both hands on the frame of the door for support, Phil Barrett pulled himself from the driver's seat and stepped out.

My mind generated quick questions. *Where are Russ and Flynn? How did Phil know he could find Kimber and me up here? Why did he park his car behind my car?*

The crickets resumed their symphony and the wind lifted a thousand million leaves all at once. The blood rushing to my ears quieted. I moved sideways two steps until I was hidden behind a tree.

Phil Barrett banged on the window of the car and seconds later tugged open the driver's door. The interior lights flashed on. I was afraid that the intrusion was a sufficient shock to give Kimber a coronary, but when Kimber popped up in the backseat, it was Phil who hopped back, startled. With the door open Van Morrison was blaring loudly enough to awaken everyone who lived within a hundred yards, I assumed that was no one. Phil reached into the car and killed the ignition power.

"You alone, Mr. Lister? I was told to expect to find both you and Dr. Gregory here."

Who told you that, Phil?

I couldn't hear Kimber's reply. He was cupping both

hands over his eyes. Finally his rotund voice crossed the dusty lot. I heard him say, "Would you close that door, please, Mr. Barrett? The lights are so bright."

Phil said, "The sheriff asked me to bring the two of you along to join Dr. Claven and Ms. Coe."

"The sheriff of . . . what?" Kimber continued to shade his face with both of his hands.

"Routt County. It's his jurisdiction. The body was found up in the Mount Zirkel Wilderness. The whole blowdown up there is in his jurisdiction."

Kimber was climbing out of the backseat. He asked, "What is that? What's a blowdown?"

I knew what the blowdown was. It had been big news a few years earlier. In October of 1997 freak winds, estimated at over 120 miles per hour, tore across the ridge tops on the western side of northern Colorado's Continental Divide. In one specific area of the Mount Zirkel Wilderness called the Routt Divide, just a few miles south of Clark, the winds were so fierce that they flattened entire forests that had once extended over twenty thousand acres. Where winds struck hardest they either felled the trees or uprooted them. Not occasional trees toppled, but every tree fell to the ground. From the air, the massive forests appeared to have been harvested by a giant scythe. Forest Service estimates had over a million trees either uprooted or sheared from the landscape in a matter of minutes. On the ground the once grand forests were reduced to immense mounds of unstable rubble.

Phil Barrett was explaining this otherworldly phenomenon to Kimber along with the news that Dorothy's body had apparently been found somewhere in the blowdown. I was astonished that her body could ever have been discovered there. Salvage loggers had cleared what they could from almost two thousand acres of the rugged terrain starting in the fall of 1998, but the majority of the blowdown was too dangerous and too remote to permit even salvage logging. I'd seen photographs and videotapes of the unlogged areas. If Dorothy's body was hidden up there, finding it would have been like trying to find a grain of rice in a chopstick factory.

"Where are Flynn and Russ?" Kimber asked.

"They've been kind enough to offer their assistance to Sheriff Pilander. He has his hands full up there." Barrett hooked his thumb across the road, in the direction of the Mount Zirkel Wilderness. "Flynn is helping to secure the crime scene. Russ is doing an initial examination of the body. Pilander is lucky to have them; there aren't a whole lot of people with their skills on call around Routt County, you know."

Kimber said, "There aren't too many people with their skills on call anywhere, Mr. Barrett."

"Of course. Speaking of experts, Mr. Lister, where is Dr. Gregory? I was told he'd be with you."

I used that as my cue to step out from behind the tree and walk toward Phil Barrett's wide back. Kimber said, "There he is."

I said, "Hello, Phil. Heard you drive up. I needed to take a leak."

He spun on me as though he were afraid I was going to hit him from behind. I was impressed at how fast he moved. With some inventive costuming, I thought, he could have another career as the mascot at a swine farmers' convention.

"Dr. Gregory, hi. I'm supposed to drive you guys up to where the body was found."

I shook my head and said, "No can do, Phil. I agreed to ferry Kimber up here to see Flynn and Russ. Now that I've done that I'm heading back down the hill and I'm going back to bed. I'm sure I'll hear all the details about finding Dorothy's body sometime tomorrow. That's plenty soon for me."

Barrett stepped back and leaned against the car. "Flynn asked for you specifically, Doctor. She even actually predicted that you might be reticent to join us up there. That's her word by the way." He smiled with his mouth closed. "Reticent."

I thought about Flynn's request for a moment. "She

was right. I am reticent. When you get back up there, Phil, please tell Flynn she was prescient." I smiled. "That's my word, Prescient."

Kimber took a solitary step forward as though he wanted to be recognized. He said, "I won't insist that you accompany us, Alan—actually I can't—but . . . if Flynn Coe has reason to believe your presence might elucidate something, I would beg that you reconsider your position. We've come quite far, literally. What're a few more miles?" As he was speaking, I was assessing him clinically. His symptoms seemed to have totally remitted.

I couldn't imagine what I could offer Flynn Coe at this particular crime scene other than a quick identification of Dorothy's body. Reluctant, I decided I would offer to do that much and then return to the bed-and-breakfast. "How far is it from here?" I asked Phil Barrett.

"Not far, but dirt roads. Fifteen minutes. Maybe twenty."

"Okay. I'll drive up there in my car. When I've done whatever Flynn hopes I can do, I'm leaving. Fair enough, Kimber?"

"I'm grateful, Alan. Thank you."

Phil spoke. "Where we're going, it's not an easy drive. The last section is definitely four-wheel country. Why don't you drive up with me, and I promise I'll bring you back down to your car whenever you're done."

It didn't feel right. I wasn't sure why.

"No," I said. "I'll follow you."

The dirt road was a well-maintained public access path that wasn't much of a problem at first. The ruts were manageable and the steep sections were short. Along the way we passed at least a half dozen ghost cabins of homesteaders whose dreams had died in the heavy drifts of long-ago Colorado winters. Phil stopped briefly at a Forest Service signpost about ten minutes from Clark. I drove alongside his Explorer. "This is where it gets dicey," he said. "Why don't you leave your car here? I'll bring you back whenever you're ready."

I said, "Lead the way, Phil."

As soon as I raised the window Kimber said, "You don't like him."

We started downhill. I adjusted the transmission, dropping it into second. "I not only don't like him, Kimber, I don't trust him. If we succeed in finding who killed those two girls, it's not going to look very good for ex-Sheriff Phil Barrett. You know exactly what I mean. And if it turns out that anyone associated with the Silky Road is implicated, which is looking more and more likely, it's going to look even worse for him."

Kimber stared out the side window at the darkness of the forest. He asked, "I wonder who discovered the reporter's body."

I said, "It's a good question. Given the terrain we're about to enter, my best guess is that there's a good likelihood that the person who discovered Dorothy's body is the one who put it there."

We drove the next five minutes in silence. I decided to let someone know where we were and checked my phone. This far into the wilderness it didn't have a signal.

As the vehicles cleared a sharp ridge-top my headlights suddenly illuminated the perimeter of the blowdown. As far as I could see in the narrow beam of light the once majestic section of backcountry forest was now nothing more than a jumble of tree trunks and branches piled at least as high as my car.

Kimber said, "Wow."

I was breathless.

CHAPTER
36

Barrett pulled right off the Forest Service access road. I followed him for another quarter mile or so down a deeply rutted lane that skirted the edge of the natural disaster. The mass of fallen trees on our left was a long unbroken wall that was almost as tall as I was. At no point was the mesh of trunks and limbs less than four feet high. When Phil stopped and got out of his car Kimber and I did the same. Barrett pulled a heavy day-pack over one shoulder and said, "It's a short walk from here. Have to climb over a few trees, though." He waved at the skeletal forest. "This is something, isn't it?"

It was something. "Where are the other cars?" I asked.

In a voice that sounded almost too natural, he said, "The others came in the hard way, from the north. We didn't discover this access until after the fact. Once you're in there," he said, pointing at the blowdown, "especially at night, it's like trying to navigate in a box of toothpicks. Everything looks the same. You'll see."

The winding path we followed through the blowdown wasn't exactly a trail. It was more like a tunnel, never more than three feet wide, at times no wider than my shoulders. In numerous places fallen logs seemed to almost cover us in a thick canopy. The aspen and fir trees hadn't just fallen where they were knocked over; instead, the ferocious winds had actually blown them like snowflakes into drifts, creating immense impassable mounts of unstable lumber. The fallen timber that carpeted the steepest slopes seemed to be staying in place despite the law of gravity.

I assumed that the salvage loggers had cleared the path we were traversing. I kept thinking of chopsticks and Lincoln Logs. I didn't have another context for what I was seeing. The terrain was as foreign and foreboding as if I had suddenly been transported to the bottom of the sea.

Our cars had disappeared from view behind us after we had hiked no more than thirty seconds. There was no opportunity at all to perceive any clues about where we were going. Phil's flashlight beam illuminated fallen trees. Thousands. Millions. Nothing else. There seemed to be as many downed trees around us as there were stars in the sky above us.

Twice we reached forks in the trail. Phil didn't hesitate either time. Kimber walked behind me, and I kept checking on his progress. He wasn't losing any ground, agoraphobia and altitude be damned. Once when I looked back at him he said in wonder, "I wouldn't miss this for the world." He was smiling like a climber approaching the summit of a fourteener.

After no more than ten minutes of hiking Phil Barrett said, "Good. We're almost there. Aren't you glad you came?"

For some reason I was as surprised to see bright light in the midst of the blowdown as I would have been to find a Burger King or a McDonald's. A pair of battery-powered lanterns illuminated a clearing that was no longer than a single-wide trailer. The light was a sultry yellow. The brilliance was disconcerting. Above us, the blown-down trees seemed to have created a precarious Tinkertoy mountain at least fifteen feet high. Rising above the immense wall of timber loomed a steep hillside that appeared as foreboding as a steaming volcano. Whatever work Kimber and I were going to be performing there, we would be performing in a wooden canyon.

Phil Barrett called out, "Hello? It's Phil. I'm back with Mr. Lister and Dr. Gregory."

No one answered his call. Phil shrugged. He turned to me. "Maybe they found something else to examine. The body's right around that bend." Kimber and I crossed the clearing. I turned and glanced at Phil. He had a bemused expression on his wide face. Kimber went ahead, entering a narrow cul-de-sac of broken trees.

I stepped into the cul-de-sac and looked at Kimber. We peered at the ground, which was littered with forest debris, then into the chaotic lumber walls, looking for a clue. Dorothy Levin's body wasn't there to see. Nothing was there to see, nothing except the look of terrified acknowledgment Kimber and I recognized as we looked up into each other's eyes.

Kimber opened his mouth to speak. But before he'd formed a word, the sound of Phil Barrett's gun cocking shattered the silence. It was the single most distinct sound I had ever heard in my life.

The next thought I had was about my unborn baby.

I heard Kimber say, "This isn't good."

He was right, of course.

Phil Barrett's voice was suddenly swollen with vitriol. He barked, "Get down on your knees. Both of you. Then crawl back over here." I looked to Kimber for guidance. He nodded purposefully. We dropped to all fours and crawled the few feet back toward Phil Barrett.

I should have listened to my ambivalence about joining Phil on this errand. *If I survive this,* I thought, *Lauren is going to kill me.*

"That's far enough," Barrett said.

We stopped crawling. Kimber asked, "Where are Flynn and Russ?"

"Do you mean were they as gullible as the two of you? Yes. Absolutely. As eager to help us out as a Boy Scout and a Girl Scout." If disdain were water, Kimber and I would have been drowning in the flood that spewed from Phil Barrett's mouth.

"Where are they?" Kimber actually sounded demanding in his retort to Phil. Given the circumstances, I was surprised by the tone.

"I'm not alone in this little scenario. When I left to go

get the two of you your friends were right here. Where are they now? Buried by lumber—that'd be my guess. They weren't my responsibility, but you two are."

Kimber continued to press. "Are they alive?" he asked.

Phil ignored the question. He reached into his daypack and tossed some locking plastic bands my way. Electricians used the bands to bundle wires. Cops used them as disposable wrist restraints. "You do Mr. Lister, Dr. Gregory. I'll do your wrists after you're done with him."

I moved toward Kimber. He offered me his wrists behind his back. I fastened the band.

"Tighter," Phil demanded.

I acted as though I were complying. "Is Dorothy's body really here?" I asked, honestly not knowing what to believe.

"Oh yes. Close by, anyway."

"You know where she is because—"

"I'm the one who put it there. That's right."

I couldn't guess why Phil Barrett had killed Dorothy Levin. To protect Raymond Welle? That made no sense. Barrett must have known that someone else at the *Post* would take up Dorothy Levin's campaign-finance crusade. So why had he killed her? I offered my wrists and backed up toward Barrett. He said, "No. First do Lister's ankles. I don't want you running off. It'll take you three bands. One around each ankle, then another one to connect those two. You got it?"

"I think so."

"Then do it. Don't try anything."

As I moved toward Kimber again his eyes told me something was up. I felt incredibly stupid that I couldn't decipher exactly what. I bowed down to begin to bind his ankles with the plastic bands. The bands weren't long enough to fit around his trousers. I lifted the left leg of his pants and placed the first band near his ankle. After I'd fastened it, I moved to the right. As I lifted the trousers on his right leg, Kimber shifted his weight and kicked me gently with his left heel.

What? I didn't know what he was trying to tell me. I

had just begun to pull the plastic band around his leg when I felt a two-inch-wide balistic nylon strap stretched taut a short ways above his ankle. Heartened, I slid my hand farther up toward his calf and felt the bulge of a gun. Kimber was wearing an ankle holster.

I looked up. Phil Barrett was distracted, dividing his attention between his prisoners and the entrance to the two trails that led through the blowdown and intersected in the clearing. He was clearly waiting for someone else to arrive.

Kimber felt my hesitation and started coughing. Phil looked at him and yelled, "Shut up!" Kimber coughed some more and I used the sound to rip the Velcro flap off of the holster. The small gun slid free. I raised it up the back of Kimber's leg and shoved it into his hand. He turned around and glared at me. His eyes screamed, *No!*

I said, "You know, Kimber, sometimes I think I've done everything right in my life and it turns out that I still don't seem to know how to avoid danger and find . . . the safety."

Kimber laughed and tried to cover the sound with another cough. I hoped the outburst meant he had decoded my message—I'd been trying to tell him that I didn't know how to release the safety on his pistol.

Barrett was staring up the hillside. He screamed again. "Shut the hell up! Both of you." From his agitation I assumed something was going wrong with his plans. As I returned my attention to the plastic restraint that I needed to fasten to Kimber's right ankle, he tapped me on the side of the head with the gun. He was ready to hand it back to me. I took it, hoping that the safety was now off. With some trepidation I stuffed the gun behind my back in the waistband of my jeans and got back to work on Kimber's ankles.

Kimber said, "What's the plan, Mr. Barrett? Exactly how are you planning on killing us?"

"I'm going to shoot you and then set off a charge that will bury your bodies under the timber covering that hillside. My main concern is that I don't want your bodies found. Always seems that's when the troubles begin. Without any bodies it's all so much easier. If I had it to do over again . . ." His voice drifted off.

"The girls?" I asked. "You're talking about the girls."

He was staring at the hillside. Meekly, he said, "It turned out crazy. The first one was an accident. The second one was just a stupid mistake. Me? I was only trying to help."

What?

He looked at me. His next words were clipped. "I didn't kill them, if that's what you're thinking."

At that moment, that's exactly what I was thinking. "Then why the hell . . . are we here?"

He looked away again. "I . . . helped. Afterward. I was . . . involved, afterward. I jammed up the plumbing in the bunkhouse and got all that cowboy's things moved up to Gloria's. I'm the one who moved the bodies to the lake. Had to use all back roads right up along Mad Creek and then through the wilderness. Took half the night to get there towing that damn snowmobile."

Kimber said, "And your subterfuge all worked. Of course I'm sure the fact that you were running the investigation made the task a little simpler."

Phil pointed up the hill beside us. He was presently immune to either praise or irony. "That hillside is steep. And the timber on the hillside above us is very, very unstable—too unstable even for salvage. There's a small explosive charge all set up there, ready to start a landslide of tree trunks. When the charge goes off and those trees start to roll, your bodies will be down here, ready to be buried beneath the pile."

"Dorothy's body? You did the same to her?" The question was mine.

He didn't answer.

Kimber said, "We've already collected most of the evidence at the ranch, Mr. Barrett. It's in Percy Smith's custody at the police department. I assume you're planning to kill him, too."

"I was there, remember? I saw what you got today and

you haven't collected the evidence that I care about. The box in Percy Smith's evidence locker doesn't contain shit. The girls died in the bunkhouse. That's why—"

Kimber said, "You torched it."

"I wasn't in town that day. But that's why it was . . . torched." He shook his head. "Stupid idea. As far as I'm concerned it was like putting a 'Search Here' sign on the place. Other than myself this is a cadre of amateurs."

"Ray Welle?" I asked.

"Ray's no amateur . . . but, no, he's not involved in any of this. There're no big fish in this stream at all." He actually smiled before he stole another glance up the hill. "Got you there, don't I? You thought this was all about Ray, didn't you? You figured that we've all been covering for the great Ray Welle."

I said, "Welle's not involved with the girls' deaths?"

"He may suspect something happened on his ranch, but I don't think he actually knows, no."

"Who are you covering up for then, Phil? Who's worth it?"

Barrett suddenly looked mean. "You think I've been silent this long just to serve you that news on a platter?"

"And Dorothy figured all this out?" I asked.

"The dead girls? No, she didn't know any of it. She figured something else out, though. So . . . she had to go. Want to hear something funny? Dorothy? That reporter? I rescued her before I killed her. Her damn husband had showed up at her hotel to beat the crap out of her. I thought he was trying to kill her. Turns out he was the one who took the shots during the fund-raiser at the tennis house in Denver—followed her here all the way from the District." He shook his head at the irony. "What an ass-hole. When I first walked into her hotel room in Steam-boat she thought I was the goddamn angel of mercy and he thought I was there to arrest him."

I said, "I know why her husband was furious at her. But what about you? What did she know? Was it about Gloria Welle?"

Phil looked displeased with the question, but he didn't answer.

Kimber said, "Someone will follow us, Mr. Barrett. We're a large organization with some of the most inventive forensic minds in the world. Someone else will show up to collect the evidence, whatever it is. The fire didn't destroy it. You can't put this off forever."

"I've put it off for over ten years. Your disappearance will give me . . . us . . . some time to confuse things a little more. I'll gladly settle for ten more years. Now finish those cuffs there. I'm done talking."

Instead of circling Kimber's ankle with the third band I threaded it through a D-ring on Kimber's ankle holster, slid it through the loop on his left ankle, and snapped it shut. I hoped that from Barrett's vantage it would appear to be a functional restraint. But as soon as Kimber removed the holster from his leg his ankles would be untethered.

I said, "There, it's done. Phil, you know that the girls were at the ranch earlier the day they disappeared. We know that Dr. Welle was there, too. He met with one of them."

"So?" He didn't seem interested. "Your turn to get restrained, Dr. Gregory. Stand up and give me your wrists. Move slowly. I'm feeling a mite jumpy." I stood and reached behind my back with both hands, removing the small pistol. As I turned my left hip toward Barrett, I rested the gun against my right thigh. Phil thought I was being uncooperative and barked, "Give me your other goddamn hand."

I did.

I swung my right hand across my body and hit him as hard as I could with the butt of Kimber's gun.

He fell to the ground like a bird shot out of the sky.

I froze right where I was standing. I'd hit him so hard I was afraid that I'd broken my hand.

Kimber said, "Good move. Now, get his gun, Alan . . . Alan!"

I took a step back and stared at Phil's head. Blood was

oozing from his ear and dripping down over his nose. A lot of blood.

"Get the gun," Kimber repeated.

I stooped to retrieve Barrett's handgun.

"Yes. Now bind his wrists, then get me free."

I had to flop Phil from his side onto his ample abdomen to restrain his wrists. That done, I searched his pockets, found a pocketknife on his key ring, and used it to saw through the plastic band I'd placed on Kimber's wrists. As I finished I said, "I can't believe I hit him like that."

Kimber hopped over next to Phil and began palpating the left side of his head, just back of his temple. "You crushed his skull."

The words made me shiver. I said, "Is he dead? Did I kill him?"

"No. He's not dead."

"I shouldn't have hit him so hard. Kimber, we have to get him some medical help. A helicopter or something. I think I remember the way back out of here. It's only a couple of turns. I have a phone in my car but I don't know if it can get a signal up here."

Kimber stood back up and wiped Barrett's blood from his hands on a handkerchief he'd pulled from his pocket. Kimber Lister was the kind of guy who always had a clean handkerchief in his pocket. He said, "Help for him will have to wait. I'm not leaving without Flynn and Russ."

At some level of awareness, I'd expected Kimber's protest. "We don't know where they are, Kimber. We only have Barrett's word that they're even up here, and he sure made it sound like they're already dead. We need to get help with all this. I've seen aerial views of this blowdown. It extends for miles over terrain that's more rugged than you can imagine. There's no way you and I can search it by ourselves, especially at night. The reality is that Flynn and Russ are probably already dead. And Barrett could be dying right now."

Kimber finally finished sawing through the plastic on his ankles. "You go then. Get out. Call Percy Smith in town. Take Phil's pistol with you." He pocketed Phil's keys and returned his pistol to his ankle holster. He checked Barrett's semiautomatic before he handed it to me. "It's ready to go. I'm going to find Flynn and Russ."

Above us, on the hillside, we heard voices. Kimber and I both turned out heads toward the sound at the same time. A man spoke first, followed immediately by a woman. I was able to make out a couple of words, but that was all.

I whispered, "Is that Flynn and Russ?"

Kimber shook his head emphatically. Even his most hushed whisper would be too robust for the circumstances.

I said, "You're sure?" He was.

The woman's voice again, more distinct this time. She said, "I don't want to wait."

"What?" the man replied, loudly. I knew the voice. The man was Dell Franklin. Tami's father.

The woman said, "Shut up." Was that Dell's wife, Cathy? I wasn't sure.

I took a step in the direction of the voices and Kimber grabbed my left wrist, almost yanking me off my feet. He was pointing in the direction of the trailhead opposite the way we had entered the clearing. He grabbed one of Phil Barrett's ankles and I took the other. We had managed to tug Phil's body halfway to the trailhead when an explosion erupted on the hillside to my left. I tried to make sense of the sudden noise and the brutal concussion.

Kimber and I paused. The ground below our feet started to shake as though heavy trucks were passing. The vibration soon became a rumble, the lights from the two electric lanterns flickering around the clearing. Kimber yelled, "The trees are coming down! Run! Leave him!"

Kimber was closer to the trailhead than I was and he made it to the entrance to the path in two long strides. I tried to follow him but my left foot caught on Phil Barrett's huge body. I tumbled over him. Above me, the falling trees had started to roar as they spilled down the hillside.

CHAPTER
37

Momentarily, the roar quieted and the air rumbled the way it does as a big thunderclap is starting to build. Beneath my feet the ground shook as though from an earthquake. Desperately I tried to scramble to my feet. Across the clearing Kimber was screaming something at me, but the words didn't register. The sound was swallowed by the rumble.

Pieces of trees began to cover the ground. A huge piece of an aspen trunk catapulted over me—finally coming to rest near the trail where we had entered the clearing. Others flew above my head like missiles. I was transfixed, staring at the flying trees as though they were a circus act or an athletic performance. Two feet from me the dry trunk of a long-dead fir impaled itself in Phil Barrett's chest with a thump that sounded like death. The sight sucked the air from my lungs. I looked away. When I looked back the image of the dead tree growing out of Phil Barrett's body cavity was right where it had been. I tried to scream, but I don't think I was able to force any sound from my body. If I did, it was swallowed by the tumbling trees.

When I looked up I could barely see the trailhead where Kimber had sought safety. All around me the clearing was filling with the skeletal remains of the forest. I crawled to my left, hoping for some shelter along the wall of the clearing that was closest to the hillside. Above me, the stars had been extinguished by the tumbling trees and by thick clouds of dust.

I stepped past Phil Barrett and felt along the wall of

trees, edging closer to Kimber and, I hoped, safety. Each
tree I touched vibrated in my hands. My eyes were filled
with dirt and the air was thick with debris. I couldn't see
more than a foot or two and I could barely breathe. I
thought of Lauren and the baby as I groped along the
wall. Inanely, I tried to conjure baby names. I wanted to
know his or her name when I died.

My hand touched human flesh.

Kimber's hand clasped around my wrist and pulled. I
tried to stay with him, but between us were obstacles I
couldn't even see. I tried to climb and lost his grip. I poked
all along the wall trying to find his hand again. I yelled his
name at the top of my lungs and couldn't even hear my
own voice.

A tree blocked my way at waist level. I climbed over
it and frantically prodded the air to my left. No wall of
trees! I moved another step in that direction. There were
still no trees.

Was this the trailhead?

I forced another step and ran headfirst into the trunk
of a tree. The bark was hard and brittle and a piece
broke off in my mouth and mixed with my blood. I spat
and poked my hand into the air to my right. Nothing. I
stepped around the tree trunk I'd banged into and
walked right into Kimber. He captured me in a bear hug
and without hesitation carried me at least twenty feet
down the trail. When he released me we started dodging
and skipping as fast as we could away from the tree slide.

Behind us the cacophony continued for another twenty
seconds or so. When the noise had quieted enough that
I felt I could be heard above it, I said, "Kimber, stop."
He did. I pointed behind me. "Phil Barrett's dead. A
tree pierced his chest. Right next to me. I saw it."

Kimber nodded, touched his finger to his lips, and
raised his eyes toward the hillside. Whoever had just
tried to kill us was still close by. Kimber leaned down
and touched his ankle holster, then raised his palms to
the sky. He wanted to know if I still had Phil's gun with
me. I felt in my waistband, back and front. I didn't have

the gun. I'd apparently lost it during my frantic escape from the clearing. Kimber looked disappointed.

He proceeded down the trail. I followed him until we reached a fork. One leg of the trail went uphill, the other down. I pointed toward the uphill trail. That's where we went.

We climbed. After five minutes the tunnel of fallen trees on each side of us was only a pile thigh high, then shortly after that, knee high. Another hundred yards and we were standing in a lush, living forest of healthy green aspen trees. The air was cool and the sky above the treetops was brilliant with stars. I felt as though we'd been adrift at sea and had finally floated ashore.

We'd escaped the blowdown.

We both sank to the ground. I was slightly downhill from Kimber. I tried to say something to him, something to express my gratitude to him for staying close enough to help me out of the clearing. But my throat was so parched that I wasn't able to free my tongue from the roof of my mouth.

I was surprised when Kimber said, "Stay right where you are."

"What?" I said, coughing the word as much as speaking it, and turned to look at him in order to puzzle out the meaning of his words. Behind him stood Dell Franklin holding a big old shotgun that he was pointing right at us.

I felt like kicking someone.

It just didn't seem fair.

Dell killed Tami?

From the moment I'd heard his voice on the hillside before the explosion that set the trees moving it just hadn't made any sense to me. Seeing the sadness in his eyes as he took Kimber and me hostage didn't make it any easier to understand.

Dell had us sit back to back. He stayed uphill from us, leaning against a pair of aspen trees that were growing from the same root ball. His finger rested close to the trigger guard of the gun. From where I sat the big gun looked like a howitzer. Dell couldn't look us in the eyes as he mumbled, "You two should be buried down there. Where's the sheriff? Is he dead?"

I said, "You mean Phil?"

"Yes sir."

"I think so. I saw a tree hit him." I spread my hand across my chest. "I think that it crushed him."

Kimber asked, "Where are my friends?"

Dell shook his head. Was he telling us that he didn't know or was he refusing to answer the question? I couldn't tell.

Dell was staring at the sky. I couldn't see Kimber's face, didn't know how he was reacting to the awareness that his good friends were probably already dead. I thought about the little gun that was strapped to his ankle.

In my only previous opportunity to be with Dell, he and I had managed some connection that had allowed him to talk with me openly. I decided to try to reestablish that connection. "Dell?" I said. I had to repeat his name before he'd look at me. "You didn't kill Tami, did you?"

He looked hurt. "Oh no. Dear Lord, no," he said. "Be like killing one of God's own angels."

"Then what are we doing here?"

"What I should have been doing back then, maybe. Protecting my family. It's all I have left that's worth protecting."

"Joey?"

Dell knew what I was asking. "Joey did a lot of stupid things when he was young. But, no, he didn't kill his sister."

By my count we were running out of Franklin family members. "Cathy killed Tami?"

"By accident." The word came out "ax-ee-dent."

"Want to tell me what happened?"

"No. He doesn't," Cathy Franklin said from farther up the hill. "He wasn't there that day. He didn't know about any of this until recently. But I was there when those girls died. I can tell you what happened if you want. Because this night's going to end the same way that one did—with bodies in the Mount Zirkel Wilderness. See, it doesn't make any difference. You're both going to die tonight, too."

CHAPTER
38

Cathy's voice started off shaky and high-pitched. It reminded me of water flowing rapidly over stones in a shallow stream.

"You've probably met everybody by now, haven't you?" She was directing her words to me. "You've been busy. I know you talked to Joey, figured you talked to Dr. Welle. I bet you probably talked to Mariko's parents, too, didn't you?"

"Yes. I spoke to her father, Taro. Her mother is in Japan."

"So you probably know about the girls being picked up for smoking marijuana?"

"At the hot springs at Strawberry Park."

"Right. Well, that's when it all started." She shook her head, disbelieving. "With a couple of damn college boys on spring break giving a couple of country girls some free marijuana. And now look at us." She waved her hands out toward the blowdown. "Over ten years have passed, and there's still dead bodies as far as you can see. Who would have predicted this?"

"No one," I said. I was guessing at my lines, reading the cues from her eyes.

"No one," she agreed. "No one would have predicted it."

Dell nodded in agreement. Kimber barely moved.

Cathy asked, "Did Phil Barrett ever tell you why the girls weren't arrested that night after he picked them up at the hot springs? Did he tell you that?" She sounded almost defiant.

"Yes," I said. "He did. He suggested he was being magnanimous. Didn't want them to suffer their whole lives for one small mistake."

She snickered as she walked from the heart of the woods to stand beside her husband. "Magnanimous? Phil? Let me tell you something. Phil Barrett was being a prick. There's only one reason that those girls weren't arrested. Want to know what that is? It's because I agreed to have an affair with him. That's why the girls got off that night." Dell took one hand off the shotgun and slid it to the small of his wife's back. She looked up at him with an expression that I could easily mistake for love. "Dell didn't know. He didn't know any of this until recently. I did everything else on my own. I did it to protect Tami."

I had an image of an old model train I'd had as a child. Of placing the individual cars on the track. Of aligning the wheels. That's where we were in the story. The cars were on the track. Some of the wheels were aligned, some weren't. I couldn't guess where the train was going to go.

"Phil Barrett was blackmailing you?"

She seemed to like the sound of that. She said, "I guess."

"It sounds that way to me."

She glanced up at Dell again, this time plaintively. His eyes stayed fixed on Kimber and me. We remained still at the end of his shotgun. Cathy said, "Then . . . you know what Joey did to that girl? The Japanese one. Mariko's little sister?"

Now, Cathy was looking right at me. I nodded in response to her question. She continued staring, hard. I said, "Satoshi. Her name is Satoshi. Yes, I know what Joey did to her."

"After I found out about the . . . thing with Joey and that girl, I knew that I suddenly had another child to protect."

I asked, "How did you know what Joey had done to Satoshi? Did he admit it to you?"

She appeared surprised at my question. "Joey? Joey wouldn't admit to me that he'd passed gas in a lift line. No, Ray Welle called and told me. You know he'd been Joey's therapist?"

I nodded.

"Thought you knew. That whole thing with Joey having to go see Ray for therapy had started right after the last time Joey had gotten in trouble. Anyway, Ray phoned me that afternoon—the one, well, you know— and he said he'd gotten a call from Mariko asking for his help for her little sister. She'd told him what Joey had done to her, why her sister needed his help."

"The earlier incident with Joey was the one in the girls' bathroom at school?" I asked.

Cathy snorted. "My. You do know everything."

"No," I said. "I don't." I still don't know where this train was heading once it made it around the bend.

Ray Welle had danced lithely through a slender crack in the rules that govern confidentiality. When Mariko had informed him that her sister had been raped by Joey Franklin, Mariko was no longer his patient. Her psychotherapy had terminated. Therefore, the information she shared on the phone about Satoshi being raped wasn't technically confidential. By any ethical standard, Ray Welle should have kept the news private, but legally he wasn't required to. And he didn't.

"After I heard what Joey had done, I immediately called Phil. I assumed that he and I were going to have another problem—like the one we'd had with Tami and the marijuana. I assumed I was going to need Phil's help again to keep one of my kids out of trouble." Her tone conveyed a combination of defeat and disgust. "Phil agreed to meet me at the Silky Road. To *talk* about it."

"That's where you—"

"That's where we usually met."

I tried not to look at Dell, could only imagine his outrage at this story. I asked, "Did Ray know about the meetings on his ranch?"

"I doubt it. Gloria and I were friends. . . . She was

helpful to me. She and I worked out the details, and Phil and I met during the daytimes when Ray was in town. Gloria would always let me know when those two gay cowboys of hers were going on the road."

"But there was a problem that day. You and Phil arrived at the ranch before Mariko and Satoshi had left. They were still up at the house meeting with Dr. Welle."

"Yeah, that was a problem. I expected they'd be gone already. Didn't see how it would make much difference, though. Boy, was I wrong." She turned away from us, moving close to her husband. Almost inaudibly, she said, "I don't want to talk about this anymore, Dell."

He shook his head, touched her hair. "They should know, hon. They've come a long way for the truth."

"But I don't want you to have to hear it again."

He shook his head once more. "That's not what's important right now."

I waited for Cathy. When she didn't continue on her own, I tried to prompt her. "But Mariko saw you arrive at the ranch or she saw your car, or something. Later she told Tami what Joey had done to Satoshi and told her that your car was over at the Silky Road. Tami probably wanted to confront you about Joey. Is that what happened?"

Cathy looked at Dell. He nodded to her to continue. Her voice was much flatter when she resumed her story. "Yes, basically. The two girls came back to the ranch a while later. I'm sure Tami wanted to yell at me about her brother. Knowing Tami, she would have wanted me to string him up by his toes right then and there. When she and Mariko got to the bunkhouse, I guess they saw my car. I was still . . . visiting . . . with Phil."

I watched Dell's eyes narrow. He swallowed twice. His finger caressed the trigger guard on the shotgun. I wondered exactly where and when he was planning to kill us.

I also wondered exactly what Kimber was planning to do with his little handgun.

Cathy stretched her neck, her chin as high as she could force it. "Tami walked right in on us. Me and Phil. She

didn't even knock, just walked right on in to the room."
She said it as though the big sin of that day was Tami's
failure to knock before she entered. "Me and Phil
were . . . whatever. We were . . . in the middle of things.
I jumped right up from the sofa to try to calm Tami
down. She was . . . upset, real upset. But she stepped
back from me too fast and she tripped right over Phil's
boots. She stumbled and she fell over backward. That's
when she cracked her head against the stone wall that
runs around the base of the room. I still hear that sound.
That thud. It was a wet sound and it was hard and oh,
my, it was loud. I hear it in my dreams still. I hear it on
the ranch. I hear it mostly when it rains. Don't know
why that is, exactly."

I sensed self-pity creeping into Cathy's story. I wanted
to snuff it out before it established a firm footing. I said,
"But Tami wasn't dead, Cathy. The autopsy showed she
didn't die from the blow to her head."

She changed her posture so that she was looking up
at her husband. "None of this was supposed to happen,
Dell. You know that, don't you? It was all just a stupid
tragedy. Just a tragedy." She waved her hand toward
Kimber and me. "I really don't want any more of this,
Dell. What happened, happened. It's time to be done.
Let's get it over with."

"All in good time, hon. Finish. Do it for me."

Cathy sighed and looked at her feet. "Anyway, we
thought she was dead. Tami. I felt her, her, um, arm. I
couldn't find a pulse. Phil checked her, too. He said she
was dead."

Kimber asked, "Then why—"

"Mariko." Cathy hissed the name. "Mariko came rushing into the room looking for Tami. Saw her on the floor.
Saw all the blood. And, dearest Lord, there was a lot of
blood. Some on the stone wall where she'd hit her head.
Most of it on the floor. Mariko saw it all, saw Tami, and
she started screaming. Phil grabbed her. She tried to run
away, break away from him. But he caught her. He was
holding her from behind, his arm around her neck. I

could tell that he was squeezing her too hard. I told him he was choking her. She kept fighting him though. I guess he thought she was going to run but I could see she wasn't getting any air. I told him to let her go. When he finally did let her go, she just fell to the ground like a rag doll."

I said, "Phil told us he didn't kill anybody."

"Phil Barrett's a damn liar. He killed both of them." I noted that she looked sideways at her husband when she accused Barrett.

"What do you mean 'both of them'? You just told me that Phil said Tami was already dead."

"Right after . . . Mariko . . . fell, Tami moaned. It was just a weak little cry, but it was enough to tell me that my baby wasn't really dead. Phil said it couldn't be, told me I was hearing things. But I knew what I heard and I, I wanted to call an ambulance. But Phil, he pushed me out of the way, wouldn't let me go help my daughter. I fought him to get to her or to get to the phone but he held me back and made me look at Mariko's . . . body. He unplugged the phone cord from the wall. He kept saying, 'Look at her. She's dead. What are we going to do about that? I can fix a lot of things. I can't fix dead, Cathy.' He made me think through what we'd done. He wanted me to put a pillow over my baby's face until she stopped breathing. I fought him—I *did*—but finally he told me he'd kill me, too, if I didn't shut up and cooperate. When I wouldn't do it myself, he threw me down on the other side of the room. That's when he smothered her with a pillow from the sofa."

"You saw him do that?" I asked.

She looked away and tightened her hands into fists. Her lips moved twice before the next words came from her mouth. "No. I couldn't see from where I was on the floor. But when he stood back up he was still holding the pillow. Phil was. And he was breathing real heavy."

I didn't believe her. I suspected that she had indeed smothered her own daughter. The horror I was feeling was mirrored in Dell's eyes. In that instant I was certain he hadn't yet crossed whatever bridge he needed to cross in order to accept his wife's rationalization.

Cathy's story wasn't complete, though. I asked, "And the mutilation, Cathy? How did that happen?"

She slid her hand up Dell's arm until it came to a stop above his elbow. "All the rest was Phil's idea. He planned it all in his head for half an hour or so. He just sat there and planned it all out. When he said he was going to cut off . . . my Tami's hand, I said I couldn't be a part of it anymore. That I wanted to turn myself in. He said if I said a word to anybody about what had happened that he'd make sure Joey was arrested for the rape and he'd make sure Dell knew about the affair."

"What did you do?"

"What was I supposed to do? What would be left for me if I didn't go along? I mean everything that had happened was just a terrible, terrible accident. If I didn't go along with Phil I'd have nothing—and I'd have nobody. I didn't really have a choice, did I? My Tami was already dead. If I told anybody what I knew, I'd lose my son, my husband, my whole family."

Kimber voiced what I was thinking, what I was certain Dell must be thinking. Kimber said, "She was your daughter. How could you?"

Cathy exhaled deeply and coughed as she tried to refill her lungs. I expected to hear another verse of the "terrible-terrible-accident, what-was-I-supposed-to-do" song, but she couldn't get any words out. Dell finally spoke. "Why did I want you to hear all this? So you would understand what Cathy did back then. In her mind what she did, she did to protect the kids. First she was helping Tami. Then, later on, Joey. With what he's done with his life since then, I think Joey has made all her sacrifice worthwhile." I was stunned by the words. For such a self-aware man, Dell Franklin had just engaged in a world-class rationalization of horror.

"Dell," I said, "you . . . agree . . . with what she did?"

"No," he said firmly. "I do not. I don't condone what Cathy did. But she did what she did to protect the family.

I can live with that knowledge. I can." He looked down at her and handed her the shotgun. "Now, hon, I need to tie these boys up so we can take them down to join the others in the blowdown," he said. "You hold 'em here while I get some line to tie 'em. I'll only be a couple of minutes. We can't afford to mess up anymore; we're almost out of dynamite."

"Dell, I'm tired. Let's just shoot them here."

Cathy looked tired to me.

Dell wanted none of it. "And then have to drag their bodies all the way back down that hill into the blow-down? No way. I won't be gone but five minutes."

The second Dell turned his back I felt movement in Kimber's shoulder. He was going for the handgun.

CHAPTER
39

Dell walked away from us slowly. His shoulders were hunched forward and the incline of the slope made every step he took seem a monumental effort. Not once did he look back our way.

Cathy didn't have the arm strength to keep the barrel of the shotgun pointed right at us. It kept drifting down and she kept lifting it higher. Each fresh cycle of effort lasted a shorter time than the previous one. Her muscles were fatiguing.

Kimber turned his head away from her and whispered, "On three, roll away from me."

Cathy heard him speak but probably couldn't understand the words. She raised the gun once more and said, "Don't you try anything. Killing doesn't bother me too much anymore. Killing you now rather than later is nothing more than an inconvenience. This is loaded with birdshot. I don't even have to aim."

Cathy couldn't maintain the angle of the gun barrel. Kimber tapped me with his elbow once, paused, tapped me again, paused, and finally tapped me a third time. On the last tap I somersaulted forward and started rolling down the hillside. I kept rolling while I waited for a blast from the shotgun, but all I heard was a hollow click. I hoped Kimber was getting away but couldn't risk the time it would take to look back toward him.

I heard him say, "Drop it, Cathy!"

I rolled once more before I crouched behind a boulder. Kimber was kneeling behind an aspen tree that wasn't mature enough to protect him from a blast from the shotgun. He held the pistol in both hands, pointing it right at Cathy Franklin. Her shotgun was leveled at Kimber.

I wondered whether it was actually loaded. It was a twin-barrel over-and-under model. At most, Cathy had only one shot remaining.

I picked up a rock the size of a lemon. Found a second. Cathy yelled, "Dell, I need some help here!"

My cover behind the boulder was better than Kimber's was behind the spindly aspen tree. I threw the first rock at Cathy. It landed near her feet.

She kept her focus on Kimber. "Dell Franklin, you get over here, now!" she screamed.

I threw the second rock. It thudded hard against her upper arm. She yelped and swung the barrel of the shotgun toward me. I tried to disappear behind the rock as I waited for the roar of the second barrel. Instead I heard three quick claps from Kimber's pistol bounce off the hillsides. The blasts were so close together that the echoes made them sound like a single shot.

I looked up in time to see Cathy fall. She didn't fall backward. She didn't pitch forward. Her knees softened, and a second or two later she crumpled right where she had stood. Her lips were moving as though she was in silent prayer. The shotgun reached the ground before she did.

I said, "Kimber, are you all right?"

"Fine. You?"

"Good, I think. What do we do now? Dell's probably on his way back."

Before I had a chance to reply, I heard, "How about we do this now? Why don't I take you two to see your friends? I think they'll be more than happy to see you." Dell Franklin was walking back down the hillside toward us. One of his hands was raised above his head like a prisoner's. The other one gripped a big chain saw. He took a path down the hill that let him pass at least ten feet from Cathy's body. Not once did he glance over at her. Kimber kept his gun leveled at Dell's chest but Dell didn't seem to notice it.

He looked first at me and smiled ruefully. Turning to Kimber, he said, "Thank you. Thank you both. I didn't have the heart to do that to her. But . . . I'm afraid that it needed to be done."

Kimber moved over to Cathy's body and rested his fingers against her neck. He craned his neck to look up at Dell. "Cathy thought the gun was loaded?"

Dell shrugged. "Not sure what she thought." He didn't expect us to believe him. We didn't.

"How did you know I had a gun?" Kimber asked.

"Didn't know for sure. I was afraid Cathy had managed to kill the two of you when she toppled those trees down the hill on top of Phil. Since you escaped I kind of hoped you had Phil's gun with you, but if you didn't, I figured I didn't have much more to lose, no matter what. I'd go get some line and tie you up. Work on plan B."

I said, "Flynn and Russ? They're okay?"

"I can't be sure, but they were when I left them. Let's go check. We might need this." He hoisted the big saw.

Kimber was still kneeling next to Cathy. He said, "Your wife, Dell? She's still alive."

Dell looked over, down at the mother of his two children, the blood pouring from below her sternum. His eyes were dispassionate as he said, "That's a bad wound she has. She won't be alive for too long."

Kimber said, "He's right."

I was the only one who kept looking back at Cathy. The callousness of the decision to leave her there to die made me feel hollow and cruel. Finally, near the boundary of the blowdown, I yelled to Kimber and Dell that I'd wait with Cathy until help arrived, and I jogged back up the hill. When I got next to her, though, I saw a pool of her own blood that was floating dust and forest debris. The quantity of blood she'd lost was immense. I lifted her wrist but couldn't locate a pulse. I lowered my ear to her face but couldn't hear any breath sounds.

I trudged back down the hill and rejoined Kimber and Dell, who had waited for me. Neither of them met my eyes. We reentered the dead forest. I never thought I would voluntarily enter the perimeter of the blowdown again. The web of dead trees terrified me as we descended into the deepest drifts of lumber. Dell led us. I followed Kimber. After walking for ten minutes, Dell stopped and looked us in the eye one at a time and said, "It was important to me that you hear the story from Cathy's own lips, just the way I did a few days back. If I had to tell it on my own, I don't think I could do it justice." He shook his head. "Right about here is where Phil said the reporter and her husband are buried. Somebody should know that, look for them. Bury them properly." He pointed up the hill. "It's too dark to see, but Phil brought an entire hillside of trees down into this ravine on top of their bodies."

So Phil Barrett had killed Dorothy's husband, too. What was his name? Oh yeah, Doug.

We walked on. I felt numb. *What had Dorothy learned that warranted her murder?*

Another ten minutes passed. We weren't covering much ground. The path wasn't clear; broken trees and stumps littered the way. Kimber said, "Dell? Earlier? You were supposed to kill Flynn and Russ?"

"Yes. That's the way Phil had it planned. I was supposed to take care of the two of them and he'd take care of the two of you. We'd let the forest bury the bodies. While he was down in Clark picking you up though, and while Cathy was busy setting the charges on the hillside, I tied your friends up, moved them someplace I thought would be safe, and fired a few shots into the air. Even though Cathy set off the charge, they should be okay where I put them. We'll see real soon. We're almost there."

*   *   *

It took thirty minutes of the deafening roar of the chain saw to free Flynn and Russ from the spot where Dell had sheltered them from the cascade of broken trunks and limbs that the explosives had sent down the mountainside. The lacy web of timber that had imprisoned them in a crevasse at the base of a high rock face was almost eight feet deep. Each time the saw quieted I told Flynn and Russ another part of the story we'd just learned from Cathy and Dell.

Flynn and Russ finally crawled up through the narrow opening that Dell created with his saw. They were both filthy but neither of them appeared to be injured. Flynn climbed out of the cavern first, then Russ.

Flynn went to embrace Kimber. During the frantic effort to free Flynn and Russ I hadn't noticed his withdrawal from our activity.

"Alan," she said. "Look at Kimber."

I turned toward him. His arms were crossed over his chest. His eyes were orbs of pure fear. "I can't breathe," he said. "I think I'm having a heart attack." His hands were shaking. Despite the chill of the night, beads of sweat dotted his upper lip and brow. He was gasping for breath. "I can't stay here. I've got to get out of here."

I climbed closer to him. "It's a panic attack, Kimber. This will pass. You're going to be okay. They always pass, right?"

"No, no. I'm not going to be okay this time! This is worse. I feel like I'm going to die up here. I have to get away from this place. Right now, please. I have to go." His eyes scanned the hillside, searching for imaginary dangers.

I knew I had to grant him whatever control I could. "That's fine, Kimber. Where would you like to go?"

He didn't hesitate. "Back to your car. I like it in your car. Right now I want to go to your car."

I needed a helicopter to locate my car. I didn't even know which way to look for it.

Dell Franklin's mouth was open as he stared at

Kimber. Finally, he said, "We're not too far from it, actually. Your car."

"Can you show us?"

"Sure."

Kimber said, "I'm dizzy. I can't feel my hands."

"You'll be okay, Kimber."

"No, no. I won't. I'm afraid I won't."

Dell led us to my car. At times Kimber jogged through the narrow paths between the fallen trees. At times he cowered and waited for Flynn or me to steady him. The relief I felt at finally clearing the perimeter of the blow-down was enormous.

I kept waiting for Kimber's panic attack to abate. But it showed no signs of lessening.

I fumbled for my keys. Kimber climbed into the back-seat, begging, "Music! I want music. More Beethoven. Boz Scaggs. Somebody, I don't want to die back here."

I turned to Flynn and Russ. "We shouldn't all pile in there with him. He needs space. I'll drive him down to town and try to get him stabilized. Dell, where are the other cars?"

"A quarter mile from here, around the edge of the blowdown. That's all. You go ahead. The three of us will follow you in my truck."

I turned to Russ and Flynn. "You're sure?"

Russ said, "Go. You're the best one to be with him right now."

Dell said, "The closest place you could take him would be my ranch. It's the first ranch past Clark. You're welcome to take him there."

Kimber yelled, "No! No place new. It will make it worse. Turn the music up. Drive, please, drive."

I offered a sad smile to Dell before I climbed behind the wheel. I said, "Thanks for the offer. You need to finish telling Russ and Flynn the story and get the local sheriff involved. I'll get Kimber to town and try to calm him down."

PART SEVEN

Welle Done

CHAPTER
40

By the time Kimber and I descended from the edge of the blowdown and reached the town of Clark I figured that his panic attack had exceeded an hour in duration. As far as panic attacks go, sixty minutes is a long time. I asked Kimber if that was typical for him. In a voice as cold and sharp as an icicle he told me that it didn't matter, this time was different, he was sure he was dying.

I was starting to worry. Although panic attacks are terrifying for the victim and scary enough for anybody in the vicinity, they are usually, ultimately, harmless physically. But that isn't always the case. Occasionally the physiological stress that an attack places on the body can cause severe consequences—heart attack, stroke, even in rare instances, death.

Ten minutes farther down the hill toward Steamboat, Kimber sat up suddenly in the backseat and said, "Alan, I don't think I'm going to make it to town." I had to admit that he appeared ready for death. He was ghostly white and his respirations were rat-a-tatting like a machine gun. He looked out the window and asked, "Are we close to Welle's ranch?"

I was perplexed by the question. I replied, "Reasonably. A couple of more minutes."

"Go to the ranch, then. Please. The Silky Road. I liked it there today. I think maybe I'll feel safer there. Maybe I'll get better there. Please."

Although familiarity sometimes has an ameliorating effect on panic episodes, I wasn't convinced returning to the ranch was the wisest course of action. "We're only fifteen or twenty minutes from town, Kimber."

"I don't think I can make it twenty minutes. My chest."

I started to argue that there was no one at the ranch who could let us through the gate. He told me he didn't care. We could break in. He'd explain it all later. "I've lost feeling in my toes and fingers. Just try it." He was begging.

Remembering that this man had helped save my life only a couple of hours earlier, I drove to the gate of the Silky Road and hit the buzzer. While I was waiting for a response I checked my watch. It was almost dawn. The only thing that was keeping me awake was the adrenaline rush I was having in reaction to Kimber's panic attack. Sylvie finally answered my beckon after a minute or two. She had obviously been awakened from a sound sleep. I couldn't imagine that she would grant us entry if I told her the truth, so I identified myself and said that Phil Barrett had asked me for a ride home from town and explained that he'd lost his keys and couldn't recall the security code for the gate.

She asked if Phil was drunk again.

I said he was.

She mumbled something profane and told me she'd go over and unlock the house for him. Give her five minutes to get dressed.

The gate eased open and I pulled inside and drove up the lane. I told Kimber to stay down in the backseat until I knew Sylvie was gone. I didn't want her to get a glance at Kimber. She wouldn't be fooled; Kimber looked nothing like Phil Barrett. Sylvie arrived at the front door a minute after I did and as she unlocked the door asked if I needed help getting Phil inside.

I said, "This isn't the first time, I take it."

"Hardly," she replied.

"Go back to bed. I'll get him in even if I have to use a wheelbarrow."

She laughed good-naturedly and climbed back into her car to return to her house.

"Kimber," I said as I leaned into the car, "we're here. Where exactly do you want to go?"

"The study. Same place I was today."

I supported him from the car and guided him to Raymond Welle's study. I didn't know how I was going to explain this incursion to anybody. I'd already decided that the moment the panic attack abated I was going to pack Kimber back in the car and drive him down the hill to the bed-and-breakfast so I didn't have to explain the lie to anyone but Sylvie.

Once inside Welle's study Kimber knew exactly what he wanted to do. He plopped down on Ray Welle's big leather sofa, curled up in a ball, and pulled a blanket over his head. I asked him about chest pain. He waved at me from under the blanket. I asked him if he needed an ambulance. He said, "No." I flicked off the room lights and left him.

I succumbed to my fatigue the moment I was alone. I moved to the living room, kicked off my shoes, and sacked out on a couch. Within minutes I was almost asleep; in fact I was so close to sleep that I was certain the sounds I started hearing were a prelude to a dream.

A door closing gently. Water running. Someone shuffling feet on a hardwood floor. I opened my eyes. Damn. Kimber must have gotten up to use the bathroom. *Maybe,* I hoped, *he's feeling better already and we can go back to town.* But I thought that the sounds that I'd heard had come from the other end of the house. My heart started racing. I listened intently.

Who could be here? Sylvie was down the lane at her house. Phil Barrett was in the Mount Zirkel Wilderness with the trunk of a fir tree planted where his heart and lungs should be.

I tried to swallow but my throat was so dry that I coughed. I constricted my throat as tight as I could but I coughed again, not only failing to muffle the sound but also announcing my presence to whomever it was that

I'd heard moving around the house. I stood up and moved closer to the central hallway. The clerestory skylights above my head were blue-black and the first soft gray light of dawn was filtering into the corridor. I saw no one lurking down the hall. I listened some more and heard no sounds coming from anywhere in the house. My heart began to slow.

It must have been Kimber that I'd heard. I stayed planted where I was for another long minute, heard nothing new, exhaled in a long sigh, and decided that I needed a bathroom before I fell asleep. From the forensic search the afternoon before, I remembered that there was a powder room just a few steps farther down the main hallway toward the master bedroom. I went there and unzipped. Midstream, seconds after I started to pee, I heard, "My, but this is convenient. God does answer prayers."

I tried to stop peeing but I couldn't. I was that frightened by the gun that was pointing at my head.

"After you've finished up there and tucked everything back in place, why don't you just put your hands behind your head?"

I zipped, and laced my fingers behind my neck.

Raymond Welle said, "That's right. Now come on out of there."

He marched me to the living room and sat me on a sofa directly across from him. He was wearing a soft woolen robe over a pair of pajamas and the kind of step-in slippers that my father used to wear. He said, "So, who are you tonight? Goldilocks? What? Were you planning on going from room to room trying to find which bed was ju-u-st right?"

I didn't know how to respond. I said, "I can explain all this, Representative Welle."

"Save it. I don't care for your rationalization, Dr. Gregory. All I care about right at the moment is that I seem to have an intruder in my house in the middle of the night. I have a weapon in my hand. And I have the right under Colorado law to use that weapon to protect my property. That this particular intruder has proven to be one major pain in the ass for the past few weeks is just frosting on the cake."

Welle was sitting with his back to the front door and to his study. It was clear that he didn't realize I wasn't alone.

"Sylvie let me in."

"Did she? Under what pretense? I doubt this visit is covered by the search agreement I signed with Locard." He laughed. "Makes no real difference. Sylvie didn't know I was coming in to the ranch. I didn't arrive from Washington until almost two. From my point of view, the situation is quite simple—you are a burglar. Or maybe even an assassin. You do know there have been recent attempts on my life, don't you?" He smiled at the irony.

I didn't like the direction of the conversation. I said, "Phil Barrett's dead, Ray. That's why I'm here."

"What? What do you mean Phil's dead?" He squirmed on his chair, squared the gun at my chest.

"You know the blowdown on the Routt Divide?"

"Yeah. What about it? I had to pressure the Forest Service to allow salvage crews up there to clear some of those trees. Reduce the spruce-beetle problems and the fire hazard. Why?"

"Phil died up there earlier tonight. Somewhere in the middle of the blowdown. A bunch of trees slid, one of them fell on him and crushed him."

"Fell on him? What was he doing up there at night in the first place?"

"Trying to cover his tracks. He killed those two girls, Ray. Mariko and Tami? Phil killed them." I stared at him, trying to gauge from his reaction whether or not the words I had just spoken constituted news to him. I couldn't tell. I continued, "The girls died in your bunkhouse. Phil was having an affair with Cathy Franklin. Her daughter walked in on them. Things got out of hand."

He didn't react right away. When he finally spoke, he asked, "This happened right here on the ranch? No, I don't believe it." I thought his protest was a few degrees shy of convincing. He paused, thinking about something. "So was it Phil who torched the bunkhouse? That was his doing?"

"I'm not totally sure. Phil denied it. If I had to guess I'd say it was Cathy who set the fire. She actually admitted to the killings, though. And she's the one who implicated Phil."

"Cathy did that?" He shook his head. "Helped kill her own daughter? I thought she loved that girl. How does a mother do that?" He appeared to get lost in contemplation and I wondered if he was looking for a new theme to use on the campaign trail. The gun barrel wavered a few degrees. If he'd fired it right then it would have missed me. "You know that Phil was pretty desperate for me to rescind the agreement I signed allowing the Locard people to search the ranch. That's why I flew back here tonight, to work all that out with him. Congress is still in session. I really should be in Washington right now. But . . . I guess she figured you boys were about to find something that would point a finger at him about those killings." Ray continued to seem pensive. I guessed that he was trying to figure out exactly how much I knew about what. My best strategy for staying alive involved not helping him with his quest.

He asked, "So is Cathy dead, too? Another tree fall on her?" He wasn't trying to disguise his suspicion about my story.

"No trees fell on Cathy, Ray. But yes, she's dead, too."

"You kill her?"

I shook my head.

He nodded as though he understood something. I couldn't guess what. "But the killings. It was just her and Phil? Doesn't go any farther. Dell?"

"Dell didn't know."

The politician in him had started calculating the impact of these developments on his self-interest. "With these confessions in place—Phil's and Cathy's—I imagine Locard's work on this case is done, finished. The rest of the search of the ranch won't have to take place tomorrow, will it?"

"I imagine not, but it's not my decision."

His shoulders sagged. He rested the handgun on his knee. "Well, it is up to me. I'll just put an end to it myself. Nonetheless, this will be a circus for the press. Phil dead. Ancient murders on my ranch. A member of my staff involved. I think I'd better get on back to Washington. I don't want to be held captive here at the Silky Road when the media craziness starts percolating over what Phil once did. I'm going to need some professional help with this from my press people."

"If you shoot me you won't be going to Washington for a while, Ray. There'll be a few questions." He yawned. I fought not to mimic him. The room had brightened further with the advancing dawn. The brightness was disconcerting; I still wanted to sleep.

"Who knows all this?" he said. "What you just told me? About the girls and Phil and Cathy?"

I didn't want to answer truthfully. I said, "A lot of people know. Phil had lured all of the Locard people up to the blowdown. They all know. Why don't you just let me go? You won't have the satisfaction of killing me, but it will be much less messy for you than the alternative."

"You may well be right about that. But the truth is that this opportunity may be too good to pass up. See . . . there's that other problem."

I was surprised. "What other problem is that?"

Some flaky sleep in the corner of one eye was bothering Welle. He scratched at it with the nail of his pinkie. "I don't especially appreciate all the questions you've been asking people about Gloria. My wife? You had that boy's uncle send me a letter wanting to see the records from Brian Sample's old psychotherapy, right? That wasn't a good idea on your part, didn't sit right with me. That's one sleeping dog you should have just let lie."

I recalled Sam's warning to me after the incident at the tennis house in Denver. "Tell you what, Ray—since it bothers you, I'll stop asking."

He laughed. "I wish it were that easy. But I don't think you'll stop. Why? I don't think you like me. I don't think you like my politics. I don't think your wife liked having me in her fancy family. Yeah, I know all about your wife. You know what else? I don't think you even like having me in your sanctimonious profession. I don't think either of you wants to have me in the Senate. So, no, I don't think you'll stop pestering. You'll just keep digging and picking at it. Won't let Gloria rest until you make something tragic look like something sinister."

"You have my word. I'll stop."

"Sorry." He wasn't. I could tell. The gun came back up off his knee.

I argued. "You can't stop the questions by killing me. There are others who know everything I do."

He narrowed his eyes and rubbed the stubble on his chin with his free hand. The sound was audible. "I don't think so. Some of this—the part about Gloria—only another psychologist would figure." He stood up. "Now you get up, too. It won't look good to shoot you while you're sitting on the sofa."

I stayed where I was and reviewed my options. I could yell for help from Kimber. Ray would probably consider it a diversion and shoot me anyway. The possibility also existed that Kimber remained so incapacitated by his panic attack that he might prove to be of no help. Either way I didn't see how it was going to increase the odds of my survival.

I could run for it and hope Ray was a lousy shot. An errant gunshot would probably rouse Kimber from his stupor and he'd run out and confront Ray, at which point one of them would shoot the other. Another possible lousy outcome.

"Up," Ray said. "Might not look good to kill you there, but I'll do it. Don't test me. Now get up."

The circumstances were eerie. I was so tired that I thought I hallucinated a tray with Red Zinger and Girl Scout Cookies on the table between us. Without thinking, I blurted, "Where do you want me to go exactly,

Ray? The closet in the guest room? So you don't have to watch what you're about to do?"

He blanched and a breath caught in his throat. His hand shook.

Until that moment I hadn't known what the stakes were for Raymond Welle. But suddenly I did.

My murder would not be the first one Ray Welle had planned at the Silky Road Ranch.

CHAPTER
41

Ray's eyes stared past me. I was tempted to look over my shoulder to see what he was focusing on. He said, "You can't prove anything." He had started breathing through his mouth, the long exhalations coming from deep in his gut.

My feelings about the gun pointing at me were flip-flopping as much as the politician who was pointing it at me. One moment I felt totally intimidated by the threat, the next moment I felt totally liberated by the certainty of my death. During one of the liberated moments, I said, "That argument alone tells me I don't have to prove anything at all. It's as good as a confession."

He straightened his shoulders, trying to look congressional and imperious. The gun and the pajamas detracted from the image. He scoffed, "And what good does it do you? Now that you know—so what? You get to die a righteous man? Does that feel good? You fool! I'm so glad for you. Will that make your widow happy? Now stand up!"

I did stand. I needed to keep Ray talking and was rethinking whether or not to call for Kimber's help. "Why did Brian do it for you, Ray? I don't get that part. Was it the transference? Was he that crazy?"

Ray took a step back from me. First one foot, then the other. He was gripping the pistol so tightly his knuckles were turning white. "No, he wasn't crazy. He was the most suicidal son of a bitch I saw in my whole career. But he wasn't crazy. Not at all. Brian Sample had not only decided that he wanted to die, he'd also decided that he wanted to die a righteous man. That's why he did what he did."

"And killing Gloria made him righteous?"

"Are you kidding? Brian knew that killing Gloria for me was only the price of admission." His mouth widened into a tight smile. "You only have bits and pieces."

"No," I admitted. "I don't know what happened."

He tsked. "I'm surprised at you. Phil eventually figured it out, every last bit of it. He's not that bright a guy, so that surprised me some. But he was here that day so he had an advantage. But you? I've been guessing that you had it all."

"Phil knew?"

"Yeah, he knew I arranged to have Brian kill Gloria. And me? I'd suspected all along that he had something to do with those two girls dying back in 1988. Left the two of us in a kind of a standoff. Remember the cold war? Our nuclear policy with the Russians? The tacticians called it 'mutual assured destruction.' MAD. If they tried to blow us up we would blow them up. And vice-versa. It was a perfect stalemate. That's what Phil and I had, our own little mutual destruction pact. MAD right here on Mad Creek. When I got elected to the House, we decided to reduce the tension a little and become allies. It turned out all right, I think, for both of us. But now Phil's dead. The rules are going to be different, I suppose. I should enjoy a little more freedom now that Ray has unilaterally disarmed."

"He killed Dorothy Levin for you."

Ray Welle raised an eyebrow. "*For us.* He killed Dorothy for *us*. She comes here for one weekend and manages to puzzle out way too much of what had happened to Gloria. So Phil eliminated her. He did it for both of us—let's just say that over time our interests had converged."

I was shocked at the motive. "Dorothy wasn't killed because of the campaign-contributions story?"

"That? No. What she had on me? It's all smoke. House Ethics Committee might have slapped my wrist.

But that was no mortal sin. No, she was getting close to figuring out what happened with Gloria. She had the insurance angle down and was asking way too many questions about me and my practice. Kind of like you are, except she was a little smarter."

Ray had lowered the barrel of the gun so far that it was pointing near my feet. I scoured my memory for details of the floor plan of the house, trying to imagine a route for an escape attempt. I doubted that Ray Welle was a skilled marksman. The more distance I could quickly put between us, the better my odds would be that he would miss when he fired at me.

His next words stunned me from my reverie like a slap across the face. He asked, "Do you know the hardest thing about getting away with murder?"

I said, "Excuse me? What?"

"The hardest part of this whole experience—the whole thing with having Gloria killed?" He could tell that I didn't have a clue what he was talking about. "I mean killing someone and not even being considered a suspect? I mean never suspected at all—ever. You know what the hardest part is?"

I was flustered. He seemed to want an answer so I took a stab at it. "I don't know, the guilt?"

Ray Welle laughed at me. "Bad guess. I figured you for being a little more intuitive than that, Alan. But, no, I'm not prone much to that particular reflection. Remorse isn't one of my things. So let me tell you just so you'll know. The hardest part about getting away with murder—I'm not talking about the details, mind you, I'm discussing my personal feelings here—the hardest part is not being able to talk about it.

"Me? I'm a talker. Everybody says that about me. They couldn't shut me up when I was on the radio. The Speaker couldn't shut me up when I was on the floor of the House. I was out of order more than a deck of cards. Truth be told, I even yakked too much when I did psychotherapy. But I haven't been able to talk to anybody about this. Not even Phil. We talked about lots of things over the years, but we never talked about getting away with murder. Neither of us. There was a time I needed to talk about it so badly I thought about going into therapy. You know, just to have a chance to spill the beans to someone and leave him sitting there with his mouth hanging open. But that impulse always passed. The result? There hasn't been a word spoken in all these years, until here today, with you."

What was I supposed to say, that I was honored? The more he told me, the more certain I was that he was planning to seal my lips permanently. On the other hand, as long as I could hear him talking, I was still alive. There was that.

"Why, Ray?"

"Why did I have her killed? Is that what you mean? She was bailing out on me, on my dreams. She was going to pull the plug on the money I needed for the ninety-two congressional campaign. I couldn't raise the money without her name and her influence. And even that wasn't enough for a decent campaign. I needed her personal contributions—as my spouse she could spend as much as she wanted. And soon enough, I figured, she was going to start making noise about a divorce. When she left me I would have been sitting with my half-assed practice in Steamboat, my quirky little local radio show, and almost no money. Gloria had to die. It was the only way I could see to guarantee my future. Although I couldn't touch her trust, the rest of the assets would be mine. I hoped that would be enough."

"And what was in it for Brian?"

"I promised to convince the coroner that he was no longer suicidal the day that Phil's boys shot him dead on the ranch. That way his family would get enough life insurance money to start their life over again. Without my intervention with the coroner the insurance company wasn't about to pay on his policy. No way. Brian understood that. Basically, he killed Gloria for me and I agreed to make sure his family were taken care of."

"Your idea or his?"

He lifted the gun so it aimed at my gut. I could feel my bowels pucker. "Brian wasn't the brightest bulb in the scoreboard, if you know what I mean. He didn't have what it would take to come up with this."

"What about shooting her in the closet? That was ad-libbed, I take it?"

Ray shook his head. "No, we worked that part out together. Brian wasn't an eager participant. Even at the end, he wasn't at all sure he could look Gloria in the face and kill her. I understood; I don't think I could have done it either. We had to come up with an alternative."

"Why did he do it?"

"I convinced him that no one would really blame him, that everyone would think he just snapped from all the stress. It was a sacrifice for his family."

I considered Brian's desperation. "A cop friend of mine thought the closet was suspicious. The fact that he shot her through the door. He had a whole lot of trouble with it."

"You know, when Phil first came in the house he had trouble with it, too. If I had to do it over again, I would have insisted Brian shoot her face-to-face." He broke into a broad smile. "And look!" He waved the gun at me. "I *do* have to do it over again. I need to remember my lesson. Let's go find a good place for you to die. No closets for you."

It was time for me to do something. Trying to run seemed absurd. Ray Welle was standing seven or eight feet away from me with his handgun leveled at my chest. He might not miss. That left the Kimber option. If he was to be of any help, I had to pray that his panic episode had abated.

I said, "I didn't come here by myself, Ray. You and I aren't alone in the house."

He barely heard my words. He was looking out the big windows of the great room, gazing toward the lane. Two vehicles were approaching the house. One was a Steamboat Springs police vehicle driven by Percy Smith.

The other was a familiar Ford Taurus driven by Russ Claven.

Ray said to himself more than to me, "Sylvie must have called them. They think you're holding me hostage." I wasn't about to remind Ray that Sylvie didn't know he was on the ranch. I was certain Ray didn't know who Flynn and Russ were; he probably figured that they were officers who had accompanied Percy Smith and the other uniformed officer.

I had reached a different conclusion about the arrival of the police than Ray had. I was thinking that Kimber must have realized what was going on and called the police. *They know that Ray is about to kill me.*

The cars stopped about a hundred feet from the house, and the four occupants all exited on the far side of their vehicles. The solitary uniformed officer had a rifle with a scope. Percy Smith was armed with a cell phone.

The telephone rang inside the house. The peal seemed to clang around the cavernous space like a church bell.

Ray said, "If I'm a hostage, I don't answer the damn phone, right? Right. Let it ring, let it ring." He turned to me. "Back up. We're going into the hall so they can't see us through the windows."

He backed me up into the hallway that led to the master suite and ordered me to stop just opposite the powder room. He said, "Sit."

I did.

The phone finally stopped ringing.

Ray said, "What were you talking about before? About not coming to the ranch alone?"

"I'm terrified. I was just trying to buy some time. You know, distract you."

He stared at me while he tried to cinch his robe tighter without interfering with the aim of the gun. "I don't know whether or not to believe you."

Good, I thought.

"And I can't exactly go wandering through the house searching for someone, now can I? I can't. The police would see me moving around and know that I'm not really a hostage."

I was beginning to recognize my leverage. It was paltry, but it was something. I said, "But neither can you risk the possibility of there being a witness already here in the house. Someone who might see you murder me in cold blood."

The phone rang again.

"I have to ignore it, don't I?"

I didn't respond to Ray's question but I counted the rings. After twelve rings, the sound stopped. I waited an inordinate time for ring number thirteen to begin.

Ray Welle narrowed his eyes and said, "I wonder if that someone else you're talking about picked it up." Keeping the gun aimed at my chest, Welle backed into the master bedroom and lifted a cordless phone from its charger. He was walking back toward me as he touched the button that would open the connection. I half expected that Kimber's indelicate whisper would carry right back down the hall.

But all I heard was dial tone.

Ray lowered the phone back to its cradle. Looking down at the lights lit up on the base unit, he said, "Someone's on the other line."

I said, "What?"

"You weren't lying before. The second line's lit up. Someone's on the second phone line."

Kimber, what on earth are you up to?

"Where is he?" Welle demanded.

"I don't know."

"Bull. Doesn't matter. I'll find him. There aren't that many places in the house with extensions on that line."

His eyes took on an evil cast. "Get up. Come with me. I know just where to put you while I sort this out."

I opened my mouth to scream a warning to Kimber.

CHAPTER
42

The closet.

The guest-room closet.

As Ray marched me closer to the wooden door I felt repelled by it as though it and I were magnets with opposite charges. My steps shortened the way my dog Emily's do when I'm leading her somewhere she doesn't want to go. My weight rocked back on my heels.

Ray Welle said, "Open it."

I said, "I can't." I was as helpless as a four-year-old being asked to volunteer an arm for a shot.

He said, "I know a little something about the psychology of motivation," and shoved the barrel of the gun between my shoulder blades.

His strategy worked. I reached down for the knob and opened the door. Instantly, an overhead light lit the small space. The switch must have been built into the doorjamb.

Ray said, "Look at that shelving, that detail, the edge work. Even in the damn closets. That was Gloria's thing. Detail."

"It's very nice," I stammered.

"Get in."

"I—"

"Get . . . in."

I stepped in. The gun in my back was, once again, a significant inducement. Ray slammed the door behind me. The light blinked off. I heard him fumble with a key. As he turned it in the lock, I felt as much as heard the bolt throw.

What, I thought, *no chair?*

Would the gunshots come immediately?

I didn't know. One argument I was making to myself was that Welle couldn't really afford to shoot me through the door. If he did, he could hardly argue that he was protecting himself or his property from an intruder. He'd have to come back and get me, then march me someplace else before he shot me.

The closet was large enough for a chair but not quite big enough to get a running start to bust the door down. I tried three or four times to no avail. Each time I rammed against the door with my lowered shoulder I bounced harmlessly back off the pine. With the heel of my stockinged feet I managed to crack one of the door's raised panels, but I couldn't get it to bust out.

I needed to warn Kimber that Ray had gone looking for him. I started screaming, "He locked me in the closet! He's by himself in the house! He has a gun!"

I repeated the refrain twice, then a third time, pausing between warnings to listen for the sound of gunshots in the distant parts of the house.

I heard nothing.

The shelves in the closet held little. Some folded linens. A down pillow. The built-in drawers were empty, awaiting Ray's next guest's clothing. I climbed the lower shelves to run my hand along the upper ones. On top I found two empty shoeboxes and a tied bundled of satin hangers.

The phone rang again.

It rang and rang. This time no one answered.

Kimber?

With a foot on a shelf on each side of the closet, I felt along the ceiling for the light fixture to see if there was something up there that I could break off to use as a tool to get out of the closet or, if Ray Welle came back, as a weapon. But there was no light fixture; the closet bulb was enclosed in a recessed can. A few inches behind it I felt a ridge of wood, a strip of molding. I traced the molding with my fingers—it framed an opening about two feet square—and moved the palm of my hand to the recessed center of the square and pushed. The panel gave just a little. My heart jumped. This little door meant attic access.

This little door meant freedom. I climbed up another shelf in the closet for leverage.

The door proved hard to budge. I was afraid the shelves were going to yield before I was able to push it open. Finally it gave, and I poked my head into the attic.

The place was huge. The true size of the house wasn't apparent to someone walking through it on the main floor. Inside the house, walls divided the rooms and the true volume of the space was disguised. But the attic had no dividing walls; one immense cavernous vault capped the sprawling home below. And although the house was technically a ranch, with all its living space on one floor, no such limitations ruled the attic space. The height of the attic varied tremendously, not only to accommodate the vagaries of the home's roofline, but also to accommodate the varying heights of the ceilings inside the house.

What I needed was a circulation vent—a louvered opening—that I could remove or kick out to permit myself egress from the attic. To find a vent I had to get from the center of the house to the perimeter. I began to raise myself to the lip of the opening to begin my search.

In rapid order, three sharp blasts from a gun pierced into the enclosed space in the closet. Immediately all strength left my arms and legs. I fell from my perch near the ceiling and tumbled to the floor in a heap. My fall destroyed the bottom shelf and made a racket. I moaned.

While I waited for more shots I held my breath. But the next sounds I heard were footsteps retreating and an amplified voice from outside the house. One of the cops was calling something to someone inside the house on a loudspeaker. I couldn't understand the words. Finally, I exhaled.

The gunshots had destroyed enough of the door so

that light was entering the closet. I could reach my hand through one of the openings and almost touch the door-knob, but not quite. I persisted, slicing my forearm on the splintered wood. The key was still in the lock. My arm tendons screamed in protest as I twisted my hand to turn the key.

Through the open attic door I heard footsteps above me. Someone was running fast toward the far end of the house, above the master bedroom. More shots rang out. The blasts seemed to follow the footfalls across the roof.

I felt blind. Activity was going on all around me and I could only guess what was actually happening else-where in the house.

I pushed the closet door open and prepared to make a run for safety. But before I took off I looked back into the closet. Had I not been climbing to the attic, the shots that had been fired through the door would have hit me. For sure.

I saw no one as I made my way first to the laundry room, then to the mudroom. I flung open the mudroom door and sprinted toward the police car with my hands high above my head. In what felt like slow motion, I watched two rifles rotate toward me. I dove to the ground screaming, "No! It's me! Help!"

Someone barked, "Hold fire!"

I looked up and back at the house. Russ Claven was crouching on the roof, staring down at the clerestory win-dows that lit the long central hall. He was tracking some-one's movements below. I wondered whether he was tracking Kimber or following Ray Welle. Russ scam-pered catlike farther down the roof, hovering at the sky-lights above the master bedroom. He pointed straight down and nodded his head.

I climbed to my feet and ran like the wind to the protection provided by the parked cars, arriving just as Percy Smith was directing his officers to take aim with their rifles in the direction of the master bedroom suite.

I hugged Flynn. She asked if I was okay. I asked about Kimber.

I could tell from her expression that she was hoping that it was I who knew about Kimber's well-being. "We don't know," she said. "We lost contact with him."

A large picture window looked down the lane from one end of the master bedroom. For a split second Ray Welle stood in that window and peeked through the drawn curtains. His eyes seemed to be searching, until finally they found mine and locked. He blinked twice and shook his head maybe an inch each way.

"There he is, in the bedroom window," I said, just as the curtain fell back into place.

"I saw him. He's gone now," said Percy.

On the roof Russ Claven had started gesturing frantically toward the far end of the house. The side closest to the deck. The side nearest the woods.

My brain was working faster than my mouth.

"No!" was all I could spit at first. "No!"

Percy Smith stared at me. "What the—?"

In less than two seconds Ray Welle was out on the deck, firing wildly toward the police cars. I ducked from the fusillade and said, "Percy! He wants you to kill him! Don't do it!"

"What?"

One of the cops said he had the target.

I yelled, "He wants you to kill him! Don't do—"

The cop fired his rifle. The other cop pulled his trigger so closely afterward I could barely feel a gap between the concussions of the blasts. I watched in horror as Raymond Welle tumbled over the edge of the deck and landed with a thick thud on the lawn.

I'd imagined the scene so many times, I felt as though I'd been there before.

Percy Smith said, "Hold fire. Get the ambulance up here."

To Percy I said, "It's exactly what he wanted you to do."

Percy replied disdainfully. "What? You think we shot

him? He's not dead. We fired way above his head. Just scared him half to death." To his officers he said, "Keep him in your sights."

Russ had scampered down the roof. I watched as he dropped from one of the copper gutters to the deck just as Ray Welle was struggling to his knees, searching the ground for his handgun. Russ vaulted the deck and flattened the congressman before he had a chance to retrieve the weapon.

Flynn grabbed my hand and said, "Come on. Let's go find Kimber."

I ran after her back into the house.

CHAPTER
43

Flynn and I found Kimber propped up against a wall in the foyer of the house. He'd been shot once in the left shoulder. From the mess on the floor around him I assumed he had lost more than a little blood.

When I dropped to my knees by his side he said, "I told you I was dying. I just didn't expect it to be so traumatic." He was calm as he made his joke. The symptoms of panic had evaporated.

Flynn took one of his hands and said, "You're not dying, Kimber. You hear me?" Without turning to face me she ordered, "Alan, get Russ in here."

Kimber's voice was tentative and weak. "God help me. She's calling a pathologist. Maybe I'm already dead."

I was encouraged that he was continuing to find humor in his predicament, but Flynn was determined in her response to him. "You are absolutely not dying, Kimber. You just keep breathing. We'll do the rest."

As Kimber opened his mouth to reply, his head fell suddenly to his chest. The whine of an ambulance siren filled the narrow valley. Flynn mouthed, "Hurry!" I ran to fetch Russ and to guide the paramedics back to Kimber.

Once my quick errand was completed Percy Smith wouldn't let me back into the house. He left me leaning against the hood of one of the police cruisers as he explained why I couldn't go back inside. My adrenaline was spent. I had barely enough energy to stay vertical, let alone to argue with him. He moved me into the backseat.

I half expected to be cuffed but I wasn't. At least not right away.

I dozed off in the back of Percy Smith's police department SUV on the drive into Steamboat Springs. Once inside the building I fell sound asleep while the local authorities were assembling the cast they had chosen to interview me for details about how Kimber Lister and I had spent the previous twelve hours or so.

When I was finally approached again it was by a Routt County sheriff's investigator who was flanked by both a Steamboat Springs police detective and an FBI agent. I shook myself from my stupor and asked about Kimber's condition. None of the cops answered me. I asked about Kimber's health. They declined to tell me that, either. Their demeanor convinced me that I might still be in some legal jeopardy for defending myself against Phil Barrett up in the blowdown, so I asked to be allowed to make a phone call. They exchanged wary glances before they assented. I used the opportunity to phone Lauren. She listened to my lengthy story with remarkable patience and restraint, inquired twice about my well-being, and ordered me not to talk to anyone until she was by my side. She promised she'd be in Steamboat within four hours.

The cops weren't happy with me when I told them that at the advice of an attorney I was choosing not to speak with them, at least temporarily. Percy Smith was recruited to try and goad me into cooperation. They could not have known that he was absolutely the wrong emissary. After I refused to change my mind, it was clear that the cops remained unhappy with me. I knew that the alternative was my wife being unhappy with me. My decision to stay silent was not a particularly anguished one; I wasn't planning on going home with any of the cops.

Before I nodded off again, I wondered about Flynn and Russ and Dell Franklin and whether they were secreted away close by. I doubted that if I asked the cops

I would get a straight answer. I didn't ask. Instead I curled up and slept on the floor in the corner of the interview room until my wife arrived.

Lauren poked her head in the door around two o'clock in the afternoon.

She brought concern, a sweet smile, a little shake of her head that amply conveyed "You are so pathetic but I love you anyway," and lunch in a bag. I was grateful for three out of four. After Lauren kissed me she informed me wryly that she should also have fetched a toothbrush and a razor.

The most important gift she bore was her legal acumen, which she feared I greatly needed.

I asked about the baby and how she felt after the long drive. As she touched her belly her eyes told me everything was fine. She explained that she had called Sam and asked him to drive her over the Divide so she wouldn't get so exhausted by the trip. Satoshi had insisted on coming along, too. I was comforted to know that Sam was close by and hoped I would get an opportunity to be the one to tell Satoshi exactly what had happened to her sister.

I was also hungry for news.

While I ate, Lauren talked. She wasn't able to provide much of an update on Kimber. All she knew was what she had heard on the car radio on the drive up from Boulder—that he had survived his gunshot and was in surgery at the local hospital.

Raymond Welle's detention by the Routt County sheriff was the day's big event. Lauren's impression was that none of the national news organizations had pieced together the intricacies of the story. No one was yet reporting anything about the two girls who had died in 1988 at the Silky Road Ranch. And no one was reporting anything about the crazy denouement in the blowdown on the Routt Divide or the discovery of Dorothy Levin's body. But having a United States congressman under suspicion in the attempted murder of an ex-FBI agent was big enough news for the time being. Lauren said that she expected dozens of satellite crews to descend on Steamboat within the next few hours. She also said that she was sure that the right-wing blonds on the cable news talk shows were already piecing together the skeleton of a "make-my-day" defense for Welle to employ for shooting Kimber. Shortly after they had all checked in for about the hundredth time on the Monica Lewinsky pathos, Lauren had decided that she wasn't fond of the right-wing blonds on the cable news talk shows.

I asked what defense Welle might concoct for arranging to have his wife, Gloria, murdered by Brian Sample.

Lauren smiled and said she couldn't think of a single one.

It became clear that Lauren wasn't at all concerned about the ill-advised decision that Kimber and I had made to enter Raymond Welle's home while seeking shelter from the storm of Kimber's panic attack. Based on my rendition of events she was far more concerned about my claim of self-defense for burying the butt of Kimber's gun into the side of Phil Barrett's head. She pointed out that my only corroborating witness was unconscious the last time I had seen him. After a few more questions, our much-too-brief reunion was over. Lauren kissed me again and left. She had some negotiating to do on my behalf.

The minutes passed like a gallstone. Waiting, it turned out, had been much easier when I was asleep.

After a half hour she returned.

"I need you to think carefully," she said, her back to the closed door. "Have you told anyone but me about Welle's responsibility for Gloria's murder?"

"No. I didn't have a chance to say much of anything before they started treating me like a criminal."

"And you're absolutely certain about what Welle told you?"

"Yes, he confessed to arranging Gloria's murder. It

was an insurance scheme with Brian Sample. Ray walked me through motive, plan, everything."

"You'll testify against him?"

"Of course."

Her eyes brightened. "Good. The police don't seem to know anything about it. I'm going to offer them a little trade. I think it will be your ticket out of here."

"Great. Any news on Kimber?"

"He survived the surgery and corroborated your account of Phil's death."

I hissed, "Yessss," as I thrust my fist into the air like Sam always did at Avalanche games.

She walked up to me and ran her fingers from the back of my head to the base of my spine and embraced me tightly. "I don't usually do this with clients," she purred.

"But occasionally?"

"I try to take it one client at a time."

The interview with the assembled authorities lasted over three hours. Lauren stayed with me for the duration. The discussion covered the entire previous night. The meeting with Rat. The trip to Clark. The blowdown. Phil Barrett's demise. Cathy Franklin's demise. Douglas Levin's stalking of his wife and shooting at her at the Welle fund-raiser in Denver. Barrett killing Dorothy. The apparent discovery of Dorothy Levin's body. Rescuing Flynn and Russ from their Lincoln Log jail. Kimber's panic attack and the decision to seek shelter at the Silky Road Ranch. The confrontation with Ray Welle and Welle's admission that he had arranged for his wife's murder. The closet.

Everything I knew. Three times.

At ten minutes after six they handed me an envelope with my car keys and my wallet in it and told me I was free to go. I'd find my car outside in the lot.

Sam was waiting for Lauren and me at the bottom of the concrete steps. "If you were my kid," he said with a big smile when he saw me, "I wouldn't let you go out of the house without a helmet on."

"Or at least a lawyer in tow," I said as I kissed Lauren on the cheek. "Thanks for driving her up here, Sam."

He shrugged. "Gotta keep that baby of yours happy. I take it you're free to go?"

"Apparently. I traded my freedom for that of a congressman."

His eyebrows reached for his hairline. "Welle?"

I nodded. "He murdered his wife, Sam."

His eyebrows reached for the sky. "No? I told you the story of that kidnapping was goofy. You have details? You know how he did it?"

"I do. How about I fill you in a little later?"

"Sure." He pointed toward his Cherokee. Satoshi was sitting on the front seat. She waved. Sam said, "Satoshi's anxious to hear what you learned about her sister. Are you up to it?"

"Yeah. Let me get a shower, wake up a little. I want my head to be clear when I tell her what happened to Mariko. Ask her if that's okay."

Sam sauntered over and spoke to Satoshi before he returned to my car.

"She said that she's waited years and that minutes and hours are irrelevant."

While I was spending my day in custody, the bedrooms at the B and B had been shuffled. Satoshi was going to share Kimber's room with Flynn, and Sam was bunking with Russ. I was delighted to make room in my bed for Lauren.

I showered for almost twenty minutes. The shower could have been better only if Lauren had offered to soap my back and any other parts of my body particularly in need of attention. But she didn't.

Russ had made arrangements with Libby for us all to dine together privately in the breakfast room of the B and B. As barter he had offered her gossip-laden details that wouldn't be in the next morning's paper about what

had transpired in the blowdown. Libby had made some
calls to get enough food delivered for a feast and was
supplying the beer and wine herself. Russ suspected that
she was angling for an invitation to the repast. But it
wouldn't be forthcoming. He asked me what I thought
about Libby attending. I voted no. He asked me if I
wanted to invite Percy Smith. I voted no again. This was
going to be a very private party.

The aromas of nourishment greeted me—I thought I
smelled abundant garlic and a blast of curry—as I tow-
eled off from my shower and began to shave away the
whiskers of the last thirty-six hours. I scraped my face in
short strokes in an effort to keep my hand from shaking.
The reality of what had transpired since the previous
sundown was descending upon me with a gravity that left
me fighting back tears. I felt a sense of guilt about what
had happened to Kimber but found most of my compassion directed to Dell Franklin, who seemed the most
complete victim in the whole tragedy.

Lauren could tell that I was taking too long in the
bathroom. She finally entered without knocking and embraced me from behind. "We're all okay," she whispered. "All three of us." I stopped fighting back my
tears, and together we slunk down to the damp floor.
We huddled together on the tiny octagonal tiles until
most of our fears were soothed away.

CHAPTER
44

The night started in the kitchen of the B and B and I ended where everything having to do with me and Locard and the two dead girls had begun—on Joey Franklin's time-share jet. The party that occurred in between wasn't a festive affair. It was more like a hybrid between sitting shivah and attending an Irish wake. There was no shortage of lives to celebrate and unfortunately no shortage of lives to mourn.

There were a lot of stories to tell.

The first thing I did after I finished dressing was search out Satoshi. I found her where she had been waiting for me in the parlor. I took her by the hand and led her into the deserted kitchen of the B and B so we could be alone.

She hopped up to sit on the lip of the granite-topped island. She said, "I have a feeling I shouldn't be standing."

I sat on a stool. "I probably shouldn't be standing either." I caressed my tired eyes with my knuckles. "Are you ready, whatever that means?"

Satoshi nodded. "I've been waiting a long time."

"Okay." I started with "I know how your sister died," and told the story of Mariko's senseless murder deliberately so that Satoshi could chew each detail separately and digest it slowly, the way she had nibbled away her carton of yogurt the day we'd first met at Stanford.

She wept almost nonstop while I spoke, but she refused my offers of comfort.

"They were both heroes," she said when she was certain I was done. "Mariko and Tami."

"Yes," I agreed.

Her next question surprised me in the way that people often do. She asked, "What's going to happen to Mr. Franklin? Do you think there's a possibility that I can talk to him?"

I said I didn't know. I said it twice. Then I added, "He knows what Joey did to you, Satoshi. He just found out."

She raised her chin, stretching her smooth neck. She lowered it, and turned her head once left, then right, before she said, "Your voice? I'm beginning to know its melodies. You're wondering if I've changed my mind, if I'm going to press charges against Joey, aren't you?"

"Yes. I am."

"I can't prove what happened back then. And if I accuse Joey, you know that he'll deny it." She examined the flesh on the palm of her left hand as though God's own advice was inscribed there. "What I'm thinking right now is this: My parents managed to survive this tragedy with one child remaining. Perhaps so should Dell Franklin."

She smiled at me with warmth, but no mirth, and asked to be left alone for a while.

When I rejoined the group, Sam and Lauren were listening to Flynn and Russ describe how they had been lured to the blowdown to help with the recovery of Dorothy Levin's body. Flynn excused herself at the conclusion of that part of the story so that she could keep a promise to visit Kimber at the hospital. Everyone but Sam was done eating before it was my turn to describe how Kimber and I had been lured to the blowdown and what had happened afterward in the Routt Divide with Phil Barrett and with Dell and Cathy Franklin.

It was near midnight before Russ answered the last question about what had transpired after dawn with Raymond Welle at the Silky Road Ranch.

Lauren said, "I'm ready for bed, I think. If I'm this tired, the rest of you must be exhausted."

"I sure am," said Satoshi, who had finally rejoined the group.

Just then Russ's cell phone chirped in his pocket. He stood and carried it to the bay window before he began speaking. I couldn't hear many words of his conversation.

When he walked back to the table he held the phone out in front of him and said, "Apparently Flynn and I are going back to the District tonight. Kimber wants to be in his own fortified castle—which isn't surprising—before the press discovers everything that happened here. He apparently talked the anesthesiologist into giving him a scalene block—it's a nerve block of his arm and shoulder—so he's not going to be in any pain for the next ten hours or so. The surgeon isn't thrilled about his leaving, but . . ." Russ shrugged his shoulders. "Kimber's hired a nurse to accompany him home. Dell Franklin arranged to have Joey's jet waiting at the airport. I'm supposed to go upstairs and pack up Flynn's things and meet them at the plane."

"Is Dell out of jail?" I asked.

"Apparently on personal recognizance."

"Thank God."

Lauren turned to me and said, "We need to say good-bye to Kimber, Alan. It's important."

"And I'd really like to meet him before he goes," said Satoshi. "I want to thank him."

We made it to the Yampa Valley Regional Airport about forty-five minutes later. Satoshi, Lauren, and I spent the drive crammed together in the backseat of Sam's old Cherokee.

The jet was ready when we arrived. So was Hans. He stood tall at the top of the short stairs with his hands behind his back.

Flynn greeted us on the tarmac. Her eye patch was plastered with tiny iridescent stars. It looked just like the night sky above the Routt Divide. She said, "Kimber's already on board. He'd like to meet with Satoshi alone before we take off. Because of his . . . uh, condition . . . he's never had the chance to meet any family members after Locard has finished one of the investigations. It's important to him that he talk with her."

Satoshi hesitated. She gestured toward the jet with her chin and said, "It's not really Joey's plane, right?"

Russ said, "Nah, it's a rental."

She mouthed something to herself and climbed the stairs to the cabin. Hans escorted her inside.

Flynn said, "He seems fine, Kimber does. He has an IV running. But because of the nerve block the nurse said the pain won't start until after he gets home."

"Is his shoulder going to be okay?" Lauren asked.

"Apparently. But the recuperation is going to be painful."

I helped Russ transfer the luggage to the plane. Sam and I promised to ferry the Taurus over to the rental car company lot and drop the keys into the after-hours box.

Ten or fifteen minutes later, Satoshi emerged from the jet cabin and asked us all on board. "Mr. Lister wants to say good-bye to everyone."

Lauren preceded me up the steps. At the landing she paused and made a little sound that was somewhere between a yelp and a coo.

"Are you all right?" I asked, startled.

When she turned to me her face and eyes were lit with a smile. She lowered both hands to her abdomen and said, "Sweetie, the baby just moved."

It took us a minute or two—maybe three—to make it the last few feet through the door. The plane seemed much smaller with so many people on board.

Don't miss

Stephen White's new hardcover

The Program

in stores now!

CHAPTER ONE

Almost Fat
Tuesday

ONE

"Remember this. Every precious thing I lose, you will lose two."

The man was a good target.

Tall, six-five. Wavy blond hair that shined almost red in the filtered February sunlight. Ivory skin that refused to tan. Green eyes that danced to the beat of every melody that radiated from every tavern on every street corner in the always-tawdry Quarter. Even during a crowded lunch hour in the most congested part of New Orleans you could spot him a block away, his head bobbing above the masses. And on the eve of Fat Tuesday, the Quarter was flush with tourists; each of them was flush with anticipation of the debauched revelry that would only accelerate as the Monday before stretched into the Tuesday of, as almost-here became Mardi Gras.

The other man, the one with the gun, knew that in a crowd like this one, he, on the other hand, would have made a rotten target. He was five-eight with his sneakers on. What hair remained on his head was on the dark side of brown. His creeping baldness didn't matter much to him, though, because the Saints cap he was wearing shielded his scalp from the sun as effectively as the distinctive steel-rimmed Ray-Bans shaded his eyes. The khakis and navy-striped sweater he was wearing had been chosen because they comprised the de facto uniform-of-the-day among the male revelers wandering to join the crowds on Bourbon Street.

The late morning had turned mild, and the man's windbreaker was draped over his right hand and arm, totally disguising the barrel of his Ruger Mark II as well as the additional length of the stubby suppressor. His left hand was shoved deep in the pocket of his khakis. He had been briefed on the tall man's destination in advance and kept his distance as he followed him. At the intersection where Bienville crossed Royal, the man with the silenced .22 would begin to close the gap on the man without one. That would give the assassin a little over a block to get close enough to do his job.

The tall blond man had come from his office near City Hall. His wife had wanted to meet him downtown and accompany him to the restaurant. But he'd declined her offer. He'd made prior arrangements to stop on his way to their lunch date at an antique store on Royal to pick up a nineteenth-century cameo he knew his wife had been coveting. The cameo was a surprise for their anniversary.

The errand on Royal hadn't taken the man long, though, and he was turning the corner from Bienville onto Bourbon ten minutes before he was scheduled to rendezvous with his wife. With an athlete's grace and a large man's strides, he dodged slothful tourists with their to-go cup hurricanes and quickly covered the territory to the entrance of Galatoire's. Briefly he scanned the sidewalk and the teeming street in front of the restaurant. His wife wasn't there. He didn't even consider looking for her inside: Kirsten had a thing about sitting alone in restaurants. He hoped she wouldn't be too late; the line for lunch at one of New Orleans legendary eateries was already growing.

They had been in New Orleans for six years, and this would mark the sixth time that they had celebrated their anniversary at Galatoire's. He was the one who insisted on returning year after year. She would have preferred going to a restaurant that actually took reservations. But he prevailed. He was the keeper of the traditions in the family. He was the romantic.

The man with the windbreaker on his arm window-shopped two doors down from Galatoire's, using the storefront glass to reflect the position of his prey. He didn't worry about being spotted. There was no reason that anyone would focus on him. He was a middle-aged guy loitering on Bourbon Street just before lunch hour on the eve of Mardi Gras. One, literally, of thousands. Finally, the beeper in his pocket vibrated. With his fingertip he stilled it and began to scan the street for Kirsten's arrival. His partner up the street had paged him from a cell phone. The page was his signal that she was approaching.

She, too, would have been a good target. Like her husband, Kirsten was tall. And she flaunted it. Two-inch heels took her above six feet, and the skirt of her suit was cut narrowly to accentuate her height. The jacket was tailored to pinch her waist and highlight her hips. Her hair was every bit as blond as her husband's, although the sunlight reflected no red. Kirsten was golden, from head to toe.

She carried a small gift box, elaborately wrapped. In it was a key to a suite at the nearby Windsor Court Hotel and a scroll with a wonderfully detailed list that spelled out all the erotic things she planned to do to her husband's lean body between check-in that evening and dawn the next day. She'd had the list drawn on parchment by a friend who was a calligrapher.

The man with the windbreaker spotted Kirsten down the block. As he had been told to expect, she was approaching down Bourbon from Canal. A moment later her husband spotted her, too, but he was reluctant to leave his place in line at Galatoire's. He waved. She waved back. Her smile was electric.

The man with the windbreaker on his arm moved closer to the tall blond man, simultaneously lifting his left hand from his pocket and placing it below the jacket. His right hand was now free. He stuffed it into the pocket of his trousers the same moment he spotted his partner moving into position behind the woman.

Timing was everything. That's what he'd been told. This wasn't just about the hit, it was also about the timing. Timing was everything.

Kirsten Lord was about fifty feet away when the man

with the windbreaker stepped into position no more than
two yards to the left of her husband, Robert. The position the man took was slightly back from Robert's left
shoulder. Kirsten dodged tourists and closed the distance
between herself and her husband to twenty feet. Impossibly, her smile seemed to grow brighter.

The man raised his left arm, the one shielded by the
windbreaker, so that it extended across his chest. Below
the jacket, the barrel of the sound suppressor was now
pointing up at a forty-five degree angle toward his right
shoulder.

Kirsten's eyes left her husband's for only an instant,
just barely long enough for her to notice the small man
with his oddly held windbreaker. She met the man's eyes
as they danced from her to Robert and back. She noticed
the awkward way he was holding his arm, perceived the
evil in his grin, and in a flash, she processed the peril
that the man presented. The bright smile she was wearing
for her husband left her face as though she'd been
slapped. The gaily decorated box flew from her hand.
Instinctively, her tongue found the roof of her mouth
and the beginnings of a horrified "No" left her lips just
as the man in the Saints cap pivoted his hand and wrist
at the elbow so that his silenced weapon emerged from
below his jacket.

Out toward Robert Lord's head.

With the voices from the throngs on the street mixing
with the music coming from the myriad clubs mixing with
the rest of Kirsten Lord's plaintive "NOOOOO," the
hushed shots from the silenced pistol were barely discern-
ible, even to Kirsten. She thought they sounded more like
arrows than bullets. Another witness later described them
as two drumbeats.

Both shots found their marks. The first slug entered
Robert's head just below his ear, the second higher, in his
cranium. The load in the Ruger was .22 caliber. The slugs
possessed neither the mass nor the velocity to find their
way back out of Robert Lord's head after they pierced his
skull. No grisly hunks of cranial bone cascaded against the

plate glass of Galatoire's front window. No bloody gray matter fouled the clothes of the locals and tourists standing in line for lunch. Instead, the two slugs banged around inside Robert Lord's head, mixing the contents of his skull the way a ball bearing blends the contents of a can of spray paint.

The hit was supposed to be clean. And it was.

The timing was supposed to be perfect. And it was.

Kirsten fell to her knees at Robert's side just as his legs were collapsing below him. One of the two shell casings was still dancing on the concrete, finally coming to rest near the crook of Robert's neck. Kirsten seemed oblivious to any danger she might be in. No one around her seemed to be aware that her husband had just been shot. She no longer recalls what she said to the strangers who stared down at her with shock and pity on their faces.

When she looked up to identify the shooter, to confront the shooter, to accept the next bullet, he was gone. There was no way she would have known it, but by then his Saints cap was off his head, his pager was down a sewer, his sunglasses were off his eyes and he was around the corner, walking placidly down Bienville toward Dauphine. That's where the third member of the team was waiting with a car.

The band in the bar on the corner was playing some better-than-average zydeco, and he decided that the longer he was in New Orleans the more he liked it.

His instructions had been to make sure that the lady saw the hit. He knew he'd done well.

She'd seen the hit. No doubt about it.

TWO

*"Remember this," he'd said, pointing at me over the
defense table. "Every precious thing I lose,
you will lose two."*

Less than a month after they slid my husband Robert's
body into the only empty slot left in his family's tomb
in the Garden District's Lafayette Cemetery in New Orleans, I packed up my daughter and moved what remained
of our life north to a little town called Slaughter, which
was bisected by Highway 19 about halfway between Baton
Rouge and the Arkansas state line.

We made the move in the middle of the night. In hom-
age to my paranoia, I'd driven all the way to Picayune,
Mississippi, before I backtracked into Louisiana and
charged north to Slaughter. My old boss in New Orleans,
the district attorney, had arranged for a Louisiana state
trooper to tail my car all the way to Picayune and then all
the way back as far as Baton Rouge. I bought the trooper
a cup of coffee at a truck stop outside Baton Rouge, and
he finished two pieces of pie—one apple, one lemon me-
ringue—before I allowed myself to be convinced that we
had not been followed.

Somewhere between the outskirts of Baton Rouge and
the town limits of Slaughter, I stopped calling myself Kirsten Lord and started calling myself Katherine Shaw. I
chose the name at my husband's funeral. The inspiration?
The name was written in pencil inside the prayer book that
was in front of me in the pew at the church. "Katherine
Shaw" it read. The name was written in a child's hand,
neatly, in pencil, and I prayed that the Katherine Shaw
who'd sat in that pew and sung the hymns in that church
and who had spoken the prayers wouldn't mind that we
now shared her name as we had shared that holy book.

Trying to make the urgent move to a new town a game

to my ever-cool daughter, I'd allowed her to choose her own new name, too. Her class in school had been studying the Olympic Games in Sydney, so my daughter was now Matilda. I wasn't fond of the name, but consoled myself with my glee that her class hadn't been studying the Nagano Games or Salt Lake City.

Together, Matilda and I danced off to Slaughter. *". . . You'll come a-waltzing, Matilda, with me. . . ."*

When I agreed to go into what I told myself was temporary hiding under the protection of the State of Louisiana, one of the reasons I'd chosen to move to Slaughter for our new home was because it was the kind of town where strangers were noticed. Where unfamiliar cars earned a second glance. Despite my still raw grief over Robert's death, I did everything I could to befriend our neighbors, and I quickly became known as the mother who watched her daughter enter school each morning and who was waiting outside the door ten minutes before the end of classes each afternoon. The routine I followed didn't vary despite the fact that the upstairs window of the house that I was renting had a pretty good view of the front door of the school. For my state of mind those days, a pretty good view wasn't good enough. A half block away was a half block too far.

School ended for Matilda on a much-too-sultry-for-early-June day. But the kids didn't notice the heat. They were energized and intoxicated by the prospect of their upcoming summer of freedom.

Matilda was planning to go home from school with a friend, the first social invitation she'd received since becoming the new kid in class so late in the school year. Upon learning of her plans, I invited the new friend's mother over for coffee and sprinkled the conversation with a manufactured concern that my estranged husband might try to abduct Matilda. A custody dispute, I implied. The new friend's mother said not-to-worry, she'd keep a close eye on the kids. She pressed for some dirt about my estranged husband, and as I struggled to invent details to satiate her, I wished I'd come up with a different story.

Eight, almost nine-year-old Matilda sensed my apprehension about her visit to her new friend's house and informed me that she could walk all the way there without a chaperone.

"Really," I said, feigning surprise, though I'd expected to hear words a lot like those from my much-too-independent daughter.

"You won't wait for me outside school?"

I raised a hand in honor and stated, "I promise."

"Mom, you *promise*?" There was a time in the not-too-distant past that she stomped a foot every time she used that tone of voice.

I asked, "Will you call me when you two get to your friend's house?"

"Do I have to?"

"Yes, you do."

"Then I will."

"Matilda, you promise?"

"Mom."

The phone rang at eighteen minutes past three on that last day of school. "Hi, Mom," said Matilda. "We're having lemonade and those little cookies just like the ones that Grandma used to make. With the jam in the middle?" "Grandma" was my mother. She'd died the previous April. My unfinished grief over her death had already been trampled over by the brutal pain I felt trying to absorb the responsibility and loss I felt over Robert's murder.

So. Matilda was enjoying an after-school snack in a home that was three and a half blocks from our rented home, yet I couldn't bring myself to sit down and rest until I'd heard my daughter's voice on the phone. Once I did hear the sweet melody of her call, I lowered myself to the Adirondack chair on the front porch and resumed my daily afternoon vigil. What was it, my vigil? I sat on the porch and watched for strange cars driven by small men wearing chinos and carrying windbreakers.

Or I watched for anything else that might feel out of the ordinary. I told myself that my task was like Supreme Court Justice Louis Brandeis's assessment of obscenity—I couldn't quite define what I was looking for, but I was positive that I'd know it when I saw it.

As I sipped my tall glass of sweet tea and the ice jiggled in the glass, the sound I actually heard was the tinkling of the spent .22 shells as they danced on the concrete near my husband Robert's head.

That, by the way, is a killer whale.

I felt the distance from my daughter deep in my chest as though it could be measured in light-years and not small-town blocks and imagined what my life would be like with just one more loss, and I couldn't imagine that it could still be called living.

I caressed the cameo that hung around my neck—Robert had bought it for me for our last anniversary—and I thought about justice. The concept was distant and imaginary, as full of promise as the Tooth Fairy or the Easter Bunny, and just as elusive.

That's what I was doing when the portable phone rang on the table beside the chair.

I said, "Hello," my attention momentarily diverted from my emptiness and my vigil on the street.

Matilda's friend's mother said, "Is this Katherine? Katherine, this is Libby Larsen. Now tell me once again what does your ex-husband look like, exactly? I think there's a—"

"There's a _what_?"

"It's one of those big SUVs," she said, drawing out the last letter, the _V,_ as though its agent had succeeded in negotiating top billing. "It's a black one. Big and shiny."

"Where?"

"Under the magnolia in front of Mrs. Marter's house. It's—"

"Are the girls okay, Libby?" I was trying hard not to let my fear ignite panic in my voice.

"They're right here on the living room floor playing with—"

"I'll be right there," I said and threw down the phone. Once inside the house, I wasted ten steps running to get my keys from the hook in the kitchen, before deciding it would be faster to walk—no!—run, then thinking twice and backtracking for my keys after all because I might need the car to chase that SUV.

I was fumbling to get the key into the ignition when I remembered to run back inside and get my gun. Arriving at the locked case in which I kept it, I realized I'd left my keys in the car's ignition and had to retrace my steps all over again. I was losing minutes when I didn't even have seconds to spare.

"Remember this," he'd said, pointing at me over the defense table. "Every precious thing I lose, you will lose two."

The man's words had chilled me for a minute that day in court, but I'd shrugged off his threat. It certainly wasn't the first threat I'd ever heard from a desperate con that I was prosecuting.

I figured that it wouldn't be the last.

But then the man in court had sent the man in the chinos to New Orleans, and he'd killed Robert right in front of my eyes on the sidewalk in front of Galatoire's.

And now there was a big black SUV parked under Mrs. Marter's magnolia tree, and I was sure it was driven by a small man wearing chinos, but I kept thinking it's way too warm for him to be wearing a windbreaker.

The entire three-block drive I wondered what he would be draping over his arm instead.

Here's a beluga:

Before we were lovers, or even friends, even before I knew I wanted him to be my lover, Robert and I shared our first long weekend away at a mutual friend's cabin in the mountains of North Carolina. Robert and I arrived separately, and we were two of ten people sharing the spacious vacation home. The second night of our holiday, after an evening of revelry that included a sojourn in a steaming hot tub on the edge of the adjacent woods, Robert pulled me away from the group and, with the softest amber eyes in the world, told me that I had the most lovely back he had ever seen.

That's right. He was talking about my back. His first heartfelt compliment to me was about my *back*.

If the man had been paying attention that night, and I assumed that he was, he'd had the fleeting opportunity to see my breasts, to gaze at the full length of my legs, and to study the then still-youthful contours of my ass, yet the man I would soon choose to marry wanted to reflect on the beauty of my *back*.

These are the types of things I remember now. Even at moments when I'm careening around corners and speeding three blocks to save my daughter from assassination.

I don't understand.

It's just a beluga.

The natural route to Matilda's friend's house caused me to approach the big SUV—it was one of those obscenely immense Ford things—from the front. I screeched my Audi to a stop halfway between the stubborn-looking snout of the monstrosity and the front door of the house that held my daughter, and I parked on the wrong side of the road, something that just isn't done in Slaughter.

Two men sat in the front seat of the huge vehicle. One wore a ball cap, and both shaded their eyes with sunglasses. Beyond that, I couldn't tell how tall they were or what clothes they were wearing.

Libby Larsen stood on the edge of the large, tidy lawn in front of her house, shading her eyes with the hand that wasn't supporting the toddler perched on her outstretched hip. I turned to face her and watched her mouth something. "Is that him?" she was asking.

I shrugged my shoulders as I walked toward her. She tried not to move her lips as she said, "Don't look, but they're getting out of the car, now."

I barely understood her words but knew what to do next.

"Why don't you go back inside with the girls, Libby? Do you have a cellar? Pretend there's a tornado drill or something, will you do that? Take them down to your cellar. You hear anything out of the ordinary, don't hesitate to call 911."

She didn't know me well enough to know my determination about things, but she attended to my words as though I were a preacher who knew the path to eternal bliss, and she skipped away to find the girls and squirrel them into the cellar.

The two men who got out of the SUV weren't anywhere nearly as tall as it was. They both walked my way. There was no hurry in their steps. Neither of them was carrying a jacket or anything that could be used to shield a silenced handgun, though the one who was wearing the ball cap seemed to have his left hand tucked back behind his buttocks.

I watched that one, the one with the ball cap, as I fingered the trigger of my pistol, which weighed heavily inside the front pouch of my sleeveless sweatshirt. The sweatshirt had been Robert's. I'd cut the sleeves off for him. On the front was embroidered LSU, his alma mater.

The man I was watching closely raised his free hand, the right one, and tipped the ball cap my way, saying, "Ma'am."

I nodded, trying not to be distracted from the hand that was still hidden behind his back.

He said, "We'd be looking for Missus Marter," while tilting his head back in the direction of the magnolia tree.

"Yes," I said.

The other man, the one without the cap, said, "We tried, but she's not answering her bell."

I replied without allowing my attention to waver from the man with the ball cap. "Then I imagine she must not be home. Is she expecting you?"

"Indeed. Our appointment was a while ago." He tapped his watch.

"Appointment for?"

"Air-conditioning. She wants a bid to install air-conditioning."

"I'll tell her you came by. Do you have a card?"

The man with the ball cap moved, his hidden hand thrust forward with a suddenness that caused me to jerk my hand and tangle the pistol in the fabric of the pouch of my sweatshirt. I couldn't extricate the darn gun. It took too many seconds for my eyes to recognize that the hidden hand, now extended my way, held nothing more than a business card.

Leaving the pistol tangled in the pouch of my sweatshirt, I reached out and took the card from him and read it. "You're with Buster's?" I asked. Buster's Sheet Metal and Air-Conditioning. I thought I remembered seeing a sign on a ramshackle building over by the supermarket.

"Yes."

"Missus Marter will be sorry she missed you, especially on a day as wicked as this one. The summer will be a long one, don't you think?"

"Fierce," he agreed.

You betcha.